MORTAL ENEMIES, UNDYING PASSION

"Did I ever tell you how beautiful you are, Margery?" Richard whispered.

"No, you forgot to put it on today's list." She had a choice: she could be cold and hate him or she could give in to the wild feelings that were pulsating through her and yield. His eyes were dilated with desire, his skin flushed with the intensity of his lust. Her hand streaked to her sleeve, the silence split by the rasp of steel as she unsheathed her dagger.

His advance was checked. "Now, that was something I did forget."

He took a step closer, close enough to touch. She could feel the vitality, the heat, the determination that emanated from him, and knew a curiosity and a longing that was as old as Eve's. He could have twisted the knife from her fingers, but he drew her to him, heedless of the dagger.

"Did you truly think to withstand me, Margery? I'd hunt you to the ends of the earth."

His words were breath on her face as he held her back from him. "You have been under my skin so long, to possess you has been a compulsion in me. God knows I have tried to free myself from this slavery, but you are so desirable."

She would remember the words later, but now she was a lute beneath his fingers to play on as he pleased.

The dagger fell to the floor with a clatter as his mouth came down on hers. . . .

THE MAIDEN

—and—

THE UNICORN

Isolde Martyn

🐓

BANTAM BOOKS

New York   Toronto   London   Sydney   Auckland

THE MAIDEN AND THE UNICORN

First published in Australia and New Zealand in 1998
under the title THE LADY AND THE UNICORN by Bantam Australia,
a division of Transworld Publishers, Australia.

Bantam paperback edition / August 1999

ISBN 0-553-58168-6

Published simultaneously in the United States and Canada

Bantam Books are published by Bantam Books, a division of Random
House, Inc. Its trademark, consisting of the words "Bantam Books" and
the portrayal of a rooster, is Registered in U.S. Patent and Trademark
Office and in other countries. Marca Registrada. Bantam Books, 1540
Broadway, New York, New York 10036.

To those I love—
they know who they are

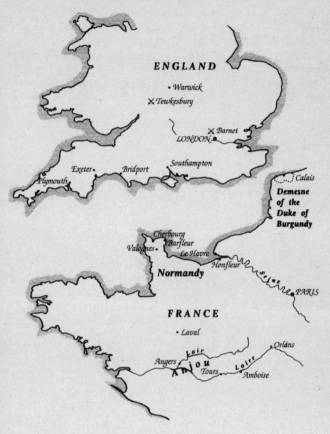

ENGLAND

· Warwick

✕ Tewkesbury

✕ Barnet
LONDON ·

Exeter ·   Bridport   Southampton

Plymouth

Calais

Demesne
of the
Duke of
Burgundy

Cherbourg
Valognes · Barfleur
Le Havre
Honfleur

Normandy

Seine

PARIS

FRANCE

· Laval

Angers   Loir   Orláns
    Anjou
     Tours   Loire
       Amboise

Margery's world, 1470 – 71

CHARACTERS 1470–71

All the people in this story actually lived except for those marked*

Margery	an orphan of unknown parentage, raised in the household of Warwick the King-maker, and attendant on his elder daughter, Isabella, Duchess of Clarence
Ankarette Twynhoe	tiring lady to Isabella, Duchess of Clarence
Richard Neville	Earl of Warwick. Known as "the King-maker" because he deposed King Henry VI of the House of Lancaster in 1461 and crowned Edward Plantagenet, the Yorkist claimant, as Edward IV
The Countess of Warwick	his wife
Isabella ("Bella"), Duchess of Clarence	elder daughter of the Earl of Warwick
Anne Neville	younger daughter of the Earl of Warwick
Richard Huddleston	King's Receiver
Matthew Long*	Huddleston's servant
Alys*	Margery's maidservant
Edward IV ("Ned")	Yorkist King of England, crowned by Warwick in 1461
George, Duke of Clarence	younger brother of the Yorkist King Edward IV and son-in-law to the Earl of Warwick
Richard ("Dickon"), Duke of Gloucester	youngest brother of the Yorkist King Edward IV, and future King Richard III
John, Lord Wenlock	Acting Governor of Calais
Philippe de Commynes	Burgundian diplomat and chronicler
Thomas Burdett	friend of George, Duke of Clarence
Wyke* *Littlebourne**	retainers of Thomas Burdett
Louis XI	King of France (the "spider king")
Charlotte	his queen
Jean Bourré	Treasurer of France and adviser to King Louis XI

William Mennypenny, Lord of Concressault	adviser to King Louis
Charles, Duke of Guienne	brother to King Louis XI
Tom Huddleston *Will Huddleston*	younger brothers of Richard Huddleston, in the service of Lord Montague, the Earl of Warwick's brother
René, Duke of Anjou and King of the Two Sicilies	
Jeanne de Laval	his Duchess
John, Duke of Calabria	King René's son
Margaret d'Anjou (the "Bitch of Anjou")	King René's daughter, the exiled Queen of England, and wife of King Henry VI of the House of Lancaster, who was deposed by Warwick in 1461
Prince Edouard	her son, heir to the House of Lancaster
John de Vere, Earl of Oxford	exiled Lancastrian lord and brother-in-law of the Earl of Warwick
Jasper Tudor, Earl of Pembroke	exiled Lancastrian lord, half brother to King Henry VI
King Henry VI	husband of Margaret d'Anjou, deposed King of England of the House of Lancaster, held a prisoner in the Tower of London by King Edward IV
John, Lord Montague	the Earl of Warwick's younger brother and also friend to King Edward IV
Error*	a deerhound of lovable nature

PRELUDE

In 1470, England had been ruled by the House of York for ten years. Edward IV, the Yorkist king, is twenty-nine, handsome, affable, capable, and has tried to reconcile with the supporters of his enemy, the House of Lancaster. The deposed king, Henry VI, is safely a prisoner in the Tower of London and both Margaret d'Anjou, Henry's strong-willed queen, and his only son are penniless fugitives in France. It looked like the House of York had won the infamous Wars of the Roses.

Thus, in March of 1470, King Edward is not expecting the greatest threat of his reign to come from two men on his own side. One is his younger brother, George, Duke of Clarence, a twenty-one-year-old envious of his brother's crown. The other man is Edward's cousin, Richard Neville, Earl of Warwick, the mighty noble who crowned him king and had thereby hoped to control him.

Warwick has become angry with Edward for many reasons: the King has refused to take his advice and prefers friendship with the Duke of Burgundy to an alliance with King Louis XI of France; Edward does not want his younger brothers to marry Warwick's two daughters; and there is gossip that the King has abused one of Warwick's kinswomen.

The rift between Warwick and King Edward is almost irreparable. And, unfortunately for Edward, Warwick and Clarence have joined forces. Warwick has already gone against the King's wishes and married his eldest daughter, Isabella, to the Duke of Clarence. Now he is spreading rumors that Edward is illegitimate, and promising to make Clarence king. The pair have been fomenting rebellions and unrest, and Edward is determined to put a stop to it. For the moment, Warwick and Clarence have been forced to flee south with the King's forces in pursuit. They have collected their wives, Warwick's youngest unwed daughter, Anne, and others of their households—including Margery, the heroine of our story, a young woman of questionable virtue who is tiring lady and companion to Isabella.

Meanwhile, in France, King Louis XI will be gleeful when he hears of the latest problems for the House of York. He will revel in seeing England unstable once again because he wants the sympathetic House of Lancaster back on the throne. If he can manipulate circumstances to ensure that the English monarch is his ally, he will be able to seize Burgundy and consolidate the kingdom of France without fear of retribution from the powerful English army.

But the Yorkist Edward lacks neither friends nor lovers, and a daring plot is about to be set in motion . . .

THE MAIDEN

—*and*—

THE UNICORN

CHAPTER
1

March 1470. If she had organized this rebellion, decided Margery, as she pulled back the canvas flap of
the Countess of Warwick's chariot, it certainly would not
have been in cold, miserable Lent.

"Go on, girl! Find out why we have stopped," snapped
the Countess.

Margery sighed at the puddled, miry road awaiting her,
but she gathered up her skirts and climbed down. It always
seemed to be her misfortune to deal with mud, whether it
was verbal or squelching around her wooden pattens as it
was now. That was the trouble with having no lawful parents, no dowry, and very little future. And here she was,
hungry enough to eat two breakfasts, in a town she did not
recognize, surrounded by weary foot soldiers who had been
trudging the churned road south for over a week—the tired,
drooping tail of her guardian, Warwick the Kingmaker's
defeated army. She could see the halted column of men and
wagons stretching down into the narrow main street of the
town. Somewhere, at the head of it, the Earl of Warwick and
the Duke of Clarence, his son-in-law and brother of the

King, were probably persuading the local mayor that their
soldiers were in too much haste to molest any townsmen's
wives or daughters.

Margery set back her hood. The rain had blown away
and a watery sun deigned to briefly bestow its blessing. It
was a joy to feel the fresh wind on her face after the cloying,
perfumed steaminess of the women's enclosed chariot, and
there was a tantalizing, yeasty smell of fresh bread coming
from somewhere.

She turned her head, meeting in surprise the full clear
stare of a man who had halted beneath the archway of an inn
courtyard on her left. It was his expression of intense astonishment directed at her that made Margery reflect his stare
as if bewitched. She had a strange sense of having experienced that gaze before.

An impression of underlying pride, authority, and self-
control reached her. Perhaps it was merely his pleasing
height or the way he stood, his broad shoulders thrust back,
the long riding cloak carefully thrown across his breast and
over his shoulder. Did the somber black folds hide some
indication that he was no friend to the King's enemies?

His alert, intelligent face drew her glance up again.
Those eyes had watched her before; she knew they had.

"Mistress, mistress!" One of Warwick's servants plucked
at the tippet of her sleeve and she turned distractedly, dragging her thoughts very slowly back to her errand. "My lord
Earl says the ladies may rest. Please you to bid them to enter
here." The lad indicated the half-timbered thatched hostelry
on her right, from whence an edgy landlord and his anxious
staff had ventured, eyeing them with cautious anticipation.

Margery nodded and glanced swiftly to the other side of
the street but the stranger had gone back into the rival inn.
With an unconscious shake of her head as if to push her
memory of him to the back of her mind, Margery forced
herself to deal with the present. She pulled aside the heavy
canvas that had kept the fresh air from the chariot. Her mistress, Isabella, Duchess of Clarence, would be relieved at
her tidings.

"Good news, your grace. My lord has sent word that we
may stop at the inn here."

"Jesu be thanked," murmured Isabella. "I shall die of

suffocation if I have to stay in this wretched monster a moment longer," and she began an ungainly descent down the back steps of the chariot.

"Margery, take her arm!" Isabella's mother, the Countess, had been fussing ever since they had left Warwick castle. Isabella, eighteen years old and heavy with child, wrinkled her nose at the mud as Margery helped her down, and waited beside her, stretching her aching back, while the cart issued the rest of the women onto the street like a chrysalis yielding a myriad-colored insect. In a confusion of velvet and brocade, the Countess, her younger daughter Anne, and their ladies clustered noisily about Isabella before they escorted her into the hostelry.

Margery tarried and darted a swift glance at the other inn across the way. The stranger was no longer visible. She searched the shadows, still sensing his presence.

"What are you staring at? Have you no appetite?" Her friend, Ankarette, the Duchess's other attendant, tugged at her arm.

"There was a man . . ."

"There is *always* a man, Margery, but there is little chance to break our fast. Make haste. Who knows how much time we may be allowed here." With a sigh, Margery followed her into the chaos of the inn.

Inside, it was as if a giant had kicked open a nest of human ants. Hungry soldiers were crowding in behind the ladies and jostling for the benches. The air was heavy with wood smoke, brewed ale, sweat, and the vinegar in which the men had soaked their brigandines to keep them free of lice.

Margery had every sympathy for the inn servants struggling through the ravenous throng, their faces strained. The needs of the noble ladies must be met first. The Duchess was already being conducted to the best bedchamber and a procession of ewers, platters, and privy pots were on their way up to her.

"Wishing you were back at the nunnery, I daresay," Ankarette exclaimed to Margery as they reached the steps. The room upstairs proved to be as tightly packed with the women as the chariot had been and their tempers were as ragged as a beggarwoman's kirtle.

When the Countess sent her to fetch the innkeeper back

again, Margery took refuge for an instant on the stairs, although even there she had to press into the wall as the inn maids squeezed by.

Her head was spinning with the noise of it all. The convent at Nuneaton, where she had spent the last six years, had at least held peaceful corners into which she could melt, whereas each moment since she had been plucked from her bed at past midnight several days before had been filled with haste and uncertainty. When the Earl of Warwick had commanded her to rejoin his household for Yuletide she had agreed wholeheartedly, but not to this flight in foul weather with King Edward's army baying at their heels, or the Countess's scolding tongue.

During the journey the Countess had frequently made tart allusions to Margery's sinful past as if the failure of her husband's rebellion against the King was all Margery's fault. Everyone in the Earl's household knew she had been banished to a nunnery for being found in the King's bed, but it was not her fault that King Edward—her beloved Ned— had thrown off Warwick's guiding hand.

Ned had been nineteen when her guardian had made him king, but he was twenty-nine now and Warwick was still trying to lead him by a leash. It was not surprising that they came to blows when the Earl declared he would uncrown Ned and make George and Isabella king and queen instead.

Margery sighed at the folly of it all but she was caught up in the treasonous tangle like a lamb in a thicket. Because she was the bastard of a fallen noblewoman, she had been reared with Warwick's daughters as their companion and attendant and she loved them both. That was why she was here now, ravenous as a beggar and growing fractious, sharing their flight and uncertain destiny out of loyalty and a certain desperation. Where else was there to go?

As she reached the bottom step, she was nearly thrown off her feet by a young esquire in his haste to hurtle past her up the stairs. The soldiers were suddenly scrambling from the trestles in panic and confusion. Recognizing one of the older men who was anxiously cramming his sallet back on his head, Margery swiftly pushed her way across to him. "God have mercy, what is happening, Master Garland?"

"There's word the King's men are but a league away," he shouted at her above the tumult.

"Surely that cannot be true."

Will Garland rubbed the back of his hand across his weary brow. "Lass, if we are caught, 'tis treason."

Margery bit her lip, doubting the rumor; Ned was known for marching his men to the edge of endurance but surely even he could not perform miracles.

She was about to grab a trencher of bread before the soldiers seized it all, when a stout man-at-arms, a head taller than those about him, struggled grinning through the crowd toward her. His surcoat was painted with the black bull, the device of Isabella's husband, the Duke of Clarence. The soldier halted in front of her, gave a gap-toothed smile, then bent his head and said loudly in her ear, "Mistress, can you tell me where I may find Margery of Warwick? The Duke of Clarence commands her attendance."

"Well, you are fortunate. Here I am. What business does the Duke want with me?"

"He desires your word on how his lady fares."

No doubt the Duke was busy with his men at the front of the column and it was far easier to send for her—they knew each other well now—to make a report to him than come in person to see his peevish duchess.

Margery did not have time to reflect that the man's helmet sat ill upon his long hair as he took her arm and pushed through the throng toward the courtyard. Her only anxiety was that she had no wish to find herself separated from the other women, especially if the pursuing soldiers were closer than they had earlier believed.

"Wait, surely there is no time for this," she exclaimed, shaking off the soldier's hand as they went outside. "The men are saying the King's army is but a league away."

Her burly escort was unconcerned. "Nay, 'tis some panic monger. It's up to my lord Earl to give the word, never fear."

"Why are we going this way?" He was conducting her through a gateway into the muddy back lane.

The fellow grinned at her. "Because I'll wager it would take us a sennight to traverse the town otherwise. There's a flock of sheep driven in for market day and a dozen stalls and all our carts and men besides. But if we go round the back of the main street, we shall be there in a thrice. Bustle, mistress, we have not all day." He courteously gestured her to walk ahead while he closed the wicker gate behind them.

The miry lane was deserted save for a loutish fellow standing at the head of a horse and cart. Margery glanced at him, wondering how she would squeeze past the vehicle that almost filled the narrow track. It was then her escort's hand whipped from behind across Margery's mouth and the other man ran toward her and grabbed her behind the knees. As she opened her lips to scream, a foul-tasting rag was thrust inside her mouth. She writhed as the men heaved her onto the cart. They swiftly dragged a sack smelling of earth and stale vegetables over her head before they hastily bound her wrists and ankles.

Although trussed and deprived of sight and balance, Margery made as much noise as she could.

"Cease that caterwauling, girl, or we'll take you somewhere truly quiet." The menacing tone of the second man froze her struggles. Her heart thudded with fear. They were pulling another sack up over her feet and cramming her skirts into it. More bags were flung across her. "Now you lie still and if I hear one groan, upon my father's soul, you'll rue it!"

The cart jerked forward. The wooden boards jarred against her shoulders. The noises of the town ceased and she could hear birdsong. She explored with her feet to see if there was any way she could roll herself off the back of the cart, but a full sack lay across it, blocking her movement.

Shivering, she tried to anticipate what might happen. At least they did not know she had a dagger strapped to her calf. It was impossible to reach it now and cut herself free. She must be cunning and wait for the right opportunity, feign foolishness or whatever the moment demanded. For now, she had to stanch the rising panic within her. The thought of what these wastrels might do to her needed to be set aside. She tried to pray as the nuns had taught her, preserve her strength, but it was hard and the cloth in her mouth was almost unbearable.

The rain began anew, spitting against the sack, the drops

growing heavier by the minute. Soon the wooden boards were awash and water started seeping into her gown along her back.

Margery had never before been so physically anguished. She was hungry, the planks bruised her, and it seemed as though her captors, in a spirit of purest malice, were jolting her over every rut and pothole in the shire. Not only were her wrists bound so painfully tight but her ankles too were aching and numb. Folk often said limbs might be lost if the blood was not allowed to flow. Could this be true?

She lost account of time but at last the lurching stopped. There was a judder as a man left the cart followed by the sound of a gate being opened, then feet leaping onto the carter's board again, and the crack of a whip. The wheels bumped forward across yet more ridges that rolled her from one side to the other. Finally the cart jerked to a halt. Hands roughly pulled the sack free of her legs. A callused hand groped upward along her stockinged calf and she thrashed about violently.

"Leave well alone, you whoreson, or he'll have your hide for his next pair of boots. Give her to me!" It was the man in the Duke's livery who lifted her. She could recognize his odor.

"And?" A new voice cut the air, curt, fair-spoken, and self-assured.

"We were not followed, sir. And she came like a dog to a bone, you might say."

"You have done well. Give her to me and go in. Fellow, there is ale and payment for you inside." She was flung over a new shoulder and the sack fell away from her head. "By Christ's blessed mercy, man, you have bound her like a witch. Let us get these tight bands off her with all haste. Out of my way!"

With her hair tumbled over her face, all Margery could see was a hoof-churned yard, muddy with fresh cow dung, and the rain spattering into the puddles. The farmyard smell flooded her nostrils. She could not hold her head up longer and her face was tossed against the cered soft leather of the man's cloak. Then a monstrous cold black snout thrust itself into her face and a giant tongue molested her hair and brow. Margery brought her knees wildly into the belly of the man carrying her—he staggered for a second, recovered himself, and cursed the dog, yelling for someone to secure it.

Her feet bumped the doorpost as he carried her in and she struggled like a snared wild animal. He swore, not finding his task easy as he began to mount a staircase. Kicking open a door, he heaved her down awkwardly on what when the world righted itself appeared to be a bed.

Margery shook her hair out of her vision and blazed a furious pair of blue eyes on her captor, only to discover it was the traveler from the inn, the stranger who had been unable to take his eyes from her.

He removed his sodden hat and riding gloves, discarding them on a carved chest that lay along one side of the room, and she saw he was younger than she had first thought. Droplets of water trickled from his long cloak and he untied it, dropping it carefully across the chest. Less formidable without it, he wore no surcoat that could give her some inkling of his allegiance. While the steel spurs on his heels betrayed that he was no knight, the black velvet cote with silk-lined sleeves and the dark green pleated short doublet reassured her that he was of gentle birth. Even the faint aroma of expensive musk reached her. But money and velvet could hide a fiend as surely as homespun.

He turned his attention to her, staring with an inscrutability that sent cold fear streaking through her. But Margery had never lacked courage and she suppressed her terror, instinctively using her wrath as a defense. It was humiliating that she was still gagged and powerless in his presence. She made an angry moan, squaring her shoulders, defying him despite her helplessness.

To her mortification, he continued to study her. "Whoever advised you to wear scarlet was no friend, mistress."

It was hardly the remark she was expecting but the arrow hit the target of her shame. Margery could have spat fire at him if her mouth had been free of the gag. She hardly doubted that cloth of gold would have ill suited her in her condition, especially when she could feel a thick smudge of dirt drying on her left temple and her freckled cheeks were dry and dusty from the sacking. Earthy fibers still dappled her shoulders, clung to the ruined red velvet bodice, and played hide-and-seek in her tangled fair hair. As for her skirt, it was a sodden map of mud spatters.

She glared at her enemy, inwardly fearful of his intent but determined not to show it. Small comfort that in normal circumstances she would not have judged his face as that of a ruthless abductor of women. To be sure, his mouth was cold and controlled but his eyes held no ill humor and had she met him at Middleham or Warwick, she would not have been ashamed to tread a measure with him.

He was watching her again with that same calculating quality that she had sensed as familiar. A tight smile of satisfaction began to curve his mouth. He moved purposefully toward her.

Tensing, she recoiled, jerking away from him like a caught fish struggling on a dry rock. She had not survived this long to be taken and used like a whore.

He grabbed hold of her, and despite her squirming, his fingers persisted in their purpose. Grasping the back of the gag, he pulled it down around her neck and untied it. Then he took hold of her shoulders and forced her back. Panic seized her but his face was not dark with lust. He was far too intent on plucking the cloth from her mouth. Free to speak, she could not utter a sound. It was as though her mouth had been scoured with sand.

Straightening, he pulled a leather flask from the breast of his doublet and unstoppering it, held it to her lips. "Drink, it will restore you."

Margery turned her face away from him. It was the only disobedience she could manage. He sighed and with his left arm under her shoulders, urged the mouth of the flask between her resisting lips. Most of the fiery spirit spilt onto her chin and wasted itself down her cleavage, but some of it moistened her parched throat and sent a bolt of heat into her breast.

"Again!" She turned her face from the flask, tears of anger on her cheeks. He swore, his face adamant, and Margery, panting, held his gaze defiantly but found no mercy. He forced the liquid into her again, which made her cough and draw back. "More until I say stop!" She shook her head but the spirit was reviving her. He compelled her to

swallow gulp after gulp until, satisfied, he drew back and
stood up.

"Who are you?" she managed at last, her voice cracked
and husky.

He leaned over to pull her up into a sitting position, then
grabbed her heels and swung her legs onto the floor. "I
doubt it would mean anything if I told you."

Someone was outside the open door. She heard the swish
of a woman's skirts. Her captor strode to the threshold.
"Bring some salve and hot water. This lady must be bathed
and her wet garments removed. And find her some clean
underlinen, if you can." He looked back around the open
door at Margery. "Perhaps a bucket of hot water rather than
a ewer," he amended.

The servant's feet scampered down the stairs and her
abductor came back into the room. "You need a bath but it
is too much work for them. If it were summer, I should dunk
you in one of the horse troughs."

He drew a rondel dagger from the scabbard on his belt,
his look calculating. She flinched but he grinned and went
down on his haunches before her, lifting her skirt to saw
through the vicious cords.

Glossy brown hair curled damply about his collar and fell
forward hiding his face as he concentrated on his task. She
winced as he carved slowly through each rope and he looked
up briefly with some concern, his long clean fingers tucking
his hair back behind his ears. His green eyes were fertile
with intelligence and there were creases of kindly humor
about them even if he was not smiling now. The unsoiled
lawn shirt laced neat against the fur collar of his cote assured
her further that he was a man who did not want for servants.
It was then she took in the metallic detail of the chain that
hung from his shoulders beneath the cote, the meaningful
intertwining of suns and roses, the King's device.

"Sweet Jesu, you are the King's man. Ouch!" Pain drove
the breath from her as her blood coursed freely.

Her enemy ignored her words, intent on removing her
shoes and her one remaining patten, seemingly oblivious of
behaving as a servant. His fingers tested her flesh through
the wool hose and calmly massaged the life back into her
feet. Pins and needles made her wince and then she writhed

away from him as his fingers slid against the leather sheath about her calf.

With an oath, he unbuckled the strap from around her leg and balanced the small sheathed dagger on his palm. "Thank God you did not have time to use this. Is life at Warwick grown so dangerous that you must arm yourself like a whore?" Then with an impatient sigh, he rose gracefully to his feet and resting a knee on the bed, turned her and cut her wrists free. She gave a whimper as the rope fell away leaving her with bracelets of skin rubbed raw. He frowned and stood back. "I hope you will not be scarred."

Appalled, she thrust out her wrists toward him. "How dare you do this to me! I am worthless as a hostage. If this is some petty delaying strategy so my lord of Warwick will not reach his ships in time, you are a fool."

"Quite probably," answered her captor, his expression as unfathomable as before. "I see the life has flowed back into your tongue as well as your fingers, Mistress Margery."

The reminder that he knew her name reduced her to silence, pinioned her mentally as he seemed to know it would. Why did he want to abduct a bastard with no property to her name? It could only be for some perverse reason. Well, the Devil take her soul if this nobody laid another hand on her without a struggle.

"If you want my virginity," she hissed, "you are six years too late."

"Yes, I know." She had wanted to shock him but it had not worked and his expression was clean of emotion. It was she who was stunned. His voice was cold, his tone impertinent, as he added, "It must have been very frustrating for you, so many years of praying. Was it worth all that trouble?"

Outrage shook her and with a force she had not believed possible, given the treatment he had dealt her, she hurled herself at him, her palm aiming at his insolent face. He grabbed her to defend himself, his grip sliding onto her lacerated wrists. Margery gave a shriek of pain and with an oath he instantly let go of her as if she had burned him. The hurt dealt her mind a dazing blow and she subsided onto the bed, fighting back her tears of humiliation.

"Settling in, mistress?" A maidservant came cheerfully

in bearing a tray set with an earthenware pot, a folded napkin, and a basin of steaming water. Before the girl could set it on the bed, the largest hound Margery had ever seen came bounding into the room. It eyed the bed and took a flying leap. The maidservant shrieked, the man made a grab for the basin, leaving Margery to fend off a scrabble of paws and tongue.

"Sede!" he roared at it. The hound sprang down and sat to attention, thumping its tail cheerfully on the wooden floor. Its untidy gray pelt and the look of hope in its limpid eyes as it surveyed Margery somewhat unknotted her terror.

The maidservant crossed herself, her eyes round with horror, and Margery, who had hurled herself into a kneeling position with a scream, untangled her limbs from her sodden skirt and the coverlet.

Her captor merely set the ewer calmly back on the tray. "The hound will not harm either of you. You, girl, unrobe the lady."

"No!" exclaimed Margery, fiercely putting up her arms protectively across her muddy bodice.

"Come, remove your clothing before you take a chill. That gown's for burning. I dare swear it is older than you are."

Margery's cheeks flamed. "What is it to you?' she snarled.

"I am used to mixing with gentlewomen who do not reek of the farmyard, but if you prefer to smell of horse dung or whatever—"

"Horse dung! It was vegetables and *you* had me trussed within those sacks." She could not believe the arrogance of the man.

"Quite. Remind me next time I abduct a woman to do it with perfumed coverlets."

"You make a practice of it?" Her voice was high and shrewish as her mind rebelled against the bizarre conversation.

His smile was hard. "I hope this is the only time, but it rather depends on certain other factors. You will oblige me in this or you shall not be fed. It is quite simple." Their fierce glances locked like the antlers of two fighting stags.

The maidservant shifted her gaze from one to the other, bewildered by the exchange that had suddenly lapsed into silence. "Mistress?" She dipped the napkin in the hot water, waiting for her to hold out her wrists. Margery wordlessly complied. Even the slight touch on the broken skin made her flinch.

As Margery's enemy gathered up his cloak and hat, another woman, elderly, with a bunch of keys rattling on her belt, bobbed a curtsy to him on the threshold and came in.

"Ah, Mistress Guppy." He bestowed a smile on her. "Here is our somewhat muddied guest." Pausing at the doorway, his hand on the latch, one leather boot tapping impatiently, he informed Margery, "You *will* humor me in this, mistress. Rest assured, other more suitable clothes shall be found for you."

"And I'll have none."

"Then you'll have none. So . . . enjoy your fast."

The woman gravely looked from him to Margery before she closed the door behind him. "Mistress, you had best do as you are bid."

Margery waited until she heard her captor's feet descend the stairs before she spoke again. "Is *he* the master here?"

The older woman nodded. "Aye, he is now, mistress, since this morning. One of the King's officers. This manor, Sutton Gaveston, by rights belongs to my lord of Warwick."

"Belonged," corrected Margery with a sigh. "My lord is now an attainted traitor and his lands are forfeit."

"Ah, we guessed as much," murmured the girl, her hands twisting in the linen cloth tucked in her belt. "May we help you free of your gown, mistress? It looks fearfully sodden."

"And this officer's name?"

The older woman tilted her head, "I am hard of hearing, mistress. Speak up, pray."

Margery repeated her question loudly.

"My son—the steward here—says the man's name is Stone." The older woman moved to the window as she spoke, inspecting the yard. "King's Receiver, he said he is, and he has half a dozen men-at-arms with him. They all rode in and took possession not long before that large fellow and the other wretch brought you in. Thank the Lord, that vermin has taken his cart and gone back to town. We don't want his likes hanging around the farm."

"Stone," repeated Margery, frowning as she tumbled the

word over. "I do not remember his name but the face . . ."
She spared herself the effort of recalling where they might
have met before. There was no time for wasting. She might
not have the chance to speak to the servants alone again and
they seemed friendly.

She moved across to the older woman. "Please will you
help me? I am a ward of my lord Earl and but an hour ago or
so I was with my lady Countess and the Duchess of
Clarence on the way to Exeter and then that man—this
Stone—has had me abducted and for what ill purpose I dare
not imagine. Sweet Jesu, I have to escape from here as soon
as my strength has returned."

The maidservant's eyes widened. "You think Master
Stone intends to force himself on you?"

"What other purpose could he have? He has given me no
explanation. You have seen how his men have treated me."

The woman at the shutter turned. "We have horses but I
do not recall any ladies' saddles hanging up," she said quietly. "You'll not remember me, but I served in my lord of
Warwick's household years ago afore I met my last husband
and I do know your face for all that you are no longer a
child. You were reared with the Earl's daughter, is that
not so?"

"Yes, it is so, good dame." Margery's voice was husky
with the tears that had been brimming unspent.

"Let me see your wrists." Margery held out her hands.
The woman examined the lacerations carefully.

"Bring me the salve, Bessie." She dabbed on the ointment gently. "Aye, it stings but all to the good. Just be sure
you do not break the skin again." With a deep sigh she let
go of Margery's fingers. "There is injustice here right enow.
Bessie, we must help this lady. For the nonce, my child, it
were best to obey the King's Receiver."

"Your clothing, my lady." The younger girl was still
waiting to unrobe her.

"I shall need my gown. Hide it for me. Unless . . ." She
would need to ride like a soul of the damned fleeing the
morning. "Can you find me some man's apparel? Woolen
hose and a cloak to keep out the cold and the doublet can be
anything you please."

The girl clamped a horrified hand to her mouth. "My lady!"

"What else can you suggest?" Margery countered gently. "That I should stay here and submit to ravishment? If I am to escape, I must ride unimpeded. I had rather risk my soul in Hell for wearing doublet and hose than be defiled." She slid the clammy gown from her shoulders and pushed it down over her hips.

"Aye," agreed the elderly housekeeper, "an' I should do likewise if I was in your shoes, methinks."

Margery kicked herself free of the gown. "My few possessions are with my lady the Countess." She gestured, irritable at her helplessness. "I have no jewels or coin with which to thank you, save a ring that was said to belong to my mother and truly"—her lips trembled—"I should be loath to part with that."

The old woman nodded. "Save your thanks for later, my child. You are not away from here yet and there is still work to be done before nightfall. Perhaps if we are liberal with the ale tonight . . ." She tapped a finger to the side of her nose.

Margery took her by the shoulders with gratitude. "One day, if I can, I will reward you threefold, I swear it."

Later, cleansed, fed at last, and with fresh linen underclothes, Margery curled beneath the coverlet and forced herself to banish everything from her mind. To escape she needed strength and for that she needed rest. One hour's sleep since yesternight would aid her little when she needed her wits about her.

⁓

The shadows told her it was well into the afternoon when she awoke. She opened the window shutters, shivering in the cold rush of air as she fixed the direction she must ride in. Southwest, the way the Earl had been fleeing, or north back to the convent? No, not back to the cloister. Her livelihood lay with the Earl's household. If she could leave that night, she might have a chance of rejoining the Earl at Exeter. The city was known to favor his cause and he had two ships at Dartmouth. But what if she arrived too late?

What if he had already embarked for Calais? Maybe she could take passage with some fishing vessel by selling the golden and pearl ring. The final problem of how she was going to explain her sudden disappearance to the Countess would require some careful consideration for they must be thinking ill of her seeming desertion, but she would cross that perilous river when she came to it.

Her plans were halted as heavier footsteps than the maidservant's came up the stairs and paused outside the door. The sound of a key in the lock made her tremble but by the time the door opened, she had squared her shoulders and assumed indifference.

"You slept?" It was Master Stone. She gave no indication of having heard him, and kept her face to the casement. "The gossip is I am intent on ravishing you." Margery's shoulders tensed but still she did not turn. "Well, it is not such a bad idea. What time would suit?"

She suppressed the gasp that came unbidden to her lips. Her heartbeat grew frantic but she controlled her speech with supreme effort, not deigning to turn her head. "If it pleases you to mock me beforehand, King's Receiver, then the sooner the better." She could feel his gaze searing down her spine.

He laughed but there was no mockery. "I congratulate you on your bravery but you have nothing to fear from me. I apologize for my poor sense of humor." She ignored him. "But I pray you, turn around. The light through your undergown renders you far too tempting for my present purpose." His words sent her glancing down in consternation, wondering whether he was speaking the truth. "Humor me, mistress!"

The sudden anger in his voice penetrated her confidence, undermining her courage, but she refused to comply, her stance haughty, her face lifted, her shoulders thrown back. She heard him step nearer. "You are proud beyond your station. What are you but a duchess's tiring woman?" She sensed his eyes flickering coldly over her and she flinched inwardly. His voice came closer still. "Why should *I* want the King's discarded plaything? You come dowerless and used, mistress. There are better bargains to be had elsewhere."

There was a rasp of bitterness in his voice as if he had

some personal reason for despising her. Her breast heaved
with anger but she had no answer. No one had reminded her
so bitterly of her situation. The truth was something she had
tried to spare herself but now it was like a whipcord across
her shoulder. Stanching her tears, she busied herself closing
the shutters.

"Ah, no matter, be of good cheer, wench. Perhaps it will
be summer for you again. I am taking you to your lover
tomorrow. Mayhap the King has only temporarily *mislain*
you."

The ability of this stranger to surprise her every time he
opened his mouth amazed her, but she would be cursed if
she would let him see that.

"The King?" she echoed coolly and swung around, finding to her dismay that he was standing less than a pace
behind her. She refused to meet his supercilious gaze,
staring sideways with all the hauteur she could manage but
uncomfortably aware of his height and strength; he could so
easily overpower her. "Why should the King wish to set
eyes on me again? Do you imagine there will be some
reward for you?"

But he did not answer. Her glance jerked to his face and
found him dangerously distracted with examining the half-
visible globes of her breasts above the borrowed undergown. Exposed beneath those intense green eyes, Margery
cursed inwardly, realizing too late that he could see the dark
aureoles of their peaks beneath the white linen. The studied
coldness in his expression was momentarily vanquished,
replaced by a look of pure masculine appreciation as his
gaze rose up her white throat, lingered at her lips, and
finally met her eyes.

"Some reward?" he answered finally, with a faint smile.
"Yes, there *certainly* will be."

CHAPTER

2

Richard dragged his eyes away from his delectable prisoner with an unspoken curse. He had unfinished business with Margery of Warwick.

Those enticing parted lips, the feel of her thighs beneath his as he had once knelt astride her, that gossamer honey hair—these imaginings had haunted his nights. Did she know who he was? Did she remember the intimacy of their last meeting? Oh, Christ, if the King had not . . .

Now the wench was staring at him, a faint frown creasing her brow, and he wanted desperately to slide his fingers down her half-naked shoulders, pull her against him, and feast upon her mouth.

"So you have expectations, King's Receiver." She broke the sudden silence between them, her voice husky as if she had the trouble of finding it. "Surely all this is a waste of your time. I believe the King has at least three regular mistresses."

"Playing Pandarus to your Cressida is not to my taste either," he answered smoothly while inwardly angry with himself that this bastard wench's body could excite his senses like no other woman's. He wanted to hate her for perturbing him all these years. "Besides, you may find that the Troilus of your dreams has changed somewhat." Criticizing the King eased the mental pain but not his growing arousal. Hastily, he gave her a curt nod and strode swiftly to the door.

"So you presume to know my dreams, do you, Master Stone?" The scathing tone in her voice lashed at him.

His hand hesitated upon the latch and he turned his head. "Of course not." He smiled coldly. "I leave omniscience to God."

He noisily locked the door on her and strode back down the oaken staircase, irritable as a dog with a stolen bone— growling at the world but with no time yet to enjoy his feast.

The manor tenant roll was where he had left it, awkwardly pinioned beneath an iron candleholder and a wooden salver on the steward's table. The room was chilly; the coals in the brazier neglected in his absence. He called to his manservant for wine and sat down gloomily. As King's Receiver, he was supposed to inspect the manor roll of every traitor's manor he was retaking for the King and report back to Westminster, but the cramped figures in front of him held little interest compared with the pillaged treasure upstairs.

With his chin in his hand, he stared morosely at the cold stone wall opposite, still marveling at what he had accomplished since dawn with so little premeditation.

Ever since the day of the wager with the King six years ago, the memory of this wench had been a burr beneath his girths, always there, pricking him. It had not needed that drunken bet with King Edward and the other young hotheads at Warwick to kiss every woman within the castle before the noon bell rang to make Richard aware of Margery. His appetite had been piqued three days earlier when he had arrived at the Kingmaker's castle in the entourage of the Earl of Northumberland, the Earl of Warwick's younger brother, and first set eyes on her. But then he had been too young, too unsure of himself in unfamiliar surroundings, to force her to notice him.

Just thinking about that cursed wager still made him seethe. His memory was as fresh as it had been the day after. He had been the first to reach the barn where Warwick's daughters and the other young noblewomen were

hiding in the loft. They had set Margery to act as sentry and
he could still envisage her as she had glimpsed him running
across the courtyard toward her. Instantly she had disappeared inside the barn in a whirl of skirts and shining hair.
He had caught her as she set hands on the ladder to the loft
and spun her around. It had been so easy to hook his heel
behind her leather slipper and send her sprawling backward
onto the soft hay. They had both been laughing as he swiftly
knelt astride her and caught her wrists down beside her
head. Then laughter had died between them as if time itself
had frozen momentarily. Her beautiful hair had covered the
hay around them like silken thread over morning grass and
he could see himself in those wide startled blue eyes. Her
lips had opened sweetly, instinctively waiting for him. He
knew he had her then, that it was right.

But he had savored her fresh loveliness a second too
long. Like yapping hounds bursting upon a peaceful glade,
the other youths had thrust open the door, the King ahead of
them. King Edward had flung Richard aside and claimed the
girl's kiss instead. Neither he nor Margery had seen Richard
tear angrily out of the barn.

But now, by Christ's blessed mercy, he had Margery of
Warwick in his hands again. Just recognizing the girl that
morning as she set back her hood to uncover that honey hair
had heated his blood. His body had quickened at the very
sight of her so real and merely a few paces from his touch.
She had even met his glance, albeit as a stranger, her lips
parting in curiosity, the wind lifting her hair about her
shoulders, and immediately his mind had started whirling
like some newfangled clock machinery.

"Daydreaming, sir?"

Richard's distant gaze refocused on the world around
him, the manor steward's room, and he looked up into the
grinning face of his manservant, Matthew. His hound was
there too, its nose nudging him for attention.

"I was asking you if you . . . Never you mind, sir, at least
you are not bewitched. For an instant, you looked as though
you were away with the small folk."

"I am bewitched," answered the King's Receiver, distractedly pushing his fingers through the dog's thick coat.
"And I do not like it one iota."

"But you have the girl now, neat as a fly in a web," Matthew Long pointed out cheerfully as he set an earthernware jug of wine and a goblet before his scowling master.

"You think so, do you?" muttered Richard, without raising his eyes from the ledger. "I have on my hands a female hedgehog. One look at me and every sharp quill is quivering to draw blood. I am not confident I have acted wisely." He raised his head and glared at his servant. The parchment, free of the pressure of his other hand, rolled itself back up.

"Well, that does make a change at any rate," commented his servant, lifting the poker to prod ineffectively at the embers. "All you have to do now, sir, is to take the wench to the King's grace as you planned."

Richard tossed the manor roll over to one side. "Life is so simple for you, is it not, Matthew?" he sighed. "Here am I tormented by conscience while you would have—"

"Laid the wench by now, that's for sure," muttered Matthew. He abandoned the poker, wiping his hands down the sides of his hose. "It's not as if she is an unravished maid now, is it . . ." His voice trailed off as his master's expression grew dangerous. Richard watched his servant's huge hands fumble. "Well, I don't know, do I?" the large man floundered.

"What do you not know?" asked his master carefully.

"Well, sir, you see this wench and then plague take me if we don't make off with her in the full view of the Kingmaker's entire rebel army and now you be thinking you don't want her after all. 'Tis a mite confusing for a poor silly soul like me."

"She is a used woman." The King's Receiver poured himself a goblet of fortified wine.

"But, master, you said it was the King—"

"That makes a difference?" Green eyes hard as lichened rock regarded Matthew.

His servant nodded. "Yes, I reckon so, master. I wouldn't say no to a king's leftovers, especially Old Ned's. I mean, well, he's . . ."

"*Discerning,* you mean? That's an elegant word, Matthew, but even *I* can disdain King Edward's leavings." Richard took a draft and watched the larger man suck in his cheeks.

"Ah," answered Matthew.

"Yes, Matthew, *ah*. Perhaps it is not my conscience but my pride which is at odds with the rest of me." He drank more deeply.

"Could be, sir. All I know is that I ain't seen you in such a pother for a long while. So what's to be done?"

"I think she will try to escape." Richard enjoyed seeing Matthew swallow his astonishment.

"You reckon she has the spirit for it?"

"Oh, yes, I will wager she is anxious to reach Exeter and rejoin the Earl's womenfolk before they take ship."

"So we surprise her on the stair?"

"No," corrected his master, perusing him thoughtfully, "we shall not stop her."

"Not— By the Rood, master, shall I cart you off to Bedlam? After all that hurly-burly, spreading rumors about the King's men being so close and the to-do about hiring the carter and abducting defenseless . . ." Matthew spluttered to silence. Richard waited, trying not to smile at the larger man's discomfort. "Aye, well," muttered his servant with a sulky sniff, "if you're still interested in anything else other than the wench upstairs, sir, the steward's waiting outside looking like a prisoner about to have his thumbs screwed. Shall you put him out of his misery?"

"Aye, very well, in a few minutes then." Richard dismissed him with a nod.

Alone, he emptied the goblet and buried his head in his hands. By all the Saints, what had he gotten himself into? It was against his nature to act so rashly where women were concerned. Was he going to regret his foolhardiness? But any addlepate could have seen that the Kingmaker was hurrying the girl out of the realm along with the rest of his entourage, making for Calais no doubt as he had done before when in trouble. It would have been foolish not to seize the opportunity to take the wench. After all, prising her out of the stronghold of Calais would prove costly. That was why he of all men, the reputedly calm and foresighted King's Receiver, had acted unusually. Capturing maidens was like something from the tales of King Arthur that old Sir Thomas Malory was compiling, Richard chided himself;

it was not a role with which he was comfortable. And besides, Margery, curse her, was no maiden.

If only she had not allowed the King to seduce her. That morsel stuck in the gullet of his pride threatening to choke him. Thank the Almighty, he still had a few days' grace to make up his mind about what to do with her. The die were almost out of his hand and on the table but the decision was still his and yet . . . And yet taking the wench to the King involved a risk—that the royal whoremonger would still want her. But not to take her to the King was an even more perilous enterprise—she was Warwick's ward and she was who she was. No, mayhap he had little choice, after all. The King had to be told she was in his possession.

As to the little fire-eater herself? Whether he could tame her within a few days, he doubted. Better to keep a tight bridle on her and stay master of his own passions. Besides, he needed to learn more about Mistress Margery of Warwick. Feeling a stirring in his groin was not enough. The next few days would determine him one way or another. Would it not be sport indeed to make the color come and go in her cheeks like sunshine across winter fields? And tonight, tonight he would fly her like a young unhooded falcon.

"I want her glad of my protection," he said fiercely to the empty room. "By Christ's blessed mercy, she will be glad of me before the morning comes."

Margery stealthfully followed the old housekeeper down the candleless stairs. She held her breath while the latch was lifted, but her new ally did it skillfully. Out in the yard a dog snarled, but Mistress Guppy threw him an unexpected meat scrap to content him and led Margery around the back of the barn. Behind the stable the woman's grandson was waiting with a mare saddled.

"I cannot thank you sufficiently for what you are doing," Margery whispered, her breath forming vapor in the air for it was so frosty you could almost smell the cold. "Pray Heaven he will not have you punished."

"I'm not afeared," whispered the elderly woman. "We

are the Earl's servants, at least until yesterday. We're helping you for my lord's sake and we pray you will tell him so."

"It shall not be forgotten." Margery leaned forward and brushed her lips against the withered cheek. "God keep you."

"You had best take this, my lady. 'Tis all I could find for you."

Across her palms lay a kitchen knife, its blade wrapped in a cloth. She proffered it as if it were a magic sword and Margery could not have received it more thankfully had it been Excalibur.

Sticking it in her belt, Margery shivered, wondering not for the first time that night if she was actually clambering out of a cauldron of boiling water onto the burning coals below. The wait into the dark center of the night had been hard enough but now, with the frosty breath of midnight on her cheek and the blackness of the lane ahead of her, it took all her determination and courage to carry out her plan.

With a sigh, she set her face to the southwest and led the horse along the track. The rustling in the thickets and the looming shadows dismayed her. She was not used to being alone, especially at night. Without servants to protect her, the highway was as dangerous and unpredictable as the man who had captured her.

Once past the dark copse and out of sight of the manor buildings, she swung herself awkwardly into the saddle, glad of the stirrup. It was neither easy without a mounting block or a groom's cupped hands to help her, nor had she counted on using a man's saddle. Like the Kingmaker's daughters, she was used to riding sidesaddle on a docile mount. Now she found it unnatural to sit astride and the mare, sensing her new rider's discomfort, misbehaved, wasting valuable moments as Margery sought to establish which of them was in control and to stop the creature turning for home.

The lad's directions served her well. She passed the village, averting her eyes from the churchyard. The horse was still testing her. It sensed her fear, reacting as much as its rider to every rustle, every moving shadow. As she rode past the last cottage, the beast shied as something hurtled through the air with a feline hiss inches from its hooves and a dog in pursuit came bounding across their path. At the sight of the larger animal, the cur stopped and growled, its hackles raised. The mare was agitated, edging sideways. Margery dug her heels desperately into its flanks and urged it on. The beast eventually complied, the dog snapping ill-naturedly at its fetlocks before it gave voice to a full-throated bark.

"Faster, faster," Margery whispered against the mane of the mare as if it could understand. She looked back but contrary to her expectations no sleepy scratching villager had staggered outside into the cold to investigate.

The road west led swiftly out into wooded country. It would be folly now to slacken pace. It was difficult holding on but she managed out of desperation for indeed the drumming hooves would rouse any rogue that slumbered within earshot. She slowed the horse to a trot as the road climbed steeply. An evil-looking wood hemmed her in on one side while on her left hand a dark hedgerow ran thickly. Ahead of her at the crest of the hill, she thought she glimpsed a figure cross the road, outlined against the sky. She could not be sure whether it was a hunched man or a beast. She reined the mare to a halt, listening intently but there was no sound. Noting where the figure had crossed, she edged the horse closer, pausing again to listen. This time somewhere in the woods ahead a twig cracked as it would at the passage of a man or, please God, a deer.

It left her with no choice but to gallop past as swiftly as she could. Not an easy task, given the steepness of the hill. She edged the horse forward at a slow trot for another fifty paces and paused again to listen. This time there was a total oppressive silence. With a prayer on her lips, she wound her left hand in the reins while her right hand drew the knife from her belt, shook it free of the cloth, and kept it ready.

She almost missed it—the huffle of an animal or the suppressed sneeze of a man. She knew she had to act quickly so she kneed the horse to a gallop. But as she did so, a dark wraith leaped at her as the track crested the hill and her horse reared, almost throwing her. A hand grabbed at her reins and with an oath she slashed at its fingers. A second demon leaped to pull her from the saddle. She scythed the

knife wildly through the air. Something ugly but human
yelped and fell back.

It took all her strength now to regain control of her horse
and urge it forward. The animal finally responded before the
rogues could come at her again and she broke into a gallop
and rode a mile before she drew rein by a gate in the hedge.
Her own breath came as fast as the mare's. Her body shook
beyond her control.

The knife. Where was the knife? It must have flown from
her hand as the horse had reared a second time.

"Sweet Jesu, help me," she whispered to the listening air.
"I am so useless." So useless it would be a miracle if she
could reach Exeter without being raped or gutted like a fish.
Better to crawl under a hedge and hope the world would
leave her alone. But there was one man who would not.
Only the thought of a humiliating recapture by the King's
Receiver made her edge the horse once more onto the road,
doggedly determined despite her failing courage.

Thankfully the country was more open now and fields
stretched on either side of her, silver with frost. But her discomfort was growing; the saddle chafed her skin through
the rough thin hose and she longed for the warmth of her
skirts. As the cruel cold crept about her neck like an icy
scarf, she shivered and drew her cloak closer. Her only
comfort was that she had set a little distance between herself
and the new demon in her life.

Without mishap she walked the horse quietly through the
next village but it was the top of the next hill that was her
undoing. Chains rattling in the wind made her flesh crawl.
Her hand flew to her mouth to stifle a scream. A dead man
swung from a gibbet above her head. She could barely see
him but the horrible smell of decaying flesh filled her nostrils. Retching, she dared not glance around her. The spirits
of the hanged were said to haunt the gibbet, mocking the
living. A wind gust shook the chains again and in panic she
dug her heels into the mare's flanks. The creature took off,
hurtling down the hill at too evil a pace. It stumbled in a rut
and whinnied.

Margery drew rein, her own heart thumping wildly. She
soothed the animal, cursing her own stupidity. All she could
coax out of the horse was a hobble. Dismounting, she slid

her hand along the creature's leg. From what she could tell
in the darkness, it had thrown a shoe on the hill. Should she
wait until dawn and beg the local smith to shoe it? But how
was she going to pay him? How long would it take Stone
and his men to find her?

The horse's neck was warm as she bowed her forehead
against it for comfort. She had as much chance of reaching
her guardian as flying on a broomstick. No money, no horse,
no servants. Sniffing back the tears, she wiped her cheeks
with her sleeve. She must behave like a man, yet, sweet
Jesu, she could barely think.

She turned the mare loose into a meadow, then resolutely
set her face southwest again. She would make for the nearest
religious house and fling herself on their mercy.

Starting like a frightened bird every time the limb of a
tree cracked or the shadows shuffled, she kept walking. The
cold seeped into her with every step she took and her hands
grew numb within their gloves as the dawn turned the sky to
mother-of-pearl.

Her mind too was beginning to freeze with exhaustion when the rumble of hooves pounding along behind
alerted her. The road was straight and two horsemen were
within sight before she could scuttle across the ditch and
into the hedgerow like a startled rabbit. Barely ten paces
from her, they halted, black against the sky like figures from
Revelation.

The hound came panting up. It paused looking back
toward the horsemen for approval before it sniffed its way
over toward Margery. Stone's dog, now familiar with her
scent but yet a creature used to obeying orders.

"Sede!" Margery whispered forcefully.

Miraculously, the foolish creature peered at her, offered
an apologetic whine and the briefest tail wag before it sat
down and snuffled at a tribe of fleas at the base of its spine.
Margery blessed the animal and squeezed her eyes shut,
praying the men would not hear her ragged breath. To be
caught would be shameful yet the thought of defending herself alone on the highway for several days twisted her
insides tightly.

"We did see something but I'd swear it was a lad not a
woman."

"She's here." It was Stone's voice with an edge to it. "I can sense it. Draw your sword along the hedge."

His prey shrank back. The sharp twigs poked cruelly against her back, resisting her further attempt to insinuate herself into the thicket as the loutish man dismounted and rasped the weapon from its sheath. The ploy worked. As the blade arced blindly near her, Margery gave a squeal of terror. The hound gave a yap of welcome and sprang across the long grass to enter the game, jumping up to lick her hand.

Stone rode his horse across as his servant drew her trembling from the mess of hawthorn. "Good morning to you, mistress," he called cheerfully and then, peering in the twilight, observed her clothing. "Sorry, young master is it? How very sensible." He held out his gloved hand to her. "You are a brave wench but the hunt is over. I confess I prefer my sport by day but tracking a woman has lent a different nuance. Have you worn yourself out sufficiently to be compliant?"

She slapped his hand away. Sweet Jesu, to think he had been following her all this time. "Why did you bother? What use am I to you? Pretend you never saw me and let me go free."

He regathered his reins and frowned down at her. "What? Leave you to go alone? Never. I am but a little danger compared to what you face out here. Call a truce, you innocent, and let's breakfast at the next inn."

Hunger was gnawing at her almost more than fury. She needed protection and her belly craved food, but no, not at his table. To listen was to be tempted by the Devil.

"No," she hissed, backing away from him unwittingly into the arms of his clod of a servant who caught hold of her around the waist. She struggled to free herself, cursing them both.

"How is it you are not riding?" Stone's voice was sharp. "Where is the horse you stole from the King's manor?"

"Stole!"

"Borrowed, then."

"She cast a shoe. I turned her loose into pasture back along the road."

"With the saddle still attached, no doubt. By Christ's

blessed mercy, mistress, you have less worldliness than a louse traveling on a pilgrim. Long, you will have to go back for it. We are not going to leave a valuable mount for someone else to pilfer."

"Aye, sir. Shall I toss the lass up to you then, master?" Margery squirmed wildly in his arms.

Stone's disdain was audible. "No, it will not please her. Let her walk."

"She'll bolt, sir. I've no stomach for chasing surly wenches across sodden fields this time in the morning."

"Oh, very well, secure her," growled his master. He bent and extracted a length of rope from his saddlepack and tossed it to his servant. Margery shuddered at the thought of anything about her wrists again and writhed within the big man's clasp but he surprised her, looping it instead around her waist, then he reduced the slack and handed the end to his employer.

"Must I, Long?" Stone's voice was bored. "How very tiresome. Are you sure you prefer this, mistress? I should have thought you would be footsore by now."

Margery swore at him, an oath eavesdropped from the Warwick stables. It angered him.

"Walk then, you shrew. I care not." He nudged his horse forward gently with his heels and the tether tensed. Appalled at her mortifying predicament, Margery threw her weight away from the rope, trying to hold back, but she was drawn after him like a slave at his horse's tail.

"I'll never forgive you for this," she railed.

Stone turned his head. "Forgiveness has not been asked. The choice is yours."

Long mounted, grinning cheekily as Margery furiously jerked at the cord with both hands. Stone regarded her indifferently over his shoulder. The two men exchanged glances. The servant chuckled, touched his forelock to his master, and turned his horse back down the road.

"May you rot in Hell, Master Stone! What have I ever done to you?" Margery shouted at her abductor but he ignored her and set his face forward.

She stumbled behind him, the dog loyally keeping pace with her. The constant tug of the rope helped her tired body

keep going, but in not choosing her own speed her balance
became precarious over the ruts. Several times she staggered and nearly fell. Her feet were sore indeed for she was
not accustomed to much walking and she felt the tendrils of
weariness plucking at her.

Her fury and hatred focused on his unfeeling back and
tears of shame blinded her. She fell finally and stayed there
weeping angrily into the frost-hard dirt, not caring. The rope
slackened. She was conscious of Stone loftily waiting for
her tantrum to cease while his dog licked at her hair and
hands with little crooning noises.

"You wish to ride with me now?" his voice inquired
politely.

She cursed him roundly and staggered to her feet. She
let him drag her another hundred yards and then pitched
her weight against the rope. He twisted in his saddle. She
was faint with hunger and her stubborn energy was finally
exhausted.

His smile broadened with satisfaction. His stallion
danced patiently beneath him as she dragged her feet to
its side. His arm came down and coiled around her waist
and with great strength he lifted her easily before him and
slipped the rope from her.

"There is no shame in surrender, lady."

Margery leaned back against him in sheer exhaustion and
gave in. She had neither energy nor mental power to fight
him. If she resented his arms gently enclosing her and his
thighs flanking hers, then she would fan the embers of that
resentment later.

"I am not surrendering," she told him wearily. "I shall
not forget how shamefully you have treated me. My lord of
Warwick will have you horsewhipped if you should fall
within his hands, you have my word on it."

"Are you grown so important? I think not." His breath
was warm upon her hair.

"He cares. He *does*," her voice faded to the merest
whisper.

Long caught up with them now, leading her horse.
Without a rider, the mare was able to walk, picking her way
delicately among the ruts.

"If the next village has a decent smithy, shall you have her reshod there, master?"

"Only if there is a good alehouse nearby. As long as the beast does not bruise herself further, we shall press on."

He slackened pace at the next hamlet, bestowed upon the slumbering inn a cursory glance, and rode onward. How far they traveled, Margery could not tell. But eventually she opened her eyes as their pace slowed. A cheerful alehouse squatted within the center of the village. In one of the downstairs windows a candle burned brightly, its impudent light defying the gray morning. Smoke puffed briskly from the chimney while the smell of fresh baked bread hung ripely in the air.

Stone dismounted and with hands on hips glanced up at the fresh garland and grinned at his servant. "Go and rouse the local smith, Long, and tell him to shoe her while we break our fast. These fine horses deserve a noble feed." His affectation of cheeriness fell across Margery's hearing like jagged hailstones.

"Aye, master, and so do I." Long's hand slapped Margery's leg. "Are you a maid, lad, to sit there waiting to be helped down. Wake up!" Margery blinked at him, then she glanced down at her cote and hose, realization dawning that she was to be treated as a man and must shift for herself. For an instant, she was tempted to grab the reins of Stone's powerful horse and try another escape but the cursed rogue was watching her as if he sensed her thoughts. With a shrug, she swung herself out of the saddle and queued up behind her enemy at the door while Long took care of the horses. Stone gave her an amused glance over his shoulder and rapped on the door with his riding whip. It was opened by a stooped innkeeper who bowed them in as if the King and his lords had come calling.

Inside it was as cozy as a Yuletide hall. A log fire blazed noisily in the grate and Margery followed the dog toward it, impatient to thrust her hands out to its welcome warmth. Her companion looked at her with concern before he gave the landlord his attention.

"Mulled ale, landlord, if you please, and oatmeal pottage." He joined her and his dog at the hearth, drawing off his black gloves and tucking them into his belt. His hound tried to lick him but he merely bestowed a halfhearted pat upon its pelt.

The wench looked unrepentant of the night's adventure, cold, hungry, and furious but with enough spirit left to thwart him still. The last thing he needed was her drawing attention or letting the alewife recognize she was a woman. She had hacked her lovely hair to chin length much to his displeasure and it was longer on one side than the other. But if she kept the long cloak drawn about her . . . yes, she might just pass as a youth providing she held her tongue. With a careful glance over his shoulder to make sure the landlord was still in the back room, Richard laid down the law. "From now on, you are my younger brother, Heaven help me! Behave out of turn and you will starve." His hand fell warningly upon her shoulder.

The girl tried to shrug his hand away. "I'll see the King hears of every word of this," she vowed, twisting her face angrily up at him. He let his fingers bite into her shoulder and put his mouth to her ear.

"If you tell aught of this adventure to the King's grace, he will compel me to marry you, I should not wonder."

Her eyes widened to the size of rose nobles and her mouth dropped open. "That is ridiculous!" she snapped, then she went deadly quiet. No doubt she was realizing it was a fearful possibility as the full tilt of his outrageous suggestion hit her. He observed she shot a sideways look at him beneath her lashes as he moved around to crouch before the fire, but he made sure his grave expression left her in no mistake that he could be merely jesting. He caught her examining his left hand as he too splayed his fingers to the warmth.

"You marry me and I shall make you the greatest cuckold in Christendom," she growled through her teeth.

"I'll see you in a madhouse first," he snarled softly, adding tersely, "and lower your voice when you have cause to speak to me. It were best you held your tongue completely, my *lad*. Wipe the mud off your cheek." He straightened up as the alewife brought in their breakfast.

"Your man back there will have a good appetite on him, no doubt, sir," she exclaimed cheerfully.

Richard beamed back at the alewife in open friendly fashion as he seated himself at the board but made sure the look he directed at his prisoner held no warmth.

The girl was no doubt loath to leave the fire but the aroma of the mulled ale prevented her from ignoring him. Lured to the table, she sullenly slid onto the bench opposite while the alewife set huge trenchers of fresh bread before them.

"I'll fetch you some cheese too. You look as though you need a hearty breakfast, young sir," the woman clucked at Margery as she returned to ladle out the hot pottage.

"My brother will not say much," Richard answered for his companion. "The boy is lovesick." He moved his leg deftly out of the way of the girl's kick.

"Ah well," murmured their hostess, grinning at the lad's fierce scowl at his older brother. "Just as well, with pretty looks like his he might tempt an unwise fancy. A blessing on your repast, sir."

Richard murmured a grace, adding as postscript, "And grant my little brother what he deserves." The blow caught him that time but he kicked her lightly back and started on his breakfast. She was still rubbing her shin when the goodwife set a homemade cheese before them.

The steaming pottage and hot spiced ale revived Richard more than baiting Margery had done, seeping through his veins with agreeable warmth. With hot food warming her belly, the girl was feeling better too, no question. She shot sulky glances at him from beneath her lashes as he carved off more of the loaf for them. The golden glow of her skin was edging out the gray fatigue, or perhaps it was the rays of the young sun coming through the window slats upon them both.

Last night had been an ordeal but it was worth it to ensure the little rebel gave them peace for the rest of the day. His eyes rested thoughtfully upon the splash of freckles across his prisoner's nose and cheeks, evidence of more time spent defiantly in the fresh air than mewed up embroidering some altar cloth. She had not followed the fashion of plucking her forehead either. That pleased him. The girl was neither vain nor did she ape her betters. On close inspection, the short hacked hair made her look more like an unruly maid scarcely turned woman rather than her true age. Certes, any woman of her years would be long wed by now and have ripened at least three babes within her womb. But this wench was special.

How old had she been when the King had seduced her? Sixteen or younger! Would the King still find her desirable if he could see her now with her hair like a boy's and weariness mixed with bad temper fouling her looks? Richard thrust his jealousy aside. If God had tripped the King in the castle yard, then mayhap the wench would have eventually given her maidenhead to him instead. God knows, he had surely wanted her more than the King.

The King's Receiver ate in silence for some while and then, the edge of his hunger dulled, he rewarded her with a more agreeable expression and tossed his salivating dog a hunk of bread. Hope of food had overtaken its desire for warmth and it sat dribbling for more.

"There will be hard riding this morning. My men will meet up with us after noon."

She checked over her shoulder to where the landlord and his wife were gossiping with his servant in the back kitchen, then without looking at him, she asked, "Do your men know you have your *brother* with you?"

"Ah, intelligent conversation, how very refreshing. No, they think I am abducting an heiress, I daresay."

"You dare a great deal, Master Stone." She raised her eyes coldly.

"I had rather dare with armed men to help me than try and protect your blemished honor unaided. Eat up, we have some weary miles ahead and I do not want you peevish from hunger."

"Why do you dislike me so?"

"Dislike you?" He was smiling wholeheartedly for the first time, his fine white teeth grinning at her. "Probably because you have done nothing but rail at me which seems totally unreasonable of you."

Margery spluttered as she took a mouthful of ale and looked tempted to fling the remains of her cup at him.

"No," he said softly. "Don't even think it."

"I wonder," she said sweetly, "how I could possibly have

enjoyed life before your appearance, Master Stone. You add
something indescribable to my well-being."

"No doubt you could find a suitable word since you seem
to have spent most of your time cavorting in the stables." He
grabbed her angry hand and held it fiercely down. "What,
hit the King's Receiver, like some common slut?"

The taunt hurt but she retaliated. "Common sluts normally hit you, do they?"

"I trust I know none among my acquaintances." His
thumb stroked sensually across the top of her hand as he
deliberately let her know by his expression that he was
examining her as a woman, assessing her, behaving like
Adam after biting the apple from the Tree of Knowledge.
Crimson flushed across her cheeks and throat beneath his
gaze. She did not like it. Let her think he might be changing
his mind about treating her like a lady.

Snatching her hand away as though he had dripped
burning oil on her, she busied herself with the bread and
cheese. Let her simmer a little more, he decided. Let her
think that the idea of marrying her, openly voiced, had lifted
the lid on a whole stew of trouble.

"Everything proper, sirs?" The alewife had stuck her
head around the door.

"Aye, and your fresh bread has revived my brother's
appetite."

He made small talk with the woman, giving his companion breathing space. His deliberate breeziness annoyed
his prisoner. Little doubt there.

When the good dame had retreated once more to the back
room, Margery maintained a grim silence, her chin in her
hand, her eyes downcast. Unobserved, Richard was free to
appreciate the fringe of gold lashes lapping the blue glaze.
Her coloring was perfect. Did she know it? Did bastards at
Warwick have a chance to see themselves in silver mirrors?
Perhaps it was curiosity that finally stung her into raising
her blue eyes. "Were you at Warwick or Middleham?"

Her question hurt. He was sure she knew who he was and
if she did not, then had that fleeting moment when he had
held her in his arms meant nothing to her? Was this another
ploy to irritate him? He felt his smile slide away. "You

know I was." His voice was soft, almost bitter. "I was at
Warwick all that week."

"What week?" she asked faintly, a frown puckering her
forehead.

"You know which week. How do you think I know you
otherwise, mistress? The week the King was with you." He
hoped to put a brutal end to this conversation; her questions
were like salt on his wounds.

"Oh," her voice shrank to a whisper and her eyes fell
before his.

"Let us go." The trestle scraped back as he rose. He
tucked his riding crop beneath his arm while he drew on his
gloves, giving her a stern glance before he strode across to
the doorway to the inner room and tapped on the door
frame. The landlord came for payment and Long followed
him in, wiping the crumbs from his chin with his sleeve.

Newly shod, Margery's horse was brought out of the
smithy but Richard was forced to sit and wait while she
made a long and silent fuss of the creature before mounting. He felt an absurd envy, not to mention impatience, at
the unnecessary delay. Watching her struggling to mount
unaided was satisfying but his irritation with life was growing apace like summer grass.

Three more days of travel lay ahead of them. The girl
was not likely to run away now but she was going to test
him to the limit. How fortunate that they had both been so
tired when he rode with his arms about her earlier else she
would have soon learned the power she had over him. He
could not afford to let her find out. Not yet.

⁓

Margery pulled a face as she eased her leg across the shiny
saddle. How she was going to endure the chafing, she did
not know. At least, she consoled herself, she did not have to
ride with *him* anymore. Did that rogue have to scrutinize her
every movement? Well, she wanted as little to do with him
as possible but her determination not to speak to him for the
rest of the morning was soon forgotten.

"But this is not the road to Exeter!" she protested as
Stone turned his horse in a northwesterly direction out of
the village.

"Lettered but somewhat untutored," applauded her captor. "Even if you can read signposts, keep your voice low."

"The master has been commissioned to take the rebel Clarence's Devon manors. He can hardly appear before the King with just yourself in tow, now, can he?" The servant, Long, pointed this out to her, with his inevitable gap-toothed grin.

"I suppose not but I thought we were going direct to the King."

"The King is not yet in Devonshire." Stone's eyes ground into hers as if he were willing obedience into her head. "If you are thinking to escape again, the sand in your glass is spent. The Earl will have boarded ship by now for Calais."

"*If* his ships have arrived there in good time. We were originally supposed to be making for Southampton."

Her captor's face became alert. "Were you now? So why did he change his plan?"

"My lord received word that it was too dangerous. He sent some of our best soldiers to steal through to Hampshire and bring our ships west. I am only telling you this because it is too late for you to act upon the information."

She was thinking rapidly, worrying what would happen if there were insufficient ships to evacuate the rebels. Would Warwick stand and fight Ned?

"No matter, mistress. We shall be in Exeter by Wednesday to learn the news."

"Three days on the road!" The mare lifted her head at the sudden jerk upon the bridle. "Do you mean I have to put up with your unspeakable company for that long!"

The stallion circled the mare menacingly until its rider was within kissing distance. "Speak to me like that one more time, lady, and I shall give you cause to exercise your legs instead of your tongue. You shall walk to Exeter if it pleases you."

Margery swallowed. She felt like driving a fist into one of those adamantine green eyes but his gaze gripped hers, his face barely a palm span away. He was invading the very air she breathed.

Suddenly the embers of her memory abruptly stirred to flame. Finally she understood the sudden feeling of familiarity that overwhelmed her. Sweet Jesu, last time they had met the knave had tumbled her down upon the floor of the hay barn bestriding her thighs, trying to bewitch her with that green fire.

She clenched her jaw. This time he had underestimated his victim. She was no longer a curious goose who was easily flattered by a man's attention and he could—well, he could just whistle in the wind until he was hoarse. She met the sorcerer full square, her eyes hard and brilliant. "You think you have unfinished business, do you not, Master Stone?" she taunted.

The imperious expression of her adversary gave no quarter. "I do not think it, mistress, I now know it."

3

Margery was as avid for news as a fledgling for food by the time they finally arrived at the northern gate into the city of Exeter—together, that was, with half of the shire and its produce. The queue was enormous. A bubbling brew of panniered donkeys, driven livestock, jammed carts, and Devon curses. They received plenty of those as Stone, armored with authority and the advantage of his soldiers, nosed his horse through the throng, his fist tight on the leading rein of Margery's horse, so she was lucky to hear the news firsthand.

The tidings were rich indeed. For once Exeter was at the heart of the great matters occurring in the kingdom and the guards at the gate parted readily with the information.

The King had come to Exeter. That was the main part. The Earl and Duke had escaped by ship so there would be no beheadings or hangings. That was the second part and the third part was that the city was so full with the King's men-at-arms that there was no accommodation left except for fleas or any woman who would share a bed with a soldier.

Stone, not seemingly put out, ordered his men and

Margery back to one of the outlying villages. Having set a guard about her, he returned to the city to seek an audience with the King.

"Did you see him?" Margery asked on his return just before nightfall, breaking her long silence.

He nodded with such disinterest that she could have shaken him.

"He will see you, mistress. But before you whoop for joy, let me tell you that he is about to leave for Southampton. I am bidden to take you to him there and I have orders to take possession of some manors in Dorset, one outside Bridport and two more the other side of Dorchester. In other words, we shall have to tolerate each other's unwelcome company for another week."

"Oh." Margery's shoulders slackened with disappointment.

"Such enthusiasm," he applauded dryly. "However, we shall go into Exeter in the morning and sleep there tomorrow night. The sooner we are out of this flea-ridden hovel the better." He raised a disgusted eyebrow at the crumbling plasterwork of the room that had been her prison for the afternoon. "Besides, I have some errands and one that touches your person especially."

"And what is that?" she asked loftily.

"To have you properly gowned again as befits your sex. You cannot attend the King's grace at Southampton as you are."

"I do not think that he would care. I am sure he would be amused."

"I doubt it." Stone's contemptuous expression spoke volumes. "How old are you?"

Margery flushed beneath his rebuke. "Pray, leave me be. I'll answer to the King for my clothes. I need some protection."

"Only from the King," he muttered and raised mocking eyes. "Even a carrot within your codpiece would fool no one." Her hand lashed out at him, tears sparkling on her lashes, but he laughed, his arm easily foiling her, infuriating her even more. "Be still with you! I thought every woman welcomed the prospect of a new gown."

"Not from you. Nothing from you."

"You have no choice so be pleasant." He strode to the

door. "Long will bring you up some supper." He opened the
door, then hesitated, his fingers playing upon the latch. "I
fancy some color that will enhance your eyes may also
sweeten your tongue."

Margery drew herself up as tall as she could, her fingers
clasped sedately beneath her breast. It was an attitude that
both the Countess of Warwick and the Abbess had affected
when they wished to preserve their authority. Her tone was
proud but icy. "Do not treat me like some silly country
maid. Do you think I am so easily pleased?"

"Yes," he snarled over his shoulder and banged the door
behind him.

Outside the room, he leaned against the wall. At last
within his keeping and yet . . . Christ, he was tempted to sin
with her. A little time in Hell for a chance to flick open one
by one the knops of her russet doublet, then slide his hands
inside her shirt. How many Hail Marys would pay for
peeling down the brown hose she wore so unabashed?

Soon, he vowed, very soon.

⁓

Margery smiled in relief as she heard his angry feet descend
the stairs. The man was infuriating but at least he was hon-
orable. He had restored her dagger to her and at each of the
manors where he had taken possession, she had been given
privacy and Matthew Long had slept guard outside her door.
True, there had been a clash between them when he had
insisted Long take the scissors to even up her hair and she
had exacted an enjoyable vengeance in casually telling him
she remembered him now—one of the youths who had held
the wager with the King.

She could swear the words had drawn blood. His gaze
had been as hard as rocks beneath green lichen. Served him
right!

With a shake of her head, Margery turned her thoughts
again to the King and what she must say to him. Ned was in
her debt for all her six years' penance. Perhaps he might
find her a place in one of his sisters' households or even at
his own court. She needed a position that would provide a
roof over her head until the Nevilles returned from Calais
and the Earl came out of his sulks and made his peace.

Without a powerful protector like the Earl of Warwick,
her past reputation and lack of parentage made her open
game for any man. When he had sent her to the nunnery,
Warwick had told her plainly that she had destroyed any
chance of a respectable marriage. And she would do anything rather than become a courtesan, trying to please some
man the whole time. Jesu, no, such a life would be just as
much an enslavement as marriage. That left becoming a nun
but . . . She sighed, yes, her whole future would hang in the
balance at Southampton but at least she would be free of
Richard Stone.

Riding into the city of Exeter next morning, Margery felt
like a child going to a fair for the first time. The city, being
the greatest in the shire and a river port besides, was far
larger than Warwick or Middleham and much more exciting. It was smoky, noisy, and full of dung from the horses
of the King's army, but stretching down the hill to the Exe
Valley in one direction and toward the towers of the cathedral, proudly rising above the gables, there were shops and
stalls everywhere.

The apprentices, catching the sleeves of passersby as
they touted for their masters, were cheerful. The King, one
lad explained in a soft Devon brogue as he grabbed hold of
the bridle on Margery's horse to slow her down, had paid
his army when they reached Exeter and the soldiers, their
quarry fled, had spent lavishly in the shops and alehouses.
Clever Ned, thought Margery, it was a subtle way to woo a
city that had hitherto been partial to the Kingmaker's cause.
Fortunate Exeter! Today its streets were mired with excrement instead of blood.

The girl within Margery could not help stealing her eyes
sideways at the sight of all those trinkets and ribbons as she
rode along following Stone. Each board that hung out on
chains from every gabled house was groaning with the
weight of its wares. How wonderful to have a bottomless
purse on your belt. But sensibly she set such thoughts aside.
Material possessions had meant little to her, for all she had
ever owned had been supplied by the Countess and, besides,
it would not do to let Master Stone notice her interest.

He saw his men bestowed at a prosperous hostelry in a lane near the guildsmen's hall. He was about to pluck her from her horse when he caught himself in time and slapped her knee playfully instead with his glove. "Come, little brother, we'll make more progress on foot."

Curiosity compelled her to accompany him though she tossed her head defiantly before she followed him into the throng, picking her way with care around the muddy puddles of yesterday's rain.

Several stalls and shops sold cloth. Stone surveyed them all from the outside and then pushed her into the largest that was set halfway down the hill.

Margery stood dazed, discovering a veritable cave of forbidden treasure. Bales of material lay horizontal against the wall. Silk, tissues of gold and silver, brocades and velvets glowed in hues as rich as gems against the duller camlet and musterdevelys. Sable, marten, and coney furs for tippets, collars, and trims sat coiled upon a sideboard like strange animals and a basket of follybells nestled beside a painted wooden box of leather points already cut into lengths for tying hose to doublets. A merchant's wife, richly appareled, was choosing buttons to edge her cuffs from the samples the merchant had tipped out onto the counter. Margery stanched her envy. It would be wonderful to afford such luxuries and take her time choosing.

Richard had his lie ready. "Some cloth for our sister's gown, good sir. She is of my youngest brother's coloring here." The merchant pointed up questioningly to a creamy white damask but his customer shook his head. "By the Saints, not that. She is too much a rapscallion to keep such a gown clean. No, white is"—he paused, grinning at Margery—"inappropriate, don't you agree, lad?" The girl's hand curled into a fist but she kept her hand to her side. No question that she itched to clout him for mocking her for her lost chastity yet again. Richard was enjoying the sport. His mother had often sent him a long shopping list of items to send back to her in Cumbria so he was quite used to dealing with haberdashers and clothiers but buying for the young woman at his elbow spiced this occasion. He could see that Margery was trying not to show an interest in the fabric that rippled across the board for their perusal but there was a brilliance in her eyes and disappointment as he rejected each.

Tantalizing Margery's womanly appetite when she was forced to play a youth's role as well as trying to scorn him was maybe unkind but Richard sensed there was no danger. The merchant and his apprentice were oblivious to the tension between their customers nor, he noted, did they even suspect Margery's gender. No one had. She played her role well, even walking with a slight swagger, aware that she could bring down the wrath of the local churchmen if her disguise was discovered.

"Then if she is hard on her clothes, sir, would you consider something darker? Is it for summer or for winter apparel?"

"A March gown that she may wear into early summer. Her eyes are as blue as the lad's and her hair this hue." He tugged at her hair and she jerked her head back with a fierce scowl.

An apprentice tumbled a bale of honey velvet across the board but Stone shook his head and Margery bit her lip regretfully. Glancing sideways at her, his thin mouth lifting into a smile, he pointed to a pale blue, the color of forget-me-nots and the apprentice sped up a ladder and brought it down. Richard held it against Margery's embarrassed face and shook his head.

"I think our sister might be pleased with this, brother," she said as huskily as she could, surprising him for it was the first time she had dared to speak in public. Pure pleasure flooded through him and he beamed down at her with seeming indulgence.

"Too costly. Another time, perhaps." Oh, the wench was disappointed. The corners of her mouth curled down and she turned away, pretending to inspect a twist of silken braid.

Richard finally settled on a well-dyed midnight blue velvet. It was a practical choice, the color would not show dirt and would sufficiently suit her but it would give her a graver mien and he was at pains to make sure the King saw her differently now. Margery was most put out and ignored him as he made the other necessary purchases on her behalf, reddening when she heard him ask for cloth for underlinen.

"They were all so beautiful," she said after they left the shop. He smiled to himself. Her admission was a minor victory.

"I agree," he answered amiably. "The forget-me-not was excellent, too excellent."

"How so?"

He shook his head at her and would not answer.

"Now we need a compliant tailor and a good lie to tell him. How opportune it rained last night." The tale that she had been sodden to the skin came easily to his lips when he knocked at the door of a pair of tailors whom the clothier had recommended.

Margery followed him upstairs to their dwelling above the storeroom where she shyly removed the cloak and looked suitably embarrassed as the two men cast skilled eyes over her. "A low neckline, sir?"

Stone shook his head, his eyes critically studying Margery's upper anatomy. "No, cut it high." Her eyebrows rose in surprise but he turned away, nursing his laughter to himself as he set half the payment upon the table.

The men, red-eyed, their fingers callused at the tips, brought the gown to the inn next morning to make adjustments and by sunset it was finished. Richard insisted on seeing Margery in it before he paid the remainder. He imperiously strode into the chamber and dismissed the pair to wait outside. They left, their looks knowing.

"They think you are my mistress." But Margery, he observed, was too delighted with the gown to pick up his verbal gauntlet.

Tight sleeves with turned back cuffs encased her arms without a crease and the rest of the fabric had been cleverly cut to fit her body closely at the waist. Instead of hiding her shapeliness, the high-necked gown emphasized it. Not exactly what Richard had intended; instead of helping her flaunt her obvious charms, the neatly stitched fabric swept down over sweet curves tormenting the discerning eye. He groaned inwardly. If he found her so tempting, how many others would? She looked delicious standing there, openly delighted like a child. The only solution would be to drape the folds of a old-fangled wimple headdress across her shoulders. That would hide the upper slope of those jaunty little breasts. And after all, that short hair needed to be hidden. Yes, that might conceal her charms from the King's lusty eyes. He would have to consult the experts.

She looked up finally and trapped his expression of indulgence. Surprise flickered briefly in her eyes. Instantly Richard's visor of inscrutability snapped down over his face. He resorted in self-defense to playing games with her again. His grave perusal made her blush angrily as he walked around her, his forefinger stroking his chin as he inspected the stitching like some guildmaster.

"Well?" she demanded. "Do you send it back? Or do you wish to examine my new undergarments too?"

Richard let his expression lighten somewhat. It pleased him when she met his verbal assault with equal strength.

"I like the gown well enough. A low neck certainly would give more pleasure to me since you inquire."

"But you said—"

"What I *say* concerns you, not what I *think*." He moved around behind her again.

"Do you always speak in riddles?" she hissed over her shoulder.

"You have noticed," he observed dryly.

"If I have gray hairs by the time I see the King's grace, it will be from having spent a week in your insufferable company."

He stopped his perambulations. "And yet I think I have done you less harm in one poor week than King Edward did." His words were softly spoken but the truth was intended to hurt her. He could not help himself. It salved the frustration that was in him, the bitter gall that she had lain with the King. "Is that not so?" He thrust out a hand and grabbed her chin. "Is that not so?"

Her eyes did not falter before his. She met his anger with fire of her own. "Perhaps, but who are you to be my judge?"

"Who, indeed?" He tossed her face up and let go of her.

"I do not know why fortune perversely tossed me in your path, King's Receiver, but I swear the day is coming when you will rue the day you abducted me."

"So you think, lady, so you think."

By the time they left Exeter, Richard had hired a maid-servant for his prisoner and lit a candle in the cathedral to Richard of Chichester, his namesaint, in the hope that his enterprise might prosper. He had also found Margery an old-fashioned wimple. She had put it on in great amusement, exclaiming that she must look like Chaucer's Wife of Bath. While it fell in dewlaps concealing her firm breasts, her captor was appalled to see that it only emphasized the wench's fresh beauty. Surrounded by the snowy folds, her large blue eyes compelled attention, lending her the heady forbidden allure of an available nun. He gave up at that point.

Margery's consistent veneer of innocence, when he knew that she had writhed beneath the loins of the King, nightly robbed Richard of his sleep; the urge to discover for himself her full capability exercised his imagination. Only iron control kept him sane within a pace of her. He resorted to courtesy and so a careful truce hung in the air between them as he grew increasingly concerned as to what report she would make of him to the King. That was the trouble with unplanned campaigns—he had made too many mistakes already.

They entered Southampton through the handsome Bargate but prior knowledge of the horror that the seaport contained led Richard to bestow his party at an inn on High Street, nestling beneath the wall that flanked the eastern moat, as far from the castle as he could arrange. It had been easier to find accommodation than he had expected; the army's weapons carts were already trundling north to London and most of the men had been sent back to their shires. My lord Gloucester's retainers were much in evidence at the castle but the King had chosen to exploit the less drafty house of Southampton's prosperous mayor. There Richard endured an uncomfortable audience informing his royal employer of his intent, which left him even more desperate to know Margery's true feelings toward her former lover.

Her distracted air over the last few days argued that she had been giving the matter much thought. It was her lack of bitterness that bothered Richard. Had she set the unde-serving royal whoremonger up in a little shrine in some corner of her heart? In his opinion, the King, having seduced her, had shown as much sensitivity as any village clod. In other words, his royal grace had completely washed his hands of her. So why did she not hate her precious Ned?

Richard gritted his teeth as they left their inn hard by Friary Gate next morning and turned into the street that ran along the inner west wall of the city. He was not proud of himself but he had one card left in his hand, a bloody card at that. Would Margery notice that Southampton had a different mood to Exeter, that the citizens shopped tight-lipped, their eyes blinkered? The route he chose was circuitous; it led past the castle that the King had shunned.

"If you will be guided by me, Mistress Margery, do not look to the western walls," he advised her with a tone of superiority that was calculated to provoke rebellion. Of course, she would look—she was a woman.

It was the stench that assailed Margery first, reminding her of the hanged man in the gibbet, making her belly threaten to return her breakfast.

"By Our Blessed Lady!" exclaimed Alys, her maid-servant, and Stone's men-at-arms swore loudly, their horses jerking and whinnying at a sudden rough handling of their bridles. A reflex almost, Margery looked, glimpsed the disfiguring insults to humanity hoisted above the ramparts, and shut her eyes in horror, her head spinning. It was the elite of Warwick's army, the men he had sent to seize his ships and sail them around to Devon. They were men she would have recognized, possibly given a name to but their heads were gone and stakes were . . .

She heard Stone curse. Someone's gloved hand grabbed her horse's reins and led it swiftly onward. Tears blinded her. Eventually when they slackened pace and the odor of rotting flesh no longer hung in their nostrils, she was able to distinguish the faintly unpleasant but reassuring smell of seaweed and hear the rhythmic wash of the waves on the sand. Margery ran a knuckle beneath her eyes and tried to stanch her crying. A man's arm came around her shoulders. it had to be Stone, trying to draw her to his shoulder but she shook him away.

"I *know* him. The King would never . . ." She bit her lip, shaking her head violently as if to dislodge those terrible images.

The horses came to a standstill. They were beyond the castle now.

"It was Butcher Worcester, they tell me." He was the most learned of the earls, but known for his violence. "I warned you not to look, mistress." Stone's voice was kind and gentle, a side of him she had not glimpsed before. He leaned across to tilt her face up. With his gloved finger, he smoothed the droplets from her cheeks and mopped her dry with the edge of the wimple. At least it did have some use, reflected Margery, surprised that her whimsical humor could surface amid more passionate emotions. She gazed gravely up at her companion.

"Your advice was wise, Master Stone, I should not have looked. But I am not a child."

"No," he agreed solemnly, his eyes gently scanning her face. "You are not a child."

"*You* think it is wrong, do you not?"

"Yes," he said softly. "I despise such cruelty."

"Then we are at last in agreement with one another, Master Stone."

A slow smile hovered at the corners of his mouth and then lit his entire face. "I am sure it will not last. Shall we go on or do you need more time? You cannot kneel before King Edward with your eyes puffed and red from weeping."

Stone was right but her appearance was of little importance now. Could the young King she remembered have metamorphosed into a tyrant?

"I tell you this, Master Stone. If my lord of Warwick ever has Worcester at his mercy, that monster will rue his handiwork," she growled. "Are we almost there?"

"His grace is at the mayor's house this morning." He pointed up the street to a high gabled house, adorned with a costly frieze of carved oak, its porch cluttered by a dozen soldiers in the King's livery and a score of countryfolk and urchins waiting for a glimpse of the royal profile.

"Of course, I see it now. I thank you for your care." With that solemn dismissal, she dug her heels into her mare's flank and urged it forward through the throng and determinedly into the bustling courtyard, dismounting before any of the King's grooms or esquires could help her. She tossed the mare's reins imperiously to the nearest man who ran forward. Then she set her face proudly toward the official who came down the steps to ask her business and swept into the mansion in his wake.

Richard hurried after her. He could not let her go in to King Edward in such a dangerous temper. "I did not know you had property in Southampton," he remarked, catching up and setting his hat straight. She gave him a questioning look. "Mistress, you are behaving as if you own the entire city."

She glanced at the official's back ahead of her, biting her lip rebelliously, before she answered his levity. "Master Stone, I thank you for whatever trouble you have been asked to take on my behalf but now we are here I can manage my own affairs."

He grabbed her arm, trying to force her to a halt. "Have a care, before you stoke your burning indignation further." She almost faltered in her step as her eyes met his. His gaze was serious, concerned. "Listen to why the King's grace has sent for you and weigh what he says." They had reached a hushed antechamber full of grave-faced people waiting for an audience and she was forced to halt her brisk pace.

"Of course." She tapped her riding crop impatiently against her gloved palm and, embarrassed, realized she should have left it with the groom.

"Wait here, my lady." The officer scratched on the doors for admittance.

"For a bastard, you behave surprisingly. They must think you at least a princess," commented Richard, both amused and exasperated.

The officer reappeared, crooking his finger. "My lady."

Richard removed the crop from her hands and bestowed it upon one of the royal pages. The guards opened the double doors. They were expected. Margery felt the stabbing jealous stares of those who had been waiting hours or even days.

Suddenly her anger cooled at the reality of not only confronting the most powerful man in England but the lover who had occupied her thoughts each bedtime for the last six long years.

The King's Receiver was watching her face solemnly. Could he read the misapprehension that blew across her mind? Her dread that the love she had felt toward the King would dominate her life again? Was it obvious? Perhaps it was, because a slow grin warmed his face.

"I am coming in with you, *my lady*," he echoed with heavy sarcasm as he thrust out his arm to her.

"For your reward, sir?"

"I trust so."

Hesitantly she rested her fingers on his gloved wrist. Stone smiled, threw back his shoulders with a proud grace, and led her in.

CHAPTER
4

The heavy doors rattled to, enclosing them in a large room dominated by a heavy oak table heaped with rolls of vellum and an assortment of inkwells and quills. A man in a cord-du-roi tabard was preoccupied in dripping hot wax upon a folded letter. After he had jabbed the royal seal into it, he straightened up, wiped ink-stained fingers on his rear, looked toward the window, and bowed.

"You have leave, Kendall."

Margery whirled around at that familiar voice as King Edward IV, her dear Ned, even more of a giant than she remembered, stepped down from the window recess. And she forgot all anger. It was her memory, not her heart, that was stirred by the sight of him. Because she was older, or maybe it was having Richard Stone at her elbow, she saw the King with different eyes.

She sank into a deep curtsy as Ned strode across to her with that lazy grace that was so deep in his nature. Behind her, Master Richard Stone lowered himself respectfully onto one knee.

Warm fingers caught her chin causing her to look up

once more into the blue eyes she remembered so well. A
strong but gentle clasp drew her to her feet and his mouth
closed down upon her lips, soft and sensuous as before.

"Well met, sweet heart."

Richard Stone tensed and fidgeted behind her, distracting
her. It was as if his presence had exorcised the magic.
Something within Margery sagged with inward relief—the
arcane invisible power no longer worked and she knew she
was free of the charm the King had wrought upon her.

Ned condescended to notice her companion as if he were
an unwelcome intruder. "Hmm, Dick lad, we shall talk with
you anon. Our brother Gloucester is anxious to know if Mistress Margery has arrived. Pray inform him so." Margery
sensed the suppressed irritation in Stone but he stood up
obediently and bowed himself out.

"Let me see you properly, Meg." A twist on her fingers
from Ned forced her to twirl around for him. "Certes, there
is more flesh on you but delightfully so. What monstrosity is
this?" His large hands deftly freed her from the wimple and
cast it over his shoulder. "You are more beautiful than I
remember, Margery of Warwick."

"Despite the six long years?"

Ned's sky-colored eyes bathed her in a kindness that was
sincere as he touched her short hair. "Indeed, all my fault
and you have paid the price. I crave your pardon." His arm
fastened about her shoulders and he turned her to the hearth.
"Make yourself comfortable by the fire and let us have
mulled wine and sweet oatcakes." He shook a brass bell that
stood on the table and a young page ran in from a door
beside the arras to know his bidding.

Margery sat down happily on a settle made luxurious by
tawny velvet cushions. She edged her cold toes to the fire as
close as she dared without scorching the leather of her soles,
then turned her head to savor the presence of the man who
had once been Heaven to her. At one time this informal
domesticity with the King of England had been her only
dream.

Beaming back at him, she saw again within his smile the
handsome, genial youth who had bent time to visit his
younger brothers in the schoolroom and Warwick's daughters in the nursery. Margery had been older than the others,

worldly enough to catch the grin that he tossed at her like a
ball above the smaller heads. Many a time he had mimicked
the posturings of the great nobles of the land to her, teaching
her they had the same weaknesses as lesser men. As his
visits grew infrequent so her pride in him blossomed as he
defeated Lancaster and became King. By the time she
reached sixteen, she was deaf to the rumors that he had been
secretly wed or that nothing in skirts south of Berwick was
safe from him.

She gave a small, happy sigh, hugging to herself the
sight of Ned with the great golden chain across his broad
shoulders and the ring of England weighing upon his finger,
grinning at her. The aroma of temporal power exuded from
him but there were subtle enemies to greatness. He might
still majestically dwarf the world around him but there was
now an increased heaviness about his girth that was emphasized by the pleated red and gold embroidered brocade doublet, and even the hint of jowl beneath his jawline.

Flinging himself into the chair opposite her with a smile,
he sprawled in the relaxed way she remembered so well, his
long legs stretched out to the hearth.

"Do I pass examination, Meg?" he mocked.

"Oh, dear," she exclaimed. "Am I that transparent?"

"I am sure that ten years of being mobbed by scrofulous
beggars, begetting princesses, and ruling a realm of willful
lords has done its damage." He was right. Time had also
chiseled cynical curves about his mouth and carved deep
lines from the corners of his eyes.

"To be truthful, you are looking heavier. Does it bother
your horse?"

The smile twitched at the corners of his mouth and
spread until it mirrored her own teasing expression and his
laughter filled the room. "No, only the Queen complains."

The page scurried in like a little mouse, set the pot of
mulled wine upon the hearth, and shifted a tray of chased
silver goblets from the table to the royal footstool. Ned dismissed him with a wave and perused her kindly.

"So now what do you want of me, Ned?" asked Margery
softly. It was a risk to call him by the name he had once
allowed her but she needed to remind him of her ruin. "Why
am I here?"

"You do not know?" He sounded surprised.

"Your grace, acquiring information from your wretched Receiver is like trying to extract a healthy tooth from a dragon."

The King lazily stretched his arms above his head, raising his eyebrows as if he were not sure how to answer before letting his arms drop and reaching out a nonchalant hand for the ladle. "Well, there are amends to make—Ouch!" He swore as the metal burned him. "But first your news."

He gave her his full attention, waiting on her himself with wine and sweet cakes and only interrupting softly now and then as she told him how she had been swiftly sent away from Warwick castle in disgrace in case she was with child by him, of the time in the nunnery and how her exile had lasted until the recent Yuletide. With care, she explained how she had spent the time since then with the Countess and her daughters while Warwick and Clarence had provoked the rebellion in the north. Then her sentences grew superlatives. The King listened frowning to her narration of how Richard Stone had suddenly abducted her and his royal jaw slackened somewhat as Margery ended, reiterating, "Ned, I implore you if you send for me again, please do not have me abducted in a vegetable sack, trussed like a fowl."

He once more offered her the plate of oatcakes before he answered. "Touching your honor, though?"

She laughed. "My . . . my questionable honor has not been touched."

"I am relieved to hear you say that."

"But what I do not understand, my liege, is why you had me brought to you."

The King did not answer at first. His chin slumped on his chest; he stared dreamily into the fire. The crackling of the logs dominated the silence between them.

Eventually he raised his head. "Your present situation concerns me greatly. With the Earl a fugitive, you need a protector."

"Why, I suppose that's true." She shrugged ruefully. "But at least I have no guardian telling me what to do."

"Oh, yes, you have, my Meg. That task falls to me. It

seems you need a husband, Margery of Warwick. A worthy respectable man to protect and honor you. You have worn a harlot's necklace because of me and that must end."

"Oh, no!" she exclaimed vehemently. "Your grace is generous but I cannot accept."

"Nonsense, Meg dear, you must allow me to compensate you for your ruined virtue."

"Ned . . . my liege lord . . . please listen to me." She leaned forward, her hands twisting in her lap. "I would rather earn my keep than be in any man's debt. Is there a place for me as a servant in the Queen's household?" She knew the answer even before her king gave a deep sigh and shook his head. "Because of my ignoble birth?"

"Let us just say that you are one of Warwick's household. My Queen is not overly fond of those who wear the Neville badge."

Margery tried to hide her disappointment. "I suppose she knows of me as well."

"Yes, I imagine she does. You see, it would not suit." He leaned back and regarded her thoughtfully. "I do have an office that you may perform. Something that you of all people could do better than any other servant we possess." There was the weight of kingship in his voice now. "If you can accomplish this successfully, we shall give you an annuity and the independence you so wish for."

"I, your grace? What could I possibly do?"

"Heal the breach between me and my treacherous kinsmen. I want you to find Warwick and Clarence wherever they are and give them letters. They have to be brought back into the sheepfold."

"Surely, your grace, the situation is past my capability as a sheepdog. You have whistled and they have made away with half the flock. If the Countess speaks true, there is too much hurt between my lord and you."

She remembered the Earl white-hot with anger a few weeks past at the mere mention of Ned's name.

"Do you want them to remain in exile, Meg, or see another war?" As she shook her head gravely at him, he sat forward. "I need a messenger that no one will suspect to carry secret letters to my brother Clarence. All of us wish him to know we still love him well despite his treachery."

"All?"

"Yes, all the brood of York. Dickon, Bess, Anne probably, although she is too busy cavorting with her lover, and, of course, Mother." He jiggled his fingers, counting off his sisters. "And Meggy, too, no doubt. Her husband Burgundy will be watching events very carefully." He clapped his hands to his cream hose knees. "That's all, sweet heart. It is not too much to ask, is it? I want you to see my brother Clarence privily and tell the wretch I shall forgive him."

Such a mission would be the answer to Margery's problems. She would be back where she belonged in Warwick's household. Stone's intervention would have been a mere hiccup. What she did not like was deceiving her guardian.

"But what of my lord of Warwick? I cannot go behind his back. If it had not been for him, I should be scrubbing kitchen floors or starving on the street."

"Oh, you may certainly bear an offer of a pardon to him but I doubt that he will give it credence. The die are cast, Meg. Warwick wanted to rule the kingdom through me but he mistook his man. He presumed too much. I am the anointed king even if he did help me to the crown." He leaned across to pat her knee. "Even you, sweet heart, were another quarrel between us. But my fickle brother is another matter. I am sure that he can be persuaded."

"Ned, I doubt that the Duke will even listen—"

The King caught her hands within his large graceful fingers. "Try. He knows that you and I are close, Meg. If you can be my voice and lure him back, then Warwick will be alone in Calais without allies and will be forced to make his peace with me."

His flattery was as heady as firewater but she could not help asking, "And if I refuse?"

Ned looked extremely surprised. "Why should you?"

"Because I . . . you must forgive me saying this . . . to be honest, your grace, I am appalled at what I saw in the marketplace on my way here. Those poor wretches were only obeying their lord."

Ned rose haughtily. "How refreshing you are, my dear

Margery. It seems the nuns made no improvement to your manners." He leaned against the wall beside the hearth, scowling at the glowing embers for a moment before he turned. "We respect your sentiments—and your courage in saying such things to our face—but those men were traitors to us. The manner of their death was not to our liking either, if you desire the truth. But before you take us to task further, consider that we could have had old King Harry put to death instead of keeping him alive in the Tower. As for my noble lord of Warwick, he had no scruples in ordering our wife's father and her brother slain to satisfy his jealousy. Do not preach to us of Warwick's purity!"

She bit her lip, her eyes downcast, wondering whether she had best fall upon her knees. "I beg your grace's pardon." Jesu, Ned could order a painful death for her with a snap of his fingers.

He stooped and tipped her face up to regard her sternly. The fury had faded from his voice. "Oh, Meg, your candid nature was a treasure I always appreciated. But, sweet heart, Worcester had to make an example of them. I must have an end to these constant rebellions. You can help me achieve this if you will go to Calais for me and there will be no more hangings. Say you will." At least he was speaking as a man again.

Margery pulled back. "This is why you sent for me, is it not? Have I a choice?"

"A choice, yes, of sorts. I am desperate enough to threaten you. If you do not wish to earn a reward by serving me then I must make other provision for you. You shall most certainly have a husband. We cannot have you unprotected in the world and we owe you that at least. How would an old man with bad teeth and a rat-ridden castle on the Scottish border suit you?"

She was not sure how much he was in earnest. There was a ruthlessness in him that she had not glimpsed before.

She rose and faced him, as much as one could face a giant. Her eyes explored his face, discovering no remorse. "You do not frighten me, Ned. I asked you for my independence. Six years I have served you on my knees."

The King smiled sardonically down at her, like a great golden cat toying with a mouse. "I shall show some leniency then. You shall have the man who brought you here."

That did touch her on the raw. Margery's bravado vanished and she stared up at him speechless. "He has prospects," purred Ned. "From what you say, he has dishonored your reputation—far more than I have—by abducting you. So let him make amends by marrying you. We shall give him lands and offices to sweeten the bargain."

"No!" She recoiled. The thought of being completely in Richard Stone's power for the rest of her life was unthinkable.

"So vehement, my sweet?" Ned's finger reached out to stroke her cheek. "Come now, you must be realistic. He is a prize for a landless lovechild like yourself. What other prospect have you of making such a match?" His tone lightened. "I believe he is from Cumbria. It is beautiful in summer, they say, although I confess I have heard it rains more there than in the rest of England."

He knew his quarry, Margery thought angrily. The threat had sunk into her as keenly as a shaft but she was not beaten.

"And he is welcome to populate it but not by me." She stormed away from him. "I had as lief lie with a wet log."

"Cruel one!" Shaking with laughter, he took a stride after her, pulled her around, swung her up into the air, and caught her to his great breast. "He is a proper man." He set her down and, bending his head, kissed her full upon the mouth. She made no resistance, her contrary mind wondering how Richard Stone would kiss.

Raising his head, the King's gaze explored her eyes and lips. "That was a wondrous week we shared but what say you to a house in Chelsea, a few minutes by boat from Westminster?"

It was like old times. Margery blinked at him in sheer delight that he should even suggest she become his mistress once again but as far as she was concerned the fire that had burned between them was cold. Smiling, she shook her head at him, her cheeks pinkening.

"Ned, put me down." She laughingly raised her hands against his chest to push him away. "Remembering what we shared sustained me through those long years of punishment but we are both changed. I love you still but as a loving subject and I will go to Calais and do as you say for England, to make a peace between you and my lord of Clarence. I can do you better service there, believe me."

"You are sure the thought of rearing little Cumbrians does not appeal?"

She turned her head from side to side and looked at him now without fear or passion. It was as if the sea had washed across what was written on the sand between them and made it whole again.

"Excellent." The chime of the hour bell distracted him. His manner became more businesslike. "Well, that is settled now. You shall take a ship on today's evening tide with a bulging purse of gold for your expenses. If any ask from now on, say you are rejoining the Duchess Isabella's household. Once you reach Calais, you must trust no one and put a guard on that warm heart and honest tongue of yours. I shall speak with you again before you sail. Go now and seek out my brother Gloucester. Blame him if you will for this enterprise for it was his notion that you should be our carrier pigeon." She curtsied. "And, Margery"—he set the wimple back over her head and tucked the fair tendrils out of sight—"if you succeed in this, console yourself that you will save many men's lives." Then with a swift kiss upon her fingers, he saw her to the door.

Once more in the outer chamber, she stood still, both excited and apprehensive of the task that lay ahead. Stone was waiting for her. He detached himself from the group warming themselves around a brazier to take her arm, drawing her to one side with ill-concealed impatience. She assumed he was angered at being excluded.

"What is decided?" he asked. "You look perturbed."

"I am to sail for Calais after all to rejoin the Duchess Isabella."

"What!" he exclaimed with an oath, letting go of her arm in amazement. His sudden lack of control astonished her. "That is too dangerous. To send you into exile when—" He strode away from her several paces, his face turned away, his shoulders rigid with fury. A royal page in the King's livery coughed politely at his elbow. The King's Receiver turned, disdain frozen on his features.

"His grace the King commands you attend him, sir."

"Does he now." His eyes blazed at her. "When are you to leave?"

"Tonight."

"Tonight!"

The page tugged at his sleeve, "Now, sir!" but he shook the boy away.

"That is outrageous. He might at least . . ." The page looked embarrassed and everyone in the antechamber became suddenly very interested in what Master Stone had to say next, but he rapidly swallowed any treasonous utterance. "Very well!" he snapped at the boy. "Mistress, you—"

"Master, the King—"

"Yes, I hear you." He started toward the doors of the King's chamber, then he swung around again to face Margery. "There is something you should know."

"His grace is waiting!" The boy's voice was peevish. The men-at-arms opened the doors to the King's chamber.

"Margery!" The voice of the Duke of Gloucester, Ned's youngest brother, made her spin around in delight.

"Believe me, you have to know—"

By the time she looked back to Master Stone, however, the doors had closed behind him. Margery, her cheeks pink as roses, was oblivious of the outraged petitioners. She was too pleased to see her old childhood friend, the Duke of Gloucester, to wonder why Richard Stone should be so angry and what he could possibly tell her that was so vital.

Richard ran through the Water Gate onto Southampton's bustling south quay and paused, short-breathed, to gaze as if blinded. A dozen vessels of varying bulk were tethered at the wharves, like cows in milking stalls, and there were more out on Southampton Water.

"Looking for someone, master?" A boy no higher than his belt planted himself firmly in front of Richard's boots.

"You know everyone, do you!" he snarled as a flat, grubby palm rose expectantly. "The carrack *Winchelsea*?" Even as the coin left his purse, he guessed the answer. A dirt-clogged fingernail pointed to a distant sail well on its way toward the Isle of Wight.

His finely clad shoulders lost their stiffness, his lower lip curled in bitter, silent fury against the King. So that was why the Keeper of the Privy Seal had been interrogating him as to the potential of every manor he had seized in the King's name. Whoresons!

Flinging his flapping cloak up over his shoulder, he strode miserably to the water's edge and down the stone steps. His dark, vehement words notched up an extra week in Purgatory and, overheard, would have sent him to oblivion in a Tower dungeon. Heedless of the indifferent waves retreating from his bootcaps, he might have stood beneath the bleak sky until the tide returned to douse him had Matthew not disturbed his misery.

"I have saddled Comet, sir. I knew you'd want to ride." Richard tore his unseeing gaze slowly away from the barnacled piers and turned sourly. His servant eyed him with caution. " 'Cept you've grand company. His grace of Gloucester awaits you."

It was no lie; a great white stallion danced proudly next to Comet at the eastern end of the quay and the slight youth who sat astride him, his fur collar risen against the bitter wind, was watching falconlike.

The King's Receiver wanted no company. He wanted to drown his fury and wake in misery with the mother of all headaches gnawing at his temples, but the King's brother, heir to the throne now that George, the Duke of Clarence, was attainted, was not a man to disobey. Dully he started walking back along the quay.

The white stallion and its rider separated from the retinue and disdainfully met him. The pale face of Richard of Gloucester looked gravely down at him. "I am sorry," said the seventeen-year-old youth, thrusting out his gloved hand.

"As your grace pleases," answered Richard coldly, brushing the Duke's signet ring against his lips.

"Come!" Gloucester dismissed his entourage with a wave and touched his spurs to his horse's flanks. Richard had little choice but to swiftly throw himself into the saddle and follow those hooves to where the quay joined the land and down across that cold glimmering left by the receding waves and through the meandering ranks of abandoned seaweeds. If Gloucester wished to command his time, he was past caring.

Spatters of sand tossed up before him, and his own horse leaped forward in chase. The Duke gave full spur and headed east through a scattering of trees to the coast road. Richard narrowed the distance, aware that two of the Duke's armed grooms were following him some twenty paces behind. The heady gallop helped some of the painful heaviness to disperse. The cold evening wind lifted his cloak and buffeted him so that by the time the Duke drew rein, Richard's face was wind-slapped and glowing.

"Feeling treacherous?" The Duke's gold-flecked amber eyes perused him critically.

Richard's jaw slackened, his thoughts running higgledy in all manner of directions. "Never tell me you are thinking of joining Warwick's rebellion, my lord?"

Gloucester's narrow mouth tightened impatiently. "Don't be so plaguey stupid, Richard! Answer my question!"

"Then, yes! Why should I pretend to you? I had what I wanted within my grasp until your brother . . . Was it too much to ask of him?" He turned his face away proudly, his soul sullen.

"This is the second time he has done this to you. I am here to ensure there shall not be a third." Richard could not answer. His head jerked around to face the Duke. The younger man was not mocking him. "I have the King's leave to put a proposal to you, Richard, one that may suit both our purposes extremely well. That is, if you are feeling wise enough to listen."

The bow that had been drawing his gut tight was suddenly released as Richard calmly met the Duke's probing gaze. "I think you may be assured of that, your grace."

"Excellent, you see I think I am going to have to arrest you for high treason."

.

CHAPTER
5

The creamy sails arched into curves catching the wind as the *Winchelsea* rounded the Isle of Wight. Margery stood at the rail of the vessel, savoring the taste of salt spray on her lips. It was almost like going on a pilgrimage to Compostela, an exciting sense of new experiences awaiting her beyond the horizon. And what was more, she was free! That was until she remembered that she had a mission to fullfil and around her neck hung a constant reminder.

It seemed that the moment Master Stone had informed Ned at Exeter that he held Warwick's ward, the two royal brothers had conceived the idea to use her as their messenger. So before she sailed she was presented with a new overgown that held the secret letters stitched into the fashionable broad brocade collar that framed the neckline. A third letter, from Ned's mother, helped give shape to a small steeple cap. It had been suggested that the letters from his two sisters should be sewn into her purfiled hem but Margery had put an end to the nonsense. Hems, she explained, inevitably became soggy and surely no one would object to the two Duchesses writing to their brother. As for the official letters for the Acting Governor of Calais, Isabella, and the Earl of Warwick, they were locked in a small coffer and the key to that was around her neck in the guise of a miniature pectoral cross.

Finally, pinned to her undershift was a St. Catherine wheel set within a vine of fruiting pears—a brooch not to be worn until she needed it as a sign to Ned's agents that she had succeeded in her mission to win over George, Duke of Clarence.

Ostensibly her mission was to carry letters to Isabella, Duchess of Clarence, from her sisters-in-law, beseeching her to persuade her husband and father to make their peace with the King and swear public allegiance to Edward once again. And surely it would be no labor to persuade the Duke to return and make his peace? But for the moment in the no-man's-land of the sea, she was enjoying herself. Even the front of gray miserable weather that was bowling toward them as the day grew old did little to stanch her cheerfulness. England, Ned, and that arrogant Richard Stone were left behind.

The twelve large towers of Calais loomed upon the little English ship as it eventually swung its stern into the narrow neck of the harbor past the vigilant right-hand watchtower. The captain, in good humor, exchanged a greeting with the soldiers on duty and invited Margery up onto the forecastle.

The town portcullis was already up, sucking a tangle of carts and laden people inside the walls, and the wharves were busy with early morning business. Quite a few ships had come in with cargo on the first tide. Bales of Cotswold wool were queued up on the deck of a Bristol vessel for the derricks to lift them onto waiting carts, while alongside a Venetian galley was unloading glass and silks. One of the crates tipped out of its ropes and the noise of its shattering contents begat a score of foul oaths.

Margery was longing to see the town. Not only was Calais the English shopfront to the customers of Christendom but it was one of the world's greatest markets. Its fairs were reputed to rival those of Antwerp and Bruges. It was also said that a man (or a woman) could buy anything in the

streets of Calais. Anything from sapphires and sables to
sausages and salt, even a pagan ebony-skinned servant from
the slave markets of Fez.

As Margery scanned the ships already anchored, their
sails rolled up tightly against the spars, the captain pointed
out the flags of Genoa and Florence, even one from distant
Russia whose ship was bearing tallow, furs, and amber, but
no Neville pennant fluttered on any of the topmasts. The
Kingmaker's flagship was missing.

A strong unease gripped Margery. Calais was devoted to
Warwick. He had governed it in the past and paid its garrison
out of his own purse when the Lancastrian King, Henry VI,
had deliberately delayed sending across the men's wages. He
must be here. He always came here when things in England
were as hot as the Devil's fire for him. Why, even Ned had
assumed that he must be here. There had been no storm in
the past two weeks to wreck his ship, but suppose they had
been attacked by Hanse ships and were prisoners? She shivered as the rain closed in and Calais slowly disappeared
behind a drizzly mist.

Of course, on further reflection, if she were wearing Warwick's shoes, maybe she would not want to blaze her presence like a bonfire. Perhaps his ship was quietly anchored up
the coast, stealthfully drawn up some tributary where it
could be left under guard while the Earl and his retinue sat in
comfort behind Calais's sturdy walls.

The captain exclaimed in surprise at her elbow. He was
expecting a pilot to row out to them, not the longboat with
men in brigandines and helmets that was fast drawing alongside. Not overly concerned, he ordered his crew to toss the
rope ladder down, muttering that Acting Governor Wenlock,
the Earl of Warwick's deputy, was carrying out his duty with
unusual alacrity. A second later he had climbed down to the
main deck and was exchanging fierce words with the officer
in charge.

Margery watched in horror as the governor's soldiers drew
their swords and the captain thrust his hands up in surrender.
With an oath he shouted up to her, "Satan take the fools!
These asses think we might be smugglin' rebels because
we're out of Southampton—men as've escaped hanging.
You'd best come down, mistress."

"So what have we here?" The beefy officer in Wenlock's livery smirked.

The captain answered swiftly, "A woman passenger, carried by the King's very orders."

"Woman, is it? They're all women these days. We found two fisherwomen last week. Grown beards in prison, they have. Get down the ladder then! Let's have a look at you."

Just as Margery reached the lowest rung, she sensed her hem lifted. She twisted fiercely around to find the captain had grabbed the man's sword arm.

"She's a lady, yer landlubberin' numbskull. Touch her and the King's grace will skin yer."

"Ha, you still say she's a wench, do you?" The knave circled Margery, threatening her with his sword. "Looks like a woman, smells like a woman, but there's sixteen-year-old rebels could pass for such. Let's make sure." He snatched at her cap and veil. It came away easily, tousling her chin-length hair. "See, a lad!" His soldiers cheered, encouraging him further. "What's needed is further examination. Lie her down, lads."

Guffaws of glee reached Margery. She turned with hot indignation upon the officer as the soldiers started forward with mischief.

"Do you value your post, sirrah?" She pitched her voice higher than normal. "I have letters from the King's grace to Governor Wenlock. Captain, bring them hither from my cabin." The captain hesitated. "Go, this officer is no fool. He surely can recognize the King's seal."

If her voice sounded brave enough, its owner was inwardly shaking. She kept her chin in the air and tapped her foot impatiently. A doe surrounded by baying hounds, she just wished he would hurry.

Alys's arrival on deck nursing the coffer in her arms caused a welcome diversion. The wench's rotund curves allowed no room for doubt as to her sex and her habit of showing a generous amount of cleavage whatever the weather ensured that loud whistles greeted her.

"Mistress?" She curtsied and the soldiers whooped.

"What say you we investigate both of 'em?" suggested one.

Margery took no notice. She pulled the cross out on its chain from her bodice and inserted it into the lock of the

coffer. Alys pulled up the lid to reveal the sealed letters.
Wenlock's man thrust in front of Margery. He grabbed two
of the letters, turning them over with a frown, rubbing his
thumb across the embossed orange wax. It was apparent he
was unlettered.

"I can smell a rat, a nasty bloated dead rat in all this.
Kings don't send women as their messengers. They send
lords with retinues. Take 'em on shore. My lord governor
will enjoy this."

"The pestilence on yer, yer rogue! Is it a fat bribe you're
after?" The captain had to be restrained from gripping the
officer's windpipe. "How much do you look for? I have a
cargo to unload and Arras cloth to take on board. There's
merchants in Kent expecting me to sail from here by high
tide tomorrow."

"Mayhap you'll be free by tomorrow. It depends on
who's tellin' lies, doesn't it? Your ship will be safe enow.
The crew can stay here under arrest but you have a lot of
questions to answer."

The captain was forced, still snarling and cursing, over
the side but at least the sealed letters seemed to have
installed a wariness into the soldiers. The officer permitted
Alys to fetch their few belongings from below. The meager
luggage did not help to impress.

"It will be all right once I see Lord Wenlock," Margery
reassured the glum captain as she joined him in the shaking
longboat.

"Will it? I doubt you'll be allowed to set eyes on him.
Still, if he should set you at liberty, pray send the merchant
Master Caxton advice of my arrest."

They were hustled through the gate, their escort full of self-
importance but no one took much notice; there was too much
business to be done. Safeguarding their prisoners through the
hordes of people, barrows, and carts was no light matter.

One young man, however, deliberately forced his black
stallion in front of them. He was entirely and expensively
clad in black save for the silver embroidery that scalloped
both the edge of his sleeves and the scarf of the liripipe that
rippled from the rolled brim of his hat. Margery met his
curious gaze and returned it in full measure, uncowed by
his close study of her. His hair was prematurely silver and

his hooded eyes were old for his young face. His glance
swept over the prisoners, missing nothing before he pulled
his horse's head around and moved the splendid beast out of
their way. Margery watched him still as his two men-
servants closed in behind him but he rode away without a
second glance.

"Bloody interfering Burgundians!" snarled the officer,
bawling at his men to clear a wider path.

Margery and her maidservant were shown into a small
room in the governor's house, unfurnished save for a single
bench. The spluttering captain had been led away to the
town lockup. The letters were given into the charge of an
officious red-haired clerk who shrugged insolently at Margery's demands.

"Good woman, I doubt he'll see you today or any day."

"On the contrary, you will ensure he does, sirrah, that is
if you seek to rise in the world. Make no doubt that I have
the King's ear. You may tell your lord and his counselors
that they spike traitors in Southampton these days. Now I
think upon it, your master's arrest of a royal emissary stinks
of treason, stinks to the vaults of Heaven. Tell him that I
remember the old days when he was glad to dine at my lord
of Warwick's table. Perhaps the King's grace has a longer
memory than your lord."

The officer's freckled face turned a red that went ill with
his ruddy head as he abruptly turned on his heel and left
them without another word.

"Mistress, that was a marvel. Such wondrous words."

"Words are useless, Alys, if no one takes any notice."

No one did. The bells of Calais tolled out each hour
increasing the women's frustration and their hunger. The
curfew bell had finally convinced Margery they had been
forgotten when the door was unlocked and the red-haired
man sniffingly confronted them, informing Margery that
Lord Wenlock had at last agreed to see her.

A smell of food lingering about the passageway and
hall painfully assaulted their bellies. The eyes of the servants, clearing away the scraps, followed them with amused
curiosity.

"Where is it we are going, mistress?"

"I care not, Alys, so long as there is some food at the end

of it. Now I know how hungry the small creatures feel in midwinter."

It was not expected—the governor's chamber. His bed, with its scarlet hangings and furs, glimmered on a wooden plinth in the soft light of the candles behind the heads of the two men who were expecting her. Neither rose, they sat behind a table, their pointed toes stretched out toward the generous fire. Like two magistrates, Margery thought, except they had the contented look of men who had feasted well. The white linen of the board bore a scattering of crumbs and regretfully nothing else save two inlaid goblets.

"Announce me," Margery commanded calmly. Astonished by her audacious sense of occasion, the officer was jolted to comply. "My lord, your excellency, this woman claims to be Mistress Margery of Warwick"—his tone dripped with irony—"ward to the great rebel styling himself Earl of Warwick."

It required effort not to show her annoyance especially as the older man, whom she remembered from her childhood, snorted, sousing her from head to toe with his rheumy glance.

Now how did the Countess always do it? She had a way of making people behave as they should. Well, it was worth a try. You had to achieve a balance of incredulity and indignation and sweep your gaze imperiously down them. Margery tried it on Wenlock and his mouth fell open, but it was the other man in the black velvet houppelande who rose to his feet and came around the table to her.

"Demoiselle"—he took her hand—"I am not disappointed." His deep gray eyes were compelling, reminding her of Richard Stone in the intelligence of his stare. It was the silver-haired Burgundian.

"You may not be disappointed, monsieur," she answered calmly, "whatever you mean by it, but I am." She turned her face to Governor Wenlock. "Is this how you treat the King's messenger, my lord? If I sound irritable it is because I am almost faint with hunger."

The debonair Bungundian let go of her hand, shaking with a mirth he was trying to hide.

"The Devil take me, Philippe," muttered Lord Wenlock, "if this is not the little baseborn wench that was sent packing for taking the King's fancy. In all my years I swear I have rarely seen Warwick so angry . . ."

Alys gave a small shriek and fell to her knees. The governor screwed up his narrow eyes farther, leaning forward to peer at Margery as if she were an exhibit at a fair, then he nodded. "Aye, it is her right enough."

Alys crossed herself, fearful no doubt they might be whipped.

"Oh, get up, girl," exclaimed Margery, then she turned back to Lord Wenlock. "Yes, you were there that week, were you not, my lord? It seems half the world was." She tried to deflect the conversation. "I am surprised not to find my lord of Warwick supping with you here. Many a time I recall you sat at his board."

She straightaway regretted her words. Wenlock appeared to wince, glancing uncomfortably at his companion. The Burgundian seemed to take no notice, however, his attention focusing instead upon Margery like sunlight through a magnifying glass.

"Will you not ask the lady to be seated, my lord Wenlock."

"*Lady!* This is one of the King's concubines."

"*Was,* my lord," corrected Margery matter-of-factly, although she felt hot blood rushing into her cheeks, "and though it was for but a week, I paid for my folly with confinement in a nunnery."

The governor raised his eyebrows. "Aye, well you look respectable enough now except that I'm told you wear your hair uncommonly cut. I imagine the nuns made you keep it short."

Her shoulders relaxed. It was a welcome assumption. "My lord, I have letters from his grace the King of England to you and to my lord of Warwick."

There was an ugly silence. Margery sensed a hatred emanating toward her from the Englishman and she could swear a smile was hovering at the corners of the man Philipe's mouth. It was he who broke the tension.

"My lord, will you not summon refreshment for the demoiselle and see her woman is fed and given sleeping quarters?"

The clerk looked to the governor for his orders.

"Yes," muttered Lord Wenlock, his fingers fluttering

impatiently in dismissal. "Do it. Be seated, mistress." A
page, quick to serve, set a stool beside the table.

"No, here, demoiselle." The Burgundian indicated the
long cushioned settle behind the table. "The fire will be too
hot for you."

Perhaps it was already, thought Margery. Lord Wenlock
was almost glowering at her as she slid in on the cushions,
while the Burgundian resumed his earlier place with his
back in the corner of the settle, observing them. Yes, he definitely reminded her of Stone except that he was wealthier
and infinitely plainer. His presence clearly aggravated the
Englishman.

Burgundy! Burgundians must come and go in Calais all
the time, considering its importance as a world market, but
this man was not a merchant. He behaved as though *he* were
the governor. Why? Calais was England's so why was it so
important to Wenlock to keep this man's good opinion?

"Philippe de Commynes, emissary of Charles, Duke of
Burgundy." It was as if the foreigner had been reading her
thoughts. Suddenly Margery grasped that it was this man's
curiosity that had freed her, but at his convenience so that he
would be able to hear why she had been sent. She bestowed
upon him her best smile, before attempting to charm her
host into better humor.

"My lord governor, there was a captain arrested with me,
a good man who gave me passage here on the King's orders.
Please could you permit his release? He has business with
Master Caxton in the morning." The governor's lower lip
curled sulkily but he nodded.

A helpful page set a goblet of wine before Margery.

"Oh, wonderful." She took a sip with delight. It warmed
her, its quality undeniable. She set it aside cautiously,
careful not to down it before her supper arrived lest her
hunger render her light-headed.

"Will you not read your letters, my lord?" prompted de
Commynes. They were lying unopened by Wenlock's hand.

The acting governor reluctantly perched a pair of eyeglasses upon his nose and myopically perused the addresses,
his chin raised as he tried to made out the words. "More
light!" he demanded testily. The flickering golden light from

the candles on the iron bracket hanging from the beams was insufficient.

Candles were set before him, illuminating the crossroads of age lines that patterned his cheeks. He must be close to eighty years, realized Margery, watching him closely as, muttering, he broke the seal on one of the letters, holding the parchment up at an angle. Then he lowered his head and, frowning, studied her anew.

"Is it possible to have lodging here tonight, my lord, and a servant to show me to my lord of Warwick's in the morn . . ." She faltered as Governor Wenlock made a show of looking about him.

"I see no earl here, girl. Do you doubt the high and mighty Richard Neville would not have installed himself in my place here at this very table if he was in Calais?" His bitter words dismayed her.

"You seem surprised not to find him here, demoiselle?" The Burgundian reached out for his winecup and watched the two of them over its rim.

She bit her lip. The elderly Englishman next to her was sweating. She could smell it and sense his tension.

"Oh, I suppose he has traveled on to Guînes," she answered brightly. It was England's other fingerhold on the mainland.

"He has sailed south," snapped Wenlock. He thrust his eyeglasses on the table. "And what sticks in my gullet is that it's clear the King expected you to find him here. What does his grace take me for? A fool as well as a traitor? You may tell him on your return, mistress, that Calais shuts its gates on traitors."

Her mouth fell open. It was the last answer she was expecting.

"I . . . I am not returning to England. As I explained, I have a letter to deliver to my lord."

"Christ!" he snarled, making the table jolt with his fist. He left the board. "Was I expected to entertain him here so that the King could force a peace? Is that it? If the King had given me some warning—Christ!" He swung around. "But . . ." he thrust a finger at Margery, only to be interrupted as a steward brought in a tray of viands, fruit, and

bread for her. He lapsed into surly silence until the servant
had gone. "Clear the room, the rest of you!" he growled to
the two pages hovering in the shadows. She guessed he
would like to have dismissed his foreign guest too.

"But?" prompted de Commynes, after the servants had
gone.

"But?" repeated Wenlock grumpily. "Aye, but! What is
her part in all this? That's what I should like to know. Why
should the King send one of his harlots—apologies—former
harlot? He should have sent Lord Howard, someone of
standing."

"Yes, why you, lady?" murmured the Burgundian.

Margery swallowed quickly. It was hardly polite to stuff
one's self when a diplomatic conversation was raging about
her. Her hunger vied with her sense of correctness.

"I was left behind at Warwick castle somewhat by accident, excellency. You see, I had an ague and was feverish
and my lady did not want me near the Duchess lest I—I cry
you mercy, my lord, I never asked . . ." Wenlock met her
gaze stonily. "The Duchess, her grace was near her time—
the baby?"

"I do not know," rasped Wenlock. "We sent her wine.
She was in travail when they hoisted anchor. She had her
women."

Margery's expression could not absolve him. Her obvious
judgment forced him to turn his face to the fire, staring into
its glowing coals, one hand above his head against the stone.

Poor Isabella. That dreadful jolting journey in the cold
and then to be in childbirth tossing upon the ocean, denied
the solid feel of land, the skill of a midwife. The Countess
wringing her hands, fretting and useless, and Anne, what
was her role? Did the Countess bar her from the cabin or
had she tried to help, to provide some order to soften the
chaos? Had they all turned their frustration upon poor
Ankarette?

"Finish your supper, woman." Wenlock was glaring at
her. "I wish to retire for the night."

"My lord, I beg an audience of you in the morning."

Wenlock merely grumbled under his breath, flung the
door open, and summoned the steward. Eyeing her unfinished repast regretfully, Margery rose and curtsied.

De Commynes must have taken his leave without further talk for he caught her up in the Great Hall and gestured to the steward to wait while he drew her aside. "I have many questions that remain unanswered. Matters in England that are not clear. We could discuss them somewhere more comfortable."

"You mean in bed?" retorted Margery, past caring for diplomatic niceties.

His eyes sparkled and his lips drew together in a mock sulk. "You offend me, demoiselle. You run like a cart before the horse."

"I have encountered a lot of horses lately, monsieur. Because I was apprehended in embarrassing circumstances with the King of England, my reputation seems to be beyond repair. People jump to conclusions. To be truthful, I am so very weary. Having nothing to do but fret is very tiresome and as you know we were confined all day awaiting his lordship's convenience until you kindly keened his curiosity." The sleek Burgundian courtier beamed at her in admiration and she knew she had guessed correctly. "So, good night to you, monsieur, I shall be happy to speak with you before I leave."

"If he lets you leave." Her surprised gaze rose. "But he will. I give you my word on it."

Later she lay considering de Commynes's presence in Calais. It was not in the interests of Duke Charles of Burgundy to see the house of York divided. Nor would he want Warwick loose gathering mercenaries especially as everyone knew that Warwick was no friend to Burgundy. The Earl had wanted Ned to marry the sister of the Queen of France. Yes, de Commynes would be pleased she was carrying a letter of reconciliation to Warwick. He would also approve the letters to Clarence if he but knew of them.

Further talk with a mellower Lord Wenlock next day and his promise to arrange passage for her to the mouth of the Seine, where it was reported that her guardian had taken refuge, satisfied Margery no end. The captain of the *Winchelsea* was restored to liberty. All was well and she had a few days respite to exploit what Calais had to offer—a choice of goods from all over Christendom.

With Alys as excited as she was and a borrowed manservant

to protect her and carry her purchases, Margery spent a wonderful extravagant morning buying both luxuries and necessities. It was a heady feeling to have money in her purse. She was wise enough to save plenty for emergencies, but Ned had been delightfully generous.

Her pleasure was compounded when a servant in the livery of the Wool Staple bade her to dinner at Master Caxton's and it was there she learned the news that gave her a clearer grasp of de Commynes's presence in Calais. The men at Caxton's table were not bound by frontiers but their liveli-hood depended on anticipating the actions of their rulers.

Warwick, she learned, had pirated some of the Burgun-dian fleet as he had sailed south and his presence on the French coast was embarrassing for King Louis since the ink on a French peace treaty with Burgundy had barely dried.

Why had the French or Burgundians never seized Calais and Guînes from England, she asked. Because, they an-swered, Calais was the ear to what was going on in England, a crossroads of gossip as well as merchandise. To take Calais was to provoke war with England and, besides, Bur-gundy and France were such a threat to each other that nei-ther could afford the weakness of fighting two enemies at once. The town was riddled with foreign agents but everyone knew it. She should curb her tongue, they warned, for there would be many interested in watching her, a rare messenger.

Margery decided that she must play the innocuous wo-man caught by accident in the web of courier interchange that spanned Christendom. Her conclusions were confirmed when Alys convinced her on their return to the governor's house that their belongings had been searched. The lining of the unlocked coffer had been gently prised up. The inter-loper's paymaster could have been Wenlock, de Com-mynes, or even an agent of King Louis. A fourth possibility occurred to her. Even in Calais there must be Englishmen who were enemies to Ned, men who had fought for Lan-caster against York. Margaret d'Anjou, the Queen of the House of Lancaster, had taken refuge in the Duchy of Bar. She too must have agents in Calais scenting out news, espe-cially as her two great enemies, Ned and Warwick, had fallen foul of each other.

Oh, Jesu, thought Margery, what have I gotten myself into here?

The next day she was bidden to dinner by de Commynes. He had taken over one of the grand houses of the Wool Staple for his entourage. The food was lavish, the wine heady, and she was glad that Wenlock and several of the other merchants were present. In spite of that, she found herself seated next to de Commynes above the salt.

"It is rare that I have had so beauteous and intriguing a guest." She lowered her eyes before the intense study. "What shall you do when you have delivered the letter to the Earl?"

"Why, take up my duties as lady-in-waiting to the Duchess as before," she replied guilelessly.

"Would you not prefer to return to England?"

"No, excellency."

"You are too modest. You cannot convince me that King Edward does not desire you in his bed. Do you not aspire to be his mistress?"

Careful, she warned herself. "To be truthful, there was a time when I should have wished that for I once fancied that I loved him dearly, but I was younger then."

He leaned closer, his words became soft breath upon her ear. "My master would be most desirous of having you resume your former intimacy with the King. Let us say that your fortunes could increase beyond your greatest imagining." Oh, Jesu, he was offering her a post of spy at Westminster. "What would you say to an elderly noble for a husband, a man who will ask no questions." Pray Heaven, he was not going to suggest John Wenlock.

"Monsieur, you overwhelm me." In several ways. Beneath the table linen his thigh was nudging hers and the piked toe of his right shoe was teasing the hem of her skirts. His hand fondled hers upon the cloth. She let him do so. Better for everyone to think they indulged in dalliance not diplomacy.

"But you will consider it, clever one, won't you? And now I have a gift for you." A bribe, a taste of things to come?

It was modest and therefore acceptable. A vial of emerald Venetian glass containing bath essence. "To put you in a

sensual humor," he whispered. "Its perfume will envelope
you and evoke delicious memories." She doubted that. For
some reason, Master Stone's threat to dunk her in a horse
trough rose unbidden in her thoughts.

The perfumed essence, when she broke the seal later,
was like the Burgundian proposal—intoxicating, exciting,
and despicable. It was tempting to use it. Yet it was a gift
from a power broker who no doubt used real people like
other men merely moved wooden chess pieces.

Alys eyed the vial with awe. "Do you want me to ask my
lord's chamberlain to arrange a bath for you, mistress?"

"No, we shall take it with us as a gift for the Duchess
Isabella."

The maidservant giggled. "Perhaps the foreign lord
hoped you would invite him to ladle it over you in person. I
mean it's disgusting really, not a suitable gift for a lady. You
can tell it's not England, can't you? I mean, Master Stone
now, he would never have given you anything so improper."

"Master Stone—and I wish you would not keep holding
him up as a paragon of virtue—was a mine of gold poorer."

"Mistress, you won't be setting this Day Commons
gentleman at a dangle for you, will you? After all, he is a
foreigner."

⚜

On the morrow, Wenlock agreed to let Margery resume her
journey to seek out the Duchess. He had commissioned a
vessel to convey her away, not from Calais but from a secret
rendezvous farther south from the harbor. Margery was on
her way there when a pincer of horsemen closed about the
escort Wenlock had provided, forcing them to draw rein.
The leader, astonishingly, was de Commynes.

He spoke to her escort leader emphatically and handed
over a bag of coins so weighty that the men from Calais
rode away with broad grins leaving Margery and her maid
hedged within a circle of mounted Burgundian soldiers. De
Commynes rode ahead and his men closed in around the
women urging them onward. They rode seaward to a
deserted beach. The horsemen dispersed, setting up a distant
cordon around them, and Margery and Alys were left facing

de Commynes. He dismounted and assisted Margery charmingly from her horse.

"Is this some sort of Burgundian outing, monsieur, someone's saint's day?" Margery asked venomously.

"I apologize, demoiselles, but I shall require you to remove your entire clothing."

Alys shrank back against Margery, casting fearful glances at the soldiers, mounted still, with their backs to them some distance away.

"Why?" demanded Margery, her arm around the trembling maid.

With an eye on Alys, he changed to simple French. "Because I want to know what papers you are really carrying, demoiselle. You have obviously worn them on your person the whole time. Do you English never take baths?"

"Yes, of course, we do!" snapped Margery in halting French. Then she gave him a shrewd look, realizing how cunning he had been.

"Exactly. I congratulate you on your intelligence. Now, undress!"

CHAPTER
6

"Your maid first."

"You overstep yourself!" exclaimed Margery.

"Either remove every shred of clothing or my men will do it for you. I have little time, please hurry." He meant it.

When she at length stood naked and cold before him, he passed her his sable-edged cloak, gathered up her clothing, and forced her to accompany him up into the sand dunes leaving Alys to reclothe herself. His adamant tone left Margery little choice.

If she was afraid, she hid it well but her fears proved groundless. The only compensation and insult, if you like, in the whole humiliating process of appearing unclothed before him was that he was far more interested in her garments than he was in her body. He spread them upon the ground and examined each thoroughly. When he found the unusual stiffness in the collar, he laughed and triumphantly slit the seams open. "So, in all, letters mostly for the Duke of Clarence in many different hands and but one for the Earl. He will feel slighted. You may put your apparel back on, demoiselle. The wind is fresh."

"You have ruined my clothing. How can I carry these letters discreetly now?"

The Burgundian laughed. "I've brought you needles and thread for the purpose."

"Am I expected to be grateful?" hissed Margery as she hastily pulled her underskirt back up over her hips. "You have dismissed my bodyguard—"

"You may have six of my men to see you safely to your ship." He lowered his voice. "My master will be pleased with the news that King Edward is likely to forgive his brother if he betrays Warwick." He sighed. "Your Monsieur Warwick is a great nuisance to Burgundy, demoiselle, and we want our ships and cargoes back from him. Now let me help you back down to the beach."

She shunned his hand. "He is merely seeking shelter along the coast of France to lick his wounds."

De Commynes smiled. "But if France gives him refuge after his hostility to our shipping, then our peace with France will be violated. *Eh bien*, I must return to Bruges. Do think on the offer I made you the other day, and before we part, permit me to say how charming you look without your gown." He possessed himself of her cold hand, planted a cool perfunctory kiss upon it. "I wish you joy in your mission. Your secret is safe with me."

Margery stood dazed as five of the Burgundians departed.

"Mistress." Alys coughed for attention. "Are we going to have to take our clothing off like this regularly? Is it some sort of custom in these parts?" Margery examined the faces of the remaining soldiers who were waiting attentively for her orders and was glad of the dagger once more within her sleeve. "I expect so," she answered Alys. "They believe English folk have tails. They just wanted to see if it was true."

"Get away, mistress, you are gulling me."

"Yes, Alys, I am."

The girl sniffed. "I wish we had Master Stone and his men with us instead. At least they spoke English and Master Stone would have never let some foreigner treat us like that."

"Little you know. I hope never to set eyes on Master Richard Stone ever again!"

The caravel *Célérité* was too small to arouse much suspicion as it pursued the coast. The exception was a large Burgundian ship that cruised alongside for a few knots before it turned its bows seaward again. But as they neared the mouth of the Seine, a vessel with grappling irons and ropes at the ready made straight for them.

"Demoiselle, we cannot withstand these pirates if they board us. See, they are in armor and there is no flag to tell us who they are."

"Lord save us, they have swords drawn and daggers in their mouths. We shall be raped for sure." Alys was trembling and Margery agreed that the likelihood of being ravaged by some of the brawny rogues grinning across the bows at her looked greater by the moment. Only at the last minute, as it came alongside and tossed across the grappling irons, did the enemy ship run up the pennon of a bear and ragged staff.

The captain of the *Célérité* was treated to the sight of his special passenger jumping up and down, waving her arms and screaming, "A Warwick! A Warwick!" as loudly as she could above the slap of the waves. The spectacle caused a stir on the enemy carrack and its captain came down off the forecastle to inspect the strange quarry, crossing himself in amazement.

"Why by my father's soul, Mistress Margery of Warwick! What in the name of Heaven are you doing off the coast of France?" It was Will Garland. "I am mighty pleased to see you so hale. There was a fine hue and cry when you went missing an' no mistake. The fairies take you, eh?"

"Oh, Master Garland, thank God! Where is my lord Earl? I need to speak with him."

"You will have some explaining to do or I am not my blessed mother's son. 'Tis lucky that the Earl is expecting us back this afternoon. You can tell your ship's master to follow us into port."

"He will not want to do that. If you fling me one of your ropes, could I not come on your ship?"

There was some laughter and consultation at this and

then one of the young seamen swung across onto the deck right in front of Margery to instruct her. Alys had appeared at this point bearing Margery's possessions. Her plumpness caused suggestions that the longboat might be better. Finally after being taught how to hold the rope correctly, Margery sprang across. It took the youth a brace of journeys to bring her coffer and possessions on board before he coaxed Alys into following her mistress. Her maid nearly landed in the Channel but bore the guffaws and cheers of the onlookers bravely. Her relief at being once more with folk who spoke the same tongue was reward enough.

It was a relief to see Warwick's proud flagship at anchor with several other large vessels with Flemish names.

"He's pirated all of those, my lord has," explained Will Garland as he grabbed hold of the ladder and steadied the longboat next to the flagship. "By Our Lady, we saw some fine action and I swear I have not enjoyed m'self so much for years. So what's to do, young Margery? We thought you might ha' made off with some young stripling."

"You are near the truth, Master Garland. Jesu, I am thankful you survived, believe me. Those poor wretches at Southampton . . ."

"Is it Butcher Worcester you're speaking of now? Is it true that the King had every jack of our men hanged?"

"It was worse than that. I—it pains me to speak of it, truly. A game beast . . . a noble stag is treated with more dignity. They were staked out, pieces of—"

"Margery, enough!"

She knew that voice so well.

She grinned up the ship's side into the freckled face of the Kingmaker. "My lord." It was after all important to sound cheerful.

"On board!" he snapped. He helped her onto the deck himself and watched her spread her salt-sprayed skirts in a deep obeisance at his feet. Snapping his fingers behind his back, he regarded her with a deep frown, but as she glanced up, she recognized in the quirk of his mouth the tangle of irritation and indulgence with which he always confronted her, save when they had brought her to him warm from the King's arms.

There was a harder set about his eyes but he looked

leaner and healthier now and judging by the number of stolen ships tethered along the quay, he was enjoying the challenge of adversity.

"If you please, my lord, I can explain my absence without your leave." Most of the seamen had halted in their deck chores and were eyeing her with open appreciation.

He ran a hand through his sandy hair, untidied by the off-shore wind. "You always can, child, but I cannot always believe you. Here is neither the time nor the place and yet my curiosity refuses to go unsated. What are you doing here?"

"They told me in Calais that the fishing is good." Her eyes met his intelligently. He drew breath and then thought better of it. "My lord," she repeated meaningfully. He took the hint.

"Garland, find a man to take my ward's maidservant to the village and you, young woman, had best not fill my ears to no purpose. Come!" He strode ahead of her onto the plank that bridged the gap between his ship and the wooden pier. The board shook so with his weight that she waited until he was across. When she had caught up with him, he turned seaward with her, away from the mending of the nets and the boy scraping off the scales of his catch, striding to the end where their only audience was a semicircle of hopeful gulls.

"You had better not be wasting my time," he warned her.

Margery wrapped her cloak about her against the breeze. It seemed necessary to be concise. "My lord, the bones of the matter are that I was abducted by a man called Richard Stone who once served you or leastways I remember seeing him at Warwick. He is now a receiver for the King and sent to take possession of your manors. Anyway, he took me to the King who gave me a letter to bear to you because he thought you were in Calais, and then when I reached Calais, you were not there so Lord Wenlock lent me a ship to bring me here."

The Earl's blue eyes frowned down at her. "Child, it is not the bones of your story that worry me, it is the flesh. You expect me to believe all this? I have never heard of any Richard Stone."

"B-but he certainly exists. He recognized me when we stopped to break our fast. Her grace had just asked me to find out where we were and he sent me a false message asking about my lady the Duchess, which I thought was from his grace of Clarence. Then he took me to your manor at Sutton Gaveston because he had already seized it in the King's name and there he kept me under lock and key until he knew where the King was. The people there, Mistress Agnes Guppy and her family, beg to be remembered to you because they helped me escape and wanted you to know that, but Master Stone caught me again."

"Margery, this so-called abductor of yours, did he abuse you?"

"No, my lord, he made no assault on my person but he was not kind. When I ran away from him in the middle of the night, he roped me and dragged me after his horse until I consented to ride with him. He was most insulting about my virtue and he knew all about my being in a nunnery because of N—the King."

"And where was *Ned*?" asked the Earl, his tone sharp. "You did say this man took you to him, did you not?"

"Yes, he was leaving Exeter when we arrived but he told Master Stone to follow him to Southampton and there . . . I saw . . ." She chewed her lips, hesitating before she blurted out, "I saw what Butcher Worcester did to our men he had captured." She watched the Earl's scowl grow heavier. "I told the King what I thought of him for permitting that. He was not pleased but I could not let the matter rest—"

"By St. Anne, wench!" Warwick cut in, squeezing his eyes tight. He shook his head at her, turning his face away, staring at the ocean. She watched him swallow, as if he could not dredge any words up. It was for his quarrel that his soldiers had died so terribly.

It seemed diplomatic, Margery decided, to display an uncommon interest in the toes of her shoes until her guardian had recovered his composure, but the spectator seagulls distracted her as they drove off a pair of newcomers, with raucous squawks and thrusting heads.

"But he wrote to me, the King, you say. Where is the letter?"

She looked up at the Earl. "I have it safe here."

"Give it me. No, use your wits, girl. Turn your back to the town. The Duke of Burgundy has agents watching me."

Margery moved close and pulled out the letter from the bosom of her gown. "He wished to be reconciled, my lord, and my lord of Gloucester told me to tell you he desires it of all things."

Her guardian made no answer as he checked the seal before stowing the letter swiftly in the purse on his belt. He stared out again across the waves to where England lay, his lips in a tight hard line, before he finally looked back at her. "You make a mighty uncommon messenger."

"Maybe for that reason, my lord, or since the quarrel between you and Ned is partly of my making. Mayhap he thought it would give me a chance to make amends and play the peacemaker." The Earl snorted with disbelief. "Well, no doubt you are right, my lord. Perchance it was merely convenient. Believe me, I do not understand how I was brought into this any more than you do." She lapsed into silence and then asked with her old spirit, "Are you going to invade England, my lord? Is the French King going to allow you to stay here?"

Warwick frowned at her frank questions but he paid her the respect of answering nevertheless. "King Louis would certainly be better pleased if we withdrew to the Channel Islands, but I am loath to put to sea again and be at the mercy of the Burgundians or Lord Howard's ships. Did you see any of them out there?"

"I am certain there is a Burgundian vessel out there now keeping watch but it let us alone."

"That would be the *Bruges*. I shall send out several of my ships and see if we can take it before the week is out." He examined her face gravely. "So what am I to do with you, child? The ladies have gone for safety at King Louis's expense to the logis royal in Valognes. You shall have to join them there and make your excuses. Whether my lady Countess will believe you remains to be seen. If she does not, then you may have to beg lodging at a religious house in Cherbourg until I can decide what to do with you."

"My lord, I swear to you I was abducted."

It was like stepping back into that terrible evening at

Warwick castle when she had faced the Earl's disbelief. This time she had to make him believe her; being sent back to a nunnery was more than she could stomach. She slid back the cuffs of each hand. "See where they tied the ropes too tight. I have marks on my ankles too."

The Earl swiftly took her wrists, swearing beneath his breath as he ran his thumb across the marks. "Why abduct you, Margery?"

"My lord, I repeat I do not know. Admittedly, Master Stone was concerned when he saw how tight they had bound me although he was extremely rude in other ways, but as to his purpose, he is Ned's servant and I assume he was obeying his orders."

"You are sure it was the King and not young Dickon who stirred this pot? He has an eye to half my lands and young Anne as well." The Kingmaker seemed to have conveniently forgotten his attempt to lure the young duke to rebellion with just such a bait. "Could it have been Anne they were after?"

Margery shook her head. "Master Stone is one of Ned's receivers."

"Aye, so maybe not, but I would never underestimate Dickon. Now if it had been him I had made king instead of the philanderer who seduced you, then the realm might have been better governed and you and I, my girl, would have been home where we belong. But I have better things to do than idle the afternoon away with ifs and buts." He put a hand on her shoulder to turn her back to the vessel.

Margery held her ground. "My lord, I do fear that my lady Warwick will not be pleased to believe me. If you could give me a letter to carry to her saying that you wish her to—"

"*Margery!*" But her pleading face moved him as it always had when she was a tiny scrap of a child. "Aye, you shall have your letter and I shall inquire into this Master Stone, you may be sure. Come, I shall dictate it presently."

Hands clasped behind his back, he began a brisk step, forcing her to gather up her skirts and hurry after him.

"My lord, how fare the Duchess and the baby?"

He halted and swung around, frowning. "By St. Anne, I had forgotten that you do not know."

"*Know*? Lord Wenlock told me that he would not let her grace on land but surely . . ." A storehouse of sorrow was in his eyes. "Oh, no, my lord, what passed?"

He began walking again as if movement could stanch the pain. "Stillborn, Margery. It would have been a boy, a future king even."

Margery crossed herself. "I am so very sorry." It was his fault, she decided, inflicting that journey on his poor daughter when she could have been safe in some abbey sanctuary and given birth in peace like any woman deserved. "Her grace is recovering?"

"Slowly, it was a heavy blow to both her and the Duke, to all of us. She would have been glad of your presence. She loves you well. Both my daughters do." He raised his head, his blue eyes glazed, then pulled himself together as they drew level with his ship.

"And the Duke of Clarence, is he here with you?"

"At present he is in Valognes."

This time he offered his hand to assist her up the wooden plank onto the ship. The sea breeze was growing stronger and she needed a hand free to keep her skirts down. The crew watched her efforts with amusement.

The Earl sent a boy to fetch his amanuensis and Margery leaned against the ship's rail, wrapping her veil around her throat before the next gust took her cap from her, relieved that she would have a letter to give the Countess.

The scribe came hurrying with an inkpot, quill, and parchment fastened to a wooden board. He squatted down on a coil of rope and took down his lord's words without even glancing at Margery until it was done, and then he noticed her and stared his fill.

The Kingmaker followed the man's glance, examining her fiercely for a moment before he signed the letter, dismissed everyone within earshot, and strode across to her. "I have a question, Margery, and think carefully before you answer me. Why did you not stay with Ned this time? You are pretty fodder. Did he not tempt you?"

"He is not the man I remember," Margery said softly, glancing down to momentarily hide her face. "Besides"—she slowly raised her eyes honestly to his—"I do not want to be a wealthy whore in some little house in Chelsea, frightened lest the Woodvilles decide not to tolerate me, afraid lest I lose my looks. To be honest, I hate being a woman, having to be all compliance. If I were a man, my lord, I would be earning my bread with my wits, using the mind God gave me. If I were a man, I could be out there with a sword in my hand capturing ships for you instead of trapped here by my sex." She glanced up at the clean, white gulls, mewling above the mast, soaring in the wind, with a sigh.

A twist of compassion curled his lips. "I do believe you mean it." Surprisingly he wrapped an avuncular arm about her shoulders. "More's the pity you are not a man, but since the Almighty has made you a woman, Margery, you must make the best of it. If He has determined you should be a wife and mother, then you must make the best of that too." She peeped sideways at him with a wry smile only to have her blood run cold. He was appraising her body.

"My lord?" She stepped away. His eyes, thankfully devoid of any wickedness, rose pensively to peruse her face. A sense of relief surged through her and her shoulders lost their tenseness. Then another alarming thought frightened her like a warning bell. Heaven forbid that he was going to suggest she climb the ecclesiastical ladder and become an abbess! Then enlightenment came. Jesu, he was behaving just like a guardian and thinking of husbands. Well, that thought had to be nipped off at bud size instantly. A refusal to take matters seriously was definitely necessary.

"My lord, do not wish me on any man if that is what you are planning. He would not thank you for it. Believe me, I am quite happy to serve your daughters. Can I not earn my keep just as your male retainers do? I have done so right willingly in the past."

The Earl flicked her cheek. "So you are now a mind-reader, little witch. Well, deny it all you may, but it's high time you had a household of your own to run. A bunch of keys at your waist is what you need, my dear, to keep you busy and your wits occupied. There will be no time then to wish yourself a pirate. Yes, I shall give it some thought!"

"Not until you have England beneath your heel again, my lord, then I shall accept no less than a newly minted duke."

He threw back his head and laughed. "Margery, my dear, you can have your King back again with a golden halter about his neck or mayhap Master Stone shackled and bound."

"Now that," exclaimed Margery, "would suit me very well!"

CHAPTER
7

Margery was happily restored to the Neville household within two days of hard riding along roads ribboned near the shabby villages by overgenerous hedges. It was raining hard when they reached Valognes. The gray town bestraddled the meeting of the roads from Brittany, the port of Cherbourg and Bayeux. Charred chalk ruins frayed its edge, a reminder of how bitterly the English and French had ravaged Normandy. Sodden peasants eyed them resentfully behind the soaked panniers and dripping stalls of the marketplace as if their small party had brought the foul weather. They found the logis royal to the east, protected by a meager river, with workshops huddling close to its walls. Inside, fires had been lit in the solar and the smoky air stung Margery's eyes bringing tears that would have come anyway as Isabella, pale and bitter from her loss, threw herself into her arms. No longer glowing with the imminent babe, she looked gaunt beside her full-bosomed mother.

If the Countess had any intention of rejecting Margery after reading her lord's letter, she must have put the thought aside for some later occasion. It was probably because the

Duchess, after howling over her loss to a new audience, had
brightened. Margery had always been able to spur Isabella
to laughter and she had done so now, sympathetically listening and then summoning Alys to bring in the puppy she
had purchased for her in Calais. Isabella instantly named it
"Tristan" and fell in love with the mischievous creature.
The Countess, with a loud sigh of resignation, withdrew and
Margery, her prayers answered, foolishly thought that her
problems were all resolved.

It was a time for confidences, for some burdens shared.
When the other women joined them, Margery took even
more care with the reasons for her absence, knowing that
dear Ankarette Twynhoe was absorbing every word like a
desiccated sponge.

Later, a hidden scrap of paper in Gloucester's tidy script
that de Commynes had failed to discover was hooked
from its cunning hiding place and delivered quietly to
fifteen-year-old Anne, bringing a bright blush to her milky
complexion.

Presenting the Duke of Clarence with his letters was no
easy matter. It seemed that Isabella had driven him away
with her tears and he spent the next three days out hunting.
Besides, it was near impossible to talk to him unobserved,
but Margery eventually managed to snatch a few private
words with him. It had required a great deal of effort. She
had managed to persuade the Countess that Isabella needed
music to cheer her. The musicians she eventually sent for
from Carentan were more suited to a Norman farmers'
Twelfth Night dance than playing for sophisticated noble
ladies, but the lusty rhythm had everyone tapping their feet
and even the self-conscious Duke could not bear to sit while
the others danced.

She liked him the least of the three Yorkist brothers.
Whereas charm was a natural spring in Ned, George of
Clarence pumped it up in a gush only when it pleased him.
Since the day he had first arrived for training in the Earl of
Warwick's household, it had been clear to her that here was
a child who had already learned how to manipulate people
with tantrums and sulks. Now, witty and willful at twenty-
one, he always served his own selfish ends. They tolerated
each other.

"I hear you have compromised yourself again, Meg. Two weeks unchaperoned with a troop of brigands thieving my manors." He grinned at her, showing the sort of teeth that distinguished Englishmen throughout Christendom. When Ned smiled, the sun shone; when George of Clarence smiled, you noticed his teeth.

"If you were not a duke, I should clout you," she replied cheerfully as their palms briefly met. "I have secret letters for you."

The remainder of their brief conversation became phrases annoyingly punctuated by spins and claps. He seemed unexcited by her revelation, as if she had brought him a cart of eggs instead of letters from a king, a duke, and half a dozen duchesses. His eyes mocked her from beneath his ruddy gold lashes as the pipes and tabors ceased, but next day he did collect the letters from where she had hidden them. She waited several days for the answer but it was as if he had forgotten, showing his disdain for his brother's offer of mercy. Well, there was still time for patience.

The year was fast ripening into early summer and the garden around the logis, which the King of France had lent the Countess, was dappled with tumbling apple blossom. The wild daffodils upon the grassy banks around the little town had withered, surrendering to yarrow, nettles, and creeping strawberries. With her mission temporarily in abeyance, Margery felt as though she had no cares in the world. But she was wrong.

∼∾∽

There was a folded letter in the Earl's hand as he awaited Margery in his antechamber at Valognes. He had sailed up the coast to Barfleur and it was the first time she had seen him again since her arrival in France. Margery thought at first the letter might be Ned's and prayed that the Earl had decided upon reconciliation. On close examination, the wax was the wrong color and the seal was smaller than the personal signet the King had used. Margery watched regretfully as he tossed it onto a pile of papers.

"Margery, be seated. Let me be direct with you. My circumstances have forced me to give much thought both to my future and the fortunes of those who depend upon me, yourself included. I fear I have been too concerned with my own affairs over the last few months to pay justice to yours."

"My lord, I am very grateful that you have given me your protection all these years, believe me."

"You have not helped my task by tarnishing your honor but I think the time to make amends on your part and on mine is now. It was my wish that you devote your life to God but the Abbess wrote to me that you showed no inclination, and there was also another consideration which is why I originally summoned you from Nuneaton."

"My lord?"

"In a nutshell, Margery, there is now an old friend at Le Havre, one who has long admired you. He has requested you in marriage. I agreed." Margery's eyes widened with horror. "I know it is a surprise but you are very fortunate, considering your past sins."

This could not be happening. "My lord, I have no desire to be wed. I thought you understood my feelings."

"What is this nonsense?" His patience evaporated like August rain on hot cobbles. "So you prefer to take the veil instead?"

Should she lie? Would hesitation and a plea for time to think upon the matter make a difference? "N-n-no, but . . ."

"I think you must trust my judgment. Who knows where we may find ourselves in a twelvemonth? This man is ready and willing to give you his name. Should aught befall him, his family will look after you. It is a better match than could be expected for you."

"You have not even told me his name, my lord. It might help."

"I stand reproved. It is Huddleston. His family are well respected in the north and have long served the Nevilles. You may have met him. He was in my brother Montague's household for some years."

She shook her head. "I need time to think upon this, my lord."

"No, child. You owe me this obedience. Your sinful doings with the King hardened me toward you but I have forgiven you. You were young and, perhaps like Eve, you were tempted. By St. Anne, I have no doubt that Ned could charm Lucifer himself, had he a mind to." The Earl paced away from her, then swung around, his fingers clasped behind his back. "I am quite resolved on this, Margery. If you will not obey me, then you shall not be welcome in my sight. Marrying you to Huddleston is the best that I can do for you. I doubt there will ever be another opportunity of so acceptable a suitor."

Margery coldly curtsied but once outside the door she picked up her skirts and ran down the passageway. Out in the orchard she sat with her back to a tree, unseen, her knees cradled in her arms.

It took her an hour before she felt sufficiently in control to return to the household. Mass was an opportunity to pray for deliverance from this elderly suitor, except she was startled by her name in the calling of banns. Now she knew how a fox felt hearing the hunting horn. And, of course, the household congregation immediately lost interest in heavenly affairs and squinted sideways.

Ankarette dug her elbow into Margery's ribs in conspiratorial fashion. "Margery, you secretive vixen," she hissed. "Thank you for telling me. I thought I was your friend."

"Secretive!" exclaimed Margery as they left the chapel. "It is not *my* doing. I have never set eyes on the wretch. I thought I should have time to consider but this is beyond endurance. I told my lord I did not wish it."

Ankarette, married to a Devon gentlemen, with several children of her own, shook her head despairingly. "Has the plague invaded your mind? I thought you had more common sense than most, you foolish wench. Accept the man with a good, sweet grace!"

"No, not me, Ankarette, I am completely bereft of all common niceties. I do not want to marry the fellow, curse him! He is old and I have never heard of him."

"You think him too old for you?" Her friend looked incredulous.

"I try not to think of him at all. Ouch!"

"It seems," muttered Ankarette, swiftly trying to untangle the veil of Margery's headdress snared unwittingly by a rosebush, "that you have hardly thought at all."

"I shall have to prevent this somehow, Ankarette. How many times must the priest call the banns?"

"Thrice, then the marriage may take place at any time. Keep still!"

"Jesu, my lord of Warwick is in haste to be rid of me, it seems."

"Perhaps he is worried that you will entice the Duke of Clarence into sin. Don't stand there looking as though you've just seen a miracle. Admit you've been sending glances the Duke's way ever since you arrived in Valognes." Margery's older friend was eagle-eyed when it came to observing a variety of human foibles.

"Oh, Ankarette. It is not like that at all." There was no answer to give. She could not excuse herself. Ankarette was the last person to confide in that she was waiting for the Duke's answer.

"Oh, I should think no one noticed except me. I doubt that the Earl has since he's hardly been here, but you should be more careful. That's good advice, my dear." She giggled. "I sound like my old granddam. Now, cheer up, it is not the end of the world to be married."

How to make the Earl change his mind occupied Margery for the rest of the day. She ate supper in the hall without savoring her food, conversed with little animation, and sat beside Ankarette that evening after the trestles were cleared away with the air of a felon condemned to the gibbet. Even the lively music of the traveling musicians from Caen failed to move her.

Ankarette twittered away, as was her fashion, while the wafers and hypocras were being served. She was in mid-comment on the appalling service of the French servants when a woman's shriek made her spill half her drink. The furor came from the other end of the hall as if the Devil himself had turned up unexpected. Another scream shrilled out close by as a huge hound, its ripped leash dragging from its studded leather collar, came scampering through—a dog so massive that everyone shrank back in horror.

The animal noticed this effect with little perturbation, took a snuffle in Margery's direction, and within seconds its paws were on her shoulders and its limpid eyes stared lovingly into hers while beads of saliva dripped enthusiastically from its tongue.

"*Sede!*" roared Margery and the animal dropped its front

paws back to the tiled floor and sat obediently in front of her. A scarlet-faced Long appeared between the skirts and houppelandes. He grabbed the dog's collar. "Pardon, madam, gracious lady. Oh, *mistress*!" His jaw dropped at Margery's fine appearance.

"Remove him from here, fellow, before someone plants a well-deserved boot on your backside," snapped Ankarette. Long needed no second bidding. Oaths and curses spat about his shoulders like large hailstones as he disappeared dragging the reluctant hound.

A chorus of praise surrounded Margery. One gentleman refilled her winecup, another fetched a bench closer for her ease, while the condemnation of the dog's owner and its lax kennelman grew apace.

Ankarette sat down next to her. "Your poor collar!" Margery squinted down at her shoulders. Once dry, the dirt would brush off easily. "Say something, Margery! You've gone the color of dough. How you were not scared witless by that brute, I shall never know."

"Leave me be, Ankarette."

It was like a dream, no, a nightmare, but as the daylight fled and the servants lit the candles in the sconces around the hall, Margery was left with a sense of unreality. If there had not been over two score of witnesses to the dog, she would have thought herself growing lunatic.

Ankarette gave a little whistle of admiration. "Now, that particular piece of steel bears further notice. They must be the party who arrived from the coast this afternoon. Finely tempered, that one. I would not mind a little dalliance with him. I'm sure I've met him before. Look around, the one in black, do you know him?"

Margery casually glanced around, then jerked her head back abruptly.

"What is wrong?"

"Dear Jesu!" she hissed. "He is here. That's the wretched knave who abducted me."

"Truly, the man with the fine calves?"

"No—yes, stop staring. I do not want him to see me."

"I think he knows you are here anyway. He's just looked this way. Breathe out, they are all going to make their bows to the Duke."

"I think I shall go." Margery rose but Ankarette grabbed her down.

"If he's one of my lord's new officers, you had better face him and have done. You cannot avoid him in a place as small as this. Besides, I should hate to miss such sport. Come, look merry, you will be wedded and bedded before the month is out so what harm can this man do you?"

"Ankarette, you have the tact of a page throwing up at a coronation."

"I shall catch his eye when he is done with my lord, just to annoy you. A little distraction will take your mind off your forthcoming nuptials."

"No, I forbid you. He will do nothing but torment me."

"Wonderful, just what you need."

"Mesdames." Master Stone accosted them later with a perfunctory bow but his eyes were alive with mischief. In his black leather doublet and shining boots, he was just as formidable as Margery remembered save that his hair was shorter, curling behind his ears now instead of at chin length. Cut to sit beneath a helmet.

Margery rose and held out her hand. "Well, here is a surprise. I expect to see flying pigs by morning."

"I am sure the local peasants will be out early with their bows and arrows if that is the case." His eyes gave her a lazy caress from head to foot that made her twitch her fingers out of his clasp.

"Though I am loath to admit it, I quite missed the volley of words," she conceded.

"How charming of you to acknowledge that."

"You are aware that your monstrous creature has already embraced me in front of the entire household and caused two ladies to swoon." She heard Ankarette splutter behind her with astonishment.

"I do apologize." The clever eyes lingered on her collar at the shoulders before they moved downward. "I understand you managed not to succumb to swooning."

Margery swept a bold eye over him, "Why, sir, it would take more than something of yours to make me swoon."

Ankarette coughed loudly and stood up. Margery glanced around.

"I do beg your pardon, Ankarette. Allow me to introduce

Master Richard Stone. He specializes in abductions, rent-collecting, and boisterous deerhounds."

Ankarette stared from one to the other in fascinated amazement, then she recollected herself and dropped him a flirtatious curtsy.

"Mistress Margery remains as inaccurate as ever." He took Ankarette's hand and carried it to his lips. "We have met before. Some years ago at Warwick and Sheriff Hutton, I recall."

"Yes, we have," murmured Ankarette. "Your father, Sir John, he is well? And what of young William and your other brother? John?"

His smile was broad. "Three brothers, Mistress Twyn-hoe, all in good health. William is busy wooing my lord of Warwick's niece or so he was boasting last time I saw him. You have a good memory, mistress. So do I, and I can recall that you dance like an angel. Would it please you to demonstrate?"

Ankarette simpered, plumper than when she had last danced with him, and let him lead her away.

Margery frowned. So the man's family aimed high if one of his kin was wooing a Neville. She must ask Ankarette which of Lord Montague's daughters was so unlucky. She summoned a passing page to refill her winecup with hypocras. As if she did not have enough problems without Master Stone to provoke her further.

One of her knightly admirers from earlier in the evening moved over to congratulate her yet again on her bravery, but her glance kept wandering to the dancers. The insufferable Stone was giving Ankarette his entire attention. In fact Margery was so irritated that she did not notice the Earl of Warwick, conversing as he moved among his retainers, until he was right before her.

He forestalled Margery's curtsy and bent his head to her ear. "Bound and shackled, I believe, was your request, Margery. So be it. Attend me tomorrow after mass." Was gloating a sin? Well, let Richard Stone enjoy the evening—he would have little reason to smile in the morning.

Ankarette was talking as she danced and Richard Stone was not answering her with yeas and nays but at length. Even when the viols and tabors ceased, their conversation continued. Ankarette appeared to be listening quite earnestly and then she suddenly clapped her fingers to her lips and shrieked with laughter. When others joined them, she detached herself from the group.

"I like your Master Stone, Margery," she announced, smoothing her silvery gray skirts, her eyes bubbling with merriment.

"He is not *my* Master Stone," snapped Margery. "You try being abducted by him on a freezing March morning. If I had a rose noble for every time he has insulted me, I should be a wealthy woman."

"Well, I vow I have not been so amused for months."

"Excellent, for I think you please him, Ankarette. He is bearing down on us again like an ill wind."

"Your turn," murmured Ankarette. Before Margery could protest she had swept off in a rustle of taffeta through the nearest doorway.

"You are annoyed, I think," stated Richard, setting his cup down on the nearest board.

Margery checked about her to see whether anyone was within earshot. The emotions she was feeling measured from a grass level of astonishment to a steeple-high trepidation; Master Stone made even the air crackle with danger. It was like being out in a thunderstorm.

She settled for a safe indignation. "To be truthful, now I am over my surprise, I am disappointed to see you of all people here. I thought you had greater sense." Her companion raised an inquiring eyebrow. "You were an officer of the King. You had prospects. Why become another fugitive dependent on the whim of the French?" She sighed. "Now your lands are forfeit, I suppose. I really despair of men sometimes. Why make this your quarrel? It is a foolish cause. I heartily pray that within the month my lord will make his peace with the King and we can all go home."

Richard leaned upon the board, shifting his cup to smudge the wet circle it had made. "I find King Edward sluggish and indolent, yoked like a carthorse to his Queen's wagon. Your guardian can rule the kingdom better."

"But his soldiering is another matter." She quickened to the argument. Ned had never lost a battle. Criticism was easy—winning a battlefield against him was not.

Master Stone languidly raised his green eyes, "Ah, you found time to discuss soldiering with him."

She thrust her chin up. "A little time, yes." She paused, bruised by the fresh jab at her past. Her eyes followed the Earl as he moved through the hall back to the dais. "Ned once told me that my lord of Warwick was one of the worst tacticians he knew and it was not surprising that he lost the second Battle of St. Albans." She returned her gaze to Stone's face triumphantly but he set the conversation sailing in another direction.

"Then you are fortunate that you will never have to ride into battle with so hopeless a leader," he answered softly.

"Oh, yes." Her tone was bitter. "The only advantage there is in being a woman." Her fingers twisted, crushing the gauzy tissue of her veil.

"Is it so difficult, mistress?" The hard, sardonic glint had softened into kindness. Almost she felt she could drown in the deep pools of his eyes.

"Yes, Master Stone, it is."

"But a woman may lose a husband or lover in a battle."

"I fervently hope so," she exclaimed, thinking it would be one way to be rid of the husband fate was about to thrust upon her so unkindly. Then imagining the face before her all bloodied and smashed, she shuddered and apologized.

"I am sure I for one shall make a fine corpse," he assured her, laughing.

"How can you jest?" She lowered her voice. "This is all so foolhardy. England will dance to the tune of Louis XI if this enterprise succeeds."

Richard Stone eyed her shrewdly, then he too glanced cautiously about him. "You are correct, of course. The situation between my lord and the King's grace should never have reached this impasse. Word was that King Edward believes Warwick will gain no real aid from King Louis because the French will not wish to break the peace treaty with the Burgundians."

"Then the King has misjudged his enemies. There have been many messengers between here and the French court. You will know that my lords Warwick and Clarence purloined half a dozen or so Burgundian ships on the way down from Calais."

He nodded. "Very clever, was it not? Deliberate provocation. Your Ned will not be pleased when he hears."

"And Louis has not turned us out of his realm, has he? He is the power broker in this affair. You see, Master Stone, have I not proved it would have been wiser for you to stay in England and watched to see which way the wind blows?"

He straightened up. "You wax too serious, lady. There is another set forming. Come, let us forget the whims of the mighty for a small moment." He put his arm beneath her elbow, turning her in the direction of the dancers. She should have declined but his touch sent a shiver of excitement up her arm. Was it imagination or did the other women glance enviously at them as they made their way through the throng? He was a new face, a pleasing one at that.

Margery regarded him gravely as she took her place opposite him at the end of the set. There was spice in any conversation with him, she could not deny it. And he was watching her again, his smile controlled but with an edge of mischief, giving her the same wholehearted interest he had given Ankarette. But there was a difference—when Richard Stone had smiled that way before, she had ended up utterly in his power. There was always that dangerous air about him that placed her instincts upon alert.

As their right hands met to clasp as they circled, she was astonished at the jolt her body felt. Like earth juddered by a thunderclap, a feeling so difficult to describe in words yet it moved from some center in her being and shivered through her body. She felt it every time he touched her.

They had reached the top of the set now and he sped her up the colonnade of clapping dancers, spun her around, left her as they each hand-chained their way down the lines to meet with hands around each other's waist to finally stand laughing, warm, and breathless opposite each other, clapping while the new lead couple took over. She suddenly wished with all her heart that they had met in different circumstances.

No, she chided herself, she must constantly remember that when he was being charming his tongue could sting like nettles if it pleased him.

When the musicians ended, there was color in her cheeks.

"Mistress." He bowed gracefully over her hand, the green eyes brimming with amusement. "I look forward to renewing our acquaintance even further."

Her tone was tart as crab apples as she sank into a curtsy. "I think there will be little opportunity, sir."

The banns were called at mass again next morning, sending Margery into such a state of inward panic that she was scarce aware of the buzz of conversation about her or a page's tug at her sleeve, summoning her to attend the lord of Warwick.

The Earl was waiting for her in his solar.

"My dear Margery," he exclaimed as she made obeisance to him. "I am so pleased at your change of heart that I have decided to hold your wedding this week. Since your bridegroom is busy on my behalf, it will be more convenient to have it all signed and sealed immediately."

Her dismay was obvious. "My lord, you ride roughshod over my feelings. I am against this marriage. What makes you suddenly think otherwise?"

Her guardian gave a snort of disbelief. "Ah, no, you merely flirt and dance with the man as if you care for him. Have you no shame?"

"I danced with one man last night. Ankarette danced with him too . . ." She faltered and her eyes flew to Warwick's as shock and disbelief flooded across her face. She wanted to sink down onto a stool; surely her legs would collapse beneath her.

"Come, let us be done with this fast-and-loose nonsense. You are marrying Richard Huddleston and have done. Ah, Richard lad, Margery is a little overcome at the haste of all this, but I have explained the situation."

Richard Stone came through the doorway, removing his plumed hat, and bowed to the Earl. If he knew Margery's appalled eyes were upon him, he seemed unruffled.

"My lord. I think it may be the matter of my horse's tail." He looked around at her now. Did the Devil look so on the acquisition of a new soul? Oh, Jesu, how could she be so stupid? His name was not Stone. Agnes Guppy had told her wrongly. After all, the old woman was quite deaf. All that time he must have thought she had been deliberately calling him so to rile him. He was Richard Huddleston.

Be calm, talk yourself out of this, an inner voice advised. Calm? When the deceitful knave was deliberately reminding her who had won all their past battles!

"No, sirrah, it is the matter of *you*! I had rather wed a heathen than be yoked to you in matrimony. As I have made very clear, my lord of Warwick, one, I do not want to marry; two, I do not want to marry this week; and, three, I do not want to marry Master Richard Sto—Huddleston."

"At least you have finally gotten my name right at last." Richard laid his hat and gloves on the table. "My lord, there has been some misunderstanding. It seems the lady thought that she was marrying someone else."

The Earl, appearing half-irritated, half-indulgent at their quarrel, glanced sharply at Margery. "Is this true, child?"

"Yes, my lord." Her fingers writhed in front of her. "You led me to expect it was someone of your lordship's years. Old was the word, you used, I recollect."

"Old!" Richard regarded the Earl with polite astonishment.

Warwick snorted. "So now he's not old, he's known to you, and he wants to marry you, though why I cannot imagine, and I want you off my hands, Margery, so there's an end to it. What pleases me and Master Huddleston shall satisfy you. I have two emissaries arriving from the King of France the day after tomorrow. You will be wed before mass and I shall feast you together with the French lords. Tomorrow, Huddleston, we shall hunt."

Margery fleetingly closed her eyes and gave an angry sigh, prepared to sweep away in dignity before tears overwhelmed her. Huddleston stepped to block her way. She refused to look at him. "My lord," he said across her shoulder to the Earl. "Permit me to speak to my betrothed privily. This is obviously a shock to her." She flinched at the word betrothed, recoiling as if he had struck her.

The Earl shrugged. "Well, I supposed there is no impropriety in that since you will soon be man and wife. You may speak with one another here but there is the contract to draw up, so make haste."

Huddleston bowed as the Earl passed them but remained an obstacle between Margery and the door. She turned away from him, her eyes on the ceiling. It was pain enough to endure being married to a stranger, but that it was Richard Huddleston! She cursed herself for a blind and stupid fool.

His voice was kind. "Mistress Twynhoe told me last night that you did not realize that my name was Huddleston. I had no intention of misleading you, believe me."

Margery took a deep breath, her shoulders proud. "Master Huddleston, I value my freedom. I repeat that I do not want to marry anyone. I will not be sold like some paynim slave to a harem. I came here this morning expecting a public apology and instead . . ." She waved her hands in despair.

"If it is the business of my horse's tail that still angers you then I admit my error. You have my belated but humble apology." The humility in his voice sounded genuine enough but she turned to see if the sincerity was in his eyes. It was, but he was playing kind, of course.

"No, it— Yes, of course it is your horse's tail and all your insults. How dared you abuse me so for your amusement because I am a landless woman and lack a father's name! Do you imagine I have no feelings because I was born in some unblessed bed?"

"Lady, you shall have land, name, and your bed will be blessed."

The blood flooded into her cheeks at the thought. "Blessed, sir, with you in it? I do not know why you have chosen me as a butt for this madness of yours but please change your mind. It will not suit. It will be a marriage made by the Devil."

He laughed and half seated himself on the edge of the table, one leg swinging. "I am resolved on it." He selected an apple from the silver platter and bit into it with his fine white teeth.

Margery's hands curled into fists at her side and she paced the room before she swung back to confront him. "Why do you want to enslave me? What have I ever done to you? Why should it be your choice? Why cannot it be mine?"

"Because I know what is best for you." Warwick's voice came from behind her. Huddleston slid off the table respectfully to face the Kingmaker. The Earl's hands settled upon

Margery's frozen shoulders, his breath was upon her cheek. "I make this marriage for you out of loving kindness, child. Trust me in this." He put a finger beneath her chin and made her look at him. "A firm hand is needed on your bridle, Margery. Once you start bearing you will no doubt calm down and become a sensible wife and mother."

"I am not a horse!" she exclaimed hotly, and snatching up her skirts, she fled.

✺

Richard left the Earl some half hour later well pleased with the bargain. Everything was going according to his plans. Warwick's fondness for the girl and his determination to dispose of his defiant ward had permitted Richard to demand a higher dowry. Of course, it was all on paper but six manors definitely made it worthwhile.

He was not expecting a slender female hand to reach out from behind a curtain and grab the coney-fur tip of his hanging sleeve. His right hand flew to the handle of his sword as he whirled around.

"By Christ's blessed mercy, lady!" He slid the sword back into its black scabbard as he recognized that the blue brocade enclosing the feminine arm belonged to the gown Margery had been wearing.

Her face peeped out at him. "Could we please speak about this matter?" Pink tinged the white around the delightful blue of her eyes, hinting at angry tears. He hated seeing her distressed but one needed to break eggs to make a custard. What was the little witch up to now?

"Right willingly, mistress, but it seems there is little more to say unless you have changed your mind. This curtain is mighty dusty. Do we have to stand behind it like lovers? Is this locked?" She gave an angry growl. He rattled the door ring. It opened onto a small storeroom stacked with broken benches, brooms, and buckets. "Hardly something out of a French romance. Would you prefer somewhere with tapestries?"

His betrothed stamped her foot at him. He grinned at her, reveling in his consistent ability to arouse the desire in her to hit him.

"I think we should discuss this marriage in a sensible

manner, sir. You will have to persuade my lord to reconsider this match."

"You want to marry someone else?" If she did, would he change his mind? There went that little foot again.

"No Master S—Huddleston, I thought I made it clear I do not want to marry anyone."

"Least of all me." He allowed the good humor to fade from his voice.

"Thank goodness, you are intelligent enough to see that."

"May I ask why?"

"*Why*?" she spluttered. "Because we do not like each other."

"I am sorry I teased you."

"Teased me! You taunted, insulted, and riled me. Your arrogant behavior was insufferable. Just because I have no parents . . ."

"And a doubtful reputation."

"Exactly. I am quite unsuitable for you. I am sure your parents—if you have not annoyed them to an early grave— would not approve."

"I admit, lady, your besmirched reputation pleases me not one whit but as to your lack of parents, I am pleased to disregard the fact. Besides, you come to me with a substantial dowry. I shall be wealthier by several manors."

"Dowry!" He could not decide if she looked like an owlet or a kitten at that point. Tendrils of honey hair were rapidly escaping from her embroidered cap. "How many manors?"

"Five so far, one more to be arranged. Now what's amiss?"

"Can you not see he's only doing this to mend my reputation and wash his hands of me. *You* have no need to marry me." His patient expression must have exasperated her further for she stuck her hands on her hips like a little fishwife. "Jesu, you are not prepared to make him change his mind, are you?"

"No, mistress, for his mind is fixed like the north star." He curbed the desire to pull her across the pace of flagstones between them so he could slide his hands down over her lower curves and cradle her hard against him. "You must be a heavy responsibility, Margery. Perhaps I should have bargained for seven manors. The sixth is for your little sin with the King."

"If I were a man, I should run you through for your continual insults."

"But you are not a man, my mistress, so why not try your woman's wiles on me instead." It was time he showed her what he wanted from her. By all the Saints, he had been waiting long enough.

"To Hell with you, Master Huddleston!"

She ran out and down the passageway before he could stop her and flung open the Earl's door. "Sutton Gaveston! Let the sixth manor that you sold me for be Sutton Gaveston!" Then she grabbed up a fistful of her skirts in each hand. "You said you did not want used goods. You said I was a bad bargain," she snarled at Richard as she hurried back toward him.

She would have torn past had he not seized her arm. He was about to kiss the anger out of her when the Earl loudly opened the door of the antechamber.

Warwick's face struggled in a contortion of anger intermingled with laughter. "Margery, enough!" he thundered.

Richard's fingers bit into the top half of his betrothed's sleeve. It was like trying to hold on to a spitting cat but he had a point to make and he made it loudly. "You said you wanted me shackled and bound. Well, I shall be, for all eternity."

Margery gave Warwick a deadly glare before she wrenched her arm from Richard's grasp.

"But I did not mean to me, Master Huddleston, not to *me*!"

CHAPTER

8

Margery fled to Isabella, not caring who saw her tears, and begged her to intercede with her father, but the Duchess pointed out that since Huddleston had ruined her anew by abducting her, it was a satisfactory outcome all around. There was no mercy anywhere.

It was then Margery decided to leave Valognes immediately. It had to be today; tomorrow all the horses would be taken out for the hunt. If she could ride away while everyone was still sitting at the trestles talking after dinner, she might manage a good start. This time she would succeed: Ned's purse still held sufficient to bribe a Norman fisherman to take her back to England and she could be in Cherbourg by noon next day.

But it was as if the Earl, or someone else, knowing her mettle, had forestalled her at every step. The grooms, busy checking the condition of the horses and their harnesses, had been given orders—no one was to be allowed a horse without a signed warrant from the Earl. No, they did not take bribes either. The gatehouse of the logis was doubly guarded too.

Miserable, Margery swiftly sought out the path around the back of the stable to return stealthfully to the tiring women's bedchamber so she might change out of her male garb before anyone discovered her absence. She did not include two of Clarence's more unpleasant henchmen in her calculations.

John Wyke and Henry Littlebourne, retainers of the Duke's friend, Burdett, rounding the corner behind the stables, deliberately walked into her at the pace of trundling cannon and snatched her cap off. "Going somewhere, lad? Why by Satan's arse, it's a wench." They circled her, a pair of human wolves in leather. "Why, the little bastard bride. Does your future husband know the King has had your maidenhead?" Wyke's hand caught her by the belt and yanked her toward him. He rolled his tongue lasciviously along his lips.

"Let go of me!" Margery swiped at his face with her riding crop.

"Bloody bitch!" He lashed out a gloved fist at her.

Littlebourne grabbed him. "You'll bruise her, you fool!" Before she could scream, he clamped an iron hand across her mouth and slammed her up against the stable wall. "Let's have a look at what's in store for Huddleston. She's not a virgin so he won't notice anything."

"Aye, but what if she squeals to the Earl?"

"The little whore will not dare. Huddleston will not marry her if she does. He may not mind the smoke but he will not want a bloody bonfire."

Wyke tried to thrust his hand within her codpiece, not finding it easy as she kicked at his kneecaps. Littlebourne, meanwhile, was fumbling inside her shirt, his lewd breath reeking with ale.

It was a deep-throated growl that froze Wyke's hand as he made to wrench down the front of Margery's woolen hose.

Matthew Long stood there, large and ponderous against the stable wall opposite, his expression as vacuous as a scarecrow's. In front of him Huddleston's deerhound was straining at the leash, lips curling back to reveal sharp vulpine teeth. Every hackle stood out.

"Fellow, you spoil our sport. Get out of here before I take my whip to you."

"All very well, sirs, but Error, this dog here, doesn't understand English. Knows Latin, he does, and he has a passion for yon lady. By all the Saints, I do not know if I can hold the beast much longer." His boots scraped the ground as Error pulled toward them.

The air was crude with expletives as they let Margery go.

"I shall remember you, fellow, and your arsehole of a dog!" Wyke shook a fist at the retainer.

"I don't know why, sirs, I'm doing my poxy best." Long grinned stupidly at their vindictiveness but a further menacing rumble and tug from the great deerhound sent them hastening on their way.

Margery slumped against the wall, awash with tears, shame, and laughter as Matthew let the dog drag him across to her. Error's rough tongue laundered her hands and washed her face as she put her arms around the animal's neck and hugged it.

"Oh, Matthew, that was cleverly done." She reached up on tiptoe and kissed his bristly cheek, sending him a fiery red.

"It was the dog rescued you, mistress. My fists would have been little use against their steel." He gave a low whistle. "The master will be mad enough to bind if he hears you have been wandering around here in that garb. S'posin' the chaplain sees you? Let me see you safely through the garden."

Let Huddleston hear, thought Margery as she followed him.

"Master says you do not want to marry him neither." They were almost at the logis.

"That is quite correct, Matthew."

"You could do a lot worse, Mistress Margery. There are plenty of knights not worthy of the name like those two ruffians back there who would make marriage a misery."

Long was right, she thought, swiftly changing back into her gown. At least as Huddleston's wife she would have a man sworn to protect her reputation and her person, even if he did not like her much. But Wyke and Littlebourne had given her one last card to play.

She was pale as the full moon as she made her way to the Countess's chamber and there curtsied. "Madam, I was waylaid by two of my lord Duke's drunken henchmen.

When Master Huddleston is informed of this matter, if he still wishes to wed me, I shall make my oath to him two days hence." Let Huddleston swallow that if it pleased him. Pray Heaven it would choke him sufficiently to call the marriage off, and providing Long kept a still tongue . . .

The Countess smiled coldly at her surrender and instantly put an end to her prowling the barriers of her freedom. She was set to work sewing, confined to the women's quarters to await Huddleston's decision. He did not change his mind.

The women around her laughed and chattered like an aviary as they discussed marriage and nuptials, their stories growing more ribald by the minute until Margery's cheeks flamed scarlet and she threw down the embroidery in disgust. She refused to eat the supper they fetched her from the hall, knowing that it would choke her.

At dawn she heard the hunt leave to the call of horns and the baying of hounds and she pitied the poor creatures to be slaughtered for her nuptial feast. The Earl's chaplain summoned her to confession and she sat unfeeling and even hated God. At dusk she heard the hooves of the horses returning, smelled the blood, heard the laughter of the men. The kitchens were busy preparing for the banquet. She could see the tallow lights glinting behind the shutters across the yard, hear the knives being whetted.

On the morning of her marriage day, the servants rose early to finish decorating the hall and carts came creaking in, waking everyone, bringing the extra ale required for a wedding feast.

The bride grew paler and more silent by the hour. Finally it was young Anne Neville who took her by the hand and led her out into the sunlight to make her a chaplet of flowers.

"Ah, there you are." Isabella found them later. "That chaplet should be much tighter, Anne, you will have to make it again. Now, I have decided to give you my cream overgown for the wedding, Margery. I know you did not care to think what you would wear but I cannot be bothered with it anymore although it is very fine. The color will become you well. Now we must go in, Mother has had a bath filled for you, make haste before it grows cold. You shall not want to be sneezing all over us."

"I wish my lady would just drown me in it and have done."

"Margery, you must improve your attitude. The French lords will be attending this afternoon and his grace my husband is very anxious that everything will go well. We shall all be under evaluation. Now promise me you will do nothing to jeopardize our chances of raising a French loan to make his grace king."

"But your grace, I was Ned's mistress."

Isabella stamped her foot. "Oh, peace, you are saying that just to annoy me. All I can say is that Ned has done precious little for you. Think on that when Master Huddleston tries to be sweet to you."

"Sweet! Tell me the Earth is not flat, your grace."

The bath would have been enjoyable if it had not been tepid by the time they had unrobed her. The only pleasure she had out of it was when Isabella poured in some of de Commynes's gift to perfume the water. The Duchess looked askance as Margery burst into a gale of bitter laughter. The women notched up her madness to her wayward nature and clucked disapprovingly.

Her hair was easily washed and toweled dry for it barely caressed her shoulders. They arrayed Isabella's cast-off overgown of cream silk over the forget-me-not blue brocade that had been stitched in Calais and the Duchess fastened a belt of broad silver platelets beneath Margery's breasts. One of the tiring women swiftly stitched a collar of white coney in a V that plunged to the waist of the overgrown. A triangle of blue brocade was fastened in to cover her breasts below her cleavage. Margery made to tug it higher. Isabella slapped her hand away.

"You have charms, show them."

The Duchess's attendants brushed Margery's hair until is was dry and glossy, then combed it back behind her ears. With a large bodkin they threaded a long string of seed pearls through Anne's chaplet, catching up a gauzy veil with every stitch. The one concession they allowed her was a veil over her face. It was not usual but Margery insisted. That privacy at least would be hers. She also desired to wear her hair pinned back but the Countess interfered.

"Richard Huddleston has requested you wear your hair loose as if you were a maiden."

Margery whirled around, a protest on her lips but her defiance gave way. What was the use? Within hours her whole life would cease to be within her control. She shrugged as they arranged the chaplet on her hair.

The stranger in the long silver mirror they thrust before her was beautiful. Neither radiant nor dewy-eyed but fair. She looked at herself in astonishment.

"Hmm," approved the Countess. "Who would believe the little scape-grace in our midst would polish up into so fine a bride?"

I should be happy, thought Margery, studying their cheerful faces. I have never looked so grand in all my life. If only they were not forcing me into this. The thought of what lay ahead sent a surge of panic through her. It was not only the public formal ceremony of possession that she must face, it was the private possession that would come later that made her tremble.

CHAPTER
9

The long fingers that Richard Huddleston held out to Margery in the archway of the chapel door were clean and clever like their owner. A single signet ring glittered on his third finger. Her gaze slid up from the edge of fine lawn at his wrist to where the embroidered brocade sleeve fell from his shoulder, its scalloped edge brushing her gown, ebony and amber against cream. She rejoiced in his brief frown of displeasure at her veil and ignored his hand. It was the Earl who lifted her defiant fingers and placed them in Huddleston's.

The strength and power in his touch ran through her arm and threatened her very breathing. She hardly heard the Latin, scarcely recognized the words prompted from her own lips. A heavy golden ring touched the tips of each of her fingers in turn before its owner slid it down finally over her fourth finger. She gave an involuntary gasp. It was as though he had snapped a collar around her neck.

Her guardian again fastened her indifferent fingers around a second ring and directed her hand. Her words were a whisper that barely stirred the gauze across her face. She was aware of kneeling beside Richard Huddleston on the tapestried hassocks for the chaplain's blessing before the household followed them in to mass.

After the chaplain gave the congregation a final benediction, her new husband rose and took her hand to help her stand. At last she looked up at him through her veil and trembled at the triumphant look in his eyes.

For a fleeting instant, the green magic of his gaze lifted them both from their surroundings and she knew that he had what he wanted, that his purpose had been relentless. In that infinitesimal moment, she was aware that in the surrender, as well as the loss of control of her life, there was a sense of belonging. But before she could seize upon the pleasantness of that tantalizing sensation, reality overwhelmed her; the household was holding its breath waiting to see if she would show defiance.

Distractedly, Margery lightly rested her hand upon her enemy's wrist as he led her down the chancel steps. Behind her was the rustle of her gown as it kissed its way across the flagstones; on either side of her brightly clothed people murmured but their faces were hazy. Outside, the world seemed truer, the sunshine dazzling after the shadowy chapel.

Richard Huddleston set back the fine veil but she refused to lift her face to his. He charmingly carried her fingers to his lips in time for the first of the congregation to be appeased. She was conscious of his arm supporting her, of the breeze blowing at her garments. Congratulations and smiles wafted in and out of her vision as if she were in a fever. She was in turn hugged, squeezed, kissed, and complimented until her head felt like a whirligig.

"Master Huddleston, you may lead us in to dinner."

Richard, relieved, bowed to the French emissaries standing beside the Earl—Jean Bourré, the Treasurer of France, and the Scotsman, William Mennypenny, Lord of Concressault, then he led the procession into the hall.

Garlands of golden and creamy daisies tumbled over the edge of the snowy white cloth of the high table and spilled intertwined with ivy from each iron candelabra. High above the great salt, braids of flowers radiated out to the walls from a central boss. Other blossoms glowed pink and almond upon the two long tables flanking the sides of the floor. Along the walls between the sideboards, the French servants in borrowed scarlet and white Neville livery stood ready.

Margery suddenly lost her distraught gaze. She stepped forward to face the servants and sank into the lowest, most gracious curtsy Richard had ever seen any woman manage. It was her thanks to them for all their labors and the servants responded by clapping until the very rafters rang.

Behind Richard, the Treasurer of France whispered to the Lord of Concressault, "*Par Dieu,* William, I think we are the interlopers at this wedding feast."

"Come, Richard!" The Kingmaker sounded well pleased. Together they raised Margery smoothly to her feet and made sure she had the hem of her gown outside her heel. "That was well done, my child." The Earl's compliment brought a tight smile but fleetingly to her solemn face, and behind them the wedding guests applauded politely.

The steward raised his wand and little page, scrubbed reluctantly to a shine the night before, solemnly carried forward a silver ewer of warm water perfumed with chamomile.

Envy bit Richard as Margery called the child by name, lovingly flicking the boy's cheek before she dropped the lavender-scented napkin back across his arm. There was no equal warmth for him, her bridegroom. He set his face in an appropriate half smile as they were escorted to share the high-backed settle on the dais, and then leaned back against the cushions, wondering if he had made an ill bargain.

Because of Warwick's haste, the girl had nothing but bad will toward him. He should have stood his ground against the disgruntled Earl, argued that he needed time for wooing. He raised a critical eyebrow at his new wife's stony profile, ignoring the shouts for bride ale as everyone settled themselves at the trestles. This marriage was a gamble. If the wench was truly wanton or still hankering to be King Edward's mistress, he had just bound the cuckold's horns upon his head with his own two hands.

Damn her! Where was the wit she usually used against

him? *That* woman he could deal with, not this beauteous, lifeless effigy. It was as if the part of her he knew had withdrawn. Was marrying him so terrible to her?

The feeble notes of shawms and small-pipes, barely audible against the beat of the tabors and the laughter, matched his weakening ardor. He needed to reawaken the courage in her, convince himself that the sacrifice he had made for this day's work was worthwhile.

Beside him, Margery was wondering how she could be so conscious of another's every breath and gesture. Her infuriating bridegroom was deliberately keeping his right arm behind her, his hand resting lightly on the cushions. She kept edging forward, her body taut as a lute string. Let him know she despised him. He might have bought her body but he did not possess her soul. True, he was behaving with decorum. Another man in his place might have let his hand adventure, but Richard Huddleston seemed indifferent. No, not entirely.

"I should have told you earlier how well your gown becomes you," he murmured when on either side of them the guests were distracted.

"Unfortunately, like me, it is used," she responded wryly and lifted her face to challenge his. But the gaze of the man who had demanded six manors for the doubtful joy of bedding her rose tardily from the low edging of her bodice, as if he intended her to observe his journey of discovery. He did not touch her; he did not need to. She felt the slow caress of his glance slide sensually up her neck and linger upon her mouth. He compelled her to recognize the controlled desire in his eyes. Struggling against the stirrings of her body, she jerked her head higher, defying his attempt to strip away her armor.

"Do you say that to discomfort me, lady?" The green eyes did not falter but it was as if the murky depth of his gaze suddenly cleared, like water letting though the sunlight. "I have found from experience that used shoes do not pinch."

She could not answer him. His meaning brought the high color rushing into her pale face. Having scored a touch, he withdrew from further verbal combat, his lips closed in a tight smile of satisfaction.

Margery took a deep breath. Alone with him, she might have tipped the soup bowl over his lap or hurled the cockatrice, could she but lift it. Sweet Jesu, before the dawn this man she could not fathom would pleasure himself within her body. Perilously, she wondered what it would be like to tangle her fingers in his hair and pull his mouth down to hers, what it would feel like to have him enter her.

Astonished at her imaginings, she gave herself a shake. She would endure Purgatory rather than submit to this man who cared not one jot about her feelings.

Warwick was watching her. He caught her chin, forcing her to look at him while Huddleston's attention was elsewhere. "Child, cease your defiance. You will one day thank me for this day's work. Drink, it will help you, and watch the entertainment. These people are here for your pleasure."

That was a lie. He was trying to impress the French lords as if the tumblers, jugglers, and a dancing dog could match the lavish feasting he had displayed in London, banquets to rival Ned's at Westminster. She distanced herself again, and across her the men verbally dissected yesterday's hunt as they ate its prizes. Later, she tried to be gracious as roasted swans and peacocks, refeathered in their intricate plumage on elaborate platters, were set before her. Yet the good wines tasted sour, the food like waste upon a joiner's floor.

As the light in the hall grew dimmer, the servants lit the cressets on the walls and the candelabras of Paris wax above the salt. Love songs and scurrilous ballads suffered from bawdy interruptions as the claret and hypocras flowed with abundance. The quips came at them continuously. She was conscious of Richard Huddleston parrying them with good nature for she was incapable of making answers. Her inner fear grew as the sweet custards, tarts, and wafers appeared. The luscious cherries shone with sensuousness. The honeyed fruits, nestling among nuts and comfits, mocked her discomfort.

At last the chief cook himself set the subtlety, the crown of the feast's gems, before the bride and groom. There was an embarrassed silence as the guest absorbed the presence of the tiny unicorn with a gilded horn resting its head upon a maiden's lap. It was inappropriate. Unicorns might be caught only by maidens, which distinctly disqualified Margery. Her unicorn-trapping days were considered by all to be long past. Ankarette gave an embarrassed cough that threatened to turn into a giggle.

Margery hastened to thank the proud master cook and Huddleston leaned forward and gave the man his hand.

"It is very . . . flattering," Margery added huskily. Indeed, it was exquisite and she felt like weeping at the honest perfection of each sugary fold. Who had inspired this kitchen genius to create such a divine but tactless sculpture? Had Master Huddleston suggested this, trying to delude himself and others that she came unsullied?

"Am I supposed to be the unicorn?" he asked gravely, with a raise of an eyebrow.

"It is impolitic but rather delightful," exclaimed Isabella.

"But Margery likes unicorns," Anne protested.

"Oh, it was your idea, was it Anne?" The Duke of Clarence smirked and the grins of the adults broadened farther.

"I thought it was a good notion for a wedding," insisted Anne, her neck and cheeks flushing scarlet with embarrassment. "You like it, do you not, Margery?"

The bride turned solemn blue eyes upon the fifteen-year-old. "As God is my witness, my lady, I like it better than anything in the whole feast and I thank you for your inspiration." Her voice was choked with an emotion she could not adequately voice.

Richard watched Anne Neville's mouth curl with pleasure and, turning, saw love and friendship for her in Margery's misting eyes.

"Master Huddleston, do you like unicorns?"

He dragged his gaze reluctantly from Margery's face to smile kindly at the younger girl. "My lady, I have never seen a unicorn I liked better."

"Well, now we have done that conversation to death," exclaimed the Duke, "perhaps we can think about putting the bride to bed. You have feasted us right *royally*, my lord."

The Countess of Warwick sniffed, sending her son-in-law a telling look that would have made a more sober man anxious, but she did glance at Margery and then at her lord questioningly.

Richard felt the cold young woman beside him tremble.

The Earl flicked the bride's cheek and turned toward the French envoys. "What say you, messeigneurs?"

The Scots lord answered. "Och, dinna rob this table too soon of such beautiful young women. For sure I wish that I was their age once again."

"I wish I was your age, my good lord, I would be rich indeed if I had your wisdom," Margery told him without a trace of flattery.

"Dinna fret, sweet lady, you are far cleverer than I will ever be, for you can grow a child within you. What man can perform so sweet a miracle?"

Richard sensed Margery quiver. She snapped her lips shut.

"Ha, but what woman can do it alone, *mon ami*?" Jean Bourré slapped the table, his cheeks rosy with the wine, and raised his goblet to Richard. "I drink to you, young man. May you earn yourself a son from this night's labors and may your wife give us a little miracle nine months hence."

Richard inclined his head in courteous thanks but he was heartily wishing it was all over. His irritation was growing. God knows it was not as if Margery was a virgin. The whole hall knew that. He was looking forward to discovering her royal bedchamber skills but the truth of it was that the little witch just did not want to surrender.

The Duke did not help. "She looks fit to swoon. Have done, my lords, let's put her to bed. Come, Meg, bestir yourself. You have to keep awake tonight."

Richard tightened his arm about her, apprehensive that it would not take much to make her run away and shame herself and him. At least the Earl, Heaven be thanked, was set to loosen the girths of the situation. Warwick rose smiling, his hand firmly on Margery's shoulder. "All in good time. Another song!" He snapped his fingers to summon one of the counter-tenors who had performed earlier.

Richard leaned across behind Margery and laid a hand upon the Earl's sleeve. "With your good leave, my lord, I think this task is mine."

The Duke shifted irritably. "By St. George, will you punish us, Huddleston, with some lovesick warbling?"

"I do not warble," retorted Richard temperamentally.

"He is not lovesick either," Margery cut in swiftly, in control of herself again. Their eyes met briefly. Like deep water, his revealed nothing to say that she was wrong.

"Give the man a lute then or would you prefer the bagpipe?" the Duke exclaimed snidely.

"A harp will suffice."

A pigeon would have taken the message to the musicians in the gallery faster than the laggard chosen but a harp was eventually procured. By which time, the Duke of Clarence was yawning audibly. "Are you not weary, Meg? Bridegroom, will you not make music with the lady instead?" Isabella hushed him angrily.

Margery, her cheeks flaming, watched Richard Huddleston take the small harp and draw a skilled hand across the strings. A rich chord prompted the noise in the hall to lessen somewhat. "You will know the words but the melody is by a Breton minstrel." He stood up to give himself more room and rested one piked foot on the settle, sweeping his hanging sleeves behind him. The strings needed a swift adjustment before his adroit fingers rippled out a sweet sad sound. The half smile flickered on his lips as he moistened them.

His singing voice was surprising, rich yet light but the words . . . the words made Margery avert her gaze instantly from his patrician profile to his fingers.

> *"I pray you, mistress, to me be true,*
> *For I will be true as long as I live.*
> *I will not change you for old nor new,*
> *Nor never love other, whiles that I live.*
> *I trust it so for it to be*
> *That it shall light on you and me."*

Her body was growing warm at the thought of those deft fingers exploring her, but the tone of his voice changed and she thought she could hear the subtle laughter in the words. He was provoking her again; demanding she answer him. Or was she mistaken? Was he trying to play the gallant?

> *"My dearest, list,*
> *By me be taught,*

For love is the sweeter,
The dearer it's bought,
For love is the sweeter,
The dearer it's bought."

In panic, she swiftly lowered her eyes to the uneaten cherries on her plate, keeping her anger sheathed. Knowing her antagonism to the marriage, the whole hall was watching her. She could hear the chuckles and the gossip. *By him be taught!* Sweet Heaven, let him try!

The gorgeous cadences died away in the rafters. For a heartbeat the hall was silent and then they thumped the boards.

"Sweetly done," the Countess applauded. "Can you sing us one more and then indeed it will be time to bed you both."

"Yes, an epic ballad with a hundred verses," Margery muttered.

Huddleston heard her. He crashed his fingers across the harpstrings, jarring his bride's fragile composure. "You need not stall your patience or mine any longer, Mistress Huddleston."

Along the table, the Duke brayed his irritating laugh. "By St. George, Meg, you have met your match. Take her to task, man!"

"And so I shall." Huddleston snatched up Margery's unsuspecting hand and proffered it to the Countess. "My lady, I give my bride to your good care."

It was the moment Margery had been dreading. She gave a desperate look around her like a condemned prisoner seeking a reprieve before the Countess and the other women led her away.

At the doorway to the bridal chamber she faltered, blanching at the folded back sheets strewn with rose petals and fertility herbs. The cloying scent of blossom mingled with candle wax threatened to overwhelm her.

Behind a screen, they removed her clothes and cleansed her again, drizzling her skin with perfumed water. She was shaking by the time they had finished and reached for her shift but Ankarette tugged it back. "Oh, do not bother with that. You will only have to take it off again to get into bed before the groomsmen arrive."

"But I am so cold," protested Margery. She was not used to being exposed without her clothes.

"Oh, let her have her way," the Countess intervened. "You are not cold, Margery. This room is like a furnace. It is your qualms about your duty to your husband, no doubt. Although I should have thought you would be the last person to feel bothered about such matters."

"As you say, madam." Margery's lips were a thin line of willfulness as she jerked her shift away from Ankarette and swiftly pulled it over her head. The fabric was of such fine quality that it hid nothing but at least it made her feel less vulnerable. She sank down miserably upon the stool. Within her was no respite. It was as if a hundred points of jagged glass were directed against her fluttering agonized spirit.

"I will do that." Isabella took the brush from Ankarette and swiftly tidied Margery's hair.

"Make cheer, you could do worse!" exclaimed Ankarette. "Oh, Lord, madam, here they come and we have not put the bride to bed. Quickly, Margery, into the sheets and take that shift off!"

"Oh, Jesu." Margery flinched as Ankarette pushed her toward the bed and struggled to disrobe her.

"No, leave her! It is too late," snapped the Countess.

Margery frantically snatched her discarded wedding gown from off the screen and clutched it to her as the chaplain swept in with two altar boys. Incense fumes enveloped them all.

Richard Huddleston arrived on the men's shoulders and was set down none too gently on his feet amid rising laughter. Margery's heart began to beat wildly. She was praying furiously that the Countess would not let the drunken throng peel her naked before her abductor.

Richard hid his urge to stride from the bedchamber and go back to England. Beneath the incense, the bedchamber smelled like a Southwark brothel and his new bride was looking as enthusiastic as a princess chained to a rock waiting for the dragon to devour her. The women had been tardy in unclothing her and putting her naked between the sheets. Now the men about him were ogling her, their bawdy comments loud as they tugged at his sleeves to rid him of his doublet.

The chaplain took the holy water from one of his altar boys. Someone pushed Margery to her knees and she stayed there, ridiculously clutching the overgown to her bosom while drops of holy water were sprinkled all over the bed.

Richard bent his knee, inwardly cursing. The chaplain splashed the water liberally over him and flicked some over the crowd for good measure before he intoned the Latin blessing once more. Then with a pompous warning that Hell was waiting for all of them, he left.

As they began to unlace his shirt, Richard saw the young Duchess pull Margery to her feet and gravely place her palm against her belly. "May you have more happiness than I in the first child you bear." With surprise, he caught the fleeting wild fear in Margery's eyes and saw her shakily lay her fingers against the Duchess's cheek. Perhaps she was not defiant after all.

"Oh, Bella." Compassion was in his bride's voice as their two foreheads touched. Tears sparkled unshed for both.

For a brief instant Richard felt pity for the little Duchess, pity for all women. What to a man was a fleeting pleasure could end in hours of travail and an agonizing death. Was that what his new wife feared or was it the act itself? He had never seen her courage ebb so low.

As the Duchess stepped back, he trapped Margery looking at him in dread like a snared rabbit. By Christ's blessed mercy, the wench was afraid of him. She knew her duty well enough surely . . . But had the King merely plundered without pleasuring her? Richard cursed. She should have given her maidenhead to him. Together they could have taught each other the delights, the arts, of love. Instead, the girl was fearful.

A merry hand tugging at the points holding Richard's hose brought him back to his own role. He thrust the drunken fingers away. It was going to be supping in Hell to deal with Margery but he was certainly not going to permit the revelers to embarrass her any further. Nor was he going to let these drunkards strip him naked as Adam and toss him into bed with her.

"Enough! Out!" Feigning laughter, arms wide as an eagle's wings, he swept everyone before him toward the doorway which they cluttered with wine-soused protests.

"But Huddleston, we have not put the bride to bed with you." George of Clarence swayed against the lintel.

"No, your grace," Richard growled. "That will be *my* pleasure!"

CHAPTER
10

Grabbing the wooden bar, Richard thrust it down onto the supporting brackets. Clearing the bedchamber had been easier than what faced him now.

He strode to the window and threw the shutters open. The cool evening breeze rushed in as if the stifling room itself were relieved to take a gulp of air. Richard took a deep breath too, steeling himself before he turned briskly toward the bed and inspected the tester. Its brocade showed no strange weight but he still slapped upward at the heavy canopy with the back of his hand. No lewd page tumbled out but a cloud of dust was awakened. His bride sneezed.

He then yanked the sheets fully back and felt between them where they tucked together. Satisfied, he brushed the mess of herbs from the heart of the base sheet and flung the bedding back over it.

Glancing sideways he was pleased to see that the trepidation in Margery's eyes had been somewhat softened as she watched his behavior in silent fascination, albeit her body was still as tense as a soldier's before battle. Grimly, he grabbed the candlestick and went down on one knee to inspect beneath the bed for piglets, grass snakes, toads, or giggling voyeurs stowed away to interrupt the bridal privacy. No one was hiding there either, and with relief in his face he straightened up and set the candlestick down upon his side of the bed.

Margery let out a deep breath.

"So you are still alive," he commented, pouring a drink from the flagon set upon a little table by the bed. "Shall you have some?"

She was frowning, watching his fingers upon the handle. At length she shook her head, seeming to grasp at the life rope of normal conversation he had flung out to her.

"You must have a good head for drinking."

Richard shrugged. "All pretense." He watched her over the rim of the goblet and, lowering it, studied her, making his own expression unreadable. By Christ's blessed mercy, if ever he had needed self-control, it was now. The silence was tangible. He watched her breath grow fast and uneven.

Surprisingly, she broke the stillness, falling back on her wit. "What would you like me to do? I left my seven veils at the convent."

"*Do?*" He let surprise into the coolness of his question while he studied her, choosing his next words, trying not to be conquered by the delectable curve of her breasts. The gown she hid behind had slithered fractionally, betraying a tempting semicircle of dark rose beneath the white lawn. His eyes slid over where his hands could not. He clenched his jaw and averted his gaze. "For a beginning you may cease standing to attention—and I am open to suggestions. You are, after all, experienced."

Margery's cheeks flamed. "I am out of practice."

It was time for the coup de grâce. He turned his back on her, filling his goblet once more to hide the battle within him. Anyone watching his steady hand might be fooled by his cold calm. It was going to take all the inner strength he possessed, every part of his considerable willpower to stanch the lust that had been consuming him. It was tempting to pit those skills that other women had taught him against whatever the royal whoremonger had taught her. But this was different. Tonight it was a nuptial bed and he was now married.

He allowed to himself that he might have erred in not handling Margery with the fawning care of a suitor, and he needed to be less hard on her. But to lose control and tumble her was to admit her mistress of his passion.

Now he could afford to be gracious and make amends. She was at last his wife for all her whorish past and he needed her compliant to make their marriage tolerable. Generosity of spirit could work in his favor and time was on his side. After all, he owned her.

"I am content to wait." He turned at last.

"To wait?" Her voice sounded shrill, betraying the alarm that must have been writhing like some monstrous serpent within her.

Richard nodded as he set the goblet back on the tray. The tension in the room was mocked by stifled giggles bubbling outside the door. Someone was sliding wafers and poking cherrystones beneath it.

He came back across to her and framed her face within his long fingers. "In the name of Heaven, cease looking as though I am about to sacrifice you on some stone or other. It has been a long day."

"You mean. . . ?" Something inside her seemed to be unwinding with relief for her expression changed to grateful astonishment. He smiled wryly, surprised at his own reaction. The magnanimity he felt was enjoyable despite the ache in his groin. His mouth tightened as he drew the ball of his thumb along her lips. It pained him to touch her but she still had to recognize his right to do so.

"That I do not desire to lie with you tonight when you are infinitely desirable? It is the common opinion out there. I could see it in their faces, every man jack of them, imagining you naked as Eve." He let go of her abruptly and turned back toward the door, as if something beyond it had distracted him. "Set the overgown aside and put something around you before I change my mind," he ordered harshly. "My wrap is on the bed, use that."

It was quieter now, the scraping of wood on stone of the servants clearing back the trestles reached them. He heard the rustle of the taffeta lining as she hastily thrust her arms through the hanging sleeves of his garment.

He turned back to her again but kept the distance of the

room between them. "In an ideal world you might be begging me to take you in my arms but that's hardly likely to happen tonight, is it?" She shook her head, biting her lower lip. "Exactly, so as neither of us are virgins and we do not have to worry about evidence of our marriage's consummation tomorrow morning, let us at least call a truce." She was searching his face, trying to decide whether she could trust him. "I told you when I abducted you that you had nothing to fear. I am not the lout you obviously imagine me to be."

His new wife drew breath to make some answer, seeking some way of couching her thanks, but as her lips parted delightfully, lusciously, he forestalled her, angry at the temptation that was nagging at his loins. "By Christ's blessed mercy, I can see I have just rescued you from the jaws of Hell. Get into bed unless you intend curling up like a cur on the hearthrug!"

He strode around to his side of the bed. She stood hesitating and they frowned at each other across the coverlet. "I suppose now with the perversity of womankind you will think me weak for not exercising my husbandly rights." Her color deepened as she trembled and solemnly shook her head at him. "Tell me, scourge me with a little truth. Is it the appearance of my person that offends you?"

She drew a deep breath. "I do not find you outwardly unpleasing."

Richard gave a bitter laugh. "How nice you are. Must I thank the Almighty for that small concession to my vanity?" He spat on his fingers and squeezed out the candle flame, his eyes not leaving her face. In the glow of the dying fire, he started to undress. "Your pardon if I remove at least my shirt." He could not tell if his sarcasm found its target. He knew she was watching him as he tugged the garment of Rennes lawn out from beneath his gipon and over his head. He tossed it across the bottom of the bed and thrust his fingers through his rumpled hair before he faced her again.

His new acquisition was still eyeing him as if he were a dangerous animal, but it did not escape him that her eyes slid down the dark hair that showed between the lacing of his gipon to where it disappeared beneath the waistline of his hose. Well, let her see what she was missing. Mayhap the little minx would change her mind. He climbed into bed and pulled the sheets above his thighs. A little time, he thought, and I shall have her where she should be. Perhaps if the Saints were kind, by morning.

Margery hesitated, then sat down on her side of the bed and raised the sheet up before she swung her legs in, careful all the while to keep his wrap about her. She slowly slid down, preserving as much distance as she could from the bare shoulders of the man who might at any moment demand his rights.

If she had had a dozen dukedoms to wager, she would never have predicted this sudden clemency. But now that she had a reprieve, Margery was feeling a little safer and brave enough to tweak the lion's tail. "Did my lord force you into this marriage? Did he have to bribe you with manors for this act of charity to a bastard like myself?"

Her new husband clasped his hands beneath his head, studying the brocade tester above them with seeming boredom. "You need some sort of reassurance? No to the first question. Yes to the second; my lord appeared to consider it a requirement. I am promised much."

"You may whistle in the wind for paper promises. I fear you have made a very poor bargain."

"You see me racked by contrition at my waywardness?"

Did nothing unnerve him? Margery humped herself onto her side. To say she was confused would have been an understatement. A wedding night was not something she had ever seriously daydreamed about but this was a strange torture. An indifferent bridegroom was the last thing she had expected and she did not know whether to be relieved or insulted that he had no wish to lie with her. Besides, Richard Huddleston was as unpredictable as an English summer. Her languid bridegroom might well metamorphose into a lusty husband at any moment during the next six or so hours she was compelled to spend lying next to him.

"Tell me about Calais, Margery. Were you well received by Lord Wenlock?" His voice caressed the darkened silence between them like velvet. Was this part of his strategy? To lull her, put her at her ease before he pounced? She considered pretending to be asleep but he would guess she was trying to gull him. Perhaps talking would keep him distracted.

"Well received? If you call being arrested hospitality,

then he was charm personified. He made me wait all day without food before he granted an audience and that was in his bedchamber."

There was a rumble of laughter from her companion. "Never tell me there is still life in that old goat? Did he try to put his hand up your skirts?"

Her tone was prim. "I know you have a poor opinion of my virtue, sir, but I do draw the line at rheumy graybeards. I suppose you heard how he refused to let Isabella bear her child on dry land. I can never forgive him for that." Huddleston made no comment so she continued nervously to fill the silence. "To make such a fuss of Isabella with trinkets when she was tiny and then to do that to her. If he had ever had a child in his belly, he would never have—"

"You speak from experience?" The icy draft of his tone chilled her.

"No!" she retorted angrily, biting her lip. Even this conversation seemed to lay traps for her unwary tongue. "I have seen babies born though. Most women have. Maybe husbands should be forced to be present instead of being barred from the birth chamber." Just the unwitting mention of husband made her cheeks flame.

"I am sure the experience would do us all much good," he agreed pleasantly, increasing her heartbeat as he included himself. A shivery heat assaulted her senses. Sooner or later this impossible man was going to thrust his seed into her and she would have to carry his child whether she would or no. Her fingers coiled into fists. Damn him!

"So Lord Wenlock sent you into France with an escort to rejoin the Duchess? You had a safe journey?"

"No, not at all. Alys and I were merely abducted by a troop of Burgundian ruffians and terrified out of our wits, but I am becoming used to it, thanks to your worthy self. I have obviously been missing out on these new ways of doing things every time one travels."

"And?" He had a habit of saying that, she noticed. "Go on, I am hanging on your every word. And?"

"And de Commynes, why he—"

"The Burgundian?" Huddleston reacted like a bull stung by a gadfly. She heard him lift his head from the pillow.

"Yes, the Burgundian envoy. You see, I met him at Lord

Wenlock's and he sent me some bath essence in Venetian glass which was very kind of him and he asked me many questions about what Ned was doing. Did I know whether he had sent out commissions of array, that sort of thing."

"While you were in the bath? So unimaginative. And did you?"

"Yes, well, I knew all the men-at-arms had been sent back to their shires. Actually I did not use the essence though her grace put some in my bath today. I had given it to her, you see."

"How disappointing."

"Had I known that we were to be shackled together in matrimony, sir, I should have kept it and broken it over your head."

"Careful, mistress. The dog beside you comes with a long leash. But do go on . . . You were saying his men abducted you. What happened then?" Richard's voice was controlled but she knew there was no way he would let her stop now.

"De Commynes—and I did *not* receive him in my bath—searched our possessions."

"So he found all the letters."

"Yes, except—oh!" Her incautious tongue had erred.

Richard was not pleased. It confirmed his view that women could not keep secrets. "It is so easy, is it not, to let something slip out? So you were carrying special letters. Did he find the King's letter to George of Clarence? I assume there was one."

Margery refused to answer. If Huddleston had just shrugged off his allegiance to Ned, he was hardly likely to share in her mission to make Clarence turn Judas.

"Are you capable of facing me?" Her new husband's voice had grown dangerous. "Did the Burgundian force himself on you? Did any of the others? You will forgive me for pressing the matter but I should like to be told if I am to foster a Burgundian cuckoo as my heir?"

Margery was tempted to torment him but it would have been like crossing thin ice. To do so would be to reinforce her reputation as an easy wanton.

She twisted around to find he was leaning on one elbow looking down at her, his face stern. She shook her head slowly, her eyes large and owlish, knowing it was important that he believe her. This talk of heirs was breeding a strange panic in her again.

Some demon in her blood affirmed that Richard Huddleston was undeniably attractive to her. The Devil prodded her curiosity further, awaking a serpent of lust within her belly. If Richard Huddleston sensed any signs of wantonness stirring in her, he gave nothing away but flopped back against his pillow, his hand stroking his hair back from his frowning brow. Margery turned away from him in relief, angry at the stirring of her body.

When he finally spoke again, it was not of cuckoos. "So the Duke of Burgundy is sniffing the air and wondering where the real danger lies. I rather think the future may be extremely perilous."

"Perilous?"

"If de Commynes suspects you to be more than you seem, then so too might others."

"I pray you do not say such things. You make me anxious."

"I like making you anxious, Margery. Your tidings, on the other hand, anger me. The King should not have involved you as his messenger. This is the second time he has used you."

"If you are referring—" Her shoulders stiffened.

"Lady, he did. I'll swear he did."

"No, it wasn't like that." She shook his hand away and wriggled to the edge of the bed but she could not escape his words.

"Come, be honest with yourself, the King was nursing a resentment against your father like a running sore. I heard him spit anger."

"*What* did you say?" she demanded, twisting around.

"Why, nothing! Who argues with kings and sleeps secure o'nights?" His gaze slid lazily downward forcing her to fiercely clamp the sheet against her.

"No, no, not that!" She could have shaken him in her desperation to wring out an answer. "It was the other thing you said. You said my *father*!"

CHAPTER
11

"You said the King was angry with my *father*!"

Richard Huddleston withdrew his gaze with a laconic shrug. "Yes." His fingers plucked idly at a glinting thread.

"Are you saying, Master Huddleston, that my father is the Earl of Warwick?"

His gaze snapped back on hers. In the moonlight coming through the window, she saw his eyes narrow beneath a frown. "Of course." Then his keen eyes pierced her. "By Christ's blessed mercy, woman, you do not mean to say that—"

Words failed him. It was unusual.

"*The Kingmaker is my father*," she mouthed, staring unseeing at the door. "Why should you think that?" She jerked her head around at him angrily. He was watching her darkly, his chin cupped in his hand, his elbow close to her on the bed. "Come, sir, it is false. This is merely some gossip that you have heard."

"Yes, it is gossip but . . . but yet not voiced. It was ever an assumption . . . oh, Margery." She was sitting up now, her face caught in wonderment as if he had given her the moon for her footstool. He would have sketched her now if God had given him a talent for drawing. It would have been something to capture her mood for eternity. Her head was delightfully cocked on one side like a little lapdog's and her chin rested thoughtfully on her drawn-up knees. Inside her head he could imagine her beliefs flung about, her mind all tangled like a ransacked room.

No, drawing her was the last thing he felt like now. Her distraction, her excitement, was tempting him. Richard could not resist playing his fingers up the tiny stepping stones of her spine to gently tangle in her hair but she shifted forward with a shrug as if his fingertips were merely a bothersome fly. He wanted to push her back against the pillows and make himself master between her thighs. He could feel himself stiffening at the thought of sliding his fingers into her while he sucked the swollen buds of her breasts into his mouth.

His hand locked around her ankle like a manacle. She was his to enjoy, damn her. The Kingmaker's daughter.

"No! Sir, I hold you to your promise." Her fingers scrambled down the bed to fasten about his, preventing him from adventuring upward. "I— Give me time." She was lying.

"Ah, time, of course." He held on tightly. His male pride and his appetite for her struggled against his honor. "Play with time as much as you please but by law you owe me a wife's duty, lady. That shall be as inevitable as the sunrise and you know it."

Margery grew hot beneath his fiery touch. *Let him remove his hand, sweet Jesu,* she begged.

Someone heard. He withdrew his fingers. With a sob, she flung herself on her side, the sheet demurely to her shoulder, but to her discomfort, he leaned across her. His fingers delicately smoothed a silken coil of hair off her cheek. "I beg your pardon. You must forgive me for my momentary lapse. It will not happen again. Let us talk then of your father."

"No! No more!" Words were easy to him. He knew how to bend them to his will. He could make swords and horseshoes from the iron of language. But his breath upon her neck was a different matter. "I . . . I do not want to talk. I want to be rid of this day."

Damnation to her, if he might not enjoy her body, he

could play with her mind and take some comfort in abusing the man who had. "Come now, I will wager you long to hear more."

She shook her head violently and edged away but his voice was at her ear now like Satan's presence in the wilderness, while his hand was within a palm span of her thigh. "I'll give you reasons no one else dared touch you except the King."

The temptation to slide his hand over her almost overwhelmed him and he flung himself back heavily against the pillow. "You know full well, Margery, that without Warwick's protection a baseborn wench like you was game for any of us. But even when he was away I would swear that you were sacrosanct."

"Oh, this is nonsense," Margery said huffily into the pillow.

"So why did no one try to lure you? It was because Warwick sat up there watching over *all* his daughters. But who was the only man who was never afraid of him? King Edward! Your precious Ned was prowling around looking for a chance to snatch a sacrificial lamb and you were it, Margery."

"That is not true and God damn you for saying so!"

"The King was searching for a way through to Warwick's soft underbelly. He wanted to prick him to a fury. Isabella and Anne were unassailable, lawfully begotten, and too young then for the King to entice—the world would have condemned him—but you were ripe for picking. Your seduction, even if you were merely Warwick's natural daughter, was calculated to enrage."

"Oh, have done! Their quarrel was over Ned's marriage to the Woodville woman. He married her secretly while my lord was negotiating for the Queen of France's sister. It was shabbily done."

"True, but taking your maidenhead in so insolent a fashion beneath your father's roof was one of the many things that broke the love and trust between them and I will swear it hurt your father as much as the rest."

Tears stung at the back of her eyes but Margery was determined to hide the pain his words were causing her. She put away the thought of Ned using her and answered as calmly as she could. "This is just surmise on your part. You have given me no real proof that the Earl could possibly be my father."

"Are you listening to me? Why do you imagine Warwick was so angry at your behavior? You are not just any bastard, you are *his* bastard! Why else would he now be dowering you so generously? Merely to rid himself of you? No, I think not. Have you no mirror? Are you not aware of the likeness? Any fool can see it. Margery, why do you imagine that you were permitted to be a close companion to Isabella and Anne and rank so high in their affection? You are their half sister, you addlepate."

"If it is so, why should he not have told me?"

Richard winced at the agony in her voice. The knowledge that she had been deliberately kept in ignorance must be like salt on an open sore. All those years of wondering. So many people misleading her and withholding the truth.

"I shall beg an audience with . . . with him in the morning. This matter must be aired." She was quiet again and he knew her mind had begun to run with the consequences like a fox with a stolen fowl.

He listened for a while to the noises outside the bed-chamber. A drunken snatch was being bawled in the hall. Below in the courtyard a woman giggled. Somewhere else a slap of water hit the ground. His new wife was not asleep. She fidgeted and one arm crept out and pushed down the heavy coverlet.

"You still think upon it?"

"I can do nothing else. You chose to keep me awake— one way or another."

"A wedding gift."

She moved onto her back, wide awake. "I always wondered why my lady Countess . . ." She gestured, seeking the right words. "Why she always held something back, why I could never please her. Now it all begins to make so much sense."

The potion of knowledge was working. She tucked her hands behind her head, oblivious to his admiring study. "If he is my father then I mean to ask him who my mother was."

"No one ever told you that either?"

She shook her head. "No one ever told me anything. I heard people whisper about me but I tried not to care. I thought maybe they were jealous because Isabella and Anne favored me and, yes, as you say, the Earl has always protected me. Do you know who my mother was?"

"No." Richard Huddleston pulled the bed curtains to on his side. Then he bestowed on her his usual close-lipped smile, a mixture of indulgence, pity, and amusement, before he turned on his side, facing away from her.

"How naive I have been," she whispered to the kindly darkness.

"But how much humbler. Your nose would have been higher than your headdress." She bit her lip, unable to choose between laughter and tears. Then she pulled the curtains together beside her against the window draft and lay down again, as far away from her bridegroom as possible.

Richard Huddleston was mentally satisfied if nothing else. She might be exhilarated with the thought of being the Earl's daughter, but the suspicions he had sown about the King would quietly spring to shoot. And soon he would make sure the world knew he was son by marriage to mighty Warwick.

⁂

He was still asleep when she stirred, awakened by a sword of sunlight thrust through the gap where the curtains merely kissed. Cautiously, she studied the sleek, healthy skin of the man beside her, the shoulders well muscled from the combat yard, the fine hand flung open-palmed upon the pillow. Her instinct was to touch him, like a child wanting to run its fingertips over the pelt of a wild creature. Unaware, asleep, he looked as unpredictable as he did awake. If she had expected to glimpse an innocence or simplicity in his features, a boy within the man, she would have been disappointed. She had no such idealism. She was caged with a sleeping leopard.

Sliding out from beneath the coverlet with all the care of a thief, Margery eased the curtain closed behind her. Alys had set out a ewer of clean water behind the screen for her the night before. Haggard from poor sleep, Margery knelt and plunged her hands into it to wet her face. The water blinded her. Blinking, she groped for the napkin only to have it placed in her hand. She started up in panic like a doe surprised at a woodland pool, but his hand kept her down. Was this being married, this invasion of privacy?

"Speak to your father this morning if you've still a mind to. He will be leaving tomorrow to spend a few days in Honfleur overseeing his ships. I have to go today."

She gazed up anew at the man who had taken lordship of her. He stood astride, his legs fine and powerfully muscled beneath the black hose. His masculinity stirred her. She grew aware of how well endowed he was behind the laces, the narrowness of his waist, and the broad expanse of his chest beneath the gipon. As if he read her thoughts, his lips twitched imperceptibly but his green eyes held no warmth. Margery was aware of the peaks of her breasts tightening against the wrap she wore. As she rose to her feet, rebelling against his hand, denying him the pleasure of straddling the world above her, her body demanded submission to him, her senses out of control, questioning what strange realm it was that held so enigmatic and unenthusiastic a bridegroom.

"No one told me that." She struggled to sound matter-of-fact.

He laughed. "Not fit tidings for a bride's ears. However, I can see the news distresses you."

"Certainly. My tears will fill at least three milking pails. When can I expect you back to plague me further?"

He rubbed his teeth with a fresh napkin, then stooped down to sluice himself vigorously with water. She swiftly shrugged off his wrap and snatched her gown from the bed. Once she had it safely over her head, she retrieved her belt from where it had fallen beside the stool. Perversely, she enjoyed watching the droplets of water fall from the curls about his forehead as he fumbled for the napkin. She picked it up and thrust it against his hand. He wiped the moisture from his face with his fingers and mopped his underarms.

"I am not certain when I shall return. It depends on the news from King Louis. You know he plays host to Queen Margaret and her son?"

The normality of conversation made her feel safe again as she hastened to fasten the belt beneath her breasts. "Yes, and makes as much trouble as he can for Ned. All the world knows the French would like to see the House of Lancaster back on the throne and yet they say King Louis has a kindness for my lord War—my lord father."

"Hmm, travelers going in the same direction may often share a bed."

She frowned. "What do you mean?"

"It is an age for wonders. Why, look at us! Paired and bedded like two turtle doves in a cot." He picked up his fallen shirt.

There were voices beyond the door now. "Have you the lies ready to trip off your tongue? They will want to know every detail, the least of which will be how I compare with the King of England."

Secured from his eyes within the covering of her clothes, she found it was possible to laugh.

"And?" he prompted.

She cast back a querying, teasing glance. "What would you like me to say? Shall I tell the gossips that you crow like Chanticleer and are comparable with a broom handle?"

He gave a roar of laughter, his eyes narrowing to such mischievous slits of devilment that she stepped back hurriedly, knocking the screen down and falling back on top of it. The basin heaved its water onto the purfiled hem of her skirt.

"Oh, the Devil take you!" she exclaimed. "How I wish I had never in my life set eyes on you!"

His hands fastened about her forearms and tugged her to her feet but he did not let her go. "I wish it so too." His laughter had vanished, replaced by such a vehemence in his tone that she caught her breath. Then he bent his head and brushed her mouth lightly with his own. Margery quivered within his hands as much in fury as with some emotion she could put no name to. She tightened her lips and pushed her palms against his chest.

Huddleston raised his head angrily, his eyes examining her face. "No? Oblige me in this or by Heaven you shall lie in your bridal bed this morning for my pleasure."

"No, please, you know my mind," she protested and then, biting her lip, she lifted her face to his. Though disconcerted by the closeness of him, she tried reasoning. "I . . . I never thought to find compassion last night but I am in your debt for that. Let me go."

"Willingly, except that I have my pride. You must obey me in this for both our reputations."

Anger at the denial of her own will in the making of the marriage, and indignation at being sold to him rescued her from the betrayal of her own body. She summoned the memories of his insults, his high-handedness, his unspeakable arrogance.

"No, I beg of you, I—" But as her lips parted to finish the sentence he kissed her, forcing her mouth open beneath his. She struggled but he held her in a grip of iron, forcing her to submit. A heat tore through her fast as a summer grass fire, searing her common sense, a blaze such as she had never experienced with Ned. She fought him, knowing he must not guess the effect he could evoke in her, but Richard Huddleston was ruthless, as if the quarrel between them was fought with lips. His new growth of morning beard rasped her cheeks. Her mouth felt swollen, used, when he finally released her to stand before him breathless and shaking with wrath.

"That's better. You look at least as though you have evidence to support whatever lies your fancy may dictate."

She deliberately drew the back of her hand furiously across her bruised lips, her breath ragged. "I think I hate you more than ever before for that, Richard Huddleston."

He shrugged and softly unbarred the door. "Behold me terrified."

"I do hate you. You are the most unbearable man I have ever met."

"Unbearable? We shall put that exercise to the testing at some future day."

Crimson with fury at his insolence, her fingers curled into claws.

He grinned and put a finger to his lips. "Calm yourself, shrewcat, if you launch yourself on me like a flailing fury, it will be in the gaze of half the household. Shall we go to meet them or wait for the invasion? Ah, too late." He reached out and pushed her before him as the iron ring of the latch slowly moved. Several teasing faces peered around the door like detached gargoyles before a half dozen of the guests from the night before burst into the room. Margery gazed at their curious faces and slackened in Huddleston's grasp, glad of the support of his body behind her.

"Come, sweeting." Huddleston hauled her after him down into the hall where a cheer went up from those still breaking their fast. He gave her a vigorous slap on the rump that drove her forward into the midst of the women. Dazed at her own feelings and rapidly trying to find the words for answers, she wanted to turn on him with a venomous look but the audience was too much for her. If she appeared as the tired addled bride, it was partly how she felt. She saw some of the tiring women disappear up the stairs to strip the sheets and gossip. Huddleston caught her glance with that maddening expressionless way he had.

"Margery." A gentle arm came around her shoulders. "Margery, lambkin, come away." Ankarette urged her from the hall, out into the sunlight of the courtyard and across into the tiny mede garden. "Sit you down. Say nothing if you please. I am here if you need me."

The kindness tilted the balance of Margery's courage. The tears came. Ankarette rocked her, soothing her with a motherly stroking on her back. "Was it such an ordeal?"

"Yes . . . no. I mean the wedding was but he did no—"

The older woman pulled back, incredulous, holding her firmly at arm's length. "For pity's sake, are you telling me the truth? Richard Huddleston? Now, you look at me square and fairly. You appear like any other bride to me." Margery turned her face away, Huddleston's kiss still fresh on her mouth. "Didn't he do anything?"

"I . . . I." Margery sniffed and dabbed at her eyes with the corner of her sleeve. Her words had already spilt out sufficiently to send her friend's agile imagination whirling like a weathervane. You could not confide in Ankarette without it rippling out to every local village. "He was very considerate, I . . . I suppose," she heard herself saying, "but he . . . I'm not usually difficult, am I?"

"You have had your moments, Margery, but no . . ."

"I am normally a cheerful even-tempered person, am I

not?" Her friend nodded. "Then why does Richard Huddleston make me want to strangle him the whole time?"

"You spent the whole night endeavoring not to squeeze his windpipe? Didn't you—"

"No!" snapped Margery, reddening. "I certainly . . . that is, do stop staring at me as though I am part of the Tower menagerie." She straightened her back. "I have something very important to ask you, Ankarette, and I want the truth. Do you know who my father is?"

Ankarette Twynhoe's eyes narrowed. "For pity's sake, how on earth can I answer that? What a question to ask a soul after your bridal night! Am I supposed to have been present at your parents' mating?"

"You are being evasive, Ankarette. Who do the servants say my father was . . . is?"

"Well, the Earl has let you off beatings many a time when my lady was in a temper with you. You have a way sometimes . . . Why, Margery? Have you found out your father's name?"

"My . . . Huddleston told me last night it was common gossip that I am my lord's bastard. He believes it."

"Well, for pity's sake! Do you mean to tell me you spent your wedding night discussing your birthright? How tedious. Ah well, each to his own."

A shadow fell across them. The two women slid off the turf seat into curtsies at the feet of Isabella.

"My lady mother is asking for you, Ankarette. Something or other she cannot find. Off you go!" Ankarette obeyed, her sulky mouth looking rather like a waterspout. The Duchess dismissed the esquire and page in attendance with a little flick of the wrist.

"You look suitably used, Margery. Not much sleep?" The Duchess, cloaked in soft velvet against the cold of the morning, made herself comfortable on the seat, patting it. Margery sat down again apprehensively. Was the day to be a series of interrogations on Richard Huddleston's sexual prowess?

"If anyone else is indelicate enough to ask me how Huddleston compares to a certain king, I think I shall do something I regret."

"You shall not include me in that threat," declared Isabella, wriggling. "Oh this seat is damp. We shall have to walk instead. I thought that at least you would confide in me. Why do you imagine I sent the others away?" She pulled Margery's arm through hers.

"But you never told me about *your* wedding night, madam."

"That was only because you were away at the convent, stupid. I shall tell you now though that it was a grave disappointment. His grace did manage something unremarkable which was a miracle considering how drunk he was, then he fell asleep instantly and snored loudly all night. It was boring. It still is and I am not missing that side of it one bit." She paused and detached herself from Margery to tuck a wisp of corn-colored hair back inside her cap. "Did I miss much with Ned?"

"Your pardon?" Margery was thrown off guard, wondering if she had heard aright.

"Well." Isabella made concaves of her cheeks as she took her lady-in-waiting's arm again and they recommenced their stroll. "I am convinced that Father would have liked Ned to marry me. All the while he was negotiating for Princess Bona of Savoy, I think he was desperately hoping that Ned would suggest it, but of course Ned usually goes for extremely mature . . ." She eyed Margery consideringly with a faint frown. "Strange that he should find . . ." Her fingers played with the petals of a creamy iris, her attention focused away from Margery's questioning expression. "Now where was I? Yes, well you know how angry my lord Father was that Ned married that grasping Elizabeth Woodville instead. Just think, if Ned had married me, there would have been no need for Father to rebel. So now, back to my original question. You shall not escape it. How did Huddleston compare?"

"Your grace, if you expect any torrid details, you may save your breath to cool your porridge. Besides, I need your advice."

"How unusual, Margery. You cannot be quite yourself. Ask away."

Margery slid her arm out of Isabella's hold. "If you

could be honest with me, I should be grateful. No one else is prepared to be. Richard Huddleston thinks I am your . . . your half sister."

She had been expecting an affronted look but the Duchess merely shrugged instead. "That's no surprise, is it?"

"Bella!" The old childhood name tumbled out. "Am I?"

"I believe so." Margery clapped a hand to her brow. "Now do not tell me you did not know. Do you imagine I should have bestowed confidences and friendship on you otherwise? Besides, being sweet to you annoys Mother. And I want you to know I am sorry I was not old enough to protect you from her anger after that business with Ned, but I confess I was rather jealous at the time. Anne and I did feel that our parents behaved unreasonably."

"But I did not know, Bella. Why was I never told?"

"Because," the Duchess said, "this is an age that delights in keeping secrets from children. It was never spoken of as far as I know. Mother made it clear that it was never to be discussed." She arched her eyebrows. "Well, I *suppose* it is true. Father has never actually admitted it but it is clear from Mother's remarks that *she* certainly thinks you are his daughter." She giggled. "Finding out that in your bride-groom's arms! You must be pleased."

"Overwhelmed."

"I should imagine Huddleston is proud of himself too. 'Tis not every man who manages to become—let me see—brother-in-law to two dukes, son-in-law of a powerful earl, and cousin by marriage to a king and half the nobility of England in one night. I was forgetting he also becomes hus-band of the King's ex-mistress too." She regarded Margery shrewdly. "Calculating man, your new husband. It is no sur-prise to me that he did his sums correctly. I confess I do not find him easy. I like to know what people are thinking behind their eyes. He thwarts me every time."

"Bella, are you implying that Huddleston married me merely because the Earl of Warwick may be my father?"

"Oh, come now, you cannot be thinking he married you for love or even lust? Marriage is for profit. You are quite pretty but be honest with yourself, Margery, unless Father had given you a dowry, no man would have offered for you.

No, do not look so nettled. By making this match, you have done uncommonly well for a woman in your circumstances. After all, Huddleston is even prepared to forget your lapse with Ned and that business with Littlebourne and Wyke two days back. I have taken his grace to task about that, by the way, and he has told Tom Burdett to scold them. Now stop being in the dumps, you may be sure that Father will put lands and titles Huddleston's way if this enterprise succeeds. And I shall ask his grace to do what he can when he becomes king. We shall certainly give you a place of honor at the coronation. I should not wonder if one day you die a baroness."

"Thank you," exclaimed Margery dryly. She let out a deep sigh. Isabella's logic explained why Huddleston had not cared to consummate the marriage. He was after her prospects, not her person. "But, Bella, what I do not understand is this. If Richard Huddleston had the wit to see that Warwick must be my father then so had others. Why has no other man ever asked for me in marriage?"

"I am sure there are several reasons. I suspect you were to be my father's gift to God. You said he told you something to that effect the other day. All noble families try to ensure one of their younger sons becomes a bishop. You know, like my uncle—*our* uncle—the Archbishop of York. Poor Father with no sons obviously could not give Anne or me to a convent so it had to be you. Personally, I have always considered that Anne would make an ideal nun. George and I have both said it to each other on many an occasion. Of course, Father did not foresee your waywardness. Your sinning with Ned was rather a blow to him but it did give him the opportunity to pack you off to a nunnery. I am sure he was hoping that if you were given enough time, you would take the veil."

"What were the other reasons?"

"Your safety. Father kept you out of the eyes of the world, away from Ned and safe from Elizabeth Woodville. She would not have wanted the King to have a Neville mistress. Huddleston must have guessed your parentage some time ago. Now I recall, he wrote to my lord about you. That's why Father sent for you from Nuneaton. By then he had given up all hope of you taking your vows. The Abbess had written to him that you were never likely to be godly. That was when he began to consider marrying you off."

"He sent for me for *Huddleston*? In Heaven's name, why did you not tell me, Bella?"

"Anne and I felt it would be cruel to raise your hopes and we were expecting Huddleston to come and visit to see if you pleased him. I am sure you would have been married to him months ago if Father had not been busy trying to make Ned behave better."

Margery put her fingers to her temples. "Anne knew as well. This is becoming too much."

Isabella patted her arm sympathetically. "I am sorry but you did ask. And you have successfully sent me down a side lane. I insist you tell me about last night."

"There is nothing to tell. The zenith was discussing my parentage."

"But you look . . . well, mauled sufficiently, to put it bluntly. I cannot imagine him behaving inadequately, a trifle cool perhaps but—"

"Yes, he was cool and very controlled. You are right in your assessment of him, Bella."

"And he's over in the courtyard now, see!" The Duchess picked up her brocade skirts and hurried across. Huddleston was arrayed in his riding garments, booted and spurred. About him were a score of men-at-arms. One of the men coughed in an obvious manner and there was a rumble of laughter as he turned from checking his saddlebags to see what was amusing the others. The glimpse of his white teeth as he grinned was predatory. Margery retaliated with a bored aloof expression and waited politely behind her mistress.

"I have been teasing your wife no end," the Duchess was saying. "How very sad that you have to leave so soon."

"They say that absence fans ardor, your grace," observed Richard dryly. Margery gave him a withering look. He had a capacity for saying what seemed to be the right thing—until one shook the memory out later.

"Then I shall leave you two together to make your reluctant farewells." The Duchess lifted her skirts and swept elegantly back toward the hall, giving Margery a feline grin as she passed.

Exposed to his inspection, Margery gave Richard a dismissive smile and started to hurry after Isabella. His hand was on her arm instantly and he whirled her around, possessing himself of her hand and carrying it to his lips.

"I do like an audience, don't you?" He raised an eyebrow at the waiting men-at-arms and the other knights and esquires in their vicinity, keeping hold of her reluctant hand. "My new sister-in-law is in fine fettle today," he observed. "Lady Anne tells me her grace was in poor spirits until you arrived from Calais. What ails you?" Margery had snatched her hand away at his words as if he had jabbed a needle in her finger.

"Nothing of matter." That was if she disregarded his capacity for ingratiating himself not just with Bella but evidently with Anne as well. Ambition was crawling all over him. "Good day, Matthew." She ignored the master and called sweetly to his servant. "I trust you are in good health."

"Never better, Mistress Huddleston. May I offer my humble belated congratulations on your marriage to my master."

"He likes big words." Richard moved his hand to her elbow and propelled her toward his horse.

"No, Matthew, you may not." Her gracious tone hid nothing from the discerning.

The great stallion nuzzled her shoulder. "He expects an apple from you. We all do." Richard grasped the reins and mounted easily, sliding his boots into the stirrups. Was he intending to make her feel like a mouse beneath a falcon's gaze? "The Duchess has been tormenting you a little, I think. Never mind, Margery, who knows, you may be putting flowers on my grave a few months from now. Is that what you are wishing?"

"I am praying hard to my namesaint that a bucket of horse dung may descend over your head this very moment."

"How very delightful." Huddleston nonchalantly signaled to one of his mounted men to sound the horn. At its harsh summons, two more horsemen ran tardily across the

yard. "A Dieu, lady." He whistled and his deerhound materialized from behind the stables, its grin as vulpine as its
master's. It bounded up, eyeing Margery with enthusiasm.

"*Veni!*" snarled Huddleston. Error looked at his new
mistress regretfully before he fell in behind the black stallion's hooves. His master gave Margery a taunting look
before he touched his spurs lightly to the black flanks. In an
instant they were all through the gateway, leaving a tiny
flurry of dust to settle about her skirts.

"The trouble is"—Ankarette was suddenly at her side—
"that if one is not in love with one's husband, the only
chance for satisfaction is to take a lover. I should not try that
in *his* absence. Perhaps if we ever return to England . . ."

"I am soon going back to England with or without a
Neville army. As for Richard Huddleston, may he—"

Ankarette laid her fingers on Margery's lips. "May he
miss you. I think he will. After all, did he not go to the labor
of abducting you? I cannot wait to see how you manage him
on his return."

"He is unmanageable. It is like living with the Devil."

"I have always felt a little sorry for Lucifer." Ankarette
glanced around as if a priest might be eavesdropping. "In
fact, I think he would be very amusing company. Maybe he
will give me an easier time in Hell for saying so. Stop
looking daggers at me. I think after sharing Huddleston's
bed a second night, you may sing to a different tune."

Margery's face was adamant. "There will be no *second*
night!"

CHAPTER
12

The women curtsied as the Earl of Warwick drew off his riding gauntlets and thrust them behind him onto the settle before taking the silver cup that his wife was holding out to him. There was a self-satisfied glint in his eyes as he quaffed down the contents and snapped his fingers at a page for more. He had returned from pirating without the Duke or, to Margery's relief, Richard Huddleston.

Margery gazed at the man who might have sired her wondering when and if she would be able to find out the truth from him. One could not exactly force the maker of kings into a corner and extract the intimate facts from him like a barber yanking out an aching tooth with forceps. She had been forced to wait a week already.

"Give your tiring ladies leave, mesdames."

Margery cursed silently as they began to file out of the solar. Gathering up her embroidery, she sank again into a deferential curtsy before the Earl. At least he noticed her for he lowered his cup to study her with a faint smile. Then with a backward flick of his hand he gestured to her to return to her stool by the window.

Margery did not feel like sitting down. It was hard not to crush her needlework between her fingers. How could she remain as outwardly calm and still as a set custard when inside she was boiling over. Was she his daughter? She fiddled with her hands when she was talking just like my lord did when he sat at board, but had she that stubborn jawline?

With no mirror of her own, Margery had never spent hours squeezing and examining her face as Isabella had. Her fingers unwittingly ran over her lips and down to trace her chin.

"Mistress Huddleston! Are you gone deaf?" The Countess sent her a look of chastisement at her tardiness in leaving, but the Earl stilled the next tart comment on his wife's tongue with a curt shake of his head.

"Nay, she may stay. Margery, have you been bitten by some French insect?" His question snapped her out of her reverie.

"More like she is remembering Master Huddleston's kisses." Isabella's finger jabbed her fiercely in the ribs.

"Huddleston, hmm. I hope you are feeling more charitable to him and me, young mistress." Warwick unbuttoned his cote and handed it to his page before he dismissed him. Margery was the only servant left. "You speak brightly, Bella, but you have shadows like saddlebags beneath your eyes. Are the dreams still tormenting you?" Dreams of a tossing ship and a dead baby denied God's Kingdom.

The Duchess hung her head. By day she was cheerful now, but nightly she would wake screaming.

"I have told Margery and Ankarette to brew a nightly posset," the Countess was saying, "but Bella will have none of it."

"Pah, no, for it tastes foul and I wake so heavy-headed."

The Earl frowned. "You should do as your lady mother bids. We all of us have had horror in our lives, Bella. I could tell you of sights in battle that would make you ill to hear it."

Isabella swiftly forestalled any reminiscences. "I fear I keep Ankarette and Margery awake with my nightmares." It was true. They took turns in sharing the Duchess's bedchamber and broken sleep was beginning to take its toll.

Warwick's brow furrowed as he examined Margery.

"Aye, so I perceive. Have some consideration for your women, Bella, and overcome your fears."

"What is the news, Father?" Anne obviously had had enough of Isabella's woes. She pushed away her sister's new puppy, tired of it nipping at her pointed slippers.

"Ha! Well, I have had word that there are troops drawn up on either side of the border. Out of pique the Burgundians have arrested all the French merchants visiting the Antwerp Fair and have made more attacks on French ships." He pushed with a self-satisfied grin. "But it appears Charles of Burgundy is reluctant to jeopardize the treaty any further so King Louis has decided to risk inviting us openly to his court at Amboise. We leave within the week." He waited as if for applause. There was a stunned silence.

The Countess pulled a wry face. "My lord, it is out of the question. We have not the apparel for court appearances."

"Nan, Nan, do not look so anxious. It is a dowdy court. Queen Charlotte is a little pudding of a woman, homely and kind. You will like her, I promise. Beside, I have a surprise for you. I did not tell you that there was a cargo of silks on one of the Burgudian ships. By noon tomorrow it shall all be at your disposal."

A gasp of excitement came from Anne but Isabella surprisingly showed no such pleasure. "And are his grace and I welcome at Amboise too?" Her tone was sharp.

The Earl bestowed his most winning smile upon her. "But of course, my dearest. He and I need to persuade King Louis into providing us with aid and, let us be resolved on this, Isabella, I have no intention of leaving Amboise without Louis's guarantee so you must smile and be gracious and your husband will have to convince the French court that he will make a more compliant king than Ned."

"George can charm anyone when he sets his mind to it."

Warwick caught the Countess's glance. "Is that so? To be frank, I do not think the Duke impressed our recent guests. Mayhap you will need to exert a more favorable influence on him—more of your time perhaps—but we shall speak of this privily, you and I."

Isabella's mouth squashed into a rosette of sulkiness and she looked to her mother for support before she retaliated. "Considering how you monopolized their time, my lord, he had little chance of proving himself." She shrugged as her father's mouth curled down.

"Isabella!" The Countess swiftly joined her husband in a show of unity before he could make an answer. "You may be a duchess but you are young in these matters. Take what your father says to heart. George cannot afford to make any errors from now on."

Anne raised her head from fending off Tristan snapping at the tassels on the tails of her girdle and shot Margery a meaningful glance. George of Clarence might be promising to be obedient to Warwick but he could be more willful than Ned. After all, he had been the brat of the family.

"Will *she* be there?" Anne was voicing what her mother and sister had left unasked. What of the woman Warwick and Ned had deposed, the defeated queen of the House of Lancaster?

"The Bitch of Anjou? No, little one, she is back at the court of her brother, the Duke of Calabria. I doubt she will come within leagues of me but it is an interesting dilemma for the King of France having Margaret d'Anjou and myself both supplicants for arms."

The Countess's hands fluttered. "I am not happy, my lord. I know you are good friends with King Louis but after all is said and done that woman has had his ear these last years and she is his cousin."

Anne scooped up the wriggling tangle of teeth and claws and thrust the puppy into Isabella's arms. "He has done precious little so far."

Warwick had not spoken. He was looking at his youngest daughter with the same expression with which he had studied Margery on the deck of his ship. An ice-cold shudder of foreboding streaked down Margery's spine. In the search for an ally, Warwick had an unmarried daughter to barter, an heiress to his great wealth.

"Margery? *Margery!* At least have the manners to listen to what is being said." The angry voice pierced her thoughts like an arrow.

"I beg your pardon, madam."

"Oh, do not waste your breath on *me*." Sourly, the Countess swept across to the casement and plucked irritably at the tapestry canvas that Ankarette had been laboring over.

The Earl's face as he glanced at his lady's sulky shoulders reminded Margery of an unrepentant dog that knows it is in trouble for running amok among the sheep, but has no regrets. "I was saying, Margery, that I have been conversing with Master Huddleston. I intend to recognize you as my daughter."

Margery sprang to her feet, pure happiness flooding through her. It would have been natural to have flung her arms in the air and whooped with sheer joy, but the angry woman at the window would have snipped her down to size. Instead she beamed at the Kingmaker, proud to the tips of her toes. She might still be a bastard. Nothing could change that, but at least she was the bastard of the most famous Englishman in Christendom.

The Earl stepped forward and clasped her shoulders. His unshaved chin rasped her as he kissed her cheek. "The good tidings shall be proclaimed at supper this even." His blue eyes smiled down at her reassuringly and holding her hand tightly in his, he turned her to confront the Countess's offended frown. "We are none of us children anymore." He looked around gravely at each of his family, particularly singling out Anne. For an instant the smile vanished from the girl's eyes as if she sensed something serious was happening to further change their lives. "Had I been more open about the past I might have saved this first child of mine her fall from grace." His beringed fingers rose to stroke his love-child's cheek.

Beneath the sweetness of the news, Margery had an inexplicable aftertaste of waste—the image of a distorted upturned hourglass, its sand running fast, dismayed her. Would it be possible for this busy man to give her time to learn to love him as a daughter should? Guilt seeped through her that his caresses came too late for her to forgive him like a good Christian should. To have left her in ignorance all her life had been an unnecessary cruelty.

"So, have you lost your silver tongue, Margaret *Neville*?"

She fell to her knees. "My lord, I thank you with all my heart for your kindness." She carried his hand to her lips. "As God is my witness, I never knew this until Master Huddleston told me what he suspected." She caught the

Countess's bitter gaze and held it. "I had no reason to be proud, but I am now."

"Do not think to puff yourself up with airs and graces, girl. Remember you are only a Neville bastard . . ." The Countess drew breath to add something predictably needle-sharp, but the looks of the other members of her family quelled her.

"It is just like the King Arthur legend when Sir Gareth discovers he is a king's son." Anne came across to bend down and put her arms around her half sister. "I am so very happy, Margery. You have always been like an older sister in my mind."

"Isabella, you accept this?" Warwick's tone was of command rather than petition.

The Duchess set down her dog and swept forward. She stood looking down at Margery, her expression haughtier that her mother's. "What, this upstart serving wench of mine? This wanton lawbreaker, this disrespectful apology for a woman? Of course, I accept her! Have I not always treated Margery as a sister too? Get up, you wretch, so I may hug you!"

The Earl swung around on his wife. "Nan, you must forgive the past. It is high tide with us."

The Countess gave a sigh of annoyance but she came across to Margery, her skirts hissing across the rushes.

It was diplomatic to curtsy again, to look reasonably humble.

"Rise, child." The grown child rose, eyes still politely lowered as the Countess of Warwick bestowed a cold kiss upon her forehead.

"Excellent." Warwick, satisfied, turned away and began to tell his legal daughters what to expect at the court of France.

His wife confronted his bastard. "Look at me, Margaret Neville!"

Margery looked her fully in the face, remembering the older woman's grudging tolerance over the years. Fire to water. At last, she could speak her thoughts. "Madam, I thank you for giving me shelter all these years but I beseech you ever to remember that it was not my fault that I was unlawfully conceived. I am the fruit, not the flower, and therefore do not blame me."

The Countess was unmoved. "Gall, more like. I pray that you will never have to do what I am doing, Mistress Huddleston, acknowledging the living proof of a husband's infidelity. Understand how hard this is for me now that you have a husband of your own, and expect nothing more." With that, Warwick's lawful wife turned away. It should not have hurt Margery but it did, like a lash.

"You may *all* have new gowns," her new father was saying and he swung around on her. "Margery, for the love of Heaven, do not choose scarlet this time. Neville women have never looked well in red."

She tried to find her voice. Tears pricked behind her eyes. Scarlet, the color of ribaldry, dangerous, carnal. The scarlet of lords-and-ladies berries, of holly, of blood. Now deliberately turned on her, the plump white skin of the Countess's back, bulging above the low neck of the summer gown, was in itself a goading. It was tempting to say brightly that Lady Warwick had always told her that red was her color and she should wear no other.

"I say that purple is what we Nevilles hanker after." Isabella tucked her hand through her father's arm. "Do we not, Father? But when is Master Huddleston allowed back to his bride? You could have at least allowed them a full day to themselves."

"Hush, Bella, you little cat. Well, Margery, he will be back soon enough. Growing impatient, my little witch?"

Isabella waggled a finger in Margery's face. "You are blushing again. I never knew you could until Richard Huddleston arrived in Valognes."

"Please do not mock me, Bella." Margery sidestepped the Duchess so that she could face the Earl. "I am no fool, my lord. Master Huddleston married me merely to become your son-in-law."

Her new father shrugged. "Time will tell. I married the greatest heiress in the land for political ends but I have learned to love her well." He stole an arm around his Countess's thickening waist and turned her around to face him. The older woman's expression was complacent like a

cat that had just filled its belly with the choicest fare. The
Earl chucked his wife beneath the chin and turned his head
to Margery. "Make the best of your situation, my child.
Your man has hardly had a chance to prove himself to you."

Nor would he, if she had any say in the matter. If Richard
Huddleston had desired her, he hardly would have spent
their marriage night discussing his father-in-law. And this
news that they were to leave for Amboise was definitely
welcome. With luck she would not see Huddleston again for
weeks. Even if he did return in time to journey with them,
from the little she knew of royal palaces, servants slept in
any available corner and he would have a meager chance of
compelling her to share his bed.

And, for the nonce, if Richard Huddleston did come back
expecting a wife instead of a warming brick he would find
her, unobtainable, in the bedchamber where the other ladies
slept, or else in Isabella's bed. Oh, yes, she was quite safe.

She could not scream, she could not breathe. She was
dreaming, dreaming that a fearful monster had swooped
down, casting a hood over her head and drawing a cord tight
around her throat with its golden talons. Her body thrashed
wildly. The common sense half of her mind told her she was
remembering Huddleston's abduction of her. The other half
wisely woke her. It was actually happening.

A tall, hooded figure as faceless as Death was bending
over her. She could not cry out to the sleeping women
around her because Death had his gloved hand tight across
her mouth. He was pinching her nostrils shut.

"Stop threshing around or you will wake up the whole
gaggle," Death whispered. He sounded like George of
Clarence. Unable to breathe, she ceased struggling and
nodded frantically, conscious of an inexplicable sense of
disappointment.

He let go of her. "Be swift, Meg. Just throw a cloak on
and come."

"Are you mad?"

He shook his head and laid a hand upon the blanket.
Margery swiftly snatched it to her, thinking he was never

going to understand her exaggerated gesticulation but at last she heard a soft hiss of laughter and he obeyed.

Her overgown had fallen in a tumble of clothes. She pulled it over her bare skin and flung her cloak about her head and shoulders, drawing it across her gown.

The Duke was waiting to grab her by the forearm. "Quickly!"

She shrugged him off. "Your grace, you may have thought that amusing but you nearly scared me witless."

"Nonsense, Meg," he whispered. "Marriage must be making you boring. We are going up the tower."

She groaned. "Oh, no, my lord, can you not think of somewhere less imaginative."

"Where is your sense of occasion? I have not had a secret assignation since I came to France."

"You have an answer for me?"

"Hush, I shall tell you in good time."

Margery was truly irritable by now as she followed him into the night. The gusty wind was feeling up her skirt and if the inside flagstones had been chilly beneath her feet, the cobblestones were knobbly, gritty, and cold as he hurried her around the outside of the logis and then up a stairwell she had not known existed. It was hazardous to climb the spiraling stairs without a taper. She sighed and trudged cautiously after him, her skirt lifted to her knees.

"You are not fit enough, that is the trouble." He smirked as she finally joined him in the turret.

Margery glowered. "I am sure we could have done this in daylight."

"Not with what I want to say to you. Stop grumbling and come and take a look, it is quite tolerable."

The window was no mean split in the wall to guard against arrows but about two spans wide. It had lost its shutters so they had a clear view of the courtyard in front of the logis and the town lapping around the wall. Valognes slumbered without a snore. Only a distant dog's bored bark against the wind and the gurgle of the river reached them. Nor was there a glimmer anywhere save for the chapel and the gatehouse. The door to the latter opened. One of the soldiers stood silhouetted against the torchlit room behind him.

He said something to someone inside, then moved to relieve himself against one of the hedges that separated the yard from the logis garden. Two other men moved into the doorway before she turned away.

The Duke had shaken back his hood and was kneeling. A flint flamed within his hands. His face, lit from below, turned into a macabre mask as he set the stubby candle between them.

Margery shivered, more with instinctive misapprehension than because of the draft. Frowning, she knelt down and waited for the Duke to speak. It was hard to believe he was trying to make himself king. In the long black gown, he looked like a lanky student.

Persuade him, Ned had said. Persuade him? Oh, yes, in a chilly turret at Heaven knows what ghostly hour.

They were kneeling facing each other like two lovers at a betrothal.

"I take it you want to talk about Ned," she began primly.

"Him! Perish the thought! No, I want to talk about Bella and me."

"*Bella,* George? You wake me up looking like Death personified to talk about Bella."

"Ankarette says I should just be patient but I am not that kind of man." Boy, she corrected him unspoken. "Bella will not let me into her bed. You saw what she was like to me the first week you were here. She is afraid to conceive again. The old man tells me he had words with her yesterday but she will not listen to reason. Do you not see I have to have an heir. Losing the babe at Calais was the Devil's work." He shifted into a sitting position, clasping his knees.

"You should say prayers that she survived." Margery felt like a pious old dowager as she said it.

"I do, Meg, I do, but your father has some secret vow to see his blood wear the crown. I have to have a son. He will lose all interest in making me king if I do not. Well, do not stare at me as though I had two heads, say you will help me."

"Have you tried to talk about this with Bella?"

"She will not listen. You know how she flinched when I tried to put my arm around her last week in the hall."

"You had drunk a firkin dry and your breath was enough to set fire to thatch, your *grace*."

"Very well, I accept your rebuke." He smiled, a man's smile not without some charm, but he was a pale reflection of his brother. "What I have always liked about you, my dear cousin—or should I call you sister now?—is that you have no regard for rank. Look, Meg, you are experienced and I want you to help me improve my . . . well, you know what women like. If you could tell me what Ned did with you—" He broke off, staring at the sleep-tousled hair that still barely touched her shoulders and her attempts to keep her cloak modestly across her unbelted overgown.

Jesu, I must be really looking the wanton, thought Margery. I think I have just made a mistake that would compare with Pharaoh's crossing of the sea in pursuit of Moses.

He was undressing her with his eyes. She drew her cloak demurely about her, scowling at him. "Ned was an exception, your grace, and I spent years doing penance for what amounted to very little practical experience. All I can do is promise you that I will speak to Isabella." Her tone grew brisk. "Now, have you given further thought to your brothers' messages?"

"Ned and Dickon sent you to persuade me, so do so! Or do you only specialize in kingly lovers?"

"I specialize in husbands." Margery felt like giving his ducal milk-white cheek a hefty slap.

"*I specialize in husbands,*" he mimicked. "Well, I am a husband and you are a cut loaf. What are you scared of? Whelping my brat? Think of the irony of it. A boy half Plantagenet and half Neville and your father will be powerless to use him because you are born out of wedlock. By St. George, the old fellow's face would be worth a king's ransom." He grinned. "That's why I waited for tonight until old Huddleston was back in Valognes to talk to you. If any of those peahens had awoken, they would have thought it was him."

Huddleston was back! If this came to his ears . . . Margery was tempted to whack the Duke very hard. "My lord, firstly, if you were not a duke and, secondly, stronger than me, I should squeeze you out of that window headfirst and hope you landed head down in the thorniest rosebush."

"Jesu, you have spirit, Meg, I could not have imagined Bella or Anne saying that to me or having a tumble with Ned like you did." He regarded her with the expression of a hopeful wolfhound. "Let's do it now, can we? I have had to be celibate too plaguey long with her parents in tow. We could lie down on my cloak."

"Let us talk about what I want to talk about and *then* I will clout you."

Instead of letting her brisk cheerfulness run off him like droplets on oiled leather, his eyes narrowed to malevolent slits. "Clout me? I will get you dismissed if you do, dear Meg, even if you are the Kingmaker's love-brat and, what's more, I will certainly have you banished from my wife's service if you do not promise to unbar her door to me tomorrow night." His tone hardened further. "I can, you know. If I let drop to my mother-in-law that you have been making improper suggestions to me." It was outrageous but the Countess would be only too willing to make mischief out of the insinuation.

His eyes leered. "I could *make* you, you know, if I really wanted to." His fingers flickered out jeeringly at her and she jerked her head away from his touch, thankful it was a sober twenty-one-year-old she was dealing with, not a drunken one. He was not jesting and he scared her. The envy of Ned that she had seen incubating ever since he had come to Warwick's household as a page would make him ruthless in doing anything to anger his brother—taking her by force would be a petty revenge. How could she say no to the Duke of Clarence without rubbing more salt into his offended vanity?

"It is tempting and I am honored by your request for help from me, but I could not betray Bella's trust. Now," she added cheerfully, rising to her feet and folding her arms in a businesslike manner, "have you thought about your brother's offer? If you were to leave my father, he would be forced to come to terms with Ned and England would not be split by war. As it is, there will be a great number of the common folk summoned to bear arms and many will be killed when they should be home working on their farms and looking after their families."

"What was that? Did you say something?" There was an

iciness in his voice now. He rose to loom over her. "May-hap your luscious naked body straddling my loins might improve my hearing." His laugh was sibilant, a hiss of menace as he reached out a teasing hand to her hair.

She recoiled as if he had strung her. Her eyes were wide. Oh, she had been so deceived by his boyishness. If she could draw her dagger from the scabbard on her calf before he seized her . . . She shrank back against the cold stone and edged along the wall toward the stairs.

He watched her and then with a swift lunge he gripped her wrist and twisted her hand behind her back. She gave a yelp. "I am going to be King of England, my sweet bastard, and Louis of France is going to help me with arms and money. You will see." Then he laughed and let go of her. "By St. George, Meg, I think I have made you afraid of me."

"Yes." She growled, rubbing her wrist where he had bruised her.

"*Yes,*" he echoed. "Oh, breathe out, cousin, you see you must stop treating me like some rebellious codling."

"Well, you have definitely convinced me." She swallowed her fear but would not look at him.

"By St. George, I think I prefer your wit to your humility." He stepped back from her, his arms raised in mock surrender. "There, I shall not torment you further. You want to know what I think about your lover's magnanimous message, Mistress Carrier Pigeon?" His face was cruel in the tiny frantic flame. "If all the fires in Hell were lit under Ned, it would content neither your father nor I."

She crossed herself. "That is a damnable thing to say."

"I mean it, Meg. Ned can go—" His grin was a demon's, his gesture emphatic.

"I see. If that is your final word, your grace—"

"*I see,*" he mimicked. "Yes, so there's an end to it. Now about the other matter. Tomorrow night."

"Ye—" She froze. They both did. It had sounded like the accidental scrape of metal against the wall.

He put his finger to his lips. They waited. He knelt noise-lessly and pinched the candle out. They both heard the distinct sound of someone moving farther down the staircase.

Margery cursed under her breath.

The Duke edged around to the window and glanced out

of it from the side so that he could not be seen. They waited but only the whispering of the wind through the newly leafed trees reached them.

He let out his breath in a long sigh. "Do not worry. Let us wait for a few more minutes and then I will go down alone. Here's the flint. Keep the candle with you for the stairs, but snuff it out before you reach the courtyard. If it is safe for you to follow, I shall give you an owl hoot."

At another time she would have laughed. His owl hoots took her back to the days of hide-and-seek at Sheriff Hutton. Yet now, Jesu, what a different world! Here he was, attainted, his dukedom lost, meeting her virtually on a rooftop in some insignificant French town, and she a bride in name only. "Till tomorrow, and be sure to unbar Bella's door." He arranged his hood so that it hid his face and then curled his fingers in a mocking wave before disappearing into the black gloom of the staircase. The owl hoot finally came.

Some sixth sense of impending disaster sent a shiver of fear down her spine as she felt her way down. A horn lantern would have been a blessing. The candle flame dazzled her as she edged her way down each step and sent horrific shadows everywhere. A rat streaked across her bare foot. The surprise of it nearly pitched her down the twisted hollow stem of the tower. A faint sound made her shudder. She faltered and a draft blew the flame away, leaving her in utter darkness.

⁓

Richard stepped back into the shadow of the porter's lodge as a figure, far too tall to be a woman, came stealthfully out of the tower and slid in and out of the shadows like a wraith. It stopped, looked about, then, turning, incredibly made the cry of a night owl.

A tight smile twisted Richard's mouth. Curious, he watched the man disappear into the shadows. What mischief was George of Clarence up to? A further movement drew his attention. Someone else was lurking in the shadows watching. Richard edged through the dark on the opposite side of the courtyard toward the tower door and waited.

A third but slighter figure let itself out and stood for a second giving Richard sufficient time to glimpse a skirt. As the woman reached out to tug her hood further forward, his heart gave a painful lurch. He knew that gesture. Christ, his untouched, king-handled bride had been meeting with the Duke.

Fury fizzed through his veins like the fiery local apple brew. As quiet as a cat, he edged swiftly around the other side of the courtyard so that he was now behind Margery. She was moving slowly along the logis wall. As she reached the next doorway, his hand slid down over her mouth and he yanked her back against the stone ribs of the narrow porch.

"Do not dare scream," he said quietly in her ear. To his amazement, she slackened within his grasp instantly, but her heart was thumping as wildly as a captured rabbit's against his sleeve. He slowly removed his hand but did not let go of her. He felt her breath struggle to become even again.

"I thought you were in Honfleur," she whispered with matter-of-fact cheerfulness as if they had met at supper.

"Obviously. What were you and your high-ranking friend doing up there—sketching the constellation of Cassiopeia on vellum, or were you teaching him how to launch a broomstick?"

Witch, that's what she was. The wench deserved a broomstick across her naked rump. God knows he was a fool for yoking himself to her.

She was trying to wrench her arm free. "How clever of you. It's the way you point the handle."

"What!"

"The twigs too, there is an art." He responded with a growl that drew a swift torrent of words from her. "Sir, I can explain but I am not going to. You almost scared me to death jumping out on me then. What are *you* doing? Spying on me?"

He felt her cross her arms between them, hugging her shoulders. The little wretch was chilled.

Spoken aloud, his answering curse would have scorched her ears. Richard was amazed that he could answer calmly. "You think innocent outrage makes the best buckler? Someone is in the courtyard watching us."

She stiffened within his arms. "Oh, Jesu! So it was not you." Damn her! The presence of some unseen onlooker bothered her more than his did.

"Do as I say, Margery. Take my hand." He appreciated
the fact that she did not argue. A cold little hand fumbled
and half wrapped its fingers around the warmth of his. Her
trust blew away some of his anger. He wished there was
enough light so he could read her face.

Without warning, his grip tightened. He hauled her out
across the courtyard at a run. Margery gave a shriek of
protest as she nearly tripped over her hem, which set the
dogs off in the kennels. She was forced to race along with
him, snatching up her skirt with her free hand. He stopped
abruptly at the entrance to the garden and her momentum
carried her straight into his arms. He lifted her high above
the ground despite her protests and whirled her around as if
she were no heavier than a babe.

"Put me down!" she protested, not caring who heard.

"Are you befuddled yet?"

"No. Oh, no, not more, stop, stop." He spun laughter out
of her.

She hung on to him dizzily, trustingly, as he set her back
on her feet. Delightfully bewitching, his and not his. She
had been up in the tower with the future king of England.
The agony of anger twisted the knife in him but reason prevailed. He had to convince whoever was watching that he
had just come down the tower staircase, that he had been up
there with her.

The new moon was hidden but the little light escaping
through the clouds showed her hair wantonly tossed. If I
could trust her, he thought, this would be magic.

"It seems we are having an assignation. I wonder if that
has convinced whoever is watching." He hoped there was a
sackload of indifference in his tone. Had she wriggled close
against him, she would have known better.

"Can you see where he is?" she asked, tapping her fingers for attention against his breast.

He turned her slightly. It would be easy to lie but he was
sure whoever it was still skulked. "I think so." He could see
her parted lips clearly in the silver light, moist, waiting. "No
doubt this will displease you, Margery, but I am going to
kiss you. You had better not resist if we want to deceive
whoever it is watching."

She curled her lips inward for a second, deciding. "Very well, it sounds sensible."

Sensible! She was about to find out how wondrously sensible. He brushed his lips against her, gently this time. Amazingly her soft mouth opened under his and he had the entry he desired. She tasted as innocent as she had a week ago. A tempting sweetness that could make him drunk for her. No telltale smell of recent carnality, no dampness on her gown. His relief was a pleasure in itself.

For a moment she seemed to melt within his arms but when he moved his hands discreetly down over her cloak and splayed his fingers around her buttocks urging her toward him, she tensed, trying to draw back without making it obvious to whoever was observing. Straining back from him, she pushed against his chest with her forearms, unaware that doing so only pressed the lower half of her body tantalizingly against his groin. Regretfully he drew back from her, lifting a hand to smooth her hair back from her face.

He ached to be able to heave her into his arms, carry her across into the garden, and plunge himself into her soft white body. If he had his sleeping chamber to himself, that might have been a possibility.

"Is he still there?" Her voice was businesslike with a delicious hint of breathlessness. Her fingers brushed at her skirts as if she was embarrassed.

"Don't look around. Here." Swiftly he thrust his hands inside her cloak upon her waist to turn her. By Christ, she had nothing on beneath her gown!

Margery stiffened, aware from his oath that he was about to personify a Deadly Sin—either Lust or Anger. She trembled, but being Huddleston, he surprised her. For an instant longer, she felt his fingers tighten and then he removed his hands as if she had burned him.

His voice was stern and astonishingly controlled. "I ought to beat you, really I should. Your honor and mine, does it mean nothing?"

"Sir, I have not had any honor for so long that I scarce remember what it feels like. I have not been unfaithful to you if that is what is bothering you."

"Bothering me? Oh, hardly *bothering* me." He thrust the knife home farther. "If you have any wits at all, you'd hardly be unchaste with our marriage sheets scarce creased. Let us try the mettle of this spy." He gripped her upper arm and urged her toward the garden.

"No, I need to go back. If I am missed they will think—"

He halted, amazement in his tone. "You are a married woman."

"But . . ." She was afraid of him, of herself. She was cold and tired and confused.

"You are lawfully allowed to be with me. Whatever you were doing with Clarence is sanctioned by my being here now. With good fortune, whoever is spying on you will think that it was I who was up there playing broomsticks with you and, with luck, we shall have suffocated this rumor before it has time to draw breath."

He was right. His unexpected presence and swift action had saved her from both gossip and suspicion.

"It is very kind of you."

"Kind!" he exclaimed incredulously as he tugged her between the huge manicured hedges. "Anyway, why are you so fearful of me? There is a heavy dew and puddles on the ground."

"What of that?" she asked nervously.

"You fear I might tumble you on some gritty, dirty apology for a mede? Strangle you more like, and I prefer my pleasures in a bed. Come, let us entice our spy onward."

There was no sound save the swish of her gown and the crunch of his boots upon the gravelly path between the boring neatness of the ankle-high herbs. They passed the turf seat beneath the rose arch, squatting dew-spangled, pretending to be a meadow bank.

"If we stand in the shadows under that apple tree, we can see if anyone has followed."

She followed him obediently. "Are you cold?" He offered her the bargain of the shelter of his cloak along with his arm but she solemnly shook her head.

"What *were* you doing out here, sir?"

"It is a strange world, mistress. I am a married man and yet there was no wife warming my bed. Unpardonable of me perhaps but it left me with a certain restlessness."

"You were out seeking a woman?"

He did not answer. His cold silence was as unpleasant as the damp dirt beneath her feet. Margery felt guilty at having asked. "How long must we stay here?" she asked testily.

"As long as it pleases me." There was danger in that voice.

"Sir, I—" She stopped instantly. "Look!" A shadowy figure was blatantly staring out across the garden, seeking them. They both tensed.

"Sir! Master Huddleston, are you here?" The lilt of a western dialect reached them. Richard stepped out onto the path. "Ralph?"

A man in brigandine and sallet, a sword in his hand, came closer. "Oh, sir, it is you. We thought—"

"Too much time thinking. You should have been out of the guardhouse in an instant. I could have boiled an egg by now waiting for you."

Margery moved out of the shadow unexpectedly and slid her hand through Richard's arm.

"Aye, Master Huddleston." The soldier touched his hand to his forehead respectfully. "I beg pardon for disturbing you. I did not know it was you who had a woman with you."

"I am Margery Huddleston." It was the first time she had called herself so.

"God's truth!" You could almost hear the sudden slack in the man's jaw. "By Our Lady, mistress, I did not mean to imply that . . . Your pardon, sir, I—"

"Did you see anyone else?"

"I thought I heard other footsteps towards the chapel. We went that way first and . . ."

"And?"

"And we heard a woman laughing a few moments ago. That's all, sir." He touched his helmet in deference and hastily departed.

"Fortunately Ralph gossips like any woman. It will be all over the hall by the end of breakfast that Master and Mistress Huddleston were responsible for waking half the household. Such is the stuff of courtly romances, except that we are unfortunately married." Huddleston's amusement was genuine.

"Please, will you see me back, sir? My feet are frozen and I have had more excitement than I care for."

His warm fingers touched her hand. He must have felt
the gooseflesh. Before she could stop him, he had an arm
beneath her knees and had swung her up into his arms. The
sensation was pleasant and to have protested would have
been ungracious. He had, after all, saved her reputation. She
slid an arm up about his neck as if they had been doing that
sort of thing for years. As long as it gave the situation some
normality, it blew out the fire that was set to light the blaze
within her.

"You see, I did not spy on you." She felt his voice
vibrate in his chest next to her elbow.

"I believed you," she answered.

"Why?" His voice was cool. She did not dare look at him
but she felt the tickle of hair at the nape of his neck on the
back of her wrist.

"Because from the little I know of you I do not believe
you would do anything that dishonorable. But what's more
to the point, do you believe me?"

"I can tell that you have not lain with the Duke." She was
relieved at the absolution but he was not finished with her.
"You cannnot, Margery. While you hold me at arm's
length, you dare not. I should know any child you conceived
was not mine."

By the time he set her down at the entrance nearest the
women's staircase and opened the door for her, she was
grateful but resolute.

"Lady." One hand detained her, gripping her upper arm,
and he examined her face as she knew he would. He must
have felt her trembling. "My patience with you is as
shredded as a beggar's blanket. I shall see you back to the
women's quarters now, but tomorrow you had better have a
good excuse for the night's adventure. We shall talk of this
at length, believe me."

"As you wish, sir. Please, may we proceed?"

"My pleasure," he said coldly. "Shall Warwick's daughter
take my hand or would she prefer me to carry her up the
stairs?" Margery hesitated, then set her hand in his. There
was pleasurable reassurance in his touch but then her hand
quivered within his; she knew the upper passageway was lit.
Now he would truly see her shameful state, her hair tangled,

her gown loose. At the door to the women's chamber, she hesitated before going in, choosing her words carefully.

"Thank you for what you did," she whispered.

Richard's gaze was stern. He had missed nothing and his voice was frosted with disapproval. "It was entirely selfish, believe me. I have no wish to wear the horns. At least have a care for my reputation by preserving yours."

"It shall not happen again, believe me, sir," she answered stiffly, her eyes downcast with seeming meekness.

But before she could escape, Richard took her chin in his hand, tilting her face up to the flickering flames of the wall sconce. It was necessary to play the master, to make her realize his lordship over her was not make-believe.

The wench would have pulled defiantly away had he not held her like a willful mare. What had she accused him of? Treating her like a horse? Well true, she had been bought but he still had to win her trust so she would let him ride her, and Richard wanted her writhing with delight when he took her. By Christ's blessed mercy, he would make her body yearn for his hands upon her again.

"Margery." The insistence in his voice made her raise her eyes reluctantly like a mischief maker caught out. "You are married now whether you will or no. Your pardon for this, but our marriage has to have some saving grace."

Her enticing lips parted in surprise as the fingers of his free hand slid inside her cloak and curled about her left breast. He knew she would not dare scream. His other hand held her fast as she struggled furiously to pull herself free. His thumb stroked the exquisite peak through the thin sheath of silk.

It was an agony of frustration knowing he had to let her go within the instant. Searing desire would be his only bed-fellow for what was left of the darkness. She was angry as she writhed out of his grasp and escaped through the door. He had heard the fury in her breath but he had roused her, by all the Saints, he had. The tip of her breast had ripened lusciously to his caress. Tomorrow?

Tomorrow he would make sure of her.

"In the dumps?"

"Yes, Ankarette, there have been demons at my elbow all day."

"Not enough sleep or is it more trouble from that lout Littlebourne?"

Margery sighed. Let her think that. The Duke had deliberately chosen an ill-mannered messenger to remind her she must attend Isabella's unrobing that night. And her other large problem sat at ease at the men's board on the other side of the hall.

Several times, to her shame, Huddleston had interrupted her looking his way, his face inscrutable. She had forbidden Alys to transfer her possessions to the bedchamber he had suddenly, and no doubt expensively, procured. And, unhappily, her attempts to make her excuses to him earlier in the day in the common gaze so he could not throttle her were stillborn.

With a deep breath and her heart beating like a stick on a tabor, she finally rose from the bench and crossed the hall to discover her husband was busy explaining some sort of battle strategy to his neighbors. Three ragged pieces of left-over trencher were advancing around two pewter beakers to attack a convoy of cherries.

The knight next to him noticed her and elbowed him in the ribs, exclaiming here was a pretty new scabbard for his weapon. Huddleston frowned and turned his head, his gaze falling from Margery's headdress, with its lappets and gauze veil, to her feet peeping out beneath the heavy border. Because the weather had turned fickle, she was wearing the blue velvet he had bought her with the King's gold. His eyes ran over the fur trim she had added to the collar and cuffs. Did he miss nothing?

Margery cursed inwardly at his examination of her, but it was the warm calculation intensifying in his gaze, the memory of his prying hand upon her breast that drove the betraying blood into her cheeks and sent twists of sensuality coiling through her loins.

How she managed to find her voice when he raised a questioning eyebrow was a miracle. "Sir, I would speak with you urgently."

Someone at his table chortled, "Go, sirrah, you are a married man and must obey."

With a lazy grin, he clapped his neighbor on the shoulder, extricated himself from the bench, and made his way down the outside of the screen that had been set up behind the diners. Margery hurried down the inside of the hall. They met at the end.

"Is the logis on fire?" His smile would have melted candles. To her, it was yet more provocation.

"Last night . . ."

"You feel an explanation is due?" He offered his arm but she refused. He gave an almost imperceptible shrug. "I shall provide one in due course."

"No, I—"

"Ah, you wish to offer me one?" He appeared charmed at the thought. "Then I suggest you let it simmer. Here is neither time nor place."

"I should like to dance with you anon, if it please you, sir," she said in a small voice.

"Really?" His disbelief was evident. "Is there any other service I may also do for you?"

"I knew you'd be difficult," exclaimed Margery. She turned away angrily but in an instant his hand was beneath her elbow.

"Her grace is beckoning you. We shall meet later. Be sure of that."

Isabella was scowling as Margery sank onto a tasseled stool at her feet. "I wish we had not come in to supper. I knew it was a mistake. Ankarette says she is getting a megrim too but she can still attend me later. I am sure you will want some time with Richard. Fan me a little, Margery!"

"If Ankarette is poorly, then I will take her place tonight."

"Tired, are you?" The young Duchess gave her a sharp prod beneath her belt. "You are a dark horse, sister, and a liar too. Stealing out at night to meet your husband of all people! All that foolish talk of disliking him so. And I watched you eyeing each other all through supper. Keep fanning! My poor head! I hope I shall be well enough to make the journey south tomorrow."

George of Clarence asked his duchess to dance but she refused, pouting. Margery received his meaningful glance and sighed.

The time between hour bells limped. From where she sat at Bella's feet, Margery could see Huddleston enjoying himself hugely. He was with a witty group. Gales of laughter reached her now and then making her doubly wretched. As the candles were lit, her spirits sank. He was ignoring her but she knew he was waiting. The covered hole in the ground was there. All she had to do was walk across the forest floor.

Richard Huddleston offered his arm to Anne Neville and led her out in a stately measure that demanded a huge amount of bowing and smiling. Margery tried not to watch but her gaze was drawn to him like a moth to the light. You could do a hundred times worse, Ankarette had warned her. From his leather shoes with their modest piked toes to his beaver hat that was neither too high to be excessive, nor too short to be uninteresting, he was a fine-looking man. The padded doublet, familiar to her from their wedding day, sat comfortably across his broad shoulders and ended decently at well-muscled thighs. She felt herself blushing again.

When he finally made his way across to her, she tensed, sharpening her wits. The very air seemed to crackle.

"Your grace, please it you to give my wife leave." Oh, he could kiss a woman's hand with such a courtly grace and Isabella simpered predictably. She darted a feline look at her half sister, obviously toying with the idea of refusing permission yet she gave it graciously.

"I am very tired, sir," Margery tossed over her shoulder as she stepped down onto the tiled floor of the hall. "Perhaps we can speak of this tomorrow." She felt angry that because she was a woman, she had to justify herself. It did not help that every fiber of her being was becoming increasingly sensitive to his closeness, aware of the physical strength, determination, and maleness of him.

"Tomorrow we all leave for Amboise. Oblige me or you may regret it otherwise." He took her elbow and compelled her out of the hall. In the passageway, she shook her arm free instantly they were alone. He ignored the rebuff and applied an urgent hand to the small of her back instead.

"Ankarette had agreed to sleep in the Duchess's bedchamber so we can have a fruitful discussion of your activities last night."

Margery froze. So he had Ankarette's complicity. Well, he could whistle in the wind. This wife was not going to oblige. If she did not obey the Duke, she had no doubt that he would poison her reputation.

She paused with an exasperated sigh and said with brittleness, "Oh, come, sir, you married me to become son-in-law to my lord, is that not enough?"

Before she knew it, he had tossed her over his shoulder, knocking the breath and the feigned sophistication out of her. "Put me down!" she hissed, wriggling. "Or . . ." Jesu, this was not going to plan.

"Or?"

"I shall kick you very hard somewhere."

A servant brushed past, discreetly ignoring them as he lowered her to the ground, his laughter a soft growl. "You did not manage it last time I carried you."

A sharp retort died on her lips as a new voice accosted them.

"Mistress Huddleston!" The words were echoed by a different voice, unpleasantly rasped.

Margery whirled around. She shivered every time she heard those voices. Littlebourne and Wyke had followed them out of the hall and were smirking in the shadows.

"Having trouble, Huddleston? I hear the saddle keeps slipping?"

However much she resented Huddleston's interference in her life, Margery loathed these two more and the last thing she wanted was for her husband to be bested by the Duke's bullies. With a disdainful smile, she stepped in front of him as they swaggered toward her.

"The Duke says to remind you of your promise to serve him this night, lady." It was said lewdly to antagonize Huddleston.

He stepped calmly alongside her but Margery swiftly set a reassuring hand upon his arm, preventing him from any intention of drawing his sword.

"Of course, Master Wyke," she answered languidly. "How could I forget? Assure the Duke that I shall obey him, but the night is young and I have a little business of my own. Now, excuse us." She slid her hand seductively up Huddleston's sleeve.

Wyke reached her first and grabbed her right wrist upward, forcing her toward him. The thick heavy lips almost spat at her. "Then best be quick, Meg. The Duke grows impatient."

Beside her, Huddleston seemed icily unmoved but she feared for him. At any instant a flame of fury would ignite his sense of honor. She had to snuff it, and fast before they hurt him. With a haughty glance down at the fat glove upon her arm, she tried to think of words that would best the lout.

Then suddenly in a swift movement she was released. Huddleston had Wyke against the wall, his hand upon his throat, while his other hand held a naked blade pointed at Littlebourne. The spluttering torch in the iron bracket threw his face into angry relief.

"It is the Duchess's sister that you address, Wyke. Remove yourself, hence. You too, Littlebourne! You keep me from my pleasure." With a snarl, he let go of Wyke and faced them both, his sword moving like the tail of an angry leopard.

They retreated toward the hall, hands raised away from their scabbards. Their faces were mocking, but Huddleston watched them go with seeming indifference. Finally, he sheathed his weapon and thrust Margery ahead of him up the staircase.

"Goodness, that was quite impressive," she exclaimed brightly as they reached the next floor; inside, she was gelatinous.

"What did you take me for, for Christ's sake, woman, a milksop? I do not need your skirts to hide behind, I thank you."

"I can see that," she agreed. Being protected so swiftly was rather pleasant.

"And what in God's name was that all about?"

Margery bit her lip. "The Duke commanded me to attend her grace this night."

Her husband's face was cold as steel. "How very convenient for you, but on the contrary, you will favor me with your presence, lady, and willingly."

"Sir, I—"

"Pray enter."

She followed him meekly into the small upper bedchamber in silence. He struck a flint and lit a wall torch. This time there was no luxurious four-poster bed, only two small cots. What made her falter in the doorway was the sight of some of her possessions piled in the corner and her next day's riding apparel neatly arranged along a narrow chest. Saddlebags, presumably Huddleston's, slumped drunkenly against the far wall.

Her husband rearranged her so he might close the door. The click of the latch behind her was unnerving. Did it feel this way to be closeted with the Devil?

"Now, delight of my harem, perhaps you would care to tell me what you were actually doing last night. Is Clarence learning to fly the broomstick or were you teaching him something else?"

She gave him a sweet smile, and stooped to deliberately busy herself with hunting through her clothing for her little wooden jewelry box to check its contents. "No," she

murmured, pretending to be distracted. "He is getting the
way of it beautifully. I advised him not to sit too high up but
he is not very good at it." She straightened up and turned
toward the light. If all her jewelry was there she would not
have known, she was too conscious of the man the Holy
Church had chained her to.

"Flying?" Richard Huddleston calmly took the box from
her and flicked its lid up, inspecting its contents and lifting
out the St. Catherine brooch. Plague take his curiosity! she
fumed. But it was all his. By law, everything she had was
now his.

"No, taking advice." She took back the brooch, briskly
removed the box from his hand, and bent to hide it between
the folded linen. The man was a menace and he was
standing far too close. She crouched down and pretended
she was checking that all her other belongings were safe.

"Margery, you cannot go up into a deserted tower with
another woman's husband," he stated gravely somewhere
above her.

"I know, but I cannot help being rebellious, Master Huddleston. It must be my new father's blood." She knew it
was a foolish, brazen thing to say when two strong hands
grasped her beneath her arms and yanked her swiftly to her
feet. His breath moved the wisps of hair that were escaping
from her cone headdress while his hands, ungloved, stabled
themselves upon her ribs. The closeness of his body against
her back made her tremble, but she tried desperately not to
show it.

"I seem to recall you threatening to cuckold me if I ever
found the courage to marry you. Is that what you are doing
with Clarence—exacting your revenge?"

She calmly removed his hands, turning to face him with
a wriggle of her shoulders. "Having lain with a king, sir, do
you not think a duke would be lowering my ambitions? I
had actually set my heart on the Emperor Frederick.
Clarence? No, I thank you, he lacks maturity." But her gibes
merely trickled off Huddleston like raindrops down a rich
man's windowpane.

His green eyes gave her a long hard look, then his mouth
quirked into a tight smile. "What is the matter with you?"

He watched puzzlement pleat her forehead. "Have I gone deaf?" he asked softly. "I do not think you answered my question." He took a few paces away from her before he swung around like a lawyer warming to an argument. "As I understand it, Warwick's natural daughter (and my wife) stole out of the Duchess's women's bedchamber, had an assignation with the Duchess's husband, was followed and observed by one or more persons including myself." His eyes pinioned her. "I want to know what you were doing and why you were followed."

"The Duke invited me."

He applauded her sarcastically with a brief handclap. "And?"

"We talked."

He moved in front of her, hands on his hips and feet astride. "How foolish of me to think otherwise. Is that what you will do tonight when you have finished with me, *talk*?"

"Do not patronize me!" With an effort, she fought down her temper and managed to sweep nonchalantly across to the window. "We often talked at Warwick in the old days." It was a discarded morsel of information, tossed over her shoulder. "Talking to dukes does not awe me, sir." Nurse that! she thought. For all Huddleston's high prancing ambition, he had never shared the confidences of the King and his brothers like she had. "He wanted my advice. It was about Bella." She darted a sideways glance at the door and was startled to find him so close behind her again. Damnation! One should always watch the enemy. Except it was hard. Facing him made her nervous.

His presence behind her reminded her of being his prisoner at the manor farm. She remembered the insults and set them ready like weights to be catapulted against his wall. Meantime, her fingertips idly played with the curled handle of the lower shutters.

"Lady, you will not lie with George of Clarence."

Margery's chin rose defiantly and her shoulders jerked in an uncaring shrug. She hoped her coldness found a soft part beneath his armor. It did. Pricked, with a muttered oath, he swung away.

Margery let out a quiet gasp of relief, appalled that her

body had been waiting for him to touch her, yearning for the feel of his hands. Never, never must she let this man see the growing effect he was having on her. That knowledge would cost her her freedom. To be rid of the marriage, she must keep him beyond arm's length.

She heard him lay the sword down on the rushes and fling himself on the bed. The silence was tangible. Margery stayed at the window, her back to him. It was tempting to glance at the door again. Not long, not long.

"Are you waiting for the Duke's windmill mind to stop turning?"

His use of words disarmed her but she schooled herself to turn around slowly, pretending she did not understand him. He was sprawled on the bed, propped on one elbow, his hand supporting his head. "The footsteps I heard were not some ghostly wraith. Someone suspects you of something. Maybe it is merely one of the Nevilles' envious servants hoping to reveal that you and Clarence are conducting a liaison and thus discredit you, or it could be more sinister—the French, the Burgundians, Margaret d'Anjou, or the whole lot together."

Jesu, the man was too perceptive, too canny.

"Or even the Emperor or Ned," murmured Margery provocatively, seeking to prod him down a more emotional passageway. "*He* must have agents here too." She faced him with a bravado that was as fragile as a wren's egg.

"Ah, the hub of our little talk, I think. Are you sent to France to make Clarence forsake your father?"

She looked down on him innocuously while, inside her, consternation hissed and bubbled like an alchemist's cooking pan. "The hub, indeed, sir. Would I betray my father?" Her tone carried a surprised but scornful edge.

"Since he has only bothered to own you for a week, perhaps you would. I think you need to be honest, lady." His eyes perused her as if he sat on some manor bench to hear and determine her case. How dared he sit there and judge her? Her righteous anger bubbled out before she could stop herself.

"With you, Master Huddleston? Since when have you been honest about a single thing since you—since we met. I have no idea how *your* windmill mind turns save that your head is certainly full of oiled cogs and wheels."

"I am sure that at least you know how some of me works." The glint of the hunt gleamed in his green gaze, setting her insides somersaulting. He sat up and swung his long limbs to the floor. His long fingers began to unhook the knops of his doublet. Things were swirling out of control again. She was forgetting how clever he could be. "I wish you might trust me a little, Margery. I did you good service last night." He eased his arms out of his cote and then tugged off his doublet, tossing them onto the other cot.

Margery's eyes swept sideways to the latch, then she fidgeted, concerned not only about the lightning that was jerking down her spine but how she was going to talk herself out of his expectations. Time was running short. "You make your meaning plain, sir, but you did give me your promise that you would allow me time to be reconciled to our marriage. Will you not escort me back to Isabella?"

He gave a sigh and looked at her as though she had the understanding of a village simpleton. "Damn you, no, I will not. You need to stay here to allay suspicion. What in Heaven's name do you think I arranged this for—my pleasure, with *you*?"

Ignoring her wide-eyed consternation, he tugged open the laces of his lawn shirt. How long could she endure this game and deny him mastery. And if she surrendered, how would he treat her then?

"I do not understand you." It was a *cri du coeur*.

He raised an eyebrow at her. "The night is not over yet, lady. What do you not understand?"

Some demon in her prompted honesty. "For one thing, whether there is blood in your veins or river water," she blurted out, and then wished a flagstone would slide open and swallow her into an oubliette.

"Why, you contrary wench, so you do want me to prove my manhood?" He sprang up and moved toward her with a deliberate swagger, making her retreat until the wall was pressing into her shoulder blades. Could he read the panic illuminated in her face? Perhaps, for he advised her softly, "Hark to me, *wife*, I will not have gossip that I wear a

cuckold's horns nor will I have you wandering in the dark
for some ill purpose. Confide in me or obey me. Does the
truth sit so ill upon your tongue?"

Margery moistened her lips. Why had she provoked
him? "There is nothing to confide."

He insinuated himself even closer, his grin broad. Wide
sleeves walled her in. The musk he wore filled her
breathing. "Then obey me. Stop looking at me as though I
am an ogre. I swear to you I shall not demand my husbandly
rights until"—he smiled like a torturer—"until you tantalize
me beyond endurance and tonight you will. As you have
just demonstrated, you enjoy playing with fire more than
you know."

He was going to teach her obedience. She knew it. He
might not compel her but his promises did not prevent him
from touching her.

At last there were voices in the passageway. Her eyes
swiftly glanced beyond him.

"Expecting visitors?" His cold gaze scythed her. "You
were ready for this, were you not? I suppose you had Littlebourne and Wyke posted to follow us out of the hall. Was
their attempted molestation of you the other day set up in
front of my servant to make me change my mind about marrying you? Do they snuffle like pigs in your—"

"*No*!" screamed Margery. Her palm was caught a skin's
width from his face. His fingers bit into her wrist.

"Swear so, on your very soul!" He jabbed her fingers at
the silver cross about her neck.

"I swear it. I would never do that to you."

"Would you not? I wish I knew." Green fire smoldered in
his eyes but a sound outside the door halted whatever purpose he had in mind. "You vixen," he said softly and
stepped back from her. His expression had lightened but the
gleam of battle still glinted in his eyes. "My dear," he said
loudly, "there is a scuffly sort of noise at the door. Are we
expecting mice? Oh, I will swear we are." He unlatched the
door and flung it open.

Alys, taken unawares with her arms full, gave him an
apologetic shrug and decked in under his arm. Matther Long
was behind her, a waterfall of women's garments rippling
over his sleeves. He flushed as his master reluctantly

removed his arm from barring an entry and turned to Margery. "Anyone else coming, sweet heart? Falconers, butlers, the odd spit boy?"

"Maybe," she answered sweetly. "The boy, however, canceled."

Huddleston swore, subsiding on his bed, his face in his hands.

Alys, looking uncomfortable in the role of accomplice, curtsied guiltily before him. "Truly sorry to disturb you, sir, but they said if my lady was sleeping elsewhere then so must I."

Huddleston uncovered his face. His gentle expression for Alys was to goad Margery. "Alys," he answered sweetly, "how could you possibly disturb me? *My lady*, is it now?" He scowled at his wife.

Margery rescued the pannier that her maidservant was clutching defensively to her bosom and dumped it by the wall. As she turned, her husband's ironic expression threatened her. He hoped she was wondering how much longer she could survive this battle of wits, waiting and wanting.

"Master?" Alys prompted.

Richard Huddleston's grin was, he hoped, disturbingly broad. "I do not bite, Alys. As you are here, Long, you may remove my boots." He braced himself as his servant knelt and tugged at each boot in turn. Master and man beamed at each other in mutual understanding. "As for you, girl, you may, of course, lie at *my lady's* feet tonight, but you arrived too early. My lady and I have—how did you put it earlier, Margery?—*a little business yet*." He stood up and unlatched the door for them. "See Alys comes to no harm, Long, and return with her in an hour."

"**B**ut . . ." His wife's cherry lips parted in astonishment as she watched him close the door behind them. He leaned back against its boards, coolly regarding her, his arms folded.

"I wish I had never felt you beneath me that day at Warwick. Come here!"

Oh, she knew now that the game was up. All that was left to her was the dagger up her sleeve. He saw her swallow nervously but she came dutifully across to him. "I am not returning to Honfleur, Margery. I am going to Amboise with you."

"You are?" She moistened her lips and looked up at him wide-eyed. He was growing used to the feigned innocence. A fool would have mistaken it for shyness. He placed his fingers on either side of the slender column of her neck. Tonight, he would put her through her paces.

"So, my sweet wanton, have you not yet got my measure?"

Her blue eyes widened farther. She smelled of flowers. His left hand moved behind her head but his right smoothly slid to where touching was overdue. She resisted, her breast quivering deliciously against his fingers while beneath the heel of his hand, her heart fluttered in dainty panic.

"Are you prepared to honor your marriage vows to me?"

She took a deep breath. "You said there were better bargains to be had elsewhere. So why eat your words? I am handled goods, Master Huddleston. Why did you not pick a virgin heiress?"

"You want reassurance, lady? You want soft words from me?" He ran a thumb along her lips. "Soft words are *earned*." Her heart was now thumping like a tabor to a whirling country dance. He felt powerful, conscious of her femininity, her fragility. He was lord over the air between them, willing her into his space. "Why not hand the keys to me tonight, Margery? The treaty is made."

Tiny fans of dark gold came down, veiling her eyes. "This city will stand, sir."

"I see." He let go of her coldly. "You disappoint me. I thought you had more courage and intelligence."

"I have!" she exclaimed hotly, starting back.

"Indeed?" How dare she withstand him when he could have taken by force what she owed him in duty? "You have the opportunity to sweeten your tongue, behave in wifely manner, and have me like clay—here!" He held out his open palm, his fingers half-curled, and then reading the adamantine look on her face, snapped his fingers into a fist. "You are a fool, lady. I offer you peace and you ride at me with a lance." Sullenly he turned away, folding his arms fiercely. Maybe indifference would goad the wench more than strength or soft words.

"Sir." Sadness lined her voice. "I respect you for all you rode roughshod over me. Perhaps, given time—"

"Time, in case you may not have noticed, is not in great abundance, nor is privacy."

'Sir." Was this Margery? Husky, pleading? That was new for her. What was the little vixen up to now? Curiosity half turned him. She was trying to make a speech, standing there in her blue velvet like an irresistible gift waiting to be opened.

"Why should I make it easy, Master Huddleston? When we were in England, you bruised both my body with hard

riding and my feelings with harsh words. It was as if you
hated me. Do you hate me, sir? Is marrying me some kind of
further punishment?"

"No." It was a sigh. No, but he would not have her know
how much he wanted her completely his, body and soul. By
Christ's blessed mercy, he desired mastery over her but not
if it meant surrendering his power over himself. He would
be the lead horse pulling the cart of matrimony. "I mean you
no harm. Have I not proved that?"

A tiny pink tongue flickered over her lips. The blue eyes
were desperate. What did it take to put a different passion in
them? She came forward like a solemn petitioner. "I would
be happy to have your friendship, sir."

Friendship! And trust, no doubt, while she met Clarence
by candlelight and was closeted alone with kings. Trust! He
looked down at her, his eyes cold. "I cannot give you my
friendship, Margery."

She would have stepped back but his hands lightly cradled her shoulders.

"Why ever not?" She seemed ablaze with astonishment.

"Take this for answer, lady."

Richard's mouth came down on hers. He knew she
fought against responding. He framed her face between his
hands so she could not escape him, and demanded entry.
When she denied him, he held her back from him, examining her with the exhilaration of a forester pursuing his
quarry. "Margery, I want you so much." This time he had
her bewitched as he drew her to him again and touched his
lips to her throat. His voice was a whisper as he stroked her,
soothed her, willed her. "Let me through, Margery. Give me
the city and you shall have good lordship." His sensuous
gaze forced her head back as if he held sharp steel against
her throat.

Slowly he drew his thumb downward. The tight bud of
her breast was ripely engorged. The fabric had become a
taut, tantalizing barrier. "You like this, my lady wife?" Her
eyes widened as if in surprise at her body's stirrings and her
lips parted. He took advantage, his mouth demanding,
taunting, tasting her. With a moan, she tried to pull away
from his hold but he held her fast. The pupils of her blue
eyes were growing dark and huge.

Unbelievably, her little hands stole up over his chest and around his neck and she arched back into his arms, her eyes closed. It was as if her body was lighting torches and unlocking her lips and thighs to welcome in the conqueror. It was easier than he had dared imagine. He gave a murmur of satisfaction against her forehead as he felt the sheath of thin velvet brushing the hairs of his chest.

"Monsieur, 'uddleston. Mistress Margery, are you awake?" A pounding shook the door at the small of his back and Richard let go of his wife with an oath, almost dropping her. Her eyes snapped open and the dreamy glaze changed to appalled surprise at the fury she must have seen in his. She thrust a knuckle to her mouth and turned away.

With an oath, he violently grabbed her in front of him, about the waist, and flung open the door. One of the Duchess's young French maids-in-waiting almost tumbled in. She instantly grabbed at Margery by her hanging sleeves. "Please, madame, 'er grace bids you come straightaway."

The girl was quite convincing; even Richard had to admit that the smudge of dried tears beneath the beseeching brown eyes looked authentic. How many more had his little witch-wife bribed to save herself from pleasuring him?

Curse her! Curse her! He held her tight before him like a hostage, his fingers pressing into her ribs as painfully as spurs on a horse's flanks. "Can there be more?" he murmured softly into her ear, his tone larded with sarcasm. "Is Ankarette to set fire to the arras if this plot also fails?"

Confused, the French girl raised a pleading face to him. "You also, monsieur, the Duchess begs you come. We all do."

"*Me?* What is this?" His grip slackened.

Margery came to life, bursting out of his grasp. He thrust himself away, his back heaving as he regained mastery of himself.

"Blanche, you must ex—"

"Just come, now, *now!*"

"Go, then. We will follow." Her voice was quietly brisk. He heard the latch. "Sir?"

He looked over his shoulder. Margery was holding his boots out to him.

"Vixen! So what else is planned?" He ignored the

footwear and her flushed face. "Is the Duke of Burgundy invading at midnight?"

"Oh, yes, there will be a thunderstorm at any moment, the ceiling is to leak over your bed, and I have given Matthew three pennies to collect all of Error's fleas and hide them under your mattress. Oh, for the love of Heaven, Richard, I do not like the sound of this. Please, I beg you, come."

It was the first time she had ever called him by his given name. The frustration fell away from him. For a moment they stared at one another. There was no antagonism or smugness in Margery's face but a desperation. Wordlessly, he reached out and took his boots from her. As he pulled them on, she picked up his cote and, with a sweet wifely gesture, held it out to him.

"I will deal with you later, my darling dear," he snarled, thrusting one arm through a sleeve and pushing her out of the room with the other.

Blanche was waiting for them anxiously in the passageway. Richard followed the two women in silence. Another sniffling wench met them at the doorway of the women's bedchamber and he groaned inwardly. His temper was still loose; Margery could have been soft, fragrant, and willing within his arms now. Why did these wretched women want *him*, for Heaven's sake? Had she planned this?

"Hush, Cecily, now what is the matter? Where is Mistress Twynhoe?" Margery put an arm around the girl's shoulders, hastening her out of the echoing passageway into the antechamber.

"With her grace. Mistress Twynhoe told us to fetch you."

"I recall Blanche said it was the Duchess who required us," corrected Richard, stepping into the room after them, his irritation scarcely visored.

Margery glared at him with a mixture of impatience and consternation. "Who is in there with her?" The girl Cecily shrugged and merely blubbered more. Margery let go of her in frustration and ran across to the inner door.

"Ankarette? Bella?" She rattled the ring latch.

There was a sort of muffled sob and the door opened a thumb's width, then widened. A female arm grabbed

Margery inside and half of Ankarette's face appeared in the gap.

"Go to bed, Cecily! You too, Blanche! Master Huddleston, enter, if you please."

He did so reluctantly and was instantly plucked into air that vilely stank of someone's regurgitated supper. The door was closed hastily behind him before the younger girls could see inside. "Thank God you have come."

"By Christ Almighty!" muttered Richard, taking in the destruction in the room.

It was as if a savage wind had scoured the chamber in its ferocity. Hangings had been ripped from the walls, half the bed's canopy had tumbled in. Shards of precious glass lay between flower stems on the fur rug and in the midst of a heap of velvet, taffeta, and woolen stockings, the eighteen-year-old Duchess was weeping.

"Oh, Bella." Margery's voice was appalled as she bent and gathered her distraught half sister into her arms.

Richard turned in amazement to Ankarette. Not used to seeing her without her elegant cone cap and veil, he hardly recognized the wild-eyed woman with her hair loose down her back. She looked haggard and older than her thirty or so years. A wooden figurine of the Holy Virgin, he realized, was clutched defensively in her hand and a dark red bruise was spreading halfway along her jaw. Her eyes, he realized, were fixed upon the wall behind him.

He turned. George of Clarence was drunkenly propped against the wall, a bloody cut congealing on his forehead. His stained shirt was open, flopping over his hose. Whether he was more drunk than stunned was barely debatable. It had never taken the Duke many drinks to become argumentative.

"I am not leaving here, Hud-Huddle . . . until my wife has pr-promised me a son an' that that bitch Anka-rette won't let me near her."

"Oh, Bella, I am so sorry. I should have been here, I should have been here." His wife rocked the weeping girl.

"You t-traitress," spluttered the Duke, his venom now directed unsteadily at Margery. "Bitch, I told you I'd have you dismissed if you did not let me in."

Richard took a deep breath, wondering what they were

expecting him to set aright first. The Duchess seemingly had
won a temporary victory. It was the spreading bruise dealt
to the Duke's honor that swiftly needed salve.

"By the Saints, is there any wine here? What you need,
my lord, is a drink."

Isabella stopped sobbing into Margery's bodice and
stared at Richard in amazement.

"A drink!" Ankarette spat at him in disgust. "You men
are all the same. Just look at this fine duke, will you,
Margery. The flower of knightho—"

"Aye, a drink," Richard interrupted sternly. "See to it,
Margery. Do it!" His wife's glare turned from indignation to
a degree of understanding as he jerked his head at her. She
gently set aside the Duchess and scrambled to her feet. As
she stepped carefully across to the door, Richard held out
his hand for the figurine. "Ankarette?" The skepticism in
the older woman's eyes flickered and went out. Biting her
lip, Ankarette handed him the holy statue. He set the injured
Virgin back in her wall niche, now looking as though St.
Joseph had not been pleased she had told him about the
Annunciation.

"You are disgustingly drunk." Margery's voice lashed
the Duke before she opened the door. Richard moved back
between the pair of them as a stifler.

"You were supposed to be here, M-M-Meg. You were
supposed to c-counsel wis-wisdom. It's all your fault."
Richard pushed his wife out of the door and was braced to
catch the Duke before he fell. George turned toward the
heap of clothing and sniffed at his Duchess, his voice sulky.
"It . . . it was not just your s-s-son. He was my babe too."
He staggered toward Isabella. Richard moved beside him.
The wobbling continued and the Duke flung out an arm for
the bedpost. "Leave me alone!"

There was a kick at the door. Ankarette opened it. She
grabbed the tray from Margery and thrust it into Richard's
arms. "You men are all the same under the skin. Take your
filthy wine. I hope it chokes the pair of you."

"It was all I could find," Margery said quietly at his
elbow.

Richard calmly set it upon the bed and poured the Duke a
full cup. He handed it to him before filling his own. "To

your next son and the future Prince of Wales, your grace!" He downed his wine in an instant. The Duke's eyes did not waver from his as he did the same. Richard refilled their cups to the brim. "To your royal highness!" Some of the wine spilled, further staining the Duke's costly shirt. "To your success with King Louis!"

The three women watched, fascinated, as George of Clarence finally crumpled slowly to his knees, his left arm still clamped to the bedpost. He was lullabying himself asleep with some tuneless rigmarole they could barely hear.

Richard rescued the half-empty cup and set it on the tray. Isabella instantly rose and came across to peer at her husband.

"Is he safe now?"

"He will have the mother and father of all headaches tomorrow and will curse the hours he must spend in the saddle. If you would kindly remove the tray, madam, I will lift him into bed."

The eighteen-year-old Neville nose crinkled in disgust. "I do not want him in my bed. He stinks."

"I shall cleanse him, my lady. Can one of you find me some water while we set this room to rights?"

Ankarette pulled a face at Margery as she corrected a footstool. "I can see now why you did not want to wed Master Huddleston. Do they breed tyrants in Cumbria?"

Margery found a jug of water that had miraculously survived and carried it across. Isabella merely stood and watched as Richard pulled back the bedding and rearranged the pillows before he dragged Clarence up onto the bed.

"Madam, you must take care that his tongue does not fall back into his throat else he will choke and die."

"You mean you are going to leave him here for the rest of the night with me?"

Richard had removed the Duke's slippers and began to untie the points that were still holding the ducal hose. "This is where he desired to be." He straightened up and looked down gravely at the little duchess. There was a hint of shared blood with Margery but more of the Countess in the girl's face. "Your grace, a little deception would be advisable. Let his grace awake as if he had—shall we say—achieved his objective. If we remove his clothes and you are

sympathetic to him in the morning, I will wager he will
remember none of this."

"Sympathetic!" snorted Ankarette, coming across to
glare at the unconscious man. "He was a monster."

"That is my advice," retorted Richard curtly. "If you
can think of a better way to deal with the future king of
England . . ."

His meaning reached Ankarette. She chewed her lip
angrily but nodded. "Oh, you are clever, Master Huddleston. I suppose my future is now in jeopardy."

Margery tipped some water onto a sponge and waited
while he tied his hanging sleeves behind his back before she
handed it to him.

"You are in no danger, Ankarette," Isabella protested.
"You were doing your best for me."

"He fell, madam." Richard made it a statement as he
swabbed the Duke's face and wiped the mixture of wine and
supper from the pale hairless chest. "He fell and hit his head
because he had been drinking. The fault was his."

"Yes." Isabella brought her fingers together in a steeple.
"Yes, Master Huddleston is right. That is exactly how it
happened."

"And the chip in Our Lady?" Margery lifted the statue
and ran a finger over the Virgin's head.

"I leave that to Ankarette's devising. She will, of course,
have to explain to the curious how she came by her bruise."
His eyes met Margery's for a brief second of understanding. Ankarette's tongue usually waggled in other people's
matters.

"We shall think of something." Isabella seemed to be
able to confront the damage now. "Do you think George
will remember which of my ladies was in attendance, sir?
Shall we say that Ankarette fell down the stairs?"

Richard wanted no more of the business. "You will need
to put ointment on that cut, my lady, and restore this room
to rights. I can probably rehang the King of France's curtains and the arras."

While Ankarette hunted for the salve and Margery
picked up the shards of glass from the fur rug, he and the
Duchess finished undressing the Duke. It took time. It was
like stripping a corpse and Richard found the task dis-

tasteful. He only hoped the Duke's memory would prove as confused as the tangle of the bedchamber.

Isabella was superlatively grateful. But if ever she became queen, would she bother to remember? He doubted it as he stood up on the bed, straddling the Duke, and tidied up the bedcurtains. No one liked to be reminded of previous embarrassments.

"Madam, I shall leave you." He did not know where the rest of the strewn clothes and finery belonged. "Margery?"

His wife's eyes grew round as gooseberries. Damnation on the wench, did she think he still ached to bed her? And yet the notion was not unappealing.

"No, I beg you, Master Huddleston. *Richard.*" The Duchess set a gracious hand upon his sleeve, her eyelashes fluttering. "Richard, please, will you sleep in the outer chamber tonight in case he wakes?"

"He will not, I assure you." Out of the corner of his vision, Richard saw Margery clap a hand to her lips and turn her back. The little witch was laughing.

"Shall you disobey me, Master Huddleston?" The Duchess fixed him, her mouth in a pout.

"No, madam," he sighed and brushed his lips across the back of her proffered hand.

It was a relief to escape into the outer chamber. He looked around and sat down wearily on one of the empty beds. Cecily and Blanche, still awake, were instantly out of bed and on either side of him as he fended off their questions. It restored his belief in the state of things and he was quite pleased when Margery came out a while later and found them still making a fuss of him. Dark shadows underlined her eyes but her amusement was fresh enough.

"Blanche, Cecily, we must all get some sleep if we are to leave tomorrow. That is usually my bed, sir, but you are welcome to it. I shall take Ankarette's." Her fingers slowly undid the band that held her headdress and she ran her lithe fingers through her hair for pins, seductive blue eyes taunting him wantonly. Oh, she could do it now to torture him, knowing she was safe. Was this how the King had seen her? Mischievous, seductive?

Richard thought rapidly—to save his sanity—of sieges, decrepitude, altars, anything. Anything that would stop the

rising heat, the aching for release. By the Saints, he would
pay her back mercilessly for this night's work. "This
arrangement should please you, sir. It will be like sleeping
in a paynim harem for the night."

He hoped his gaze scorched her, that she would lie
awake aching for him.

"Is it true that the female slaves are supposed to wriggle
up from the bottom of the Sultan's bed?" Cecily sat up
giggling.

"No, that is the duty of his wives and concubines,"
Margery answered confidently. Richard watched with pleasure as she met his raised eyebrow and blushed livid as she
realized what she had said. There were no more alluring
glances after that. She snuffed out the two candles that lit
the room. The sound of her sliding down her garters to
remove her stockings pained him.

When finally Blanche and Cecily slept, she came and
stood at the foot of his bed, unwittingly tempting him further. "I am sorry that you were hauled into this. You acted
with great ingenuity and foresight."

"Praise coming from you? It was hardly unselfish,
believe me. I cannot afford to make so powerful an enemy."

"To be truthful, I am not easy about him becoming
king."

He laughed softly, bitterly, at the circumstances in which
he found himself, in exile with a rebellious wife to tame and a
fickle wine-bibbler to placate. "Are you not, Margery Huddleston? Well, let us see what his most Christian Majesty of
France has to say in the matter when we reach Amboise."

15

At least the journey to Amboise was without incident. Margery conceded on the last day. That was if she discounted the Countess mislaying her favorite ring, a cart mysteriously disappearing overnight, and the damp sheets that marred the hospitality of the abbey where they had stayed two nights ago.

The grumbling, which had begun then, had stoked the complacency of the English visitors. Warwick's entourage, as many travelers do, spent their time comparing their own land favorably with that they were visiting. Such self-congratulations, Margery noted, skirted the fact that they themselves were beggars on the King of France's hospitality.

The Duke, with as much discretion as a flea on an archbishop's forehead, had declared that the farms in France were less prosperous than their English counterparts. He was unfortunately right. The buildings were meager, the thatch threadbare and untidy. Few yeomen were to be seen, and the peasants haymaking in their lords' meadows were more raggedly garbed than any Margery had ever seen in the Kingmaker's fields. The men, mostly bare-legged and unshod, wore unbelted loose smocks looped up into their breechclouts. The women laborers were pronounced less comely than their English counterparts, although Margery observed the Englishmen noting the naked sun-brown legs beneath the hoisted kirtles and the flesh showing beneath the loose lacing of the bodices.

Where her husband's looks sped, Margery had no inkling, for Richard Huddleston did not travel with them. He rose earlier always, bidden to ride ahead with the King of France's officers to ensure the coming night's hospitality was adequate. He never sat long at supper either. He was giving her time and space but she sensed that like a patient hunter, he would eventually close in.

As the pilgrims to King Louis's gold left the apple orchards and the small high-hedged fields of Normandy, the land flattened and the whisper of the vast fields of waving seed heads betokened a good harvest. Near journey's end, they glimpsed the towers of Tours, but took a road past vineyards to the southeast. At noon of the last day, they found Huddleston and some of the other knights awaiting their company beside a small tributary with the news that the French dignitaries would be with them within two hours and that they were now but three miles from Amboise.

The convoy of carts and riders halted and the chests were unlocked. A pavilion was swiftly thrown up for the ladies to exchange their riding gowns for courtly garments. The slap of water on male skin filled the air. Blushing maidservants carried ewers from the stream to the Countess and her daughters while the ladies-in-waiting lifted out the newly stitched gowns from where they had been lain so carefully after pressing. Some of the fabric had fared ill but it would have taken too much time to have lit fires for the flat irons.

For the Countess, the tiring women shook out a dark blue brocade with sweeping dalmation sleeves and a heavily embroidered border of emerald leaves and golden daisies. For her eldest daughter, Ankarette lovingly brought an overgown of lavender, spangled with tiny gold and silver stars and edged with a broad collar and stiff back-turned cuffs in cloth of gold.

The simplest kirtle was Anne's with its round, modest

neck. Blue threads adorned the folds of snowy shimmering silk with tiny meadow speedwells, the only ornament a belt of small white and gold enameled platelets that clasped about her slender hips. Unwed, she wore her blond hair free beneath a satin cap latticed with tiny gems.

Her mother and sister needed more imposing edifices. The Countess fussed loudly about the construction going on above her brow. For years she had followed the fashion set by the late Queen Ysabeau of France—the steeple henin—but her daughters had at last persuaded her to adopt the more modish butterfly headdress that at least did not rise to such monstrous, uncomfortable heights.

While Isabella was having a final tantrum about her eyebrows, Ankarette and Margery were at last free to hastily change their attire. Margery was permitted much less extravagance than her half sisters, but the Burgundian dusky dark rose overgown that Alys hurriedly tugged over her head was the finest she had ever worn. Grumbling as she pinned, Alys lamented that her mistress had insufficient curls to whirl into a chignon beneath the high, flat-topped cap surmounted by a stiff wire loop. It was not very comfortable. The top of the wire reared like the antennae of a butterfly above the cap. Over it Alys draped a delicate veil of cascading gauzy tissue so transparent that it revealed the darker hue beneath.

Margery rose, unconcerned about applauding her own reflection, which was just as well since Isabella was monopolizing the polished silver hand mirror. The decision as to whether Ankarette should come and fasten a sapphire brooch with teardrop pearls in the center of the Duchess's cap did not concern Margery, but she was irritated by the Countess's pleas for reassurance on the new-style headdress from every woman in the pavilion.

Only when a dab of rouge had been administered to each cheek did Warwick's wife finally rise satisfied to inspect her daughters and their attendants. It was inevitable she found something to criticize about her husband's bastard. Sweeping a haughty eye down Margery's overgown with its tiny white and pink marguerites, she sucked in her plump cheeks. "Yes, we all know you look very fine, Mistress Huddleston, but at least try to behave like a lady. You are

supposed to thrust your belly out in deference to Our Lady
and keep your hands clasped upon your girdle as you walk
and your eyes modest and downcast. Remember, it is a
royal court."

"Madam." Margery dropped her a swift curtsy and thrust
her way out of the warm perfumed tent, her shoulders
heaving in fury. It was such pretense. Were they all expected to behave as though they were heavy with child the
whole time they were at Amboise? Was it out of holy reverence or merely because Queen Charlotte was almost near
her time that the French court ladies were said to be walking
so? Ridiculous!

Anne stuck a concerned face around the flap of the
pavilion.

"Do not worry over me, Anne."

"It is only because Mother is in a pother herself."

"I know. I am used to it."

The younger girl grinned and ducked back inside.

A half-dozen whistles made Margery turn her head. She
was the first of the ladies to emerge and the freshly shaven
horsemen had noticed her. No doubt the Countess would
now accuse her of behaving wantonly. She almost turned to
go inside and then decided to stand her ground.

Acknowledging the whoops with a slight curtsy, she
walked around the tent to fix her attention stonily on the
gaudy awkward chariots in which the women were to ride
the last mile. They were awful. She would have much preferred a palfrey instead of this crossbreed of a merchant's
covered wagon and a Corpus Christi mummer's stage.

"You look very fine." A huff of hot air reached her neck.

She turned her head, startled to find herself face-to-face
with the shining black head of her husband's horse. Richard
Huddleston tugged on the bridle and walked the stallion
around her as if she were under inspection. Had the whistles
made him come over to stake his possession, to scatter more
holy water on her delicate reputation?

"It looks uncomfortable. Is it?" He frowned at the wire
that circumnavigated the outside of her headdress.

"Yes, a penance for respectable wives."

"The Countess is making life hard for you?"

"Yes, and it is hot." His grin disarmed her while his

entire appearance inspired a longing that she was afraid to put a name to. How could she find a man she disliked so appealing to her senses? From the gleaming black leather boots that fitted his calves like a second skin, her gaze swept up over his black-clad thighs, rose over the mulberry and white embroidered doublet with its hanging sleeves to the plumed cap. Across his shoulders sprawled a gold chain with the arms of his house suspended. He had worn it on their wedding day but she had refused to notice it.

"What is the motto of your arms?"

He leaned down good humoredly and held the pendant out to her. "*Our* arms, lady. Can you understand it?"

" '*Soli deo honor et gloria.*' Only to God belongs the power and the glory," she translated. "At least it is modest." The lettering was warm beneath her fingertips and then, of a sudden, she was conscious that he was enjoying a privileged view of her décolletage. Swiftly letting go, she stepped back hurriedly into Ankarette who had come looking for her. Her husband laughed at her confusion, his eyes sparkling approvingly at her. "A good translation. I did not know you knew any Latin."

"There is a great deal you do not know, sir." Her hands curled into fists.

"I shall enjoy finding out. Mesdames, your servant." A gloved hand mockingly touched the beaver brim of his hat before his spurred heels caused his beautiful horse to prance away.

"That man is a fine judge of horseflesh," declared Ankarette. "For a mere husband, he takes an uncommon interest in you, Margery."

"He thinks he plays me like a fish."

"Then let him haul you in or some other woman will take his line."

It was not easy, Margery reflected, as she eventually followed Anne into the chariot. Marriage was supposed to be a contract. In England, Huddleston would have taken her to Millom to introduce her to his family and there would have been a pattern of conventional behavior to follow, but here in France she was not being poured into any mold. Her new husband appeared and disappeared like a counter beneath a conjurer's cups on a market stall. She was neither wife nor maid. One minute he tormented her into a fury, the next he had her senses reeling and her body aching.

"Did I show you what Master Huddleston brought me?"Anne Neville tapped the brooch on her shoulder, a tiny, shy, white unicorn in enamel with a blue jewel eye, kneeling on grass.

"He gave you that?" Strange that Margery should feel the needle of jealousy.

"Not exactly gave. I believe he extracted it from the Burgundian merchandise. It was because everyone laughed at me at the wedding except the two of you. You frown, Margery, are you surprised?"

"It is a kind thought."

"Did he not mention it to you?" It was one of the many things that Master Richard Huddleston had not bothered to mention but Margery was too overwhelmed by the sudden bustle about her to think further than the moment. Word of the French lords' imminent arrival was heralded and swiftly the Countess and Duchess were helped aboard.

"Do you like his grace's hair cut so?" Isabella asked meaningfully, her glance enveloping Margery and Ankarette. The new ducal fringe hid the bruise extremely well. George's hair was the color of ginger root, lacking Ned's wonderful auburn or Dickon's dark ruddy tones, but in the French sunshine it gleamed well enough.

"He looks like a future king," answered Margery truthfully.

Indeed, the Duke did look magnificent. To advertise his royal blood, a ducal circlet glinted around the crown of his cream beaver hat. From his short cloak of cloth of gold over the cream and gold brocade doublet down to his Spanish white leather boots, he looked every inch a Plantagenet. At his side, Warwick sat astride his beloved white stallion that was caparisoned in black and silver. He might be eclipsed by the Duke's youth but for Margery, the Kingmaker had a presence that George of Clarence could not match.

The Earl crooked his finger now and the clarion sounded. The English retainers moved swiftly into their ranks and the Clarence herald rode ahead. The Duke and Earl urged their horses forward and behind them, like a massive folded peacock's tail of glistening gems and brocade, came their retinue. The pennants were hoisted proudly, reiterating the fierce bull and the bear with the ragged staff upon the embroidered tabards of the esquires, pages, and grooms.

The French lords had drawn rein and divided, lining the highway like trees. Through the Valois ranks rode the panache and power of the houses of Plantagenet and Neville and, on either side, each French noble swept them a low obeisance as they passed. At the end of the welcoming line waited the Admiral of France, husband of King Louis's bastard daughter, and the Archbishop of Narbonne. If Philippe de Commynes had any Burgundian spies lurking, they would be most alarmed: Louis of France was officially welcoming the mighty English rebel so lavishly that there could be no doubt that the treaty with Burgundy was as dead as Charlemagne.

The procession that now numbered two hundred halted briefly at two bridges that bestrode the Loire and Margery had her first glimpse of Amboise. Upon the farthest bank, the château sunned itself strategically along the soaring cliff. A fat, white, corbeled round tower grinned down at them like a merry snow mannikin. It was surprising that no religious spires or secular turrets vied with the fortress. From the Ille St. Jean that linked the two bridges, she could see there was an ecclesiastical cluster of buildings to the west, but the commoners' buildings, edging the river around the rooted walls of the château, were insubstantial—hostelries for the most part. The town, if it could be called such, did not lack for residents for there was a large crowd drawn up, but the bulk of inhabitants evidently resided or worked within the castle bailey for the creamy battlements were iced with people. Gold and azure banners and pennons were everywhere, fluttering upon the turrets or hanging down from the windows. It was very flattering.

"This is a welcome that would not disgrace his Holiness," declared the Countess smugly. "You can see how much they respect your father here."

Isabella and Anne exchanged glances. The French heralds in their blue tabards emblazoned with the gold fleur-de-lis were waiting.

"I think this will prick the Duke of Burgundy beyond

endurance," murmured Margery as she assisted her sisters
from the chariot. "Sweet Heaven, is *that* the King of
France?"

A man was bustling toward the Earl, his head thrust forward like a chicken's beneath a beaked black hat orna-
mented with saint brooches. Beside him lolloped several
large hounds with huge heads and floppy ears, and sepa-
rating him from the common people marched a bodyguard
with plaid baldrics.

"*Mon cher compère!*" The voice was clipped.

Margery watched her father kissed on both cheeks with
instinctive unease. It was not exactly that Louis XI looked
malevolent—he was dressed like a dowdy nobody in houppelande, hose, and ankle-length boots all the same dusty
insect black. His dull brown hair was lank about his shoulders but his eyes were unpleasantly mischievous, missing
nothing.

"The contrast is notable," murmured Huddleston's voice
in her ear as she waited in attendance upon Isabella. "Is this
king also worthy of your amorous embrace?" He had unob-
trusively moved up through the throng. Not one to let an
opportunity pass him by, Margery reflected cynically.

"No one could surpass Ned." It was sweetly answered
but she was too troubled by her instinctive dislike of the
King of France to quarrel further. It was not surprising that
his enemies spoke of Louis as "the Spider"—maybe it was
the way his black-gloved fingers knitted and reknitted like
the busy front legs of a spider, or was it for another reason?
Men said the sticky threads of his web stretched into all corners of Christendom, that his agents were wherever deci-
sions were being made—in the houses of the merchant
bankers of Augsburg and Florence and the privy chambers
of his fellow rulers. The world whispered that he kept his
prisoners in wicker baskets, hung from his castle walls.
Well, if he did, thought Margery, fearful it might be true, he
had tidied them away for the afternoon.

"An extra duty that his surliness will not bow lower than
waist height," wagered Ankarette, as the Duke of Clarence
faced the King. It was a miracle for any brother of Edward
of England to bow the knee before Louis but somehow the
Duke managed it; he needed the money. Isabella sank down

gracefully at his side, as regal as a princess. A silken moth at the edge of the web.

The Countess joined her lord, her plump face solemn with nervousness but her head proud. After all, it was her father, Richard Beauchamp, who had trounced the French and ordered the faggots to be lit beneath Jeanne d'Arc, the soldier-witch. But the person who seemed to arouse the greatest interest was, surprisingly, Anne Neville, a slight figure as she glided forward to stand beside her mother, her gown whispering across the carpet, her hair a waterfall of gold over her shoulders. Louis inspected her with the same intensity that most men show on choosing a wife, while Warwick stood at his side beaming like a summer sun.

It was clear that there was a rapport between the Earl and the King. There was no formality in the way they joked together. But then Warwick's glance found Margery and he gave her a nod of summons. Everyone's heads swiveled around.

"Jesu!" whispered Margery, as a murmur ran through the French courtiers. "I do not want this. How in Heaven—"

"Courage!" You are Warwick's daughter!" Richard Huddleston reacted instantly, his confident fingers grabbed her hand and tugged her forward. Margery perforce fell into step beside him. Had she been a rabbit, she would have disappeared into the nearest burrow rather than have suffered the shadow of this royal bird of prey.

"My natural daughter, Margaret Neville, and her new husband, Richard Huddleston."

"*Bienvenue*, Madame 'uddleston, monsieur." The King's voice was rich with interest as they both knelt. Unwilling to raise her head, Margery was conscious of the royal fingers flexing in front of the tip of her nose. "*Beau sire*," she murmured.

Huddleston rose to his feet beside her, the pressure of his fingers on her elbow urging her to rise. Then suddenly she was almost thrown backward as a great hound sprang between her and the King. On every side, the King of France's dogs leaped at their leashes and the noise was deafening.

Margery shook in horror at Error bouncing around with no regard for majestic niceties. The pink tongue was an insult, the happy innocent eyes an outrage.

"Your pardon, most Christian Majesty." Huddleston grabbed the animal's collar, snarling a swift command. Error sat and wagged his tail at the King of France and Margery watched incredulously as the cunning face before her softened into admiration. It was love at first encounter.

"Yours, young man?"

"Your majesty is correct. A badly behaved deerhound. His name is Error."

"He is a prince of dogs. I never saw the like." Louis was rapt.

"Then he is yours, sire."

Louis of France reached out a gloved hand and caressed Error. He was cheerfully washed in return and did not seem to mind the drips of canine saliva flicking onto his scuffed boots.

"You expect a dog to serve two masters?"

"*Beau sire*, I expect him now to serve you."

"You breed these giants?"

"Yes, *beau sire*."

"You will acquire me a breeding pair?"

"Consider it done, your majesty."

"Excellent. Then I shall borrow him till then and try him in the hunt." The King looked around at the Earl with a smile and Warwick's shoulders lost their stiffness. "But next time, Monsieur 'uddleston, you look to your dame. She is not pleased with you for ordering him set loose. He could have spoiled her gown."

Richard for once went as scarlet as a summer fisherman and Margery found the courage to smile back at the King of France.

They were dismissed. Richard's gloved hand fumbled for hers. She almost snatched it away as they deferentially backed across the roadway to their previous place. Margery made sure they sank back into the ranks out of view. She was not just angry, she was mortified! Not only had her upstart husband managed to get himself noticed by the King of France ahead of his betters, but to have had the gall to deliberately plan it all! What humiliated her most was that King Louis had seen through his scheming.

"How dared you?" she hissed at Huddleston under her breath, as everyone craned their necks for a glimpse of them. "Of all the pandering, toe-licking, calculating . . ." Words almost failed her. "Poor Matthew could have been whipped within an inch of his life for letting that beast off." Huddleston was not looking at her but he slid a finger around his neck to ease his collar. His sudden high color and the beads of moisture on his forehead were traitors. "Is there no end to your ambition?"

His defensive reply revealed he had not parried the shaft entirely: "And you are now an earl's daughter and proud of it so do not prattle to me of ambition, mistress. You were but a bastard tiring woman before I wed you. A little gratitude would not go amiss. Besides, my Error is the 'prince of dogs.' "

"Then go home to Cumbria and sit in a bog and breed the monsters!"

"That is not only what I will breed."

"Oh!" exclaimed Margery in disgust. If she had not been wearing satin shoes, she would have aimed at his shin.

Ankarette tactfully pushed in between them, beaming like a saint in Heaven. Someone half clapped but was hushed.

"You have three very beautiful daughters, *mon compère*," the King of France was saying in slow French so that the English visitors could get the gist. "And I also. But with *le Bon Dieu's* blessing, France will have a dauphin very soon. Come, messeigneurs!" He held out an arm each to the Duke and to Warwick. Thus linked informally, he led his guests on foot along the road of crimson fabric that had been laid between them and the town.

"Did you know Queen Charlotte, who is supposed to be almost bursting with child, is going to meet the Countess at the front door of the château like a cheerful farmer's wife?" Ankarette whispered.

"I imagine the effect will be spoilt by her fifteen maids of honor," muttered Richard, clearly out of temper. "If it is anything like the English court, not one will be any more virgin than my wife is."

It was a long afternoon. When the introductions to Queen Charlotte were done, Warwick and the Duke shared a loving cup with the King and his closest advisers before everyone was invited to take a goblet of wine and raise it to peace and amity. The phrases unsaid were to wish the downfall of the usurper Edward of York. If Isabella had hoped they would drink to the Duke and herself as future King and Queen of England, she was disappointed and could be seen fanning herself, a sure sign in her that she was irritated.

Outside where the ladies were taken to be tempted by sweetmeats while their ears were seduced by sweet music, it was easier to try to forget what it all might mean. Queen Charlotte, round and ripe like a peapod about to burst, wisely left politicking to her husband and was happy to listen to the Countess's experience of childbirth. It gave Isabella good reason to excuse herself, taking her two sisters with her. In her wake, Margery kept a fixed half smile on her face, while beside her, Anne fidgeted with a lily someone had presented to her. It was no longer England. The banker, the diplomat, the host, was the smiling, busy King of France.

"Do not look so pained, Bella," pleaded Margery. "I am sure your every expression is being noted."

The Duchess sniffed. "Well, no matter, they will think it is because of the loss of my baby."

"If they even know. For my part, I wish we had not come." Anne glanced about to make sure no one was within earshot.

There was an uneasiness among the Neville entourage, Margery sensed. At Valognes the English at least had the semblance of being in charge of their own affairs, but here at the court of Louis XI the reality of their dependence on his goodwill was revealed.

"Be thankful you do not have the headache as well," snapped Isabella. "I wish I could go and lie down. Babble, babble, babble and I can barely understand a word of it. I suppose it is to be tedious like this from now on. How I shall bear it, I do not know. By Our Lady, one even has to be careful where one walks. Now I know why the Queen is reputed to have so many shoes."

She was right, there were dogs everywhere and the kennel-boys discreetly circulating with pans and scoops were not particularly efficient. The Duchess twitched her skirts away from an interested black nose. "They say that six bitches share the King's chamber and not one of them is the Queen."

"Bella! Be careful!" Margery warned. "Some of these ladies may well have a smattering of English. Besides, you will have to be gracious if you want King Louis to lend you money."

"I suppose so. Oh, Lord, more French dames with a surfeit of hypocras and doucets." But since one of the French noble ladies exclaimed over Isabella's brooch, the Duchess was mollified and allowed herself to become the center of attention once more.

Anne Neville looked around her with a discerning eye. She was growing up fast, thought Margery.

"You know what I should like above all? To go back to England and have some say in where I lay my head. Why is it that I have a sense of foreboding, Margery?"

Her half sister tossed back a ball that had rolled across to her feet. One of the Queen's dwarves grinned. "I feel it too, Anne. A sense of losing control. Oh, why did my lord have to present me to *him*?" As she watched Louis and her father step down into the courtyard, an icy chill ran down her spine and she added softly, "No, I lie, King Louis asked for me to be presented. Anne, he *knew* about me."

"Of course he did. I expect Lord Mennypenny told him about the wedding. I rather thought his majesty did you great honor. Still, he is said to know everything about everyone which means that he may also know that you and Cousin Ned . . . oh, I see. Yes, it is unfortunate."

Margery bit her lip. She did not like to confide that she felt danger closing about them, as if they were venturing deeper and deeper into a dark, menacing forest.

"Well, we must survive as best we can," Anne was saying. "If we are sweet to the French, they will lend us arms and we can go home."

Margery frowned, "But what then? Ned has never lost a battle." And she watched Anne's fingers finally snap the stem of the lily.

◦⟁◦

Richard found Matthew Long staring hard at the huge beasts in the moat. "A real lion, master! Look at the size of those there claws!"

"And I shall feed you to him, piece by piece, if you deny me an honest answer! What madness possessed you back there?"

Matthew straightened up, his skin a dull red. "It was not the dogboy's fault, sir."

"No, *yours*!"

Long's eyes flickered about them before his huge hands fumbled in his pouch and swiftly thrust a coil of leather into Richard's hands. It was Error's leash, neatly sliced through at the collar end.

Richard swore. "You saw someone?"

"The lad thinks it was one of the Duke's swine. Says how some rogue cuffed him to the ground from behind and cut the dog loose before he could find his feet. Shall you beat him?"

"No." Richard sighed.

"I think, sir, 'twas to punish me for interfering when those plaguey rogues were molestin' the mistress afore your nupitals."

"And now I have lost my dog and my wife thinks I planned the entire incident."

His servant rumbled with laughter. "Shall I enlighten her?"

"Oh, no," snarled Richard. "I care not what the wench thinks."

"I think, master, pardon me for boldness, that you should not be talkin' that way. The mistress acquitted herself right well in her finery today an' I think that, given time, you will as likely be pleased, for all her wayward tongue. What with her bein' the Earl's by-blow and having good childbearing hips, everyone has remarked as how you have probably gotten yourself a fine bargain."

Richard shook his head in wonderment. "Well, Matthew, thank you for sharing that morsel from your vast pantry of philosophy." His face hardening, he clapped a hand upon his servant's shoulder. "Take especial care from now on, Long." And he left him with the lions.

cᗡ⌒

Margery, making the inevitable visit to watch the feeding of the great beasts, noticed her new servant on the edge of the fascinated crowd.

"Mistress." Long touched his forehead deferentially.

"That was a foolish business with the hound, Matthew."

"Aye, mistress, I said my prayers, I can tell you. Though 'twould have been the kennelboy who'd have had the thrashin'. One moment the cur was there and the next instant some poxy varmit had hacked through his leash and that did it. There's no stopping the beast when he's loose."

"Hold, Matthew. Are you saying someone else freed Error?"

"Saints preserve me, you never thought I *let* him off, did you, mistress? Lady, your pardon, but neither my master nor I are that addlepated. Still, all's well. You should see where the great lolloping cur is housed. Better off than I am or many a Frenchman. Packed like piglets in a sow's womb we are, whereas the plaguey hounds are all in a kennel the size of a blessed manor hall with a brick wall at one end and a huge, new fangled fireplace. Have you seen your sleeping quarters, mistress?"

"Not yet."

"Alys says it is the same—not an inch to scratch."

Well, thought Margery as she followed her sisters into the Great Hall for supper and found to her astonishment that for once she was seated next to her husband, it was definitely a time for a spoonful of ashes and a wisp of sackcloth.

"You must be sad at losing Error."

His chin was cupped gloomily in his hand while his fingers drew plow furrows on the cloth. "The King is welcome to him. He was a gift from my father, but his education was unfortunately neglected. My mother spoiled him."

"And I suppose the King is welcome to me as well. I am not trained either. At least your horse behaves."

He raised an eyebrow and studied her suspiciously. "Is this a kind of apology? I gather Long must have lit a candle of innocence for me on your altar? I told him not to bother."

Margery's eyes sparkled, her lips moist and teasing. It

was safe here to provoke and withhold. "Behold me an abject penitent if it please you, sir, but I should warn you my humility is of short duration."

"Then until the next hour bell, lady." He set a goblet in her hand. "Let us be at peace."

"Who cut the dog free?" She tapped the metal against metal. "Your health, sir."

"Truth is hard to come by these days." His green gaze caressed her face but not with gentleness. His voice was low. "Does it matter? Perhaps a certain person lusted after the beast and set an agent to cut it loose, or Long and I have enemies."

Margery glanced around to see if their neighbors had caught his gist but anyone watching would have seen a husband dividing a portion of spit-roasted capon for his wife. She took care not to glance toward the high table. "Surely you jest?" Her fingers trembled as she took the proffered morsel from the tip of his meat knife.

"I should advise you to weigh each one of your words like a miserly goldsmith. The balance is everything—to be seemingly at ease but to divulge nothing. This is Amboise. Have you not observed it holds more cages and dungeons than Valognes?"

Richard noted she could barely swallow the white meat down. "Why are you telling me this?" she asked.

"Because what spatters you with mud now inevitably sullies me. It is a pity there is no trust between us." He summoned a page to refill his goblet with Chinon red.

She spread her fingers across her winecup. "There could be, sir, if you would agree to free me from this foolish hasty marriage of ours."

"And begin again? You want me to woo you like a village maiden, pretend that your Ned never charmed you onto his daybed?"

He knew it was not what she meant. "You do not give up easily."

"Oh, I was trained as a soldier. Failure is unacceptable."

A sigh escaped her. Gauzy lashes fluttered modestly like iridescent insect wings. "I wish I knew why you want me stumbling behind your victory chariot."

"Fishing, lady? Because victory would be sweet and

Matthew Long assures me you have good childbearing hips." She choked on her wine and had to be thumped carefully between her delectable shoulder blades. He let his fingers linger longer than they should, but when she looked up at him her eyes were sparkling with laughter. But what she read in his smoothed the mirth into gravity.

"I can hear the laughter and the music," she said softly, her blue eyes dark as lapis as her gaze flickered across his face like a shadow. "I can see the light of many candles but I am on the outside in the darkness and the porter does not answer. The lord of the house has commanded him to keep the gate shut. Why is that, do you imagine?" Her lips parted, soft, giving.

For an instant Richard was taken aback. Eventually he would have found the right answer but the little witch's face crumpled into mischief and he could not tell whether for a fleeting instant she had been in earnest. His fingers imprisoned her chin and he found he could laugh with her.

"Delilah!" His hand drew her face near and he saw her swallow nervously. Perhaps tonight. There had to be somewhere in the castle he could lead her. Then suddenly the dreamy look snapped out of her eyes and she jerked her head back.

"I—I have to—your pardon."

Before he could detain her, she had scrambled free of the bench. Raw pain assailed him as he watched her hasten down the hall with white-knuckled hands grabbing her skirts as if a demon were after her.

She did not return and when he inquired after her the next day, the wench was indisposed. That it was the sudden onset of her monthly course, not his unacceptable company, which had caused her hurried exit was little balm. He disliked the way the other ladies firmed their ranks and barred him access to his wife. That and then having to be in constant attendance on his new father-in-law, ready to give careful answers on estimates of armor, crossbows, and biscuits had him seething like milk before a custard.

By the end of the week, he needed to quarrel with someone.

CHAPTER
16

"Ankarette has offered to take your duty for today so make ready," Richard Huddleston growled at Margery some four days later as he passed her on his way out of the Great Hall. "And pray, do not argue, I need a day free from loans, army provisions, maps, and maybes. I shall expect you at the stables as soon as you can."

It would be refreshing to be actually told that she was expected to ride, thought Margery. She assumed that was meant, unless he was planning to chase her through the hayloft for sentimental reasons. It would have been courteous to have asked if it was agreeable to her or even to have waited for an answer.

"A plague on him!" Margery swore through her clenched teeth and went off in search of Ankarette. "Did you have to agree?" she exclaimed wryly. "You know that spending the entire day in Huddleston's company thrills me to the very depth of my being!"

"Well," retorted Ankarette, "I should be delighted to spend a day in *my* husband's company and he is tedious and talks of nothing but milk cows."

Margery's sarcasm abdicated in favor of sincere remorse. She put an arm around her friend. "Your pardon, I should not complain."

"Oh, complain all you like if it helps but you really should make the best of things."

Suitably chastened, Margery exchanged her damask kirtle and thin leather slippers for her green riding gown and boots and sought her husband outside the stables. Long promptly materialized with three saddled horses but there was no sign of Richard Huddleston until the next quarter bell when he appeared with two dogs and a small cart in his wake. It was driven by a falconer accompanied by two youths. Behind them was a rail on which five hooded birds of prey perched, tethered and disgruntled like a row of magistrates on a bench before breakfast. The discordant bells on their legs mocked their pomposity.

Margery frowned at the cruel talons and sharp curved beaks but at least the birds would be chaperones. Everyone knew that men did not hunt women at the same time as they hunted game, otherwise she would have been tempted to leave Huddleston to ride with his ill humor for company.

Her husband looked ready to check any protest on her part, an eyebrow flexed to parry criticism. He raised a leather falconing gauntlet to the brim of his green hat in salute before he swung himself into his saddle. Long helped his mistress mount and followed after them at a respectful distance, attempting to chatter in loud, distorted French with the falconer who turned out to be a Scot.

Below the castle wall, the sloping town market square of sorts was untidy with laden barrows. It smelled like a great lord's kitchen, the yeasty aroma of fresh bread twisting in and out of the rich breath of roasting meat and beneath it all the stink of composting vegetables, rank meat, smoke, and human waste.

Richard drew his sword and merrily lanced a pear off a stall, tossing down payment. He presented it to his new wife. She unskewered the gift gingerly with polite thanks, her mind elsewhere.

"Why are there no stone buildings, do you think, sir? There is stone aplenty to be had."

They had reached the bridge. He set his hand upon her

reins, checking they were out of earshot. "A sensible question. Rumor has it that if a dauphin is born, the King will pull each dwelling around the castle asunder lest plague carry off the child. But there are some he cannot harm. You cannot see them from the castle walls but if you follow the road that runs south, you will find houses carved out of the cliffs. Such dwellings are common in this area and less costly."

"How? Like caves? You have seen them?"

"Not from the inside but I intend to."

"What freedom you have as a man," she sighed. "You can do what pleases you."

"It would please me to—" But he bit back his words, schooling his features into respectful gravity. "I can escort you if you wish. Give me a few days to arrange such matters."

It was excellent that she interested herself in such curiosities; it also gave him further opportunity to steal her away from her duties. There were other matters that deserved her attentiveness.

Across the bridge, beyond the peasant hovels, they finally smelled the blessing of the sweet summer air. Margery's soul, freed of the château, stretched invisibly in temporary delight beneath the cloudless hazy blue of the sky.

"The birds belong to the Lord of Concressault. I promised I would exercise them for him," her husband told her over his shoulder as he slackened pace. So things had changed, after all. For an instant, Comet's swishing black tail ahead of her palfrey had reminded her of the road to Exeter. "I will say this now, Margery, and have done. Next time you rush from my presence in such panic, I want reasons and I will not be banned from direct converse with my wife. If we were home in Millom . . ." He sighed as if he saw the crackle of rebellion beginning to smolder in her face. "I see you do not care for falconry but I need the sport after days of constant negotiating and I would think you need to fly just as much as the hawks."

With that, he touched his spurs to his stallion and the splendid harmony of equine sinew and muscle set a challenge to her palfrey. The wind billowed Margery's light summer cape and veil out behind her and drove the roses into her cheeks. When he slowed his horse to a trot, she was not far behind him and the grin he gave her warmed her unaccountably more than the sun.

He spent the morning putting the short-winged hawks through their paces with the falconer following on foot like a persistent peddler, a constant half pace from his spurs. The birds gripped grumpily onto a wooden frame that hung from the man's shoulders, fluttering furiously now and then to keep their balance. Long and the apprentices cheerfully ran hither and thither bagging the game. Despite the beauty of the morning, Richard was saddened; Error should have been there rolling in the grass and outpacing the other dogs.

Margery winced every time the birds made a kill and after two hours grew hungry and fractious. Huddleston had surprised her with a lady's hawking glove and taught how to hold her wrist but she had felt no rapport with the handsome goshawk. Her husband's businesslike tutoring brought her an exhilaration that the sport did not. To have him touch her without the usual battle of wills afforded her an unlooked-for pleasure.

"You do not approve?" Huddleston finally, to her relief, slipped the leather hood swiftly over the last, sated hawk's head before it could snipe his hand and set it back on the frame.

"I know how the small birds felt." Before she knew it, his gloves were about her waist and she was swung out of the saddle. Did he hear the rumbling in her belly? Had he instructed Long to bring food?

"Ah, we harp upon the same theme again, do we?" He dislodged a pebble with the point of his boot before fixing on her face. "Lady, face the realities of this world. If it had not been I who had tied your jesses to my glove, it would have been another. It is a wonder Warwick did not dispose of you in marriage sooner."

"He was hoping I would take the veil." She brushed away a persistent fly and was surprised when he pruned a switch from a sapling and proffered it to her like a rose.

"So why did you not? In time you could have become an abbess with land to administer, a multitude of servants, even, perhaps, a compliant young chaplain. Your passage through the local shire might have been a spectacle to behold—and you could have had books to your heart's content."

She waved the twigs like a fan. "And calluses on my knees."

"But a self-contained existence, a contract between you and the Almighty, a misericord eventually in Heaven." His irreverence had her laughing. "So why not, Margery?"

"I missed Bella and Anne and Ankarette. Besides, the contemplative life is too rigid, too disciplined. Every moment of the day was set out, whether it was weeding the Mother Abbess's herb garden or getting up at some unbelievably frosty hour to pray. Oh, it would have suited my lord to have presented one member of his family to God. Archbishop Neville—Jesu, he is my uncle, is he not?— spent three hours on my return to Warwick trying to persuade me to change my mind. It was such hypocrisy. I doubt if he even remembers what the inside of York cathedral looks like since he spent most of last year helping my lord bring the King to heel."

Huddleston was not in total agreement. "There are a lot of clergy like him. On the other hand, you need educated, intelligent men such as Archbishop Neville in positions where they can advise. We both know of noblemen who cannot order a pigsty. The only reason they can manage to stay where they are is because they were born to their positions and have well-trained commoners to keep them there."

"Like you."

"Like me. Life is very unfair. Why should the inept inherit? Are you hungry?"

"As a toothless wolf," she admitted, laughing. "Have you not noticed I have been casting covert glances at Matthew's saddlebags."

"I can see our travels in Devon have spoiled you. We shall be too late for dinner at the château. Let us return the birds to the mews and our trophies to the kitchens and then I shall introduce you to a most excellent cookshop."

"Cookshop!" exclaimed Margery in astonishment, her insides reviving at the thought.

He grinned, his hand steering her back to her palfrey. "Aye, unless you want us to trap the local salamanders. I can see that keeping you hungry is the answer. How many pastries would buy a promise from you to behave for the rest of the day?" He tossed her back onto the sidesaddle.

"I am not sure," she said thoughtfully. "How many can you afford?"

With fresh color in her cheeks, Margery looked far from famished by the time Richard finally bestowed her happily at a trestle inside the cookshop and slid onto the bench opposite. Her eyes were everywhere and he could tell she was enjoying herself. Other patrons were staring at her as though she wore her eyes at the end of two antennae but he was pleased she was too hungry to care.

They were alone at the end of a long trestle table that had been politely vacated for them by some deferential apprentices. The large room was hot and dark but surprisingly clean. The other tables were full. A party of merchants was conversing enthusiastically, happily drunk; an artisan and his wife were stolidly eating without conversation; a Franciscan was on his own in a corner; and two townsmen were doing business over sops in wine, arguing solemnly.

The serving wench ogled Richard as she took the order so he deliberately watched the wench's waggling rump retreat. In truth, Margery's pert bottom pleased him better but it did no harm to test her capacity for jealousy.

"I am sure she will accommodate you later," his new wife murmured. "Though is there not a danger of the pox or some such?"

He was mercifully saved from answering as a wooden platter of savory tarts descended between them. "These are good. I tried one yesterday. Careful that you do not burn your mouth." He could see she was so hungry that to wait further was torture. The stares continued and she was conscious of them now. The other end of the table was filling up with newcomers.

"Our neighbors are trying to calculate whether we are married to each other or conducting an *affaire du coeur*. They have decided on the former."

"You could fondle my hand," she suggested, laughing. "Would that reopen the speculation?"

"I do not feel like fondling anything of yours at the moment. I am too ravenous." He bit into the pastry. "Eat, eat!"

Margery eventually sat back replete with a tiny contented sigh. She met his grin.

"It pleased you?"

"It pleased me," she answered. "Thank you."

He reached into his pouch and laid out some French coins upon the board. Some he selected for payment, the rest he pushed toward her in husbandly fashion. "Here."

"For me?"

"Why not? The market is still open. Today is a special fair in Amboise."

Temptation fought her reluctance. "It is considerate of you but . . ." She nudged the coins back across the scrubbed wood.

"I am sure you can find some trinket to please you or do you still have plenty of your usurper's money?"

She shook her head. "Most of it went to paying our passage on the *Célérité.*"

"And you do not want to be in my debt, I suppose. How long is this squeamishness going to go on for? You are my responsibility whether you like it or not. Come, smile, and take the paltry sum, or do you want me to choose a trinket for you?" She curled her lip indecisively. "Very well, mistress, let us declare a truce still valid since we have managed to avoid quarreling up till now. You may sharpen your tongue on me again tomorrow."

She hesitated and then nodded. "A truce but only if you promise not to provoke me."

He held up his hands in surrender. "I am sure I can resist the temptation for a few hours more. What would please you—a ribbon, a ballad, a pair of tassels for your girdle? Come, the market awaits you!" He caught her hand and tugged her laughing to her feet, pleased that she stood beaming up at him.

"Since you ask, if I had a window of my own, I should buy a plant in a pot to give me flowers through the summer."

It seemed to Margery that he approved. His eyes narrowed, the kind creases there for her. She did not often see him look like that.

"One day," he answered, tucking her hand through his arm.

She had to admit it was rather pleasant to be squired through the fair. His male attentiveness, pointing out something amusing to her or steering her out of the way of carousers or around some freshly dropped dung, was a new experience for her. He showed her how to improve on throwing quoits over a stake, competed with her at the butts, and was surprised when she hit the bull's-eye better than he. They had their fortunes told by an outrageous coxcomb of a charlatan and resisted an ointment that cured impotency as well as sore breasts. Finally, as the sights and stalls palled, he bought her a sugar mouse.

She sucked its nose off on the road back up to the castle, her emotions tangled, her feet sore, and her face feeling overkissed by the sun. The breeze was gently warm against her skin and it was wonderful to know that there was a whole summer ahead.

"You will have no appetite for supper," he scolded.

"I do not mind." She stretched her arms out above her head, not caring that it was unbecoming behavior for a lady, just feeling comfortable and being herself. "It was a wonderful day. I do not know when I have . . ." Her words died.

She had caught him unawares, his gaze hungry upon the curve of her breasts above her gown. Her arms fell to her sides abruptly. It had been foolish of her to behave so.

Huddleston had the grace to look guilty. A visor thudded down hardening his features.

She halted on the cobbles, wondering whether to refuse to walk on with him. He had been lulling her into being easy with him, letting her fly like the Scots lord's hawks. He broke step and swung around, waiting for her, his green eyes regretful.

"Am I back on your wrist again, Richard?" she asked softly.

"Yes." He paused, seeking the right words as if to smooth the troubled waters between them. "Yes, just as I am back on your father's. We all have a living to earn, a duty to do." He glanced up at the steep walls, half turning from her as if to end the conversation.

Margery found herself desperate to find the chink in his armor, not to twist a cruel blade, but for once to touch the real man.

"I . . ." she faltered. He turned his head to look politely down at her. The emerald eyes glittered defensively. "I—I wish I could fathom you."

"I thought you had no desire to." His eyes were no longer hard but deep pools that could drown her at will. "My depths have no surprises but I can lend you a plumbline and tell you what to weight it with." The truth as always within cynical humor—the talons within the velvet glove.

"You promised me a truce," she reminded him sadly, walking on again. The dark shadow of the portcullis briefly chilled them.

He fell into step with her. "So I did." he said lightly as they reached the steps that led up to Isabella's apartments. "We shall eat at the same board tonight and I shall dance you to exhaustion." But the green glint of his gaze spoke differently, spoke of seduction as he bowed over her hand. "Until supper."

       ⌒☙⌒

"Are you each sick? There is no word of dissension in the air." Ankarette seated herself at supper on the other side of Margery and inspected Richard across from her. "You have both caught the sun and I hope your nose peels, Margery. Isabella has been an absolute shrew and the Duke has been out hunting with the young French lords."

"Shrewish because the Duke has not been near her all day, Mistress Twynhoe?" Huddleston felt bereft at his ignorance concerning women. "Times change."

"That's the right of it. He spent yesterday hunting for boar as well and last night carousing and she is angered that he is not spending any time with her father and his majesty. And he still has not apologized for last week because he is not supposed to know he has to. I wonder you did not see the hunting party today but perhaps they went in the opposite direction."

"*We* went in the opposite direction."

"You were not expected to attend him then, Master Huddleston? You do not enjoy the hunt?"

He shook his head. "I had hunting of my own."

"We flew the Scots lord's hawks," explained Margery

hastily but Ankarette's irrepressible dimples appeared as she looked from one to the other. Huddleston sensibly quelled further comment, brushing the crumbs from his jacket and dark green hose. "Excuse me, mesdames, I must catch the Lord of Concressault."

"I still say he has fine legs in that hose, better than my man." Ankarette glanced over her shoulder at him as he waylaid William Mennypenny. "Twynhoe has bulgy sort of calves. I am always telling him he looks better in a houppelande but he tries to ape the Burgundian fashions. At least he does not wear his tunic as indecently short as some youths and draw everyone's eyes too much to the codpiece." She had not forgotten the quarry of her conversation. "So, Margery, my curiosity is as rampant as a lion on a coat of arms. You found a haystack, did you?"

"No, Ankarette. His man was with us and the Scots lord's falconer as well as two boys to mind the cart. Why should you think that?"

"Because for an instant Huddleston had the look of a Robin Goodfellow, as if he had created a mischief in elvenland and taken great pleasure in it. So, I am wrong." Puzzlement twitched Ankarette's lips as Margery gravely shook her head. "How strange, I should have thought that was his plan."

"And you conspired in it, you traitoress. No, he never even suggested anything improper."

"Perhaps you should put a burr beneath his girth. Smile sweetly at some French gallant, make him jealous and see what follows."

"Ankarette, when we return to England I will petition King Edward to write to his Holiness and have this marriage annulled. Ned will do it too. He is in my debt."

"What foolishness. Anyway, how could you of all people prove anything? Besides, Huddleston will have you with child long before we see England again—oh, Master Huddleston!"

The icy inscrutability in his face as he faced Margery and the embarrassment in hers was obviously too much for Ankarette and with a mumbled excuse she fled back to the Duchess.

"I promised you a dance," he reminded Margery stiffly, with a curt bow of his head. She rose, offering him a polite curtsy in consolation. She could follow his example of pretending the conversation had never happened. It was safer. Besides, being sorry for his bruised feelings was a new emotion, like a brew she had never sipped. She let him lead her into the set. His glance was so cold every time they came together that her heart hurt—because the day had been precious. It was as if she had found something of value and lost it again through carelessness. But if the ground gained today could so easily be retaken, what value did it have?

They danced without words. Far, far easier just to dance. At length, when they were both hot and uncomfortable, he escorted her toward a window embrasure.

"Why did you marry me?" she asked passionately, speaking the instant they were reasonably out of eavesdropping distance.

He stopped, able to look her in the face but with a gaze more unreadable than ever. "Because I could not do otherwise." It was yet another example of his usual cryptic response to any direct questioning and she longed to crush the lapels of his figured satin jacket and shake the real answer out of him.

"Were you stung by a gadfly since dinner or which of us was it offended you?" she goaded. Was it her talk of annulment that had angered him or of fathering a child on her? All manner of reasons why he had made no attempt to lie with her flooded through her mind. Each one of them opened a floodgate of future sorrow.

"Let us leave it simply as yes, I was stung by a gadfly." He must have seen the hurt and frustration in her face for he added softly, "Life is not so simple, is it?"

She clasped and unclasped her hands, glancing nervously down at them before looking up at him again. He was waiting for her to make an end. "I—I want you to know that I enjoyed today, truly, and thank you for the mouse."

A reluctant smile twitched at the corners of his mouth though his eyes were still sad. "You have eaten it all?"

"Except for the tail," she confessed, lowering her eyes.

The soft laugh above her made her jerk her head up. The old gameplaying, resilient Huddleston was back—just. "Then if you still have it, I demand the tail as fee for my services today."

Margery gave a deep gurgle of laughter. It was a moment of unbridled merriment for them both, breaking the unholy tension. To his amazement, she pushed her fingers into her cleavage and drew out the string tail of the sugar mouse. He held out his hand.

"You are being ridiculous." She giggled and laid the string on his open palm. His fingers for a moment brushed hers as he closed his fingers over it. She bit her lip consideringly. "I think I had better go," she murmured, and with a bob of a curtsy she picked up her skirts to scurry away.

"Margery, I—" His other hand suddenly reached out, delaying her. "I enjoyed the fair very much also." Such an admission was gold indeed. "I heard what you said, Margery. All of it." Richard watched the smile die on her lips. "Rattle your chains all you like but I have you by the law and, by Christ's blessed mercy, I will keep you!"

CHAPTER
17

"**M**argery!"

Richard Huddleston waylaid her two days later as she left the chapel after mass. He managed a careful smile but the old uneasiness was there again between them and Margery was in a temper. The Countess had given her a severe sermon on marriage in front of Bella earlier that morning, using her obliquely to reprimand the Duchess.

To be truthful, Margery blamed the cannon for my lady's ill temper. The gunners had been practicing the previous afternoon and all morning. A copse behind the château had had its canopy dispatched and an ancient farmhouse had been bombarded to its foundations. The hens had stopped laying; the dovecots had all been vacated, a palfrey had reared, killing the young maid of honor who had been riding her, and the temper of the townsfolk was said to be fretted like a saw's edge. Consequently, the devotees of St. Barbara, the patron saint of gunners, were looking smug and the rest of the château irritable as misers asked to pay a poll tax.

"Sir, if you wish to argue with me, then pray go your way. My wits are frayed beyond today's mending."

Black-gloved hands barred her way. "Lady Anne tells me my lady has been unkind." He had certainly been ingratiating himself further.

She nodded like a nun in a hurry bestowing a blessing. "Yes. Now, pray excuse me, sir, Bella needs me." He made no attempt to step aside. "I assure you, sir, it really is no matter."

It was, of course. He was frowning as he studied her face. She swiftly sought to wheel the conversation down a safer, lanterned alleyway.

"How are the negotiations progressing?" She tried to sound cheerful.

"Your father and the King are like twins knit together at birth, while my lord Duke is entertained by his majesty's friends elsewhere."

Her interest was of an instant snared. "Yes, so it seems. Constantly, I would say. Has he had any discussion with them at all?"

"Barely." Sweet Heaven, what did it all mean? And she was no closer to fulfilling her mission for Ned. "In fact your father and his majesty are closeted privily today so I have leave. Would you like to visit one of the troglodyte homes?"

Perhaps Huddleston was just trying to be kind. On the other hand, he was unpredictable, just like the weather, and she did not feel strong enough to spend even an hour so dangerously. "Another day perhaps." She raised a flustered hand to her brow for extra emphasis. "I am sorry, sir, but I had rather be tranquil and bear my own company. Even now I should be with her grace and have tarried . . ."

He gently lifted her hand from her face. "It seems you do not care to flaunt your wedding ring."

Another time she would have tormented him but the criticism made her defensive. She was already so fragile that the weight of further words would make her weep again. "It—it is far too big. I am fearful of losing it and I *am* wearing it." She tugged at the golden chain that ended deep inside her bodice and eased the ring out of her cleavage.

Richard reached out to examine it. It was warm to his touch from the heat of her breasts. The intimacy ripened his resolve. She was emotional still, scarred from the Countess's scolding—more malleable.

"I thought as much. I have arranged with a goldsmith to have it altered for you this afternoon." She put up her fingers to lift the chain free of her neck but he imprisoned her hands. "No, keep it on. The merchant is expecting us within the hour. He will need to take a measurement of your ring finger."

"No." The pinkening of her tear-streaked face made her blue eyes dark, vulnerable. "Isabella asked me to fetch—"

"Forget your duty to your sisters. Besides, permission has been granted." He caught her little chin, forcing her to look up at him. "Do you not want the ring to fit?" He made his voice gentle, compassionate.

She lifted her face free of his fingers. The old Margery was stirring. So he had already decided how she should bestow her time, had he? The courteous asking had been merely froth. "Why the sudden concern, sir? You think that the appearance of your ring will render me holy and undefilable when you are not with me?"

Richard tried a smile that would strip away her armor. "Your needle is blunt, lady, but such jabs do not pain me." He took her hand. Halfway to his mouth, he turned it over so his lips met the center of her palm. Her Mount of Venus brushed his cheek. He would swear on Saints' bones that he felt her quiver. Now if he set an arm cautiously about her shoulders and turned her like the breeze gentle upon a weathervane, would she resist?

"You think you have my measure, Richard Huddleston, but you do not know the half of it." Did she realize they were halfway across the courtyard now?

"That can be remedied." He glanced down at her, grinning.

"Ha!"

He sighed. "So you still whistle to that tune. I thought you had learned to like me a little."

"There is more to marriage than liking. There is trust and sharing and children."

"Is that what you want?" He halted her.

"I wanted a fair choice." Looking up at him very firmly, Margery calmly removed his hand from her arm. "But no one, sir, has ever given me one."

"You had a choice a long time ago and you sacrificed your virtue because you were lured by a charming tongue, temporal power, and a shiny crown. I think you are very fortunate considering." He possessed himself of her hand before she could slap him, and tugged her after him.

"Did you know he offered me the position of mistress and a house in Chelsea?" she countered.

"Yes, he told me, and you refused the offer."

"He then offered me *you*, sir!"

Unperturbed, Richard tossed her a smile that had won him a woman's caresses on many an occasion. "Yes!"

They had reached the stables. Comet was saddled and dancing impatiently on the puddled ground. He lifted his head at his master's whistle, almost tugging the groom across to where they stood, and deliberately ignored Richard since Margery was opening her purse. She found a tiny sugar swan, rather bruised and covered in fluff. The eager black equine nose located the reward in the palm its master's lips had so recently enjoyed.

"You spoil him," Richard protested, jealous of the loving look she gave the beast and the fingers caressing the long forehead. They could be put to better use.

"Where is my palfrey?" She was frowning but obviously prepared to go with him. It had been easier than he had imagined.

"I thought it unfair to give the grooms extra work for so short a distance. Besides, you have forgotten you are not clothed for sidesaddle. Up with you, wife." His hands lightly touched her waist, lifted her away from the horse's head and easily onto the saddle before he swung himself up behind her.

"Is this to impress upon everyone that I am your property?" she muttered angrily. "Is Lady Warwick waving at us from a window?"

"Yes." He slid his arms around in front of her and jerked the reins. The wench felt right, comfortable between his arms albeit she was apprehensive. It would feel right waking up holding her too. "Be at ease, mistress. You do not have to give an impression of rigor mortis. They have all seen dead bodies before."

She let out her breath. "Richard, please stop quarreling with me."

"So what must I do to buy my line in your judgment

book, Margery? What do you want of me this day—a jeweled cross, a bracelet, a pearl brooch, a paternoster?"

"The truth," she whispered. Did she ever wish that their union could be deep-set in trust or was she still yearning for the King of England?

"Truth, my dear, is never perfect and I want to buy you something that is. Something of exquisite workmanship because you have never had a proper wedding gift of me." He shifted behind her, holding her protectively back against him, hoping she would soften against his body.

The guards in their blue and gold surcoats at the postern eyed them with amusement. The wench edged forward, her back proud and stiff. For an instant, Richard thought she might shame them both by casting herself off the horse and he readied his arms to imprison her, but once they were over the drawbridge, he felt the tension trickle out of her. The clean fresh scent of her filled his breathing and he could enjoy the joyous curve of the breasts, which he now owned, rising from the summer neckline. Perhaps the day might truly bring its reward.

"Look out!" Her hand grabbed the rein as a runaway piglet sped squealing across the road, chased by two raggedy children. He cursed and tried after that to keep his attention from her cleavage, but it was not easy.

He had found a goldsmith's shop in Amboise where the workmanship was excellent. Added to which, Monsieur Levallois had a vivacious second wife and a sultry daughter by her predecessor. And there were other coincidences that linked him to them but Richard did not bother to explain all this to Margery nor did he tell her he had already spent two hours with them earlier in the week lingering over wine and cakes.

They were expected. A stableboy was waiting to take his horse as they rode into the courtyard behind the main street. Before Richard could dismount, Jacques Levallois, followed by his wife and eldest child, strode out to welcome them. Adèle, his much younger wife, was Margery's age and so great with child that she could hardly curtsy to the daughter of the famous Earl of Warwick, but it was clear that Margery was flattered by her attempt. The girl Katherine's smile as she sank dutifully was selective.

Madame Levallois left them to her husband's selling ploys. As he ushered them into the downstairs workroom, their merchant host spoke swiftly to Margery in such a torrent of language that she looked as though she might drown in it. For her sake, Monsieur Levallois lightened his enthusiasm to a drizzle of words and a veritable thunderstorm of Gallic gestures. But what made her eyes go truly owlish was hearing Richard reply in French more fluent than her father's.

"I never realized you could speak French so well," she murmured as he led her across to watch a brawny apprentice, sweaty from the fire, beating gold into a setting for a cabochon ruby. Richard grinned and moved her on to where an older youth, at the end of his seven years of service by the look of him, sat chiseling facets on a topaz. Across from him, a mastersmith was setting an enameled scene of the Annunciation into agate. "I never told you about the master brewer's wife in Kendal or the recorder's daughter in Gloucester either."

"And . . ." she mimicked him.

"And my old nurse was from Rouen."

In the shop that opened onto the street, the air was cooler. Margery gravely handed over her ring and Levallois conducted her to a table covered in black baize, where an apprentice shook a row of simple silver rings off a tapering steel rod. The merchant gave her several to try for size. When he was happy with her selection, he led her to the inside counter to see his other wares.

Golden goblets, musk balls, chalices, and silver saltcellars glittered on high shelves around the shop, while at nose height, pinned upon a broad piece of scarlet felt behind the counter, rosaries of gold, lapis, crystal, coral, and chalcedony beads were roped between collars of pearls. A pendant cross framed with twined lopped branches of matted gold was fastened above, flanked on either side by two lozenged golden reliquaries depicting Christ's entry into Jerusalem and his Passion. Rows of *enseignes*, hat badges for travelers and the devout, made of gold or enameled with the lives of saints, hung on straps. Below, upon the counter, buckles, tassels, and bracelets were anchored to timber covered with velvet cloth.

Multi-drawered cabinets were now fetched to the board and unlocked ceremoniously for Margery's pleasure to reveal rows of rings lolling on ebony velvet. Smoke-blue sapphires to aid in childbirth, emeralds to ward off envy, unlucky opals hazy with hidden hues that took the breath away, and lodestars in all sizes, set into delicate twists of sinuous gold or couched in opulent rings.

"Perhaps Madame 'uddleston wishes something for her lovely throat?" Madame blushed and protested, sending Richard little covert glances from beneath her lashes. Without a doubt, his lady was dazzled and he was enjoying the fact.

Monsieur held up a succession of necklets against his daughter's throat. Katherine Levallois showed no embarrassment. Clearly, she was used to it. A clever ploy to sell women's jewelry to male customers.

Margery turned away. Such wealth and workmanship glittering around her was heady liquor for a poor woman's head, already reeling from unaccustomed flattery. Wonderment at finding herself with Richard Huddleston now when the day had begun so sourly filled her with amazement. What in the name of Heaven was she doing here? Letting the Devil buy her? These were not sugar mice before her now. His sincere enthusiasm for spending money on her was utter bribery and yet . . . She stole a thoughtful glance at him now as he jested with the merchant, at ease, articulate, so confident. He brushed a wing of lustrous hair behind his ear. The life force shone from him in the healthy pallor of his complexion, the laughing white teeth, his very strength. Jesu, sometimes is was possible to like him so much, possible to forget to fight. How was it that one could both like and hate a person to such extremes?

"Do you want a heart device set with diamonds, or there's this?" He held up a collar of three fine silver chains harnessed parallel and fingered the pendant rose as though its petals were soft and fragile. Margery shook her head. "Ah, here is beauty." Richard picked up a golden flower on a collar of two lustrous pearl strands, its center a circle of latticed gold, surrounded by an aureole of daisy petals. Standing behind his new wife, he held it hard against her throat, watching her face in the mirror that the merchant's nubile daughter held up for her.

Margery felt his breath clean upon her cheek. Sometimes— just sometimes—it was like . . . like being married. Like a marriage could be with someone who cared. The fleeting companionship fragmented as she saw the girl Katherine was tempting Richard—sending him an alluring glance one instant and then coyly veiling her large eyes with silky long black lashes the next. Margery tensed, uncomfortable. Was it all pretense on Huddleston's part, this wanting to choose a gem for her?

"No, concentrate, it's a marguerite," he commanded, his breath stirring the tendrils of hair escaping from her head-dress. "Look again! Enjoy what you see. We must be sure." The mirror showed a girl with roses in her cheeks, wide-eyed, and Richard's face behind her laughing at her confusion— behaving like a veritable lover.

Her breath came unevenly at his closeness.

"Do you not like it?" For an instant she doubted his sincerity, yet when her eyes flew back to the silver mirror, of a surety, genuine disappointment hovered in his face.

She moved forward, out of his touch and turned. "It pleases me well if it pleases you. But I am sure it is too expensive." Sweet Heaven, what was she saying? She was moon-mad, surely. To let him purchase this was to owe him. It was wrong and yet she could not bring herself to wipe the charm from that smiling mouth. He had not even noticed the French girl tucking her neckline lower.

"You may sell it if ever we become penniless. Let me fasten it properly so you may be sure it is comfortable."

There it was again—*we*—the word of unity with its implication of infinity. And his fingers, so gentle as they deftly fastened the collar about her throat. A woman's collar, despite the golden daisy the size of a rose noble that hung below it. Was this his way of demonstrating that he owned her despite her rebelliousness? First the ring that must be displayed, now this.

Unpredictably, contrarily, the thought warmed her woman's senses, uncoiling the serpent of lust within her.

"My wife shall have it. There!" One hand held her by the

shoulder and he thrust the hand mirror before her with his free hand. The gold looked well between her throat and bodice, lending her the appearance of a cosseted wife, an earl's daughter.

"It complements your wife's fair looks, if I may say so, Monsieur 'uddleston." The merchant bestowed a kiss upon the back of her hand. "*Alors*, madame, it will now delight my wife if you will go upstairs and partake of refreshment while your husband and I negotiate a price."

Margery's fingers flew to unfasten the clasp. "Sir, I beg you, keep this by you. The price may be too high."

Richard's eyes sparkled with charming mischief. "You may wear it for the nonce. If I cannot afford it, then I will come and fetch it back."

"You promise?" She looked up at him gravely and marveled at the amused tenderness in his face.

His long fingers brushed down her cheek and he nodded. "Go now, the girl is waiting to show you the way."

Katherine Levallois curtsied and gestured to the door.

Margery did not want to go up the stairs; she wanted to stay by this different Richard before his mood was blown like a pennant in a different direction.

On the next story, it was like entering another world. Furs and imported eastern coverings made the floor soft beneath Margery's fragile soles and an illuminated book was propped upon a wooden stand on a small table. Tiny diamond panes let in the sunlight from the casement and proud upon the walls were not painted arras cloths crudely daubed but tasseled tapestries in subtle hues depicting love.

Adèle Levallois left her cushioned window recess and a small lapdog rose indecisively from its basket, stretched, and waddled across to sniff at the beaks of Margery's shoes as she gazed at the tapestry.

"*Le Jardin d'Amour*." Adèle fondly stroked the chevalier who knocked upon the wicket gate, with his lover shyly tugging back at his hand, her eyes modestly lowered. "It was a marriage gift from my husband. Come, sit, we shall have hypocras and strawberries."

Although her French limped where Adèle's skipped and cavorted, Margery could grasp the gist of what she said. Although halting at first, her answers now became more sure as she happily fell under the spell of the woman's charm and hospitality. In return her hostess required gossip about the princesses, the fashions, Queen Charlotte, the expected dauphin, and the mighty rebel Englishman, *le comte Warwicque.*

It was after the city bells began to strike three that their husbands finally came up the stairs, discussing the greed of Lombard bankers, with Katherine following in their wake like a camp follower behind an army. There was a gray-haired man with them too. Adèle's father, Henri Badoux. It seemed he was also a merchant but an outsider who had come to the valley to trade.

A carafe of Touraine muscatel was sent for and Monsieur Levallois declared that they must toast the babe beneath his wife's girdle from glass goblets imported from Venice. The mother-to-be, blushing despite past pregnancies, beamed upon her guests as though they were a knight and lady magicked from some romance.

"I have a boon to ask, monsieur." She turned an irresistible smile upon Richard. "*Alors*, I want to show your wife my twins and then I wish us to play cards. We have a new set arrived from Paris. Perhaps another afternoon, Mistress 'uddleson shall visit me and we shall play picquet instead. You will translate, please."

Amusement twisted the edge of Richard's lips. "She wants you to admire her children and then play a hand of cards."

"She is so kind. May we do that?"

He swept a bow to Adèle. "We are at your command, madame."

She giggled. "*D'accord!* You will also come, Monsieur 'uddleson?"

He was too polite to correct her. "To please you, gracious lady, of course!"

The wet nurse, a girl of about eighteen years, rose to greet them. On each side of her stood a waist-high wooden cradle. The twins, no more than a twelve month, and out of swaddling bands, had wakened from their afternoon sleep and Adèle scooped up the girl-child and thrust her into Margery's hesitant arms.

She put the little girl against her shoulder where the child sucked her thumb thoughtfully at Richard. "She is heavy!"

"Your arms will grow stronger after your first child." Henri Badoux fondled the child's dark curls and lifted curious eyes to study Margery.

Richard watched his wife's cheeks flush pink. If they had only been home at Millom, she might have had a babe inside her by now. The thought of beginning the process must have showed in his eyes for she lowered hers with sweet embarrassment.

"Stop laughing at me," she whispered in English.

"Why should I when you provide me with such entertainment? Do you know anything at all about babes?"

"More than you, I wager. You want to hold her?"

"Why not, but I had rather hold you if you promise to behave."

He took the little girl gently into his arms and carried her to the window, whispering softly. The child responded with a delighted gurgle and reached up a chubby finger to his mouth. He turned his head challengingly to Margery only to catch her off guard, staring at him with an expression he could not fathom. "You think I would make a poor father?" Tiny fingers pulled at his hair.

She shook her head, swiftly drawing a smile over the sudden rawness as if it were a clean dressing.

Handing the child back, Richard sighed. Could Margery interpret the desire that must be burning in his eyes? She must know his patience was at an end. He wanted her vulnerable, confused, and so aroused that her surrender would be exquisite.

"You are most fortunate. Madame 'uddleston is a pretty and modest young woman," Levallois observed politely, after Henri Badoux had taken his leave.

Richard had returned downstairs with the two merchants to where Katherine was waiting, eyeing him slyly, her fingers stroking the frets of a lute.

"Modest?" Richard tasted the word like a new flavor. It was disturbing that what he took for artful coyness, others interpreted as modesty. Levallois, of course, did not know of her past. "I suppose, monsieur, that we all want our wives modest in company and forward in the bedchamber."

His host's eyebrows arched. "You have a bedchamber in the château? You are exceptionally fortunate."

"A bedchamber with Mistress Huddleston?" Richard's tone was wry. "No, I am unable to make my way to the garderobe without clambering over a half score of snoring knights, let alone extricating my wife from a chamber packed with a dozen sleeping women. It but wants the vow of silence and I could think myself in a monastery."

"*Malheureusement*, you suffer the penance for waiting on the mighty. But come, deny it if you will. Would you be elsewhere, young man? Is not the court of our King the heartbeat of Christendom?"

"It is, but sometimes I could wish myself a simple plowman."

Levallois chuckled and called for more wine. "This visit brings much pleasure to my wife. I should like you to stay this night with us."

Richard's loins grew taut at the possibilities. It took all his control to keep the rising excitement from his voice. "Stay? Now there's a thought. It is true we have no duties at the château, but I think we have prevailed sufficiently upon your hospitality."

The older man patted his shoulder. "Treat it as an act of selfishness upon my part because I have a young wife, a good sweet wife, whom I wish to please. We can play cards and sup together, then play again and forget the curfew. Besides, we always keep a bedchamber in readiness for guests. There is no extra travail on our part, I swear. Now tell me, does your wife play a fair hand?"

"I do not know."

Jacques clapped a hand on his shoulder. "*Eh bien*, we shall try her! Perhaps Adèle and I may conquer England, like William the Bastard, *hein*?"

Richard clinked his goblet against the older man's. "Monsieur, if it means this most excellent wine will flow in London's streets, I will personally pilot you up the Thames."

"We play cards, *oui*?" Adèle came jauntily into the chamber.

A cushioned settle, rearranged for summertime, had its back to the fireplace and here Adèle settled Margery beside her. Richard sat down opposite his wife on a cross-legged chair. He stroked the smooth planed wood, marveling at such luxury. His family had but one huge carved chair that

belonged to his father. He observed Jacques Levallois lower
his large body onto a matching chair. Surprisingly, it held.
Now if he could find an English joiner to imitate the design,
a simple x-form to balance the weight when they returned to
England . . .

"*Alors*, let us begin." Adèle gestured to her husband
to deal.

"Are we to revive *La Guerre de Cent Ans*?" Richard
asked but his eyes rested thoughtfully upon Margery, already
imagining how he would slowly slide the gown down over
her shoulders to reveal those taut, concealed breasts.

"I have often wondered about the Black Prince, Monsieur 'uddleston, I think perhaps this Englishman may have
been good at killing people but not so skilled in love. What
of his wife?"

Margery happily took on the challenge of answering. Her
French was intolerable but gently fortified by the wine, and
she decorated her language with English words and a multitude of understandable gestures. "His wife, the Countess of
Salisbury, was an extraordinary lady, so they say." Her
hands drew a curvaceous female figure in the air. "The
prince was her third husband. Her first husband was away
fighting so long"—Margery's fingers walked across the
table and then took up an imaginary sword at an invisible
opponent—"that she took a new younger man as husband."
She kissed her hand. "When her lord returned, she persuaded him to retain the other man as his chamberlain." She
held up three fingers and then made a gable roof of her fingers. "Did they understand that bit, sir? Perhaps you should
translate."

Richard was laughing so much that he could not answer.

Jacques wiped the tears from his eyes. "Perhaps the lady
was insatiable," he managed eventually, taking up the cards.

"*Can* you play?" Richard asked Margery, an eyebrow
raised.

"Because I spent six years in a nunnery? Which do you
doubt, sir—my skill or my enthusiasm?" Her lips drew
together coquettishly.

As his host dealt the pristine cards, fresh from their
leather wallet, Richard leaned forward, his arm flat upon the

cloth, his voice warm and compelling. "I hope you will demonstrate both, Mistress Huddleston."

Perversity sparkled back at him from the shining blue depths as she wriggled her shoulders into the cushions, no doubt feeling herself sufficiently chaperoned to flirt. "I do not know how well you play, sir."

"What are you two saying?" Adèle smacked Richard's wrist.

He leaned back, grinning at Margery, feeling like King Solomon, having just selected his concubine for the night's pleasure.

His wife was smiling, happy, safe. The war of wills between them was temporarily in abeyance, or was it? The little witch was constantly teasing him now with her glances, not overtly like young Katherine but subconsciously, raising her eyes to his when she played a card, like an artful courtesan to whom it was second nature.

The English began to win, congratulating each other silently with triumphant looks, sending each other messages to play high or low, creating an unspoken language where none had existed before.

That a summer storm had broken outside sending heavy rain splashing down heavily on the street cobbles beneath the gabled casement did not concern Margery, Richard observed, as he savored the aged Bordeaux. She was fast learning the French words needed for the game and enjoying herself. Did she realize yet he was going to caress her body into surrender? Oh, he would show her he had learned ways to make her arch with pleasure and plead with him to take her. Had the royal whoremonger made her cry out in ecstasy?

"We should take to the taverns, you and I," he murmured in English. "Are you as good at dice?"

"It requires no talent." She stretched like a wise woman's cat on a sunlit windowsill and then leaned forward, sliding the pack across to him. He enjoyed looking at his gift snug against her white slim throat. It was easy to slide his gaze now and again over the tantalizing gap between the necklet and the alluring valley below.

He repaid her temporary alliance with him plenteously with charm and courtesy so that she did not notice the hour bells tolling longer or that the apprentices had ceased shouting in the streets.

When the servants brought in supper, he discovered over the *anguilles* in red wine and the buttered *sandre* that there was a domestic quality about the occasion that he had been missing. It made him remember Millom. Margery might be used to large convents and great households but he recalled with a sense of loss the quiet winter evenings with his brothers before he was sent away to Lord Montague's household. There would be dogs twitching as they dreamed lying around the fire and his mother would summon their tutor to read aloud. There was always chess or . . .

The Levallois infants arrived to interrupt his reverie, looking like glossy, tiny angels, ready to be kissed and taken back to their cradles under Adèle's supervision.

Richard took his goblet to the window. The light was fading early. Soon the watch would be out, grumbling as they patrolled in the wet.

"Another game? You must give us a chance to retrieve our honor." The merchant slid his arm around his wife's waist on her return from ordering the nursery.

It was a mistake to turn his head and let his anticipation show as Margery looked to him to announce their departure. All her good humor and teasing confidence fled as if a spell was broken. She stared about her, at last aware of the long shadows dulling the chamber. He saw the rising anger in her suppressed and held.

"The curfew, we must go," she announced briskly at his shoulder.

"Not yet," he said softly in English, watching the water droplets chasing down the tiny diamond panes of costly glass. Margery ignored him and began thanking their hosts.

Richard was aware of the merchant moving across to take Margery's hand between his own. "My dear, this is too charming an evening to end so soon. It is decided you are to stay at our house tonight and then we can play some more. I swear we have not enjoyed ourselves so much for ages, have we, Adèle?"

Richard swung around. He curled back his lips and gave Margery the sort of dazzling smile that King David might have bestowed upon Bathsheba the morning after her bath.

Margery understood then the implications, knew that it had been anticipated, almost planned by the man standing opposite her but her smile could match his. She turned with a swift graciousness to her host. "Sir, you really are most kind but we cannot impose upon you further. I think my husband was unaware that I have to be back in attendance at the castle tonight." Her gaze at Richard Huddleston was level and adamant. "If you prefer to stay, Master Huddleston, perhaps Monsieur would arrange an escort for me."

Her heart was palpitating wildly. Richard Huddleston did not stir. The candlelight danced upon his hair and glinted on the chain across his shoulders but his eyes were dark. "It is too late. The drawbridge is already up." You should have thought of that, his gaze told her. This is the price of arousing me with your enticements.

She stood still, a superficial smile frozen upon her lips, watching as he strode across to the table and took up the pack of cards and held them out to her. "We stay." Then he spoke in slow French so that she would catch the gist. "The Duchess of Clarence may whip my shoulders with a kerchief tomorrow if she pleases. Your deal." Adèle giggled.

Margery's fingers crept up to the gold about her neck. Had he also bought the night's lodging when he had paid for her jewelry? She could not leave without him, without an escort—it would be rude, unseemly. And if the portcullis was already down, where could she go? She had nothing of value but the collar about her neck and that left her the target of thieves. Her throat would be cut before the dawn.

She took the cards and sat down, forcing herself to stay calm, but her fingers trembled as she dealt. He watched her like a cat waiting for a mouse to make its escape.

"The painted cards are beautiful, do you not think, Madame 'uddleson? *Moi*, I find the ones from wood blocks so grotesque." Adèle sent her husband a meaningful smile.

"They must have cost a great deal." Answering required strength. "The line is very fine. They are wearing the latest fashioned clothes too."

"Pah, the kings and varlets are mere pretty girls," snorted the merchant. "I will wager the painter was a sodomite."

"Monsieur!" reproved Adèle but the wine already had the better of her husband.

Richard set down the queen of diamonds. "This one is a beauty though, as fine and fair as any queen." His gaze warmly caressed his wife's face.

The lady on the court card was delicate, her gown looped daintily over her arm, and there was a pleased but startled expression on her lips as if some man she admired had paid her an unlooked-for compliment.

"Aye, I could bed her," murmured their host as he set down his card, "but I should not rely on the others to defend my purse in a dark alley."

Margery tried to concentrate. She knew she was playing badly. They began to lose.

"I think you did not mean to play that." Her host caught her fingers before the wrong card reached the cloth.

"You grow tired, my dear," Richard observed softly, brushing the fan of cards thoughtfully against his chin.

The warm timber of his voice and the desire in his eyes was stirring up such a turbulence inside her that Margery could feel a melting in the depth of her belly and a moistness growing between her thighs.

"*D'accord.* Let us make this the last game and we are quits."

Adèle rose as they finished, offering to stand in for Margery's maidservant, but Richard shook his head, merrily taking the candlestick.

"If I cannot help a woman off with her gown and garters, then I am no true man."

The guest room was in the adjoining wing of the house overlooking the courtyard and because the house was of new design, there was no need to pass through everyone else's bedchambers. Instead, the room led off a gallery that ran above the courtyard and promised privacy. The fragrance of rain moist upon the summer evening air barely refreshed Margery's senses. She was berating herself for drinking too much wine, for not noticing how the hours had crept away like thieves.

The chamber still held the fresh smell of whitewash but the perfume of flowers overhung the air. Creamy roses stood in a sinuous vase of curious eastern design upon the window ledge and a posy of newly gathered violets lay upon the pale green coverlet.

"I hope this pleases you." Adèle took the candle from Richard and set it upon a small table. The flame sent gentle shadows scampering across the pristine whitewashed ceiling into the dusky corners. Costly tapestries hung about the walls. The bed coverlet was turned back.

"It is a beautiful room." Richard stooped to bestow a kiss upon Adèle's cheek. "Your hospitality exceeds everything."

"Then, sleep well." Meant kindly but an empty blessing.

The door closed and they were alone. The house was silent about them save for the rainwater still dripping from the roof with the regularity of heartbeats, into the butts within the yard.

Margery moistened her lips and turned to face the man she could not purge from her life. The reckoning had come.

C H A P T E R
18

He stood with careless arrogance like a tournament hero, chin lifted proudly, lips stern but exultant as if he could hear the applause of the courtiers in the stands and the cheers of the populace, and Margery trembled, tormented, beneath his stare.

It had happened before, or rather it had not happened. Before, it had pleased him to be chivalrous but tonight was different and tonight she did not know her own mind.

"You knew this would happen." Her voice was husky, scarcely recognizable.

"Be thankful. It is better than an inn." He leaned back against the door, his eyes exploring the contours of her body like a hungry man confronted by a board laden with wondrous dishes. "I cannot wait for you any longer. This evening was agony, desiring you, knowing that within a few hours I would have you in my bed."

Strange sensations spread-eagled throughout her body as he peeled her clothing off her with his gaze.

"You promised me that you would be patient, that you would wait until—"

"—you wanted me."

"But I . . ." She felt hot and cold both in the same instant, as if she were on fire within yet glacial beneath the heat of his gaze.

"Still so diffident, Margery? Let me prove to you that for all your pretended protests I can light a fire in you this night that will keep us both warm."

It was a statement not a plea. To persuade him otherwise would have been as unwise as trying to muzzle a lion. She watched him unbuckle his belt. It fell with a metallic clang behind him. His pleated doublet was tossed aside, his burning eyes never leaving her face. He wanted nothing but surrender from her. She felt her breath turn ragged, her heart growing frantic within the cage of her body.

"Did I ever tell you how beautiful you are?"

"No, you forgot to put it on today's list."

Her hope of annulling the marriage was now out of the question—he would take her against her will if she refused. She had a choice: she could be cold and hate him or she could give in to the wild feelings that were pulsating through her and yield. His eyes were dilated with desire, his skin flushed with the intensity of his lust. Could she tell an incoming tide to turn? Her hand streaked to her sleeve, the silence split by the rasp of steel as she unsheathed her dagger.

His advance was checked. "Now that was something I did forget." Yet he took a step closer, close enough to touch. "Are you going to teach me a trick or two tonight?" His voice was light but sensual. She could feel the vitality, the heat, the determination that emanated from him and knew a curiosity and a longing that was as old as Eve's. "Are you?"

She rallied to the image she had created. "It requires half a pound of butter."

For an instant his jaw slackened, then he gave a shout of laughter and clapped his arms about her trembling body, heedless of the dagger. He could have twisted the knife from her fingers but he drew her in to his shoulder, his arms sliding protectively around her back.

"You are shaking, honeymouse." He held her tight against him.

She knew the hardness of him, awakened and ripening

against her belly; she felt the thud of his heart pulse against her shoulder. "Did you truly think to withstand me, Margery? I'd hunt you to the ends of the Earth." She could have stopped him then with the dagger, even a bodkin would have sufficed, but to stanch the mad longing to be held, to belong, to be touched, was no longer within her power. "By Christ, why have I let you torment me all these weeks?"

His words were breath on her face as he held her back from him and unpinned the cone and veil and tossed them aside. The honey hair fell and he plunged his hands into its silky mass. "You have been under my skin so long. To possess you has been a compulsion in me. God knows, I have tried to free myself from this slavery but, Jesu, you are so desirable." She would remember the words later but now she was a lute beneath his fingers to play on as he pleased.

For an instant his lips brushed hers tantalizingly and her lips parted wanting more. The dagger fell with a clatter and he laughed, drawing her toward him like a bowstring. Then his mouth came down on hers, gently at first, coaxing, persuasive, while his hands made circles, arcs, forays, reducing her body to seething bewildering sensations. She gave a low moan as his fingers sent messages through her that she had never experienced before, not even with Ned. Shyly, she slid her arms around his neck. "You want me to stop?"

Margery shook her head, knowing this was inevitable, had been so since he had seen her across the street and desired her. To be compliant at last was a relief. The cat and mouse game that had played havoc with her emotions was ending—even if it meant her surrender to the enemy. The aching in her body was growing.

"I want you willing." His voice was a low growl. "You agree? You *must* agree!" He trapped her face within the broken spire of his hands. "Look at me!" Her eyes fluttered open. The dark passion and unsheathed desire in his face made her weak with obedience. Her fingers flexed in his hair. "I am not being unreasonable?" She shook her head. "That indeed is a blessing for I fear my reason is fast deserting me."

"One thing." Her fingers stroked down his neck. Her lashes dropped like gauzy veils as she lowered her eyes.

"Six years . . . I . . ." She swallowed, hunting for the words that eluded her out of modesty.

"Lady." He lifter her face by the chin and brushed his mouth across her parted lips. "I will prise you open as sweetly as I would that oyster which conceals the most priceless pearl in the whole world. Believe me, I would not damage your pleasure in this for all the gold on Earth."

He unfastened her belt and threw it aside so that he might ease the skirts of her gown over her head. The half globes of her breasts dwelling sweetly within the silk underkirtle glimmered in the candlelight. He groaned. His mouth caressed her neck while his fingers slid the soft silk down over her shoulders and coaxed her nipples into the candlelight. "I have been dreaming of this for so long," he whispered against her throat. "If you only knew how much." He carried her across to the bed.

She lay, erotic as he had imagined, watching him pull off his boots and ease his arms out of shirtsleeves and the gipon. He had not felt so aroused in all his life. With one lithe movement, he pushed down gipon, shirt, and hose and stepped free. He stood for a moment marveling at her beauty, and that at last his dream would be fulfilled.

Margery's eyes were large as a cat's by night. She was lying so still that Richard dared not even guess her feelings. He needed her compliant but not dutiful, wanton but not lewd.

"We will not hurry this. I want you moist and open for me." He sat down upon the bed. He touched her hair and drew his long fingers down her cheeks and across her lips while he eased the undergown up above her thighs with his other hand, his pleasure audible. He rubbed the ball of his thumb across the peak of her left breast, watching her harden at his touch before he lifted her face to his and explored her mouth again. To ensure her body was a confusing, dizzying mass of sensations was paramount. He wanted her yearning and pleading for him to assuage her own lust. His left hand lifted the scalloped hem of her undergown even higher and slid upward, moving between her thighs to enjoy the center of her. She gave a low female growl as his fingers began their work. A door not used for years needed a slow unlocking.

Feeling her body swelling lusciously at his touch, ready-
ing for him, he rejoiced that she was not fighting him.
Another time he would tease her to anger with verbal thrusts
while his fingers tantalized her.

Margery's head went back and her body arched toward
him of its own volition. It had been too long. She knew now
how much she had been aching for his hand upon her.

Suddenly he was sitting back; his hands had left her. Her
eyes opened in astonishment, her body—hot for him—was
clamoring its loss.

"Were you like this for the King?" The shadow of Ned
fell between them as if his tall body stood like a colossus
astride the bed.

"Why now?" she asked, raising herself on her elbows,
brazenly studying the firm sleek body.

"Stand up, my sweet temptress. Remove your skirt."

Sulkily, sensuous, she rose languorously from the bed
and undid the laces at her waist. It fell in a billow at her
ankles, leaving her in gartered fine wool stockings and her
costly collar. Was this how a whore behaved? Surely virtuous wives were not expected to . . . He was making her
feel like a slavegirl, watching her from the bed like some
naked eastern potentate from a divan. What was she supposed to do now?

"Ever since I felt you between my thighs in that stable at
Warwick, I have planned your seduction. I have not forgiven the King of England for taking what was mine. And
you are mine!" He slid off the bed and stood before her as if
she were a spoil of war before a naked conqueror. His hand
slid between her thighs, his fingers searching out the nub of
her again, demanding, tormenting.

She caught at his wrist. "Damn you, my virginity was not
yours nor Ned's to take. It was mine own alone to—" His
mouth robbed her of further words as he pushed her imperiously down against the pillows and pushed her legs apart so
he might kneel between them.

"Your body tells me I can please you, Margery." She
writhed beneath his coaxing. Her thighs were purest fire, her
body arching as his fingers relentlessly drew her onward
until she was no longer in control and gasped in one fierce
shudder.

He thrust into her at last with exultation but she was tight, six years tight, albeit wet and willing. She tensed. He cursed and thrust again, entering her to the shaft and took care to move gently, sensing her tenderness. With another lover, he might have been more vigorous in his lovemaking, but this time he was competing with a king. He held off from his own relief, his caresses bringing her to climax again until she arched like a bow and cried out with womanly pleasure. It brought his own release and a sensation that was paradise.

Sated at last, he lifted himself onto his elbows and saw the tears, like mysterious pearls, upon her cheeks. "It has been a long time for you." He kissed them away. "It will be even more pleasurable next time."

"Too long," she whispered.

"I could stay entwined by your thighs and let the world go by."

"I pleased you?" she asked timidly, her fingers tucking back the lock of dark hair that was falling, hiding his face from the candlelight.

"Pleased me?" He carried her fingers to his lips. "How could you not please me?"

His eyes slid over the hills and valleys of her body in the light of the risen moon. All this was now his. The siege was over and the city lay open with its defense down at last.

Margery's body was still vibrating like a used bowstring, as if something within her was pulsating quietly back into place. If this man could change her like this, then his power was great indeed.

In the distance an owl hooted. "What is the matter?" he asked.

"You want my mind too, sir?" She turned wide eyes on him, no longer fearful to have his face so close.

"Oh, yes, I want that too but your soul I will leave to the Almighty. I am not yet grown so presumptuous."

"Are you not, Richard Huddleston?" she retorted dryly and received his wandering hand for her pains, teasing her appetite for more.

"Jesu, lady, you heat my blood as I knew you would. Let me still that errant tongue of yours."

Later she lay awake while he slept, his arm possessively

flung across her, knowing now that their marriage had entered different country. Could surrender be turned into conquest? Could the captor become enmeshed in the net too?

Once more before dawn, like a veritable bridegroom, he stirred and took his pleasure of her, driving her before him as hungry as he.

As the sun came through the glass, Huddleston stood up, stretching with a leopardlike grace. His body was sleek, his skin healthy and shining and the ripple of hair descending from his breast to his thigh would have pleased the most voracious of female appetites. Indeed, he looked as satisfied as a great cat that had killed and feasted.

"Rise up, sleepy one, let me see how beautiful you are in the light of day." She growled and turned over, hugging the sheet against her but he forced her to her feet.

"I do not want to go back to the castle," he groaned, winding his arms about her, burying his face in the tangle of her hair. Suddenly she felt him tense.

"By Christ! Margery!" He let go of her as if she had burned him.

"What is wrong?"

"Oh, by the Saints! *The sheet!*" His hands grabbed her elbows and shook her, his face contorted with disbelief. "Margery, you liar! You—" Words failed him for once and he let go of her roughly. "What have I done?" he exclaimed, turning away from her, his hands clapped to his head.

For once, it was she who had the reins of the situation. "You lay with your wife, Richard. You finally managed to lose that self-control of yours." She reached down and jerked her underskirt out from beneath the fallen coverlet. It was creased and she shook out its folds.

He swung around to face her, an Adam who had bitten of the apple and found he was barred from Paradise. "You lied! You lied to the whole world. Why for the love of Christ? Why did you let them do it to you?"

She stepped into the skirt and tied it at her waist. "Because no one at Warwick would listen to a bastard wench like me. You all thought you knew it all."

"Do not pack me in with the rest!"

"You were there, Richard. You did not come forward asking for the King's leftovers then." Listening to herself, she was astonished at how cool and controlled she sounded, whereas he for once was off guard. The visor was up and the chinks in his armor where a rondel of words might pierce were showing.

He turned away, running his hand through his hair. "I do not know what to say." He paced to the window and swung around on her. "But you were found with King Edward."

"Oh, yes, found, in a state of considerable undress, but we were unfortunately interrupted."

"But why did he not—"

"Tell the truth? Well, you see, no one actually asked him. My father demanded he leave and refused any explanation. I was not allowed to speak to him again." She found a comb in the purse on her belt under the debris of their clothing and began to draw it painfully through her tangled hair.

"But why did you live the lie ever since?"

"Because I enjoyed being the King's ex-mistress. It made me special. It kept all the wolves from my door—except, finally, you. You were persistent, driven by ambition. You wanted the King's mistress and Warwick's daughter. My past gave you an opportunity to feel gracious and generous. A respectable man bestowing his good name on an undeserving but well-connected wanton." She paused to examine a lock of hair that was resisting the comb. "You were so clever. There were several times when I almost gave myself away."

"The maiden and the unicorn."

"Anne was ten when I was sent away. She was the only one who questioned the lies, the only one who listened to what I had to say. I remember how everyone laughed at her folly at our wedding feast."

"No, I never laughed."

"Yes, that is true, and there was a moment when I thought you had guessed but then your vanity overrode your intelligence."

He reached for his shirt and held it to him. "You have a low opinion of me, it seems."

"No, Richard, I cannot admit to that. But does it grieve you that you were wrong, that you do not know all the answers anymore?"

He sat down on the bed and buried his head in his hands. "Why did you not trust me? If you had told me, I would—"

"You would have done the same. But I did enjoy it, Richard. Perhaps there is a harlot's blood in me. I am sorry I cannot tell you that you were better than the King of England." He groaned and shook his head but she persisted. "Comfort yourself with the fact that everyone still thinks your wife was the King's—pardon, *usurper's*—lover. Nothing has really changed. You have even married a virgin bride."

He thrust his arms angrily inside his shirtsleeves and stooped to snatch up the rest of his clothes. "You always said you hated me. You must loathe me even more now. Mayhap you shall have one of your wishes and I shall be a mangled corpse within the year." He pulled his clothes on swiftly, angrily, and when he had done, he stood and faced her, no longer bothered by her half nakedness. "Fear not, I shall trouble you no further." It was spoken with a curt bow. "I regret any hurt I have done you. That was never my intention. Here!" He snatched her wedding ring out of his purse and threw it down upon the bed.

"*Richard.*" She had gone too far in her hunger for revenge. Now that she wanted to throw her arms around him, his fierce look brooked no forgiveness.

He reached the door. "If I come through this campaign alive, we shall reach some settlement. No doubt the King will help you apply to Rome as you intended."

"But—"

"You never wanted me, did you, Margery? I have behaved like an infatuated boy throughout all this. Well, God be with you. From now on, I shall behave like a man." He opened the door and turned. "Long will come to escort you back to the castle since you cannot bear my company."

"Richard, no! It is not—" The door slammed in her face. "*Richard!*"

CHAPTER

19

It was one thing to have an angry husband but quite another to have a missing, angry husband. When Richard Huddleston did not appear in the Great Hall that evening for supper, Margery finally sent for Matthew.

"Master's not here, mistress." Long gave her his best gap-toothed grin as he stood looking down at her, his great hands fumbling with his felt hat. "Came back this morning as angry as a buck hare that's had its burrow blocked and I told him my lord of Warwick wished to see him."

"About what matter, Matthew?"

Long scratched his head. "Lord, mistress, I am cursed if I know, some news from England I reckon, but the master came out looking like a condemned man and he's taken himself off on Comet. Wouldn't hear of me going with him neither."

"Do you know where he went? Surely not back to the coast?"

"Nay, he said naught about that but for sure he'll ride for hours. Always does when he's in a pother. Did it at

Southampton. Nay, do not frown, mistress. He will survive. Always does. Has a good head for drinking, my master does."

The pangs of guilt that had begun to haunt her were exorcised instantly. "You think he has gone drinking?"

"Mistress, if he has, he could be in any tavern between here and Caen." The big servant's eyes grew serious with concern. "Is it urgent? I wouldn't wager on my chance of finding him."

"No, he may drink himself to perdition but make sure you tell me when he returns, *if* he returns and I hope he does not!"

He looked relieved. "Like that, is it, mistress?" He touched his forehead respectfully and ambled off.

"Take that silly grin off your face, Long!" she exclaimed and he turned and saluted her good-humoredly.

It was just before curfew when he discreetly reappeared at her side in the hall and, tucking his dull corn hair back behind one ear, he bent and whispered, "Mistress, he is back and in none too sweet a temper from the look of him."

"Has he been drinking?" Margery rose.

"I wouldn't swear to it, mistress, but he needs a shave. If he's been to Hell, the Devil's let him back out to annoy the rest of us."

"Take me to him."

"Nay, mistress, it were best you leave him until morning. He is not to be meddled with, if you want my opinion, but I suppose you don't."

"No, I do not. Make haste, if you please."

Richard Huddleston was on his way from the stables, a saddlebag flung over his shoulder. He was still in his brocade doublet but his black hose and boot caps were thick with dust. He noticed them waiting like petitioners, but with a raised brow he walked straight past. There was a haggard, haunted look about his eyes and mouth, like the face of a courier who had ridden posthaste for three days.

This was not quite how she had imagined matters, thought Margery, picking up her skirts and hurrying after him; what she had intended was a qualified apology but now . . . Matthew read her expression behind his master's back and shrugged sheepishly. She gestured and he nobly hastened his pace.

"Thank the lord, sir. I thought—"

Richard whirled around on his servant, as if he were about to throttle him and Matthew flung up his arms and glanced sideways anxiously at Margery. "We—we thought. . ." His Adam's apple betrayed him as he swallowed nervously. Margery shared his discomfort for Richard Huddleston looked as though he had been chased by a gadfly across the breadth of France.

". . . that you were howling drunk between some tavern wench's thighs," Matthew offered tactlessly, cautiously lowering his arms.

"As was my right," snapped Huddleston, but his attention was now centering on Margery. "So, lady, I wonder you confront me after your insults this morning."

"I thought you might have left for Honfleur, I . . ."

"Go on."

"Stop glaring at me like that. I cannot think."

"The truth at last!" He hissed and started striding toward the Great Hall again. "Between the pair of you, you might manage some intelligence the size of a walnut."

"Richard—" They hurried after him. "You are behaving as though we had caught you in some hayloft. Were you?"

"After pleasuring you all night?" he snarled over his shoulder.

"I think I should wait elsewhere." Matthew laid a warning hand upon Margery's sleeve.

Richard stopped and swung around again. "Yes, perhaps you should, Long."

Matthew was being sweetly heroic. "We were worried, sir, that you were not yourself. The Lord knows, the thought entered our heads that you might drink yourself into a stupor and be set upon, robbed and—" Matthew must have read the dangerous look in his master's eyes for, with an apologetic glance at Margery, he shut his mouth with a snap.

Huddleston took hold of her forearm and dragged her on a few more paces out of his servant's earshot. He paused at the bottom of the flight of stairs that led to the upper yard.

Behind him the dying sun was lighting up the craggy wall of
the lower yard. It threw his shadow into menacing propor-
tions. "I am my own master, lady! I do not belong to you or
to your father or to the King of France."

"Yes, you do." Margery stamped her foot. "*You are my
husband*, damn you!"

As the green gaze slid away from her face and rolled up
toward the graying sky, he appeared as fiendish as Lucifer
looking back to Heaven. "Oh, by Christ's blessed mercy,
the lady has last admitted the truth." Margery tried to pull
away from him, knuckling the tears from her eyes with her
free hand, but his fingers were still around her arm. He
inspected her streaked cheeks without compassion. "What I
say, where I go, and what I do are not your affair so if
I choose to tumble any dirty tavern slut I can find in the
town sewer and then lie with you, that is my decision, you
hear me?"

Margery shook herself free. "No, I do not hear you, you
upstart! Go and sharpen your tongue on my father's spurs!"

His face paled white with anger. Iron fingers tightened
like screws upon her arm.

"Did I tell you the King of France has asked me to
agree—for a very princely sum—that you should lie with
the Duke of Clarence from this week on to learn his mind?"
He shook her away from him.

Margery's jaw slackened, her anger blown away by the
revelation. Was he in earnest? His manner was so icy, she
could not tell. She drew herself up as grandly as the Countess.
"I hope you told him I am not a courtesan."

A stare that held riddles scythed her. Above folded arms,
he sneered at her. "Are you not? You take your clothes off
for kings and diplomats so why not dukes? By Christ's
blessed body, you little fool! Did I not warn you to be
careful?"

Margery decided it was safer for her peace of mind not to
believe him. He was playing games with her again. Setting a
bait and letting her run to it.

"Ha!" she scoffed. "Next thing they will want me sneak-
ing back to Ned to be his mistress and learn *his* mind."

Indifferently, Richard gazed above her head. "That was
aired."

She curled her lower lip down in fury, her tone smeared with venom. "So, how much did they offer you, dear Judas? More than the price of a jeweled collar, I trust."

"Offer *us*, my dearest wife." His grin would have made snakes look friendly. "Enough to make us wealthy if we live that long."

"Dear Jesu, you are hateful! What did you say to them?"

"I raised the price."

Her fist came flying through the air. He parried the strike and twisted her hands behind her back with such swiftness that she was breast to breast with him. It would have been a comfort to scream how much she hated him but the whole château would have heard her.

His smile tormented her. The green eyes piercing down into the depths of hers told her that last night's intimacy had not touched his heart, that he had given and taken bodily sensations and that was all. He had been her husband but not her lover. Now to be held so close to him without love was torture and he knew it. He must be feeling her quivering against his loins.

She dragged her eyes away from his face and heard that calm voice, soft and ironic, above her head. "Enough of this folly. Learn from your mistakes, dearest."

"Let me go!" She struggled, only to be aware that her body was reacting to his closeness, yearning for more.

"Are you referring to our marriage or to this present circumstance? I wonder. Unfortunately, I have inadvertently destroyed the one thing that could have enabled me by law to let you go. Besides, you may be carrying my son and heir within your womb so you will behave honorably, will you not, and stay away from the Duke. I want no probing from the King of France." He let her go. She rubbed her wrists and eyed him sullenly.

"Then you were lying just then."

"Was I? The King has more eyes in this castle than a peacock's tail." He raised a hand. "As God is my witness, it was known that I had quarreled with you even as I arrived back here this morning. We are watched, you and I."

Cold fear streaked a jagged path down Margery's spine. "Because of de Commynes."

"Your Burgundian? Perhaps. Who knows how the

twisting minds of the mighty work? His most Christian
Majesty would suspect a flea of treason if it jumped too
high."

The strain in his face convinced her that somewhere in
this ugly conversation was a terrible truth. "You are merely
saying all this to frighten me." She was trying to rationalize,
to brush her fears into a smooth fabric.

An eyebrow arched at her. "Your grasp of matters is
astounding. From fear comes caution if we are blessed."

Tilting her head, she examined him. Not a muscle
of understanding moved beneath her scrutiny. It was like
examining a painting, fixed and merely two-dimensional,
reflecting her own interpretation back at her.

"Jesu, sir, I came to mend matters but it seems you hate
me as much as I detest you." It was a pinprick but it seemed
to draw blood.

He moved, half turning as if wearied by her company.
"No, you inconvenience me. You, lady, are the fount of all
my problems. You and yours. I would I had never set eyes
on you again. No sane man would have behaved as foolishly
as I did. I have become your fool and I will have no more of
it, you hear me!" He glared irritably across the courtyard
beyond her, and sighed impatiently. "How shall I put it? To
be frank, your presence destroys my peace. Since I obviously
destroy yours, I think it best that we avoid each other." It was
as though he could no longer bear to look at her.

It would have been simple if she hated him but she was
past that.

"The game is finished, is that it? Now that you have what
you wanted, the excitement of the hunt is over. And, of
course, now you have acquired the trust of my mighty
father. Well, climb as high as you dare but you are still what
you are. You have disappointed me, sir. For without question, you were correct this morning—you are still a boy and
lack a man's courage. Your peevishness makes the Duke of
Clarence in comparison a saint. Marriage is not merely the
carnality of the bridal night, it is a future—one that we certainly shall not share!" She drew breath but could think of
no more words to vent the depth of her feeling. With an
angry swish of her skirts, she ran up the stairs and away
before he could see further tears betray her.

Richard reeled back against the wall, flinging up a hand to mask the top half of his face. His head hurt and tiredness sucked at him through every pore. And, as if an unfair hand had hurled sand into his face, grittiness scratched his eyes as he squeezed his eyelids closed to stanch the gathering moisture.

"Master, come." Matthew's arm came about him and he surrendered to exhaustion.

Margery leaned her shoulder against the unsympathetic stone, her listless eyes staring at the sky. When they had sent her to the nunnery in disgrace, it had hurt her but it was nothing to this, this hollowness as though God had scraped all joy out of her and replaced it with misery. No, not just misery, hunger. She wanted Huddleston desperately in the same way he had wanted her. She wanted him in her bed needing her. If he was now trying to teach her a lesson or exacting revenge, it was in full measure. The decision she made then was not out of vengeance but to set them both free.

She was as fixed as the Pole Star in her resolve next morning as she made her way to King Louis's audience chamber. There was already a queue of petitioners outside. They must have scrambled in at dawn, as ravenous as a crowd of beggars around an overturned provision cart.

Merchants, clad in finery above their station, despite the sumptuary laws, queued beside lawyers in striped gowns. Plentiful, too, were rich and poor widows with faces ranging from plump to puckered within their coifs. The fetid odor of the ragged poor hung among the wafts of musk and ambergris from the overscented.

Margery took her place and more petitioners poured in to fidget behind her. It might take all day. She had told Alys to come to her to hold her place in the line while she went to mass. That was at least two hours away. If she managed to see the King that day, it would be fortunate because it was not just the other people ahead of her who had precedence but noblemen and courtiers who had business with Louis

and were assured of entry. After more than an hour, she
grew anxious that her father might espy her there. Besides,
the man behind her kept edging uncomfortably close and
the woman before her was a babbler with a French dialect
that Margery could hardly follow.

"Mistress Huddleston?" A Scots accent warmed her ears
and she peeped upward into the blue eyes and freckled
smile of the Lord of Concressault. "Nay, lass, forget the
curtsy. What are you doing here?"

"The same as everyone else, my lord," she replied with a
wry smile.

"Does your father know you are here, lass? There are
other ways to pluck a chicken."

"I do not want him to know." She watched the Scot push
the brim of his beaver hat back and scratch at his retreating
sandy hair.

"Och, you had better come in with me. You dinna want
to be idling here all day."

She could have hugged him; instead she clasped his hand
with both of hers. "My lord, may I? That would be wondrous kind."

"Aye, lass. It is that I am a mighty curious fellow. You
will own that I have to hear what you say if I take you in?"

"I—no, what of it? I accept your kindness."

Now there was no going back but, Heaven help her, there
seemed to be only one way out.

William, Lord of Concressault, beckoned Richard across
the steps as they passed one another. "I am going across to
the mews, laddie. Care to join me if the Earl has no need of
you?"

"As always, my lord, I am at your service." He answered
cheerfully, hiding the emotions that were tearing at his con-
sciousness like carrion after a slaying. By Christ's blessed
mercy, it would be a distraction to talk of falcons, to stop
desiring and hating Margery at the same time. His body
yearned to have her encompassing him, soft and yielding; his
mind warned him to avoid her until his anger had cooled. The
normality of trivial conversation was an ointment on his hurts
as he strode along the muddied path with the Scots lord.

Like the kennels, the French King's mews smelled little. The privileged predators sat proud as bishops, each upon its perch. The royal falconers had boys to regularly change the rushes that collected the droppings.

They stopped to inspect two of the King's birds before they came to those that Richard had taken out on the happy excursion he had shared with Margery.

"And how fares the little bride?" asked Lord William, running the side of his forefinger cautiously down the back of the touchy hawk. A mews servant waited at his elbow with a selection of dead mice.

"Assertive, contrary, as fractious as any new wife, no doubt."

The blue eyes twinkled knowingly. "Leads you a dance?" Gloved fingers hovered and then selected a furry corpse.

"The news is old, my lord." Richard watched, ensnared, as the mouse was swung by its tail across to the cruel hooked beak. Another mouse was selected for the neighboring bird and the servant withdrew.

The older man studied Richard's face from the other side of the predator. "King Louis is not within her league, laddie."

Hiding his surprise was almost beyond him. Richard's eyes stared unseeing at the cruel eyes of the hawk as it ripped at the dangled carcass. "Would you care to explain, my lord?"

"Och, it is none of my business, lad. I dinna mean to poke my spoke into the wheels of your cart but—"

"My lord, are you saying my wife has spoken with the King?" His voice was matter-of-fact.

"Aye, she has that, and offered to go to England when our negotiations are finalized to become King Edward's bedfellow. But I expect you know that." It was a probe.

To swear aloud or hurl the hawk from its perch would hardly have assuaged Richard's inward anger. He swiftly chose not to react. "It is important her father's enterprise should succeed," he answered carefully.

"Then that is a relief. I dinna ken all that is going on around Amboise but I like to keep my finger on the pulse, so to speak, but if you have a hand in the matter, then I will say no more."

"It could be dangerous. I appreciate your concern, my lord."

"Nay, the English King is soft. He willna harm her, but—"

"I should prefer not to talk about it further, my lord. Wars are not fought with plumes. We all serve where we can." Whores are not married except by fools.

"Aye, I hear your two younger brothers have arrived in Bayeux."

Richard forced himself not to stiffen. His displeasure at their leaving England was still raw and painful.

"Did Lord Montague send them, or are they here under their own canvas?"

"I have not been informed but certainly Lord Montague must be wondering how his brother Warwick is faring."

"Aye, no doubt, usually where there's treason in one brother, a canny king may smell it in the rest."

"As you say, my lord, perhaps my brothers felt it prudent to leave England." The fools, the cursed fools! He had enough trouble with his rebellious little wife, without two younger brothers now panting to be rebels, and he would not be here playing the spy if it were not for her! A pox on his stupidity!

∞

He found Margery at tennez with Lady Anne and two of Queen Charlotte's maids of honor. How could she be enjoying herself when he felt angry and bereft?

"And how is Master Huddleston?" Ankarette, her eyes brimming with mischievous curiosity, linked her arm uninvited into his.

"Desirous of slapping his beloved's rump. Will that suffice, Mistress Twynhoe?"

"See, I told you." She grinned, too close for his liking, waggling her free forefinger at him. "Young Margery needs a firm hand. Had too much of her own way for one of her status and that is not good for marriage."

"Fetch her for me, if you would be so kind. Perhaps you may stand in for her."

Ankarette withdrew from him reluctantly. "You are out of luck there but I will do the office for you. Little good it may earn you, for you are not in her good books, I can tell you."

If Margery had seen him, she might not have stopped so willingly, but the instant Ankarette spoke, he watched his wife tense. She turned her head, chewing her lip. There were cries of female disapproval as she excused herself and came across to him, the wide tail of her gown over one arm, the front of her skirt gathered in her hand. Color shone in her cheeks from her exertion. By St. Richard, she was pretty! If only he had been able to trust her.

"You have been collecting feathers, I see." Sweet as marchpane laced with poison. "I have been expecting you."

He ignored the light service of humor. "Have you now? What exactly are you expecting—a surfeit of apologies? Am I to muddy my knees craving your forgiveness—one or both?" He plucked a feather from his hose. "I have been at the mews with my Lord of Concressault." He watched her gaze rise from inspecting his knees slowly to arrive at his face. Her misapprehension was evident.

"You know, do you not?"

"Oh, yes, Margery, I know." Her eyes were bright, a defiant, maddeningly beautiful blue. "Come." He held out his hand, palm up. It was almost trusting the way she laid her fingers on his. His own snapped down, and held hers fast.

"Where are we going?" It pleased him that she almost had to run to keep up with his pace and it was balm to his pride to shrug at her and keep striding.

Barking buffeted and bruised his hearing the moment they entered, for the kennel was the one place in Amboise where he could shout at her without the whole world hearing. He bribed the two kennelboys on duty to wait outside and bowed, gesturing her to lead the way to Error.

Margery ignored his insolent civility. Putting her hands to her ears, she ran across to the noisy hound, exclaiming, "Error, come lad!"

It was insane, thought Richard to be jealous of a dog that he no longer owned. Error was springing about madly on his short leash, woofing fit to burst until the instant Margery bent down and wrapped her arms about his neck, allowing the dog's pink tongue to exercise itself on her cap and veil.

"Leave that!" snarled Richard, grabbing her elbow with one hand and hauling her to her feet. "Now you will explain yourself!"

"No!" She wiggled her shoulders rebelliously. He had difficulty hearing her, even though she was shouting above the din. "And do pat him, he is waiting."

It was a foolish idea to bring her in here. "So am I, damn you! And it is my dog, remember!" But he could not resist curling his free hand around the back of the hound's head and scratching him behind the ear, which was one of Error's greatest pleasures.

"Was!" she corrected loudly.

Richard raised his head, hoping he looked arrogant. And he is still mine, he swore inwardly, and so are you, mistress!

"*Was* my dog but you are still my wife and we will remain here until you apologize. How dare you offer yourself when you are *my* wife!" She was pulling like fury, her teeth clenched. It was necessary to coil his other arm about her and yank her to him. His mouth came down on hers with a control that surprised him. What undermined him even more was that her lips, after token resistance, parted beneath his and let him through. She was trembling within his hands, out of control. He wanted to raise her skirts and sink himself into her, show her who was master. Instead he held her by the forearms and set her back from him, his breath as uneven as his temper. "You will not gull me that way," he insisted firmly.

She slapped his hands away and thrust her fists upon her hips. "You demon! You want everything but give nothing back. How could you walk away from me when you had pleasured yourself all night?"

"So this was the perfect revenge, was it, my mistress? To spin the wheel of destiny full circle, to do something that would stick in my maw to the utmost, to go to your beloved Ned once more and even be paid royally for it?" He could have shouted "whore" at her but his bitter words already seemed to sting her as much.

"No more than your own idea, Master Huddleston. You said you had raised the price for my services; well, it is now too high for you!"

He could have slapped that pert adorable face but the

folly of his own words whipped back like a tiltyard quoit to lash him instead. He stood for a moment letting the emotions chase across his face before the fury drained out of him and his shoulders fell. "Oh, God save us, Margery, you stupid little fool!"

Margery's lips parted. She looked around the room, at the floor, at the beams, and then back at him. "Do not tell me . . . But . . . Upon your soul, did you *lie*?"

Only two dogs were barking now. Error was whining, straining on the chain to reach them. As if she could not bear to meet Richard's face, Margery moved back to the animal and held the dog against her skirts as she confronted him. It was outnumbering and hurtful, as if he had lost them both. Were tears gathering in the corners of her eyes? She tugged her cross and chain over her head with difficulty, cursing as she caught it on her veil, and thrust it out at him. "Upon this, swear!"

He felt as though he were stone, nay, numb from the ice of winter. She thrust the cross at him again as though she were fending off the Prince of Darkness.

"Answer me, Richard Huddleston!"

He took the silver in his hand. "I exaggerated." His lower jaw almost trembled. She cold not look at him now, her anguished gaze was on the crossbeams. Why was it this knot of flesh and bones, this female fiend who had the body of a siren, could torture him so? Why was she making him defensive when it was she who had erred?

"Margery, by Christ's blessed mercy, you caught me on the raw last even. You should have heeded Matthew Long when he warned you. Can you not tell when a man is tired beyond reason?"

"Ha! I have not had the practice of knowing when a man is tired beyond reason. I was a virgin until the other night, was I not? Or," she warmed to the argument, "am I to be accused of smearing chicken blood upon the sheets to deceive you? You have accused me of everything else since you abducted me."

A polite canine cough echoed at the other end of the kennel. The dogs were listening attentively and the kennel-boys would be back within an instant.

"We will speak of this further, madam." Richard made a

sortie toward the double doors and halted a few paces away, swinging around on her. "I should have expected that you would seek some excuse to return to your King's bed."

Her shoulders were back, her head proud. "Why not when you do not want me in yours?" Richard surveyed her, deliberately letting her feel some heat from his gaze. The truth was obvious. Why could she not read him yet, know when he was in earnest?

"I never said that. Of course I want you in my bed."

The door ring rattled; the kennelboys were warning of their return.

"You want me, sir?" Margery's voice was cool, disbelieving.

"I can no longer remember a time when I did not want you. You are my plague, Margery, my cross. I do not know what destiny or unkind hand cursed me with such desire but cursed I am. You should have trusted me, lady." He stepped back from her before he was tempted to fasten his arms about her.

Seeing his hesitation, she turned away, cradling her shoulders as if she shivered with an ague. She met his gaze across her shoulder, tears sparkling on her cheeks. On the other side of the courtyard and from the town came the tolling of the hour bells. "Well, there is no going back, sir." Her voice shook. "You begat this strategy."

He understood. Somehow he pitied her. The yearning and the heat that he felt now burned as brightly in her face. To touch her was to ignite a fire that would burn them both.

His face was inscrutable; his soul was in torment.

"Yes, my fault. I thought I had taught you to forget the married king who did not give a damn if he took your maidenhead. But, no, I can see you still burn candles for him. Well, your heart may be his but your body is mine. I can ripen you to passion anytime I choose. However, I will respect your wishes. We had best avoid each other as much as possible from now on. I accompany my lords and King Louis to Tours tomorrow."

Margery swayed but kept her balance. "Well, excellent, sir! That will please me very well!"

The illustrious lords' departure for Tours was delayed by several days of thanksgiving and rejoicing following the birth of the longed-for Dauphin. Only the townsfolk were grudging in their celebrations. Their royal master had given orders that no more dwellings were to be permitted, confirming the gossip that he had plans to divert trade to Tours to prevent visitations of the plague threatening his precious heir.

It was also rumored before the lords set out upriver that the King was writing to the Bitch of Anjou offering her son, Edouard of Lancaster, the prestigious office of godfather to the child.

Such calculated flattery achieved its goal, as Margery discovered two days later, when George of Clarence arrived back from Tours without the Earl and stormed into the Countess of Warwick's antechamber. His face, red and perspiring, looked ugly against his gilt velvet hat and he was heavy with the odor of sweat and horses. Normally he was fastidious in his person except when his breath was soused with wine, so this unusual appearance was sufficient to

make Margery clumsily drop the little wooden bishop she
was about to move. Anne retrieved it from the rushes,
handing it back to her with a questioning glance.

"Your grace," snapped the Countess disdainfully, not
even bothering to look up from her tapestry frame, "you
might at least have shown some delicacy by changing your
apparel first."

Isabella had sprung to her feet, her countenance pale.
"Hush, Mother! Something has happened. A riding accident? Is Father safe?"

The Duke unclipped his riding cloak, bestowing road
dust like largesse upon his mother-in-law. "Oh, no accident!
He is on his way back here now." They were used to his
flippancy but there was an understatement in his voice, an
unlooked-for control that told them he was really angry.

"Not news of a Burgundian attack upon the ships?"
Margery inquired anxiously.

"No, I could tolerate *that*." The ice blue eyes fixed hers
meaningfully before he held out his gloved palm to his wife.
"Bella, you will come with me. Find me some muscat, Meg,
and wait upon us." He gave a curt nod of his head to the
Countess. "I shall leave Father Warwick to break the good
news to you, madam. I hope the telling of it plaguey well
chokes him!"

"I always thought Cicely could have brought up her sons
with better manners," huffed the Countess loudly as the
door closed with unnecessary noise behind him. "Oh, do not
look askance at me, the two of you. Go, Margery! Obey him
but do not use the good wine that my lord was presented
with at Valognes. In the humor he is in, anything that will
slide easily down his throat will suffice."

"Vinegar?" Anne asked.

The Duke had already dismissed Blanche when Margery
entered with the wine. Only Ankarette had tarried, deliberately taking her time to pack a darned veil into a chest.
George snarled at her and she left reluctantly, pulling a face
at Margery who decided it was best to set the wine upon the
small side table and withdraw as swiftly as possible.

"You can stay, Meg. You do not gossip like the other

bitches. Pour us all a cup, for the love of Heaven, I am that parched."

"Tell us what has bitten you!" snapped Isabella.

"Your father"—he grabbed the first full cup—"your poxy father is bidden by the French whoreson to Angers to meet the bloody Bitch of Anjou. While you were swanning around the gardens here discussing the height of your head-dresses, that spider has been persuading your father into considering an alliance. That was why they have been dithering around with these talks—they were waiting for the answer as to whether the old hag would consent to see him."

"*And she has*?" Margery was incredulous.

"Oh, with great reluctance apparently—the only good tidings in the entire squalid business. All these plaguey secret discussions. No wonder the French wanted me to busy myself with hunting. And I never suspected." He glared at his wife who stood still before him, her fingers in a steeple against her lips. "Did you not have any inkling, Bella? Did you not ask him what was going on? You have been at the château the whole time, for Heaven's sake!"

It was the Duke's own fault, thought Margery, sipping her wine with more control. He had been only too willing to ride off hunting boar with the other young men and come back to brag about the killing over supper. She had watched the French courtiers fêting him like a dauphin. In retrospect, it was so blatant.

Isabella was being disappointingly incredulous. "I—I will not believe it. Father would not even think of such a thing!" She lifted her cup of wine from the table with a shaking hand. "He drove the Bitch into exile in the first place. There are torrents of blood between them. Besides, Father has sworn to make you king, George. You know he wants his grandson on the throne."

"*Grandson*, madam!" the Duke hissed, slamming the winecup out of her hand. Its contents spattered across Isabella's gown. "*What grandson*? If you had welcomed me to your bed lately with kisses instead of squeamish excuses, mayhap your father would not be contemplating an alliance with our enemy." She blinked at him in shock. "Can you not understand, you simpleton? The rebellion is not just an old man's petulance because Ned has outgrown his advice and married the Woodville witch. It's not even that your father is hungry for his old power again, it is much more than that. It is an obsession, Bella, a gnawing hatred against Ned and a desire to have Neville blood wearing the crown. And it can even be Lancastrian seed, providing it's a Neville womb. Have I shocked you two innocents? By Christ Almighty, the Duke my father, God rest his soul, would turn in his grave if he knew of this treachery." He viciously seized up a footstool and hurled it at the window. Amazingly both the stool and expensive pane held.

Isabella frowned down at her spoiled gown. It was hard, after all, to defend the indefensible. "Goodness, my lord, as you say it may come to nothing and by then I may be with child." She sent Margery a look that forbade her to leave them alone together.

George turned and swooped, his fingers curling clawlike about her shoulders, his words blasts of air in her face. "But he *has agreed* to meet the Bitch, you foolish woman! He told me so. He is to go to her father René's castle at Angers." With an oath, he flung himself away from her, slapping a fist angrily into the palm of his other hand.

"Could it be a trap?" offered Isabella, glancing at Margery for verbal support. "You do not think that King René will seize Father and you will have to ransom him?"

"I hope he does," exclaimed the Duke. "The Angevins can lock him up and throw away the key!"

Isabella was struggling to stay calm, smoothing her skirts about her in the way her mother had when she was perturbed. She tried another approach to soothe him. "But mayhap Father is just planning to merely use the Lancastrians. We all know that he is the most popular and powerful man that England has seen in decades. Why, he and my uncle Montague can bring ten thousand men to the field. Perhaps when we are all back in England, he may render the Bitch and her people helpless unless they do as he says." She nodded, satisfied by her own arguments. "In any case, if there are any Lancastrians left in England, I hardly imagine they will want to fight behind my father."

Yes, he probably orphaned half of them, thought Margery wryly with a lack of filial loyalty. In any case, Isabella's

argument was too full of ifs and buts. Would all the Neville
retainers blindly follow their lord?

It was not easy to reckon up how many of the nobility
might take up their swords against Ned if the odds were sufficiently tipped against him. After nearly ten years of
silence, no intelligent lord would turn traitor to their King
unless there was land to be gained. And would all the closet
Lancastrians crawl out from under their stones if their
mighty enemy Warwick now offered to lead them? She
doubted it.

Yet . . . yet such a triple alliance of France, Lancaster,
and the Nevilles, if it were possible, would threaten Ned
more fiercely than any previous rebellion. Warwick and
Margaret d'Anjou! It was what Huddleston had hinted at on
the morning after their wedding night. Huddleston who
always seemed to know more than he should. She set that
painful worry aside for the time being.

And where did a Lancastrian alliance leave the seething
young man before her? That was a point! Her only consolation was that perhaps she would be able to send some
promising news to Ned after all.

"What are you going to do, your grace?" she asked the
Duke. He shrugged sullenly, his smile grim.

"Are we expected to go to Angers and meet Queen Margaret too?" Isabella was scowling.

The Duke glanced sideways at his wife. "Now that question at least shows some intelligence, madam. Kiss the
Queen of Lancaster's bloody hand! By St. George, I hope
not." He held out his cup for Margery to refill it. "I do not
think I could stomach it." He paced and turned. "What a
shame that I lack Father Warwick's obsequiousness. Perhaps he has forgotten what she did to his father's head,
hacked it off and stuck it on York's Micklegate next to my
father's and brother's."

"Stop it!" shrieked Isabella. "Anyone would think *I* cut
off your father's head! Why do you not shout at my father
instead? But I will wager you have not dared. For all your
pretty speeches, he still can best you. Do you think I con-
done this? Do you think I have forgotten how much that
woman hates us? Oh, how can he even contemplate making

peace with the bloodthirsty hag after what she did?" She
took refuge upon the bed, miserably cradling her arms
across her bosom.

The Duke watched her unmoved, his mouth in an ugly
sneer, but Isabella could match him for petulance. She
blinked up at the ceiling, tears dripping down her cheeks.
"He promised us England. He promised to make me queen."
Her lower lip quivered like a precocious child's who has
just had a sweetmeat removed from her fist.

"So the hammer has at last hit the anvil!" muttered the
Duke, his eyes heavenward in exasperation.

"If this should come to pass"—Isabella's voice grew
softer and she leaned her cheek against the bedpost—"*if* . . .
then all this travail has been for naught and we have cast
away our lands and our poor babe for just a dream." Her
small hand curled forlornly around the twisted wood. More
tears pearled upon her cheeks and splashed upon her bodice.
"Oh, George, he would have lived if we had not fled England. I know he would have."

Margery waited for the Duke to storm out but he surprised her. The Plantagenet face that was usually so full of
scorn softened and the fury melted like candle grease.

"Bella!" He crumpled to his knees before her, his fingers
upon her arms, and buried his head in her lap. "What shall
we do?"

Margery, ashamed at playing witness, hurriedly let herself out, squeaking as she collided with Ankarette who
materialized from the shadows like a player on cue. "Are we
needed?"

Margery shook her head firmly, grabbed Ankarette's
arm, and dragged her away from the door. "Is my lord
father returned yet?"

"Thomas Burdett reckons they were about four miles or
so ahead of the rest. What is amiss? Have my lord and his
sulkiness fallen foul of each other at Tours? Come on, surprise me!"

Margery told her the news, seeing in Ankarette's aghast
face how her own must have appeared.

"So that's how the wind is blowing." Ankarette sucked
in her cheeks. "Who would have laid gold on that wager a

year ago? No good will come of it, you mark my words. So, is the duke-who-would-be-king spewing out his venom at our little duchess or is he wanting her to pat him on the head and sing a lullaby?"

"They are both feeling very sorry for themselves."

"And only themselves to blame. Well, I think we have a duty to warn the Countess and Lady Anne of what has befallen. They will be grateful for the time to compose themselves. Come, Margery."

"No, you tell them." Ankarette would actually enjoy the task. "I will stay here. If he is drinking, he may turn on her again." She watched her friend strut off gleefully on her mission and sat down on her palliasse in the antechamber. About her, the château was strangely quiet, as if the air itself had taken a watchful breath.

Neither the chorus of dogs barking a short while later nor the hooves thundering up into the great stableyard lured her out to see her father's return. She could not bear to discover whether Huddleston was with the Earl. Like the Duke of Clarence, she was passé.

⌘

That evening no one would have guessed at George Plantagenet's inner unhappiness. In the common gaze, at the high table, he appeared to be in excellent humor, albeit his color was heightened and there was a colder brilliance about him. Margery caught him watching her as she was whirled past in a set. She danced all evening, accepting any partner, conscious of her husband's deliberate absence.

The Duke partnered her as the candles burned low and deftly swept her outside to the corbeled walk under the hard stars. Below the castle walls, the lights and laughter of the taverns were disturbing. Was that where Huddleston lurked or was he accepting the servile smiles of the Levallois girl across her family's small-table like some heathen lord?

"Meg?" Margery was uncomfortable in George's presence but duty to Ned compelled her to take the risk.

"I have been hobbled, Meg," he whispered when he was sure they were alone. "This whole business has been a feast of misrule and I the butt of the jest. King Louis has no more intention of making me a king than living his life in a hovel. He wants Margaret d'Anjou back on the throne. Unless we agree, there will be no loans."

Margery crossed herself. "But as you said earlier, Queen Margaret may not agree. Sweet Heaven, she cut off his father's—my grandsire's head right willingly."

"Yes, you might be right. The woman is perverse and stubborn. Oh, Meg," he sniffed, like a man betrayed, and took her by the forearms, "send . . . tell my brother what is happening if you have the means."

"I will, certainly, but be cheerful, my lord, it may not happen."

A door had opened, the music from the Great Hall was louder. Margery sprang back, away from him. Her sister peered around the curve of the tower looking for them.

"What are you doing, George?" Isabella's voice was suspicious as she joined them. The Duke took his wife's arm and steered her farther away from the door.

"Trying to discover if Huddleston has told Meg here anything I have not gleaned already."

"Has he?" The Duchess sounded somewhat relieved.

"No. I should be the last person he would confide in, Bella." Her tone was shrewish.

"You must wheedle what you can from him," hissed Isabella. "It is important, Margery. He talks to everyone. He is high in the Scots lord's favor and speaks French as though he was born to it."

"You must pardon me in this, I cannot help you."

"*Will* not, you mean. If you will not help, Margery, you are a baseborn traitor."

"Ah, there you are, Bella. Oh, I see I interrupt." The Countess's gaze flicked over each of their faces. "What is this about treachery?"

"Nothing, madam," muttered Isabella sullenly. "There are *some* in this castle who have forgotten where their family allegiance lies!"

The light from the spluttering cressets seemed just enough for Lady Warwick. Her eyes narrowing, she glanced suspiciously from the Duke to Margery. The Duke laughed nastily and Margery, angry, unwisely turned away from

Isabella's pouting and stared up at the indifferent stars. It was unfortunate, but what could she say?

Vengeance came on the heels of sunrise. Margery was summoned to an audience with her father. Richard Huddleston was there before her, leaning back against the table like a priest perched on a misericord, his arms folded, his expression inscrutable. Evidently he already knew why she had been sent for. She eyed his indifferent expression with scarcely concealed hostility although some instinct reassured her this meeting was not of his making. He straightened, more like a great cat stretching languidly, and gave her a formal nod.

Her father appeared to watch this byplay with little amusement. He sprawled in his chair, the ringed fingers of his right hand tapping impatiently on its carved claw.

Why was it that men always seemed to spread themselves as if their very mass could subjugate all lesser beings, Margery wondered as she made obeisance. It was like an act of power, of self-aggrandisement directed at the encompassing air. Women were not permitted to do such things. Nor did they seem obsessed with doing so.

Her father dismissed the servants and regarded the pair of them sourly. "Pour us some wine, Richard."

Huddleston turned to the tray that had been set upon the polished oak. He raised a cold eyebrow at Margery. She shook her head.

Warwick regarded her with irritation. "I am making changes, daughter. It is decided that you are no longer to be part of Isabella's household." There was a stubborn determination dug deeply around his mouth that brooked no refusal but Margery, guessing that the Countess had daubed her reputation the color of mud, faced him undeterred.

"Why, my lord? Has his grace of Clarence decided I am an evil influence on Bella? We have all observed he is whimsical even when sober. Or has Master Huddleston here decreed it does not suit him?"

Green eyes impassively met her blue fury, but the air crackled invisibly between them.

Warwick, seemingly unruffled, took a deep breath and
studied his son-in-law questioningly. Huddleston shrugged.
The patronizing masculine rapport stung her. "A phase of
the moon approaching perhaps, my lord," he offered.

Margery whirled around on him. "How dare you?" She
watched a devil's smile steal into the corners of his mouth.

"What wasp stung you, daughter?" Her father rose. "I
thank the Almighty, Margery, that you were not born on the
dexter side of my escutcheon or you would be an even greater
plague to Christendom than you are to me." He whacked her
on the rump and took the cup that Richard held out to him.
"From now on, daughter, you will serve Anne. Your duties
will begin in two days' time when we travel to Angers."

"Angers!" A whisper edged with surprise. It was true.
Her father was going to meet the Bitch of Anjou. Margery
raised an appalled face but now she dared not voice her displeasure. Her father's face was as stony as St. Peter's must
have been when he turned back Mephistopheles at the very
gate of Heaven.

"Yes, what of it?" Warwick's tone dared her to protest
and Margery, who could think of a score of reasons why her
father should never set foot in the stronghold of King René
of Anjou, darted down a less dangerous path. How could
she watch her father even touch fingers with the accursed
House of Lancaster? "I understand that the Duke and
Duchess intend to go back to Normandy." She waved her
hands, searching for more reasons. "I . . . I thought that
Master Huddleston would be returning to the fleet at Honfleur." She avoided her husband's gaze, her tone sweet-
ening. "We will be closer to each other if I am with her
grace at Valognes."

Huddleston exploded into a fit of coughing.

Warwick appeared not to notice. "Their graces will
remain here as guests of Queen Charlotte. Richard is
coming with us to Angers. His majesty has particularly
requested it."

To be thrown into closer proximity to her husband was
the last thing Margery needed. Besides, the Duke was bound
to berate his duchess further. It was necessary to try softer
persuasion: "My lord father, Bella needs me."

"Must I be frank, daughter?" Warwick was looking irritated with her. "I had thought we could decide this without acrimony. You say Bella needs you? After what she said last night to you, no, Margery, I do not think so." He took another gulp, and scowled at her.

Margery averted her profile from Huddleston's scrutiny with a toss of her head. So Warwick had been listening to the Countess. That was predictable. The Countess must have thought Bella was accusing her of trying to seduce the Duke. That was why she was being separated from her half sister. But how could she tell her father the truth without implicating Bella? "I think there has been some misunderstanding. Have you discussed this with her grace, my lord?"

"No," snarled the Earl. "I shall not hurt her feelings further by even raising the matter. Besides, she is not speaking to me at present."

He flung himself back into his chair and pointed a menacing finger at Margery, like an angry king. His mouth could be cruel, she realized. "I have been at pains to restore you to grace, girl, and I tell you this, you will not have a second chance from me. From now on, you will behave as though you are a very saint. You will not trip! The eyes of Christendom will be on the Nevilles at Angers and I want no slur, no indiscretion, not even the slightest word or deed that could provide carrion for gossips to be leveled at me or mine. You understand?"

Margery nodded although indignation and rebellion were brewing within her bosom. Yet there was more humiliation to come, her father was relentless, his imperious gaze embraced Huddleston briefly before he looked sternly upon Margery again. "You will perform your wifely duties. I want a semblance of civility between the pair of you from now on, is that understood?"

Her lips parted in an outraged gasp. She avoided meeting the ironic gaze that Huddleston had fixed upon her.

"My lord, in truth the lady feels we are better apart." It was asserted softly, foiling her attempt to discern any regret in his tone.

"A pox on such foolishness, daughter!" snarled Warwick, slamming his goblet down on the small-table at his elbow. "Your eye falls on better winnings, no doubt, as is your wont."

"My lord!" She and Richard protested as in one voice and fell silent instantly, their glances falling away from each other.

"You have been harkening to false gossip," Margery exclaimed. She glared sideways. "Does *he* complain to you, my lord? I rather doubt it."

"My lord." Richard's tone was reasonable. "I do not know what is meant here but," his glance brushed her unhappy face, "the lady . . . "

The Earl did not let him finish. "The lady errs, man. She is a child of Eve. You let her run amok just like your dog."

Richard paled, speechless with anger.

Margery raised her chin at the man who had dishonored her mother and still presumed to wrong her. "You misjudge me, my lord of Warwick! I pray to God that I am the only thing that you misjudge."

She did not even curtsy. Once outside, she sped briskly down the passageway, lashing out at a wall arras in her fury as she passed. She might have known Huddleston would catch her. His hand fell upon her sleeve as she was about to cross the Great Hall.

"I am sorry for what you suffered in there." It was said with dignity.

She discreetly removed her arm from his touch, not meeting his eyes. He had abetted her father but she was not going to demean herself by accusing him. "I am used to it."

"Then it must cease."

Her glance snapped onto his frowning face. "You mean it beggars your reputation, Master Huddleston?"

The green eyes perused her thoughtfully. "No, it belittles yours. And would you care to explain what your father was talking about?"

That was a coffin of worms best left shut. "It would serve no purpose."

How could she mistrust someone but starve for his company? His mere presence added such spice to the everyday fare of her life. She wanted to blurt out that she had missed the gleam of the hunt in his eye from across the room and the sensation that his deep glance would rouse in her. Instead she inclined her head coolly and gracefully gathered up her skirts.

He made no move to delay or accompany her, merely gave her a formal short bow and returned toward her father's chambers.

Margery hastened along the ramparts and found a place where the sentries would ignore her. Only the grotesque gargoyles below heard her muffled sorrow. Fury and frustration rose in her like bile, foul and bitter, and she knuckled the tears from her eyes. Oh, if she were a man, neither of these two male tyrants would abuse her so. Why was it women must be under the sway of men?

Her father had betrayed her again; he assumed the worst. He had enslaved her to an adventurer who had married her for ambition; Isabella was yoked to a drunken, selfish brat; and now the wretched man was dragging poor little Anne down to Angers for auction. And to tell her in front of Huddleston that she could not so much as glance at another man!

Margery savaged a corner of her veil between her fingers. Disillusionment was working in her like a slow poison. Where was the Earl's wisdom in all this? He had quarreled with Ned and now was but a pawn in the giant chess game between Louis of France and Charles of Burgundy.

As for her damnable husband! Huddleston merely wanted to control her. It had been a lie to say it was her reputation not his that concerned him. She desperately needed to escape him. When she was in his presence, she could no longer reason clearly.

Leaning her elbows upon the wall, she stared bleakly at the church across the valley. Could she take refuge there? No, she had had enough of the ways of the church. Churchmen only treasured women who starved themselves until they lost all bodily functions.

She could flee to Burgundy but the only person she knew there was de Commynes and he might still be in Calais. She could try to return to Ned—at least the French would not stop her—but Ned would not welcome her unless she carried a promise of Clarence's change of heart. It was still too soon for that. If the Bitch refused an alliance, Louis might turn once more to favor George. Anything to ferment mischief for Ned.

The forests blanketing the distant horizon were not

comforting. Just the thought of setting out alone to cross
several kingdoms when she did not speak any of the lan-
guages was daunting. That one night on the road to Exeter
had been sufficient. Oh, Huddleston had schooled her well.
He had deliberately exposed her to that adventure. Besides,
he had proved that he could track her down and she instinctively knew he would come after her. His pride would not
let her escape. She was his property even if he no longer
desired to honor his marriage vows.

She cursed him heartily, reluctantly admitting to herself
that she missed the hiss and rasp of words between them
and that her body craved his touch. *You are my plague*, he
had said.

Lust! she thought dismissively, but that passion remained simmering in her innermost being. He who had suffered in lust had passed it on to her like the pestilence, and
now it no longer contaminated him. It was she who was now
in fever. Did desire burn itself out? Did time heal? If only he
was not coming to Angers, she might survive.

Slowly the shouts in the courtyard below distracted
Margery. She had found a quiet corner that afternoon, escaping the rest of the ladies who were sitting sewing in the
gardens. Idly, she moved to the window.

Below in the combat yard, a cluster of knights and
esquires, after much discussion, was splitting into pairs, her
husband among them. The quiver of excitement in her thighs
was still disconcerting. She watched like a voyeur, unable to
take her eyes off him.

He was one of three instructors circling the yard as the
practice began, stopping combatants here and there to correct a thrust or parry. The English lads laughed cheerfully
and heeded him.

She should be hating him but her reason was telling her
that she had been the liar and deceiver and that he had every
cause to despise her. Sweet Jesu, but it was a pleasure to be
able to watch him unobserved, without the green mockery
challenging her.

The fighting pairs suddenly ceased swordplay and re-
grouped. Margery watched Huddleston strip down to his

gipon and hose, then he strode back into the midst of the yard, his sword naked, ready for combat. One of the French knights who had been bawling instructions saluted him and the pair of them moved slowly, demonstrating techniques to the younger men. Then the circle of watchers fell back, leaving the two men space for more serious combat.

Margery lingered. Not even Queen Charlotte could have dragged her from the spectacle. Was it sinful to admire the hard muscle, the long lithe body, to compare Richard Huddleston favorably against the men with protruding bellies or skinny, fat, or misshapen shanks? Her appetite feasted on his manly shoulders and glistening skin. Do I need to confess this in church, she thought, this pride in my husband's appearance? I am lusting after him. And I cannot have him, cannot build any future. I have kicked the foundation stones aside already.

Her husband's opponent was stockier and there was great strength in his blows as he belabored Huddleston skillfully. Steel rasped against steel and the circle of men shouted and cheered. Her Englishman was agile, his blade flashed swiftly, catching the sun as the two men slashed, spun, and thrust again. The Frenchman's shirt was sticking to him and Richard's shoulders took on a sheen as though rubbed with oil instead of sweat.

"Margery."

She jumped as a man's hand came down on the bare skin of her shoulder. Startled, she faced her father. He was unattended. How long had he been standing behind her? Had he seen the hunger in her face, the passion within her as fierce as the conflict in the yard below?

Before she could curtsy, his arm slid around her shoulders, returning her to the casement. "Here is sport for a summer's afternoon. This takes me back to the golden days when the little dukes came to learn arms and wait at table. Remember the practice yard at Middleham?"

"We were happy then." Her fingers traced the carved stone about the window, uncomfortable with the Earl's presence. Below, the bout was over. Her husband was leaning against the wall, his arms folded morosely while the Frenchman who had been his dueling partner was talking at him, hands gesturing. Then he nodded and strode forward to watch the new combatants. "You have watched many a fight. What think you of the standard down there?" Warwick edged in, his alert gaze flicking over the men below, noting who was present. His eyes rested pensively on Huddleston before lifting to hers.

"There is always room for practice, my lord. Some of the men could do with losing weight."

Her father stroked his chin, his expression as sheepish as an earl's might get and he stuck a thumb beneath his belt, but there was little space. "Including me. I grow fat as butter with this feasting while Clarence stays skinny like a scarecrow with hunting every day. So you think I should be down there with them this afternoon?" Margery nodded honestly, her glance upon his paunch. He grunted. "Aye, you are right but I had as lief sit at a board and present smooth arguments as prepare for battle." He pinched her cheek. "And do not mistake that for cowardice but for age. You are right though. I shall have to put in at least an hour a day if I am to take England back again from that ingrate. Although speaking of Ned . . ." He turned Margery from the window, gazing upon her with a sadness that might have been calculated. She was never sure with him; he was, after all, a creature of politics.

"My dear." His hands framed her shoulders ensuring that he had her full attention. "Margery, this is not easy." Casting his blue gaze beyond her, he sighed. "Ah, nothing is easy these days . . ." But the sharp intelligent gaze snared hers again. "I have something of import to say that requires mayhap absolution from you. Master Huddleston has spoken to me privily this day and I am grateful to him. He . . ." Letting go her shoulders, he again averted his eyes, his complexion darkening. "How may I couch this? The subtlety at your wedding feast—"

Margery cut in. "The maiden and the unicorn?"

"Aye, that was it. Huddleston told me this morning that the lady in question was in truth a maiden."

Margery's mouth tightened. Her hand was caught and lifted between his own. "My daughter, it seems we all owe you the most humble and profound apology and I am the most culpable. I regret that you suffered at my hands. No name until now and all these years a false reputation."

"I thought you wished to gift me to the church, my lord father. My sin was opportune. Your hatred burned so brightly against Ned that you needed more fuel to nourish it."

"Margery, I do not deny it, but . . ." Bowing, he carried her hand to his lips, his voice hoarse, unusually humble, "The Earl of Warwick begs your pardon." He was giving her the triumph, a paltry gift of a few cadences of breath upon the wind without witnesses, and yet part of him did seem to sincerely give. He held out his arms to her.

Tears betrayed her, sparkled on her lashes and stifled her reply. She had never seen him behave like this. No wonder he had banished his attendants from the gallery.

The strong arms folded about her crushing her against the wiry silver embroidery of his doublet. "I am not sorry I tried to give you to God. For who knows, you might have chosen in time to take the veil . . . but I am sorry for your bruised reputation." His fingers stroked up and down her back. "You have had to put up with my lady's rebukes but I shall set her straight, I promise—her and your half sisters."

Margery sensed it was time to draw away, to sniff back the tears. "Anne knew—no, she *believed* rather than knew." She tried to wipe her cheeks with her fingers. "I am so grateful to her for that. She was the only one who listened."

"Child, you wring my heart."

Fumbling at length, she drew forth a kerchief from her purse. Using it restored her enough to show some of the Neville pride. She faced him unflinching. "Master Huddleston had no right to speak of this to you."

Her father seemed surprised at her stance. "How uncharitable of you, Margery. In my opinion, your husband wishes nothing more but to set the ledger to rights." Did her father notice her anger growing? He seemed not to, sounding more like a cleric by the minute. "Truth lies hidden half the time but when it does emerge into the light of day, we should value it even if it hurts us to do so. It pains me to know how much I made you pay for your indiscretion when the guilty one walks free. It was that cursed whoreson bent on seducing you who should pay. And he will, be sure of that! I will snatch the crown that I gave him back off his treacherous head."

"No, my lord." Margery recoiled.

"No?" exclaimed her father. "What means this 'no'? He was married—a grown man—while you were . . . by all the Saints, you scarcely had dugs."

Margery was adamant. "I never wished my affairs to be any part of your quarrel with the King, my lord, and I assure you he carries only half the blame." Warwick shrugged, his expression supercilious. "No, my lord," she asserted, combating that male condescension, "I am in earnest over this. A few moments more and I would have willingly surrendered my chastity to Ned without remorse."

Warwick tossed up a dismissive hand at her and flung away, his back rigid and furious before he turned abruptly, shaking a finger at her. "Pah, the infatuated child in you speaks still. If you are presently lighting candles at the scoundrel's shrine, then you are a fool and, believe me, Margery, I thought you had more sense." Then pity crawled into his eyes as he examined her face. "By all the Saints, you foolish girl, are you still imagining Ned loves you? Is this the reason why your marriage with Huddleston tosses like a ship in rough weather?"

Margery's lower lip curled stubbornly, "The ship flounders, my lord father, as I foretold."

He caught her chin, "Oh, by the Lord, I see my blood in you. You have my damnable pride." Yes, thought Margery, facing his steely blue eyes. He studied her, bending his head so close that she could see the angry broken veins beneath his skin. "I am warning you to make repairs, child. Steer for safe harbor. Huddleston cares enough for your reputation to make it sweet."

Furious, Margery jerked her chin away and turned back to the window. Richard was still in the courtyard. He was idly looking up at the windows. She swiftly ducked back. "No, my lord, he cares for *his* reputation. By repairing mine, he does himself good service. We all know he married me in order to gain your patronage."

The Earl looked irritated. "Come, come, you mistake him. He could have married an heiress."

"He is ambitious, my lord, I swear it. He now kisses Anne's hands more sweetly that he ever kissed mine.

I wager you he will fawn upon the Bitch with equal charm."

"And so may I!" snarled Warwick.

Of course, she was expected to eat in the Great Hall, and so it was unavoidable that her husband would know exactly where she would be at a certain time. Richard paused before her outside the hall before supper, a cluster of combat companions at his back. His bow was formal, insincere, the gleam in his eye cold but predatory. "Your father tells me you take an interest in my swordplay." His deft fingers stroked down a brocade fold of her skirt with a teasing caress.

"I'll warrant she does," chuckled his erstwhile opponent, clapping him bawdily on the shoulder and sending Margery a hot stare.

She swallowed, ignoring Huddleston's gibe, as she tried to fathom that bright hard gaze, wanting desperately to feel his fingers upon her flesh again, to experience the eddies of feeling that he could conjure up like a magician.

"Swords hurt," she said dismissively to them all and walked away.

After dining she found him, disturbingly, at her elbow as she stood beside Ankarette while the trestles were cleared back for dancing. He was as stern as a looming thundercloud as he held out his hand to her. "A moment of your time."

Curious, she rested her fingers in his; her heartbeat quickened at touching him but she masked the impact. "I thought I was condemned like Socrates and not to be borne with. Have you discovered a patch of hemlock worth brewing?"

It drew a strained smile. "No, a bed of nettles. What I have to admire about you, my dear Margery, is your resilience. Come!"

Two youths waited in their path. She had a sense of familiarity and yet . . . Huddleston dropped her hand and, taking her by the shoulders, held her before him like a cloak to dry.

"Tom, Will, this is your new sister. Margery, my brothers."

Astonishment washed over her as her glance flicked back and forth. She knew from his stern tone that he had not welcomed their arrival.

Neither of the two youths was as tall as her husband, nor did they exude the calm power of command that seemed so natural to him. But she could see that well-chiseled noses prevailed within the family and that their smiles could melt hearts, even if they lacked those wondrous green eyes.

The two young men grinned at each other before the older, stockier of the two took Margery gently by the hands and kissed her cheek. "So this is the lady who cast a net over our Richard's heart."

"I did not know he had one," Margery answered gravely with a curtsy. Huddleston's hands lifted abruptly from her shoulders as if being close to her was contaminating.

The younger lad, flushing as pink as finger pads, shook her hand.

"Excuse me." Richard's voice was cool. "My Lord of Concressault is summoning me. I will leave you to be better acquainted."

"So he did not tell you we were coming. And here was me thinking he'd be that pleased to have us here." Thomas was frowning.

"Oh, not your fault, I assure you. I am the one in his bad books at present," exclaimed Margery brightly, but she was wondering the same as she reined the conversation in a safer direction. "Now I know naught save that one of you is wooing Lord Montague's daughter, Ysabel."

Tom burst out laughing. "Aye, that is Will here. We are both in Lord Montague's service. Our lord has sent us to determine what is happening here in France."

Margery smiled grimly. "My father is still negotiating. Nothing is resolved yet."

"So Richard informs us." Will frowned.

Thomas grinned. "Well, at least our curiosity is sated. We were agog when we heard that he had abducted you."

The younger lad grew bolder. "Aye, he has changed. He never used to do anything without hours of planning. If he had been the Almighty, the Earth would never have been managed in a week."

Margery did not agree. "I have learned not to take him at face value."

Thomas gave her a formal bow but his eyes were impish. "Our mother has asked us to convey her apology to you for his behavior." The humor in that was at least gratifying.

"Aye, that was another reason for coming. Our father was curious to learn what mischief our ambitious Richard had been about."

Margery bit her lip. "Will your father approve of your brother's marriage to me? Pray do not answer if you had rather not."

"Will we have snow afore Chistmas at Millom?" Thomas beamed at her. "Mistress, rest you easy. Richard has been negotiating for you since, what say you, Will? Long before Michaelmas? And our father will be pleased to hear that my lord of Warwick has acknowledged you. We were expecting the marriage anyway. Our brother is so besotted."

"Aye, we never thought that love could turn him into such a rebel," Will joined in softly. "He made it clear just now that it is his only reason for being here and we should be fools to commit ourselves to any treason until we knew the full score. Is something wrong? Will you sit?"

She shook her head but it was whirling. Richard Huddleston talking of love? What top was he spinning now?

Her voice emerged huskily. "I . . . Has Richard told you that we leave for Angers with my father two days hence?"

Will looked at her sharply. "But that is in Anjou."

"Yes, and did he tell you also that my father is to meet with the exiled lords and Queen Margaret?"

Her younger brother-in-law stared scowling at her father, comfortable at Louis's high table upon the dais, and swore softly. "Lord preserve us, Tom, what have we gotten ourselves into here?"

"Please God, nothing as yet. Oh, your grace!"

Margery spun around to find George of Clarence had been standing there smirking. With an arrogant grin at the Huddleston brothers, he took her hand and led her into the set as the musicians struck up. "Your new relatives talking treason already, tsk, tsk."

"Why are you embarrassing me further? Last night—"

"Last night, Meg, has turned out to be a godsend. Because of last night, the old man is taking you to Angers and you can be my eyes and ears. Couldn't be better if I had planned it."

"The Countess thinks I am already in your bed."

He let forth his awful whinny of a laugh that drew all eyes toward them.

"George!"

"Wave to my mother-in-law, Meg. What, no smile? You grow lily-livered, wench. What is the gossip? What says my Lord Montague?" He took her by the waist and whirled her deliberately past the Countess.

"Nothing as yet. He wants the news from here first."

"Poor fellow, caught between Brother Warwick and dear wonderful Ned. It grows more interesting by the minute."

Margery did not answer. Her father had observed her dancing with George and looked like he wanted to hammer her into the tiled floor with a thunderbolt. She was thankful when the music ended.

"Oh, dear me, here is old Richard trying to cover his horns. Take her, Huddleston, I have warmed her hand for you."

Anne was hanging on Huddleston's arm, her cheeks rose-colored from the dancing but her face was drawn.

Richard's gaze was stone. "Cheer your sister, she fears the future," he said and left them.

CHAPTER
21

"Oh, look there!" Lady Anne's voice was horrified as the barge came into sight of Angers. The company moved to one side of the vessel and had to be swiftly bawled at to stop the whole enterprise capsizing shamefully in full view of René of Anjou who was standing on the downstream wharf with his trumpeters.

Richard frowned. She was right. There was no welcome in those stones. The Château d'Angers looked as though it must have been the last word in defense when it was built to dominate the confluence of the rivers for some ancient Duke of Anjou.

Massive, unassailable towers, surmounted by the inevitable turrets, glowered down at the river from a formidable eyrie. It would have needed a hundred-foot rope to scale them. Mortared between, like curtains of stone, were massive walls, each some six hundred paces long. But there were no traitors' corpses hanging from them. Not yet.

The city lay closely, like a lover, west of the castle. Judging by the superfluity of gables and spires and the prosperous sprawl beyond its walls, it looked smugly confident that the château would protect it. Of course, it was just an illusion; continual bombardment by cannon would make any garrison capitulate eventually even if it did tie down the besieging army for some time. This castle would take months.

"It is a strategic masterpiece, my lady. The view of the country will be magnificent." Richard tried to lighten Lady Anne's gloom. Since he was officially of her household, he had done his best to keep the girl's spirits cheerful by a solicitousness for her comfort. He could tell that his behavior had met with grudging approbation from Margery although she avoided his company as much as she could.

"Evidently they have gone to some trouble," she observed.

Brazen notes were floating across the water toward them but the colors on the shore were bright and joyful. The sunlight sparkled upon jewels not steel.

"A prisoner would not have a view, Master Huddleston." Lady Anne's self-containment was at breaking point; she was not appeased. Her arm was rigid within her half sister's. The girl knew why she had been brought from Amboise.

"True, you can be a prisoner without chains," added Margery, casting her husband a bitter look from beneath burnished lashes.

"Those kinds of prisoners often build their own Hell," he retaliated. "They wear the shackles on their eyes."

"I have never seen striped towers before, Master Huddleston." Anne Neville, knowing the tension between the two of them, was tactfully toeing the conversation into a safer direction. It had distracted her from her own fear.

Richard shielded his eyes. "Slate. Probably from a nearby quarry. The builders would have used local materials if they could. The dark bands make the castle more formidable, do they not?" They did.

Anne perused the stonework with a more careful eye. "I forgot you would understand about that."

"About what? Being formidable?" Margery said.

Anne turned from the rail in surprise. "Did you not tell her, Master Huddleston? Why, Margery, his family have quarries and mines aplenty. I would guess Sir John has more income from those than wool or produce, would you not say?" She bestowed a gracious smile upon him.

"You have the right of it, my lady. As for the telling, my wife has but to ask." He inclined his head and left the rail. Oh, Margery did not like that chastisement that was so well deserved. Perhaps now she would think him less an adventurer.

Thank God she had ignored him for the most part during the journey. He had needed time to think. By Christ's blessed mercy, he wondered where their future, *any* future lay. The times were such that a man might wake and become his brother's enemy by noon. Mayhap, within the next few days, he and his contrary wife would be severed well and truly by the Yorkist king's accursed shadow. Greater matters were afoot and to hoist a canvas against the tide might be to drown.

To others observing him, he must have seemed bemused, watching the oars rise and drop in unison except for that of the bargemaster who used his skillfully to prevent the vessel jolting into the wharf. Richard scanned the castle once more with a sigh and then dropped his gaze to the glittering crowd. The barge ropes were being looped and the planks slammed across the rail.

The favorite hounds leaped ashore and, in their midst, the King of France, beaked hat thrusting forward, greeted the elegant, fattened little rooster who awaited them. There was a masculine, mutual flinging of limbs, sleeves swirling, as if they were true friends, but it was common knowledge that France wanted to wrap its arms around prosperous Anjou and not let go. Then the Earl of Warwick was given the Gallic kiss on either cheek. Another man, somewhat younger, with a ducal coronet set around the brim of his high-crowned hat was introduced. Someone said it must be the Bitch's brother, the Duke of Calabria.

Richard assisted Lady Anne down the plank and held out his hand to his wife. Margery ignored it with a sweet smile and moved up to stand dutifully at her youngest sister's elbow. His hand itched to wallop the curvaceous rear beneath those slithery folds. And he would take a wager that she had deliberately lowered her neckline to show more cleavage.

Instinct told him he should dread her waywardness. Her

present meekness in her father's presence was skin-deep. On the occasions when she could not avoid him, the little malapert teased him subtly, challenging his self-control at every opportunity, using her wit to prick him, her eyes to flash sudden provocative glances. Now that he had plumbed her delicious body, his torment was greater than before. He cursed inwardly; it had been a mistake to admit his body stirred at the sight of her.

Certes, he should never have married her. The widow at Doncaster would have brought him more manors. It was his unchristian lust for the blue-eyed Neville bastard that had landed him in this maelstrom, caught him up into the whirl of events. That was his dilemma: the depth of his miscalculation bothered him. If his judgment had been wrong with her, what other mistakes might he now make? Already his brothers were tarred with treachery, believing in his wisdom. Christ forgive him! His temples ached with the folly of it all.

The King of France was beckoning him to make obeisance to their host. His dog had already been introduced.

Close as touching, old René, King of Sicily (which he no longer possessed) and Duke of Anjou (which he did possess) was evidently not a man who spent months on campaign. Cake-colored brocade, stitched with silver and gold thread, clad an overplump belly. Wispy, effete silver curls glinted between his broad rolled brim and shining forehead as he reached up a ringed hand to mop his brow. The other hand protruded from a voluminous, perfumed hanging sleeve, edged with miniver and lined with dark blue silk.

Richard kissed the ducal ring. Above, Louis XI was fulsomely extolling the virtues of Error, and Richard, kneeling, was maneuvered into promises to the Duke.

More dogs. At this rate, if ever he was allowed back into France or Anjou, he would require packhorses to load with puppies. With another bow, he stepped back and aside for others to take his place.

King René made an interesting study: a man of peace who had survived the bloody civil wars in France and gripped his duchy still, despite his land-hungry nephew, Louis XI, as a neighbor. This man would have conversed with Jeanne the Witch Maid who had led the French against the English and triumphantly crowned Louis's father. He would have touched goblets with Gilles de Rais who had burned for sacrificing babes to the Devil. He would have opened dreaded letters over the years, missives telling him his son-in-law, Henry VI of Lancaster, was slowly losing every possession on mainland Europe save Calais, and finally that the kingdom of England was lost. How did he comfort a bitter, beggared daughter? One day, my dear, one day . . . And now one of the men who had wrenched her crown away was here within a dagger's kiss.

"What is to happen now?" muttered Margery.

Richard slowly turned his head. She was waiting for him to offer her his arm. "Ah . . . well . . . we all go to mass." They stepped off the wooden boards to confront a cobbled road that led straight up the hill through the city gate to the cathedral. It looked as though some apprentice had let spill a bale of scarlet cloth from the bishop's threshold to the foot of the hill. Impressive. And fatted with people on either side in festive mood.

"Did you know there was a St. Maurice?" His voice sounded light but it was an effort not to worry about the gilded portcullis that might trap them in this optimistic city.

"The French saint of cuckolds and doomed alliances, I hope." She let go of his wrist to scratch her nose, her other gloved hand being occupied in holding her skirts out of the puddle that lay in her immediate path.

"If that is so, I hope we will *all* pray for guidance." They trudged after Lady Anne and the Duke of Calabria; the fabric, they discovered together, was slippery to walk over with dignity, especially with the sun grilling them through the heavy embroidery.

With a lack of self-consciousness, Margery held up the courtiers following them when she plucked a sprig of hearts-ease out of the nosegay she had been given and handed it to a tiny girl who sat astride her father's shoulders. The uncalculated kindness pleased her husband. It was one of her virtues.

"What a wealth of new alehouses and stews for you to explore," she declared, staring with blatant interest down each narrow cross-street. "And I do believe they have cleaned the sewers for our visit."

Richard grinned and to annoy her touched his brim to a
generously bosomed girl who was fluttering a kerchief at
him from a beflowered casement. "Such cleanliness beto-
kens a serious attitude. The women are pretty and the city is
wealthy and definitely covetable. I wonder if there are more
kingdoms at stake than England's. Do you think they will
give us a bedchamber to ourselves, mousekin?"

"I doubt it," retaliated Margery sweetly, though she
blushed, "but you may have the dungeon next to mine."

In the cathedral, as the notes of Anjou's best choirboys
soared heavenward, Richard let his attention wander to the
wheels of tracery and colored glass crushed into the stones
high above the transept. Later, his gaze edged along the
peerless Bataille tapestry of the Apocalypse. The visions
of John, Christ's beloved apostle, upon alternate panels
of murrey and azure, stretched beyond his view: years of
stitching running around the walls, flowing away from him,
the scope and perseverance a lesson. But none of the Angevins were looking at it. They were all transfixed by their
unlikely visitor, the man who had turned their princess
hungry into the fields.

Richard could feel some sympathy for his father-in-law.
The mass was not just political. The Kingmaker definitely
needed to have God amenable if he was about to meet his
most bitter enemy—not the easiest task for anyone as stiff-
necked as a Neville. The exiled Lancastrian Queen was
expected next day and, of course, as this was her childhood
home, she would be in her element, whereas her great
enemy was a guest among strangers and would have to sus-
tain his politeness.

Warwick stood seemingly at ease between the two kings,
but Richard had learned that the stroking of one thumb upon
the other and the occasional grind of jaw betrayed moments
of uncertainty. Clearly, it was definitely going to be an
interesting week. The Kingmaker was facing his apocalypse. He was going to have to dirty his knees groveling to
someone.

Richard glanced down at his own knees and reconciled
himself to the fact that he was too. The dilemma again. This

week might be the fabric of chronicles but Richard still needed to weigh up his own options. Could a Neville-Lancaster alliance—if it actually eventuated—destroy Margery's lazy, brilliant Ned? Did *he*, an esquire, want to play for high stakes? The irony of it creased his mouth in a grim smile—the *high stakes* that held the heads of traitors on London Bridge? It was definitely time for a prayer and a request for guidance. He lifted his eyes to the glittering cross. If St. Richard of Chichester was not available, would St. Maurice be interested?

There was a brief reception at the Logis Barrault and then the visitors were escorted by the royal chamberlain across the deep moat of the castle to the best fanfare composition Richard had ever heard. It boded well. René the Beloved, they called their king.

"Wait for the drawbridge to—" Margery, again upon his arm like a tethered hawk, abandoned words and blinked in astonishment as they came out from the shadow of the formidable portal. "Goodness, gold within lead!"

He understood perfectly. It was as if the outer walls of the castle were a heavy ugly suit of armor that protected a beautiful, accomplished, young courtier. The buildings within the courtyard came from several different centuries but glass windows had been inserted into the older apartments and the new unweathered additions were built for comfort.

Along their right were trees and enticing pavilions but the procession coiled on relentlessly beneath an inner gatehouse. Its appearance halted Richard in amazement and the Angevin lord and lady following almost walked straight into them. "Would you look at that!" he murmured as Margery tugged at him. Then she followed his gaze and started to share his amusement.

Visiting stonemasons must have scratched their heads and muttered. True, it had four pointed, slate-tiled, curly-brimmed towers at each corner, but it was as if the master builder had been jesting when he filled the space between the old walls. Instead of the gable of the gatehouse rising centered above the middle of the archway entrance, it peaked on one side. Windows, actual glass windows not arrow slits, had been set in each of the building's two levels, not one above the other but at odds with the decorated gable and each other. The golden stones of the four towers were neat and shaped, the long windows had neat sills but the stone in between was all shapes and sizes. It broke every rule.

"I like it," exclaimed Margery, adding softly, "the man who paid for this had humor and taste. Do you think King René deliberately commissioned it? The stone is barely weathered."

They passed through the archway with Richard craning around as they emerged to observe the building from the other side. The two rear towers did not match. One rounded turret rose from the second floor, the other from the ground, and the latter was different from the other towers. The roofline was not seamless and rounded but hexagonal.

"I think—" Margery was gazing in admiration at the large windows that had been set in the buildings to their right that flanked a chapel—"that if the food here matches the mood of your whimsical mason, we shall either do very well or we shall be eating subtleties with salted herring."

Now it was possible, of a sudden, to forget the self-interest festering in the visitors' hearts; here were gracious apartments overlooking the river and they could smell the roses and the lavender.

In the logis royal, built by the previous Duke of Anjou, that sat on the noble right of the Great Hall, chambers had been made ready for the Nevilles. The furnishings here were at odds with the elegant chambers they had already passed through. Perhaps it was the Duchess Jeanne's influence. Costly tapestries adorned the walls and the furnishings were newfangled and exquisitely contrived but outrageously overdone—the settles were voluptuous with cushions, the padded stools with velvet seats were overtasseled, while the carvings were skillfully accomplished but overornate and obtrusive. Painted ceilings were crowded with stars. Colors competed and clashed like a huge crushed armful of summer flowers.

Margery sped to the window, exclaimed at being able to see the river, whirled and collapsed on the cushions, and then masked her mouth with her hand to hide laughter at the sheer misplaced opulence.

Huddleston, following her in, set down the small coffer he was carrying and stared about him, struggling to manage his amusement. "Why can you not meet my gaze, Margery?" he challenged, grinning.

Greeting the spontaneous laughter in his eyes, she suddenly caught her breath.

"What is it?" Her husband had seen the change in her; his eyes were kind, concerned. Measuring how truly joyful she had been in his company during the last hour was a revelation to Margery. Dear Jesu, she could count the times she had felt wonderfully happy in her life on the fingers of one hand. The Kingmaker owning her as his daughter, the market day in Amboise, and walking up the hill today. All due to the annoying mesh of male flesh and soul who was regarding her with perplexity. Sweet Heaven, she felt at one with Christ's blind beggar seeing for the first time.

Because he did not know what to say, because something had instantly blown out the joyous candle flame and it was not his fault, Richard reached out an anxious hand to her.

As if she did not wish him to touch her, she gave a little shake, stood up, and swirled out of his orbit. "Is this not . . . not . . . remarkable and . . . ?" Thrusting her hands in the air, embracing the whole room, she spun around, her pleasure a ripple of laughter again.

"And?" he asked, hilarity bubbling up like a holy well replenished by God's blessing.

"And I am just wondering how they have decorated the oubliettes."

He had neither excuse nor leisure to ask where he was sleeping until close to supper. Halting in the doorway that led off a recently finished gallery, he blinked at the wide, beautiful, testered bed. A lady's discarded riding gloves untidied it and, near the edge, a stitched wool stocking folded into a neat rectangle snoozed beside a frothy garter.

"This is my bedchamber? There must be some mistake."

The Angevin page to the King's chamberlain glowed with

local pride. "*Mais*, you are married to Lord Warwicque's daughter, *hein*?"

Richard stepped into the room, picked up a leather shoe with an embroidered tongue. "It is well," he answered, but the attendant had gone, transformed, it seemed, into his astonished wife, framed in the doorway now like a startled saint in a dismembered triptych.

"I see you have located the oubliette." Her eyes were solemn.

He was more accustomed to the mischief she had been using as a buckler and gravely raised gloved hands in surrender. "Acquit me. It is your father's meddling."

"This is not wise." How very true. "I will use the trundle in my sister's room."

"As you wish, though I think the Countess will broom you out, and won't King René wonder why you scorn his generosity? By the time the lords of Lancaster arrive, this place will be full, as crammed as a summer pie."

She growled at him, snatched up the garter, and moved past looking for her shoes.

"Humor his lordship, mousekin. We are beneath the magnifying glass of Christendom, are we not?"

"Perhaps I should steam it up for him," hissed Margery, crouching down to peer beneath the bed. "After all, I am supposed to be the whore around here."

"Enough!" The missing shoe appeared from his hanging sleeve and landed with an angry thump next to her. "Your father has been told the truth. You are the only one who persists in self-delusion."

Margery rose, brushing her skirts, and watched him huffily turn away, inspecting not only the view across to the square tower of the cathedral but the position of the window in regard to its brethren. A soldier's inspection.

"No!" It was necessary to be firm. The western sun aureoled the competent shoulders, the lordly stance.

"No?" He looked over his shoulder at her, an eyebrow facetiously raised. "What else do you suggest?" His irritation was blatant as a gaudy, painted shield. "And what about tonight? Shall we place Alys between us or maybe Long would be a better bulwark, but he snores—loudly. Do you think this bolster might suffice?" He yanked it from the horizontal. "Or maybe King René can find some ancient chastity belt preserved from the Crusades for you to borrow."

"Richard!"

"Ah, I know! The great bed of Ware still lacks a buyer. We could sleep half the castle between us. I could send a pigeon to request an estimate but they might have trouble with the spiral stairs." He folded his arms and scowled.

Margery regarded him warily. Why was it this man of all men could make her inner being awake and stretch wantonly? In his finery, embroidered and fur-edged, he was a spellbinder. Were there charms against men like him? Men whom nature had endowed with a fine blend of poise, muscle, strength? His palpable masculinity and her own desire weakened her.

Devilment and desire bested her judgment. "I hear you only came to France because of me."

Wondering what she was at, Richard folded his lips into a thin line. "My brother Tom has been gossiping." Oh, yes, he had exaggerated to Tom and Will. What could he say to them? *Go home, I am the viper in this nest of traitors, the paid-up Judas.* He tilted his head suspiciously. "What are you up to now, lady? You want a pretty speech? What was I supposed to say? 'Treason is wonderful. Do as I do.' Dear God, a fine example of a brother I am." The arms unwound, his fingers momentarily splayed, as if helpless against fortune, before he hooked his hands upon his forearms once again.

"They said you were besotted with me." She glided across to him and tiptoed her fingers up the silken ridges of his doublet to tangle in his glossy hair.

It was nearly beyond his power to keep his hands hidden in the upper reaches of his spliced sleeves, his fingers clenched. "Yes, I said that. 'Raddled with lust,' I should have added."

She was exquisitely tormenting him, lips moist and the wide blue eyes coaxing. Richard gently removed the soft hands that scarved his neck. "I have duties, lady, and they are not marital." He intended to leave her, he trusted, bereft. For if the wench thought she could manipulate him by suddenly performing her duty as a wife, then her intellect was

as thick as the wall at his back. But behind the mirror of his
face that gave her back her own enigmatic smile, he was
hopeful.

He suffered for the rest of the day, his mind an internecine
war in which resentment belabored lusty anticipation. The
enforced separation, both of mind and body from the quar-
relsome, provocative, untrustworthy little bastard wench
had at least drawn a fretwork across his wounds, but now he
was bleeding again. He wanted Margery Neville writhing
beneath him in sweet abandonment. And she knew it and
was striving to enslave him as he had dreaded she would.
She was cleverer than he had anticipated and yet she played
with that knowledge as if it were a village football, only
kicking the bladder when it came her way, making no effort
otherwise.

Oh, patron saint of trundle beds! Thank God she was
away from him, enclosed in the gauzy row of women that
sat along the opposite board. Even the delicate carp, the
spiced viands, the endless platters of delicacies could not
distract him from the horses of desire and common sense
that were pulling him in two directions.

Actually, it was a donkey that drove away his demons
and brought laughter back like the gift of God. Nothing
more than a stubborn plaguey ass with two men inside it and
a master that yelled abuse. It was an astonishing surprise
after the stately entertainments that had been intermeshed
with the delivery of each course. The final incongruity that
King René always delighted in achieving.

It tried to sit on Warwick's lap. It lifted its tail at the Duke
of Calabria and dropped cakes of gingerbread from its rear.
It emitted sounds that brought blushes and headed toward
the ladies. While it was distracted with tidbits from the
Duchess of Anjou who was crying with laughter, the Countess discreetly withdrew, firmly ordering Anne to leave with
her and Margery followed them regretfully out of duty.

The players worked hard: they sang, they tumbled, they
quarreled, they juggled, they disappeared stealthfully one
by one and returned as a host of devils to plague the two
remaining actors who were mincing up and down as fat

merchant sinners. The tridents went everywhere, lifting hems, prodding purses, scaring the dogs until the noise deafened and the two kings rose with their hands over their ears.

Afterward, Richard drank with the players, learning of their meandering travels and whence they were bound. By the time he had done with them, they were happy and soused like herrings. He let them delay him before he finally left the hall, no, not with a swagger—he abhorred swaggards.

The laughter and carousing had strapped him with a breastplate against the despair of a night alone. The wine followed by beer had numbed the aching. All for the best. The Almighty, with the charming waywardness of the Delphic Oracle, had confirmed that celibacy was to be enforced and endured. But the bells of the cathedral sounded lonely and the river Maine was a cold band of silver beneath the moon before he felt his way up the unfamiliar stairs without a candle. The thick stones of the walls were substantial, rough against his fumbling fingers, and for an instant he would have sworn on Our Lady's mantle that he had the wrong room.

Moonlight forced its way through the shutter, missing the coverlet. Margery, trundleless, lay like a question waiting to be answered, the tendrils of honey hair curling over the edge of the sheet. He held his breath. Was she sleeping?

Only a cricket rasped through the stillness. His senses told him she was still awake. He divested himself swiftly of his clothing as if it were aflame. There was no bolster.

Incredibly, neither warp nor weft sheathed her silken skin. The pristine snow slope of back and thigh lured his fingers to slide, and slide he did, one possessive hand between her thighs.

Surprised, she squeaked and wriggled but he held on, testing the moistness of that delightful chasm. What he found there pleased him.

"Your hand is cold, sir," she protested, albeit sleepily.

He brushed his lips against the creamy skin below her ear. "So, my firkin of desire, am I to slake my thirst with you now or do we quarrel first and beget a child later." He felt her tense with anger, and grinning, he withdrew his hand and turned her over, but the sheet came with her. She let her breath out as if deliberately calming herself. Her eyes, wide, watched him, but her expression, her mood, he could not read. Not yet.

Slowly he pulled the sheet away from her coy clasp and eased his gaze over the lovely curves, grateful that there was enough light to make out the contours of that delicious country. "You are curiously amenable, mistress. Are you ailing?"

"I am trying not to joust but the kerchief is down." Her voice was husky. Like scenting rain across a meadow, tears were near he guessed. Confusion, if it might be named an emotion, perhaps tormented her.

His smiling mouth found a corner of hers and teased. "I promise . . ." He made her part her lips, tasted her sweetness, then drew away to feast his sight again upon her body as he brushed his thumb over the dark peaks of her breasts as if she were the frets of a lute. "I promise that I will not argue with you for the present but as to jousting, lady . . ." His fingers stroked down her belly, across the soft tangled mound to the most intimate part of her. "As to jousting, I have a lance that needs must penetrate beneath your hauberk."

He felt her gasp and moisten further at his words.

"You are—"

"What? He bent his head to one sensitive peak.

"Outrageous."

"And very comfortable with tournaments of this nature, if you are thinking of unhorsing me in mid-gallop."

Her fingers burrowed into his hair and forced him to bring his mouth up to hers. She opened her lips beneath his.

He tormented her, one instant demanding, the next withholding, while his fingers echoed his lips until she was slippery and unfulfilled. Her fingers also grew adventurous, caressing him until he was groaning and unable to withstand her. He thrust her hand away and swiftly moved between her legs.

"Richard." She gasped, arching and writhing as his fingers worked at pleasing her, dragging her gently to the abyss. "Please, have mercy." He laughed, exquisitely torturing her before he plunged his shaft toward her womb. He felt her tremble and then sweetly convulse, bringing him his own release.

Afterward, emptied, satiated, he collapsed beside her, his face in the pillow, his breath short.

"Richard." A little hand shook him. "Please, speak, are you ill?"

"Do you mean have I splintered my lance?" He raised himself on his elbows. Of course, one forgot the lady was inexperienced in lovemaking if not in dissembling.

"I suppose I do." He heard the frown in her voice even if he could not see it in her face. "Does it hurt afterward? Are you in pain?

"Not anymore. Give me time to recover and you may alleviate any further discomforts I have yet to suffer before morning."

She gave a little sigh of relief at his laughter and then added, "We have to talk before morning."

He cursed inwardly. "You and I do not talk, Margery, we argue. You know very well that there will be no resolution of differences by morning. Just because you think you can beguile me between your thighs does not mean that there is any peace between us. This night is but an honest admission of desire on both our parts. At least your father can cease scolding like a grandam."

She thumped her pillow testily for answer and turned on her shoulder. He smiled and edged close so that his body fitted against the softness of her. She wriggled in protest but he held her close, delighting that his strength could encompass and overlap hers. He buried his face in the web of her sweet-smelling hair. This pleasure could be his every night if there was sufficient privacy—if he could forget that although her body might be his by law, her loyalty was to King Edward.

"Richard, if this meeting tomorrow should result in an alliance, will you support it?"

He tensed. What was she after now? He had already given a wealth of thought to this cause already. Now he had no wish to air the matter and certainly not with Margery Neville.

"Let it come to pass first."

"I hope it does not. Did you see how moved Anne was? Ah, I forgot, of course, you are in her confidence."

"Peace, you shrewmouse. Am I not the fortune seeker

you think me?" He sighed, shifting to rest his head back
upon his crossed wrists. "I wonder how my Lord Montague
will view this alliance if it comes to fruition. He loves King
Edward well and it will be a bitter thing to have to choose
between his brother and his friend."

"And, of course, your brothers must choose also. Will
they support Lord Montague's decision?"

"Our family have always fought on the Nevilles' side.
Mayhap they will consult our father in this, should a decision become necessary."

She turned onto her side facing him, her fingers teasing
the dark curls upon his chest. "What about you, Margery?
Who will you pray for? Your father or the wonderful Ned?"

She withdrew her hand. "I will do anything to prevent
this alliance which is why I will go to England." She was
reminding him of the pit that lay between them because he
had rejected her, always the constant jab of her duty to the
infamous Ned. Could she not grasp the nettle at last and see
that *he*, her husband, had the ordering of her life and would
outmaneuver the King of France yet.

"Hmm. And if I decide to support this alliance, lady, and
command you to support it also?"

"You cannot order my conscience." She rolled over to
rest upon her elbows, her delectable breasts creating an adit
that beckoned to pleasurable depths.

Running a finger down the valley of her spine, he quoted
softly:

> *"I wish her well, she wills me woe,*
> *I am her friend but she's my foe."*

"*Are* you my ally, Richard?"

"That depends on you trusting me."

She gave it some consideration before she added, "Would
you be brave enough to stand before the King of France and
tell him you will not let me go?"

"Perhaps if I offered him a white crocodilus and a
phoenix."

"I do not believe in such creatures. You do not have
the stomach for it, do you?" She wriggled angrily away
from him.

Must she be always testing me, he wondered irritably. He turned his head. "Do not provoke me, mistress. I shall do whatever suits my purpose." She lapsed into silence at that. He did not want to think about why he had indirectly driven her to King Louis nor why she was willing to suddenly be so dutiful. If the wench would fall in love with him, then she would be like clay to be molded.

"I should like to meet your third brother. Is he also a riddlemaster?"

"John is the epitome of charm and possesses a pleasing wit. Unlike me."

"Oh, but you are very charming when it amuses you to be so and I am grown used to your humor. When you asked me at what time I wished you to deprive me of my virtue at Sutton Gaveston, I thought you were in earnest."

"How do you know I was not?"

"Because to do so would have dishonored you."

She was right, his little witch. So she thought she had fathomed him, did she? He needed to tug at the reins again, to remind her who was lord in this marriage. His hand skated down her flank. "Mayhap there is now a child taken root within your womb." The lovely curve beneath his hand quivered and he laughed softly at the success of his stratagem. "You are grown suddenly silent, lady."

"How many children are you expecting?" she asked in a small voice."

"Well, there's the babe I whelped on a cordwainer's wife in London, and yes, I am sure I told you the recorder's married daughter in Gloucester has twins swelling beneath her girdle. Her mother was a twin also, she tells me, and then there is a noble widow who lives on a fine manor outside Doncaster. Ouch!"

Margery was leaning on her arm, glaring at him, one lovely nipple thrust entirely too close for his peace of mind.

"You really do know all these women, do you not?"

"Yes."

"You seduced them under their husbands' noses."

"It was a close shave sometimes. Once I had to escape over the thatch. But it was all in preparation for you, mousekin." He touched the tip of her breast and felt her shiver at the sensation. Her answer, however, was shaky with indignation.

"No wonder you think so poorly of women, especially married ones. They fall off their trees into your lascivious hands like plums."

"It is true, I have met few honest women. I suspect Ankarette Twynhoe only qualifies because she has a shape like a barrel and a tongue that never stops clacking."

"You are very cruel."

"No, merely honest."

"Have you some bastard children?"

"I do not know, lady, nor, I suspect, do their mothers."

She clouted him at that and he laughed as he thrust his fingers into her hair, tugging her face down to him. "I can hear the trumpets."

She tried to draw back but he held her still. "W-what trumpets?"

"The kerchief is down again."

"Such a swift recovery, sir?" Her disbelieving fingers crept like scouts down the hair of his chest and belly to discover the position of the enemy and found he spoke the truth. He knew that if it had been day, he would have seen her cheeks turn to rose.

"You see," he said softly, and had her on her back again with swift strength. "I said you were '*mon seul désir.*' " Her soft mouth yielded willingly beneath his lips. Her giving astounded him; the gentleness and the passion were the heady brew that he had dreamed of.

"Do you want me, Richard?" she asked when he let her breathe again.

"Yes, as the earth needs sunshine, but alas, the morning will come all too soon and Truth will hide her face again."

She pushed him away. "But do you want me for me?"

"Of course." His fingers were teasing the luscious berried tip of her left breast to a ripe perfection.

"No, I mean, do you care about me?"

"I think I have been asked that by every woman I have ever bedded," he answered with deliberate arrogance and in return received a punishment that was both instant and divine.

Margery woke with Huddleston's arms imprisoning her. Somewhere a rooster was issuing proclamations. She freed herself at the risk of awakening him and wriggled out of the sheets.

"This is where we have another devastating argument and come close to strangling one another." His voice found her at the window.

She turned around deliberately, no longer embarrassed to be as naked as Eve, aware of the full power of her body over him. Her gaze deliberately studied the dark river of hair that ran down the center of his chest and disappeared beneath the sheet about his waist.

He raised an eyebrow as if amused at her newfound confidence. "I cry you mercy, lady. You cannot have more. The petards and the pennons are all down and the crowds have gone home."

She frowned and sought a chastising answer. "My father will at least be pleased at your capitulation."

"What!" He was out of bed and joined her by the window, grabbing her wrists as he had done at his most bitter, so that her belly was against the hair of his. But the manacles of flesh were gentle this time. For an instant she had been afraid, and then he laughed and kissed the tip of her nose and let her go.

"Now heed me, pert one, before Alys arrives to help you dress." He held her chin between his thumb and forefinger, compelling her attention. "We may not have the luxury of a private conversation again for a while. Stop looking at me like that and hear me out. Angers will be full of eyes and ears. The world will be eavesdropping. As your father said, you must be very careful."

She searched his face, dismayed by his sternness, and stole her arms about his neck so that he too must perforce listen.

"Please, Richard, advise my father against Lancaster."

"No one advises your father. You know that." His fingers curled around her arms but he did not break her hold on him.

"No, I do not know that." She shook him. "I am merely a woman and banned from counseling. If I were his male bastard, he would at least listen to me."

"And this ridiculous conversation would not be taking place." He broke free and moved away from her to gather up his clothes. Then choosing his words with care, he set his garments on the bed and turned to her. "Listen to me. In Angers now there are Englishmen who have lost their lands because they supported their anointed king. Most of them are men who fought hard and valiantly in the long wars with France and deserve better of fortune. They believe your golden Ned is a whoreson and an upstart. So you *will* keep silent about your Yorkist loyalties, Margery, and if needs be, you will abandon them. We could be shortly witnessing a change of kings."

"Oust Ned?" She lay down across the bed and rested her chin in her hands. "Pah, you think a few ragtag exiles can thwart him?"

Her husband freed his head from the neck of his shirt and tugged it down before he scowled at her. "Mistress, are you deaf to my advice? If your sister Anne becomes the future queen of Lancaster, will you seek to undermine her and the heir she may carry? Will you oppose *her* because Edward of York once smiled at you and laid his head between your breasts?" He caught her fists before she could fling herself at him and compelled her wrists back against the sheets. She thrashed from side to side trying to free herself, trying not to meet the power in his eyes. "Lady, I think you are vulnerable in your present state of undress. You tempt me to take my hand to that delightful naked flesh of yours."

The instant he let go, Margery sprang away with a curse and sat on the edge of the bed with her back turned against him, rubbing her wrists. This was not going as she had planned it at all. She had hoped he would be more malleable. Now it sounded as though he was going to lecture her.

"If your reasoning rested upon logic, lady, instead of your feelings, then I would say your arguments had some substance." She did not answer him. She could hear him lacing up his gipon and drawing on the woolen hose. "I think you and I may never feel easy with each other until you cease to worship Edward like some pagan idol."

Too much! She jerked her head around and found him watching her.

"That is what underlines *your* enmity, sir. What hypocrisy to accuse *me* when *you* cannot forget that Ned has held me in his arms."

"Quite right." His eyes held her gaze coolly as he looped

the fastenings of his doublet over the row of buttons. "I cannot forgive his cruelty. He tried to make a whore of you to goad your father." His eyes glittered as he warmed to his argument and he leaned forward, resting his fingers upon the crumpled coverlet. "In fact, he succeeded in making you a whore, because from that day onward you saw yourself as one."

Margery tried not to let him see how his words flayed her. She turned her face away and scowled unseeing at the iron candleholder.

"Why do you persist in your support of Ned?" His tone was venomous. "All the world knows he is but a sluggard and a lecher. Follow your father's wisdom and see sense."

"Ha! Perhaps I missed all the rhetoric while I was at the convent. Tell me, was there anything in my father's speeches about allowing himself to be used as a fire poker by the King of France? The common people would rather have Ned than the Bitch of Anjou. They proved that when that let my father crown him king."

"The people will bend with the strongest wind that blows."

"They do not bend to a wind from France! And nor shall I! So, I have my answer, sir. You will support Lancaster. Anything that will bring Ned tumbling down into the dirt."

"Because of you, my sweet bastard?" His tone was scathing. The bed creaked as he took his weight from it. "Acquit me of making foolish judgments because I want some petty revenge." It was a few minutes before the door latch rattled and she turned her head.

The long fingers paused upon the iron ring. Oh, he was fine from his shining boot tips to the folded pleats of his high lawn collar. The grace of him thrilled her senses, but not his words. "It pleases me that you have learned at last to use your body, now learn to use your head."

"You arrogant—"

"Fortune hunter? If you say so."

He escaped through the door before the candlestick hit it.

CHAPTER
22

A distant trumpet distracted King René from explaining the origin of each piece of furniture that the Countess of Warwick was politely admiring.

"Madame, monseigneur, a thousand apologies. My daughter's party have been sighted crossing the Pont de Ligny and I must welcome her." If their host noticed that the Earl of Warwick's face tightened visibly at the news, he gave no sign of it. "You will like my grandson," René murmured, delaying to pinch Anne's cheek. The strong scent of lavender and musk departed with him.

The girl cursed and swung away to the window where Margery sat watching, her quiet mood unexpected.

"You will not see from here. I am going to watch, will you come?" Richard Huddleston held out an arm to each of Warwick's daughters.

"No!" Anne said shortly.

"No, Master Huddleston, it would not be seemly." The Countess was watching Anne, her mouth an upside-down horseshoe. Ill luck. "But you may go."

"As my lady pleases." His eyes lighted on his wife with a

wicked gleam but she gave a brief jerk of her head, unable to look at him.

The Nevilles had to tolerate hearing the fanfares a second time as the castle welcomed home its aging princess. The sensitive visitors could easily believe today's cheering sounded less contrived. Their consolation prize was hot coffyned delicacies that were served on the small-tables in their apartments. Their hosts had decided it was judicious to keep the English guests out of sight for a little space.

Louis of France spent the next hour in a pendulum motion between the apartments of Queen Margaret d'Anjou and those of Warwick. It had been planned that Warwick would not be reintroduced to his bitterest enemy on his own. His brother-in-law, the Earl of Oxford, who had recently defected from England, had agreed to be present at the meeting with the Queen. The two rebel earls were supposed to shortly enter the *grande salle* together, but Oxford had not arrived and Warwick's temper was growing shorter as the afternoon shadows lengthened. They waited for the Earl for two hours before Louis ran out of patience and insisted the meeting no longer be delayed. The Countess, her matronly attendants, and Warwick's two daughters were conducted down to their places to observe the historic confrontation. It was still hoped that Oxford might yet ride across the drawbridge at any moment.

The *grande salle* was already crowded as Margery entered at a discreet halfpace behind her sister. The finely clad throng parted to let them through, clapping politely. Anne waited for her, her smile clenched. "I hate this! Walk beside me."

"Have a care, Anne, some of these people may be English, remember."

A squat "x" of a chair had been set at the side of the hall for the Countess. She did not seat herself but stood graciously smiling. It was a brave performance that neither of the younger women felt like emulating, but several of the Angevin nobles glanced at each other and then came forward to pay out words with polished smiles.

"Anjou must want this very much," Margery murmured.

The fifteen-year-old did not answer. A scarlet codpiece flamboyant against mustard hose beneath a sinfully short

doublet had distracted her for an instant before she caught
Margery's eye and blushed.

"Madame, forgive me." One of the older Angevin ladies
had overheard and drew Margery apart. Her English was
heavily accented, her breath just tolerable. "If only your
noble earl can restore our princess, then Anjou will be able
to hold its own against the might of France. We fear invasion when our lord dies."

"But the Duke of Calabria can surely prevent this?"

"No, my lady, not without England on our side. The
Duke is ailing and our King is an old man. I beg you tell my
Lady Anne that we pray for her marriage with Prince
Edouard."

Margery sighed, "I shall tell her but you must understand
that she was raised to regard the Prince and his lady mother
as enemies of her blood. This is not going to be easy, least
of all for my lord of Warwick."

"We understand."

There was a temporary hush from the back of the hall
and the Angevin courtiers bowed and hastened to their
places, but the Kings had not arrived and the buzz of conversation renewed.

"Look there, have you ever seen such a fashion?" Anne
whispered, directing her sister to an effete young man with
hair down to his shoulder blades and pikes on his shoes that
were so long they were attached to his knees with tiny silver
chains. "I wish I'd seen him come in. He must look like a
duck when he walks."

"Hush, Anne," hissed the Countess. "Anyone would
think you had never been at a court before."

"Well, it is true. You never let us go to Ned's. He invited
us several times."

"Only because he knew your father would not accept."
The Countess sat down and fanned her face with her hand.
"Ned is the last person you should be talking about now of
all times! And pray refer to him as 'the unsurper' from now
on if you insist on mentioning him at all. Margery, set a
good example."

Margery was too distracted to be irritated. Two thrones
draped in heavy silk had been set upon the dais beneath
canopies embroidered with the coats of arms of each

kingdom. A third chair of state sat empty on the floor of the hall but she could see from the leopards and lilies gleaming in gold thread on the brocade that it was for the Lancastrian Queen.

"It begins." Richard Huddleston materialized at her side, too handsomely lethal for her peace of mind. His gaze noted his gift around her throat and he gave her an ironic smile.

Margery was not pleased to see him. "I thought you would be in my father's party."

"He sent us ahead. That wretch Oxford has definitely failed him. I have been playing lookout for the last hour." No wonder his brow was hot and beading. He glanced about him. "I should have worn my contrasting codpiece. Have you signed them all up for assignations?"

She smiled though her tone was icy. "How can you jest? Yes, of course, I have signed contracts. I need to gain some expertise from somewhere." He was heating her blood by letting his glance linger on her body. And he knew the full extent of his power, curse him!

The clear warning notes of the Angevin trumpeters sounded from the gallery. The Countess rose. Margery said a quick prayer for her father and turned to face the center of the hall. Stiff-backed, Anne shook like a wobbly funeral effigy.

The trumpeters produced an elaborate fanfare. The two kings walked in side by side, Louis slowing his pace to the older man's, and took their places on the thrones as the echoes died away. The Duchess Jeanne de Laval followed, her train whispering softly up the steps of the dais to stand beside her husband's throne. The French King fidgeted, rearranging the blue satin folds stitched with the golden fleur-de-lis that hung from his broad ermine collar. René of Anjou sat still as stone; only his eyes flickered from face to face.

Preceded by her herald, Queen Margaret arrived to a complex fanfare, on the arm of her brother, John, Duke of Calabria. A tiny page carried her train and behind her strode a grinning youth, his tunic stitched with the triple feathers of the Prince of Wales.

Margery felt Anne hold her breath. The lad was nothing remarkable. He would have topped young Gloucester by a

head but he definitely lacked the muscularity that years in
the combat yard would eventually bestow. The light brown
hair was neatly cut and curled in line with a jawbone that
hinted at no great strength. This was supposedly the
grandson of the victor of Agincourt, which, of course, might
be quite true. But according to his enemies—actually the
Nevilles had fanned the smoke of the rumor more than
most—he was supposed to be the son of the late Duke of
Somerset. Everyone knew King Harry VI had been reputedly mad at the time of conception. Anne's glance met
Margery's. The Prince's potential bride was not impressed.

But it was the Bitch who held Margery's interest. The
Queen had now grandly curtsied to both kings and seated
herself. Calabria and the Prince, having made their bows,
stood on either side of her chair.

Brave once, impoverished now, and as indefatigable as
her reputation, Margaret d'Anjou not surprisingly looked
older than her forty years. There could be little gold left in
her hair now for the tiny glimpse of it where her henin had
slipped back showed gray and lackluster. The burning fire
for revenge must have gradually consumed her beauty. The
plucked forehead of fashion did not flatter her; it accentuated
the deep lines of bitterness that destiny had etched across her
brow and the slashes of frown marks above her nose.

Studying her, Margery could see where the exiled
Queen's satin gown had been discreetly darned. Even the
deep, golden border was tarnished. Although her bodice was
fashionably cut away, it was sadly obvious that her scraggy
neck and shoulders had missed the salves and potions that
most other princesses could afford. The Countess of Warwick staring across at her was white, plump, and pampered
in comparison.

Having learned Margaret d'Anjou's history in a Neville
nursery, it was easy for Margery to hate her. But, trying to
be objective, she could feel sorry for her too.

Margaret had been sent over to England, at the age Anne
was now, to marry Henry VI. It must have been a jolt to her
hopes for it was said that all that Harry had in common with
his famous father, Henry V, was his name. Everyone knew
that he had been better fit for the cloister than the throne.

Margery had been told that apart from averting his eyes from every female cleavage in his proximity, Henry had also inherited a strange sort of madness from his Valois mother's family, an illness that had bedeviled Louis XI's grandfather as well. As Queen, Margaret had struggled to control the factions of ambitious nobles. She managed to form her own party of loyalists and even have a son, Prince Edouard, whom she was able to pass off as her husband's. One faction, however, led by both Ned's father, the Duke of York, and Warwick, finally evolved into a powerful opposition.

York and Warwick's growing predominance was strengthened by Henry's increasing bouts of insanity. Military conflict ensued. Battle after battle was fought until finally the Duke of York was slain in the north by the Queen's army. Before she could rush her victorious force south to crush the rest of the rebels, Warwick, with the Londoners' acquiescence, had crowned Ned as King Edward IV.

Ned had proved a far more powerful enemy. Not only had his charm and good looks enhanced his leadership qualities, but he was a good strategist. Queen Margaret, despite her loyal captains, was defeated and fled with her husband and young son to Scotland. Her husband, Harry, in his simple madness, crossed back into England and was made prisoner in the Tower of London. Margaret returned to her family and had kept an impoverished court of exiled Lancastrian lords about her for nine long years.

The timing of the Queen's encounter with her father suddenly began to make sense to Margery. Edouard was seventeen, unwed and old enough to fight. Had several years of planning gone into this? Louis and her father had been friends since '64.

Where *was* her father? Huddleston must have sensed Margery's tension. He rested his hand upon her shoulder. "Not yet," he mouthed. She should have shrugged him away. His fingers played with the wisps of hair escaping from her cap. She wished the candlestick had hit him.

Three noblemen strode, one behind the other, up through the hall, and made obeisance before each throne before they clustered about the Queen. The ardent Lancastrians.

"The heart-stealer is Jasper Tudor, Earl of Pembroke,"

Huddleston informed Margery. The Earl was kissing the Duchess of Anjou's hand. "On his left, Beaufort, Duke of Somerset. Behind them, Courtenay, Earl of Devon."

Tudor, with an easy manner, exchanged words with the Prince and then waved and nodded with a roguish grin to someone within the throng of retainers in the body of the hall.

Margery gazed at the three English lords calculatingly. Was this trio to be trusted? There was the same pride of spirit and resilience in them that was familiar in her father.

Expectancy hushed the hall. It seemed that King Louis had arranged matters in his typical manner to draw every shred of suspense from the occasion. Its unique quality went without saying but the most dramatic moment was imminent. The heralds sounded; the Earl of Warwick was announced. Heads swiveled; eyes divided between the doorway and the tense expression on the Queen's face.

"Jesu," whispered Margery. "Can one build an alliance on hate?"

"I hope so," her husband's voice replied softly at her ear, "otherwise we are all wasting our time." His hand moved up beneath the concealment of her cascading veil and settled possessively below her collar necklet. His touch heated her and a faint flush of color played traitor in her cheeks. She would have stepped away if she could but the throng was pressing around them.

The sound of one man's footsteps echoed from the entrance portal and halted. Richard Neville, Earl of Warwick, paused upon the threshold of the hall.

"What entertainment!" murmured her husband, his fingers stroking her as if she were an overspirited mare. Her profile held but inside her, hidden, parts of her stretched longingly.

The Queen involuntarily sat forward, her knuckles white upon the carved chair arms, then she sank back into the seat uneasily.

As taller people leaned forward to gape at the Earl's face, it was hard for Margery to see her father. For a moment she caught a glimpse and her heart beat with pride at the confident manner with which he swiftly scanned a hall full of his many enemies, like a bear about to face the dogs. Now she understood why he had been angered by the Earl of Oxford's tardiness. They were to have entered together so that Warwick might seem less like a Yorkist. As it was, he had been forced to enter alone.

The hall held its breath. Only the sound of Warwick's footsteps fractured the silence. Looking neither to right nor left, he walked proudly up to the dais.

Margery could not see his face as he approached the thrones but she watched the Queen fix simmering eyes upon the man who had engineered her downfall. As he drew level, the Bitch of Anjou pointedly jerked her head away, refusing to watch the Earl make obeisance to each king in turn. The Lancastrians instinctively tightened their phalanx behind the Queen as Warwick strode across to take his stand on Louis's right hand.

Then the argument for an alliance began. Charles, Duc de Guienne, King Louis's younger brother, spoke first, proposing amity, suggesting a treaty between Warwick and the Queen.

"Could the fair and much wronged Margaret, Queen of England, Princess of Anjou and Maine, be generous and merciful and pardon . . ." He was not the most comfortable speech maker. His voice droned on.

The Queen listened, troubled, looking as though her head ached beneath the heavy gold cloth henin with its jeweled circlet. She had probably been bombarded with written arguments by King Louis for days. Told that she needed a general to rally the Lancastrians and disenchanted Yorkists; lectured that it was her last chance to win England back; and threatened that there would be no arms and no money unless she made peace with Louis's great friend, Warwick.

Guienne mumbled to a close without a perforation and there was a short silence while they all looked at the tarnished Princess who sat gnawing her lower lip. With supreme effort she seemed to will herself to look at last upon her great enemy before she rose stiffly and walked forward, her train lapping loudly over the tiles in the hush. Below her cousin of France's throne she stopped to cast an arch look over the silent ministers of France and Anjou.

Margaret d'Anjou's voice was surprisingly husky. The very sound of it physically jolted Warwick and Margery wondered if the years had rolled back for him to the tense confrontations at Eltham and Westminster. "How can I pardon him?" she was saying. "All the miseries, shame, and debasement my family and friends have suffered are of his making. This is the man who dares to do what God alone may do." Her disdainful lip curled in scorn. "He has unmade a king who by right of birth and his own holy nature was, *is,* the true anointed and the only King of England!"

Old Yorkist arguments, taught from the cradle, rose unbidden to Margery's mind. Anointed, maybe, but had not old King Harry's grandfather, Bolingbroke, seized the crown by force and murdered its rightful wearer, Richard II, at Pomfret castle?

"He deposed the King's grace, my lords," continued the Queen, drawing Margery back to the present, "to set in his place a coxcomb, a whoremonger with no royal blood, not one drop of Plantagenet blood in his veins, but Neville blood certainly!"

Warwick's tanned cheeks turned a dark red as a rumble of laughter from the Lancastrians washed through the hall. It was the old tale that Ned was no son of the Duke of York but the child of a handsome Flemish archer that his mother had lain with in Rouen.

The Queen was smiling at her enemy now, her golden brown eyes provoking him to admit that the King he had set up had hounded him out of England. With arrogance, she turned her gaze upon the two kings. "In God's name, my lords, I will neither besmirch my son's honor nor my own. What would my loyal friends in England say if they heard I had become ally to the bloody Earl of Warwick!" She swept a perfunctory curtsy to King Louis and, turning to the Duc de Guienne, declared in a voice still loud enough to be heard by all, "Royal cousin, I beg of you not to ask for such an alliance ever again."

"Madam!" The Queen's shoulders flinched. "Madam!" rasped Warwick's voice again.

For a moment the Queen seemed to shake. Pembroke and one of her ladies moved forward, concern in their faces. Then the Queen rallied and turned to face her enemy, turned enough for everyone to see her face.

It was not over. It was a match between equals.

Warwick had come down the last step of the dais and moved into the center of the hall. White and scarlet, they confronted each other like figurines upon the checkerboard.

"I own that because of my armies, aye, and my kinsmen's, you had to flee into exile, but, by our Holy Lord, lady, you know as well as I do that your bad counselors plotted the downfall of my kinsmen and myself for no just reason. I would have been a lunatic indeed not to have fought back to save my own.

"Any other lord here would have done the same in my place. I acknowledge that I have erred in putting the usurper Edward on your husband's throne but, madam, I have paid for my mistake." His voice grew humbler and, with it, softer. "He has kicked me out of England like an unwanted cur and I am rewarded by his ingratitude. It is his witch-queen and her grasping Woodville kinsmen who rule England now, seizing property and goods unlawfully. Every Englishman here knows how Sir Thomas Cook was found guilty on a trumped-up charge because the Duchess Jacquetta coveted his fine house; you all know how Elizabeth Woodville sealed the Earl of Desmond's death warrant because he thought that Edward had married beneath him and said so publicly. She did not stop at his execution either but had his little sons murdered.

"Oh, yes, madam, you and your friends have good cause to hate me but you have sufficient reasons to pity me. Almighty God has punished me and destined this meeting. You and I are equal in our hatred now."

He took a step nearer the Queen but she recoiled. "Gracious Queen, what I have made I can unmake. Where I have set up one king, I can set another. You and I share a common cause against the House of York, so therefore, let us make peace and become . . . allies." The last word spoken so softly that only those close by caught it.

It was an arrogant speech, Margery thought, but then he was a confident man.

He slowly went down on one knee and wearily raised his proud face to the Queen. She was not looking at him. He took his beaver hat off and bowed his head. Taking a deep breath, he spoke hoarsely and at great speed, like a priest hurrying through mass to go to dinner. "I beg you to pardon

my past faults and to forgive me. The princes of this world
are greater than all other men upon this earth and therefore
capable of greater acts of mercy and marvelous wisdom
than lesser men. Madam, the Earl of Warwick asks your
pardon."

Sweet Heaven, it must have cost him, thought Margery. Little wonder that he had been tense and irritable for
the last week.

There was an uncomfortable silence. The Bitch was not
answering. Warwick shifted his weight slightly. The tiles
were probably biting into his knee but there was no doubt
his pride was smarting even more. Humility was not his
metier and there he was, as foolish as a lovesick swain,
kneeling in front of a capricious woman in full view of two
courts of noble lords.

Margery watched him turn his face to King Louis. The
slight nod and lowering of the eyebrows by the King signaled encouragement. The Queen moved deliberately to his
right out of his vision.

His voice was quivering with scarcely leashed anger as
he spoke again. "I do understand that it is asking a great
deal from you but I am willing to swear to be your true and
faithful soldier as his majesty King Louis can tell you. You
will stand surety, will you not, your majesty?"

"Oh, certainly," announced Louis, rising and coming
down to make a triangle. "You see, my sweet cousin, my
friend can lead your armies for you. We beg of you, Marguerite, forgive him. Mercy is given as a gift to the beloved
of Christ. 'Blessed are the merciful.' " He rested a comforting hand on Warwick's shoulder, probably to keep him
there. "The Earl of Warwick is my friend and a man of his
word. We are in his debt for many favors in the past and we
value his friendship above a peace with *Angleterre*. Pardon
him for our sake!"

Margery saw the Queen look up at her father, René, with
savage triumph. It was as if having her enemy at her feet was
like a flagon of sweet water to a thirsty man, and she was
drinking all she could hold. Still she did not speak.

Warwick shifted angrily under Louis's hand so that he
was now on both knees. It looked definitely as though the
King was holding him down. A wad of linen held firmly

over a flowing wound of anger. Unstanched, all would be lost. Louis jerked his head at his brother Guienne, and the French Prince came forward and knelt beside Warwick, rendering him less conspicuous. It was a kind thought.

"Most noble Princess," Guienne contrived to make his voice suitably choked with emotion, "I entreat you once more to pardon my lord of Warwick."

The minutes sped by. The tension in the hall turned to impatience. Huddleston's hidden fingers began anew to draw roads and rivers upon the exposed skin of Margery's back. She swallowed. Eddies and whirls of feelings moved within her, the memory of his lovemaking blushing her skin. He thought himself sure of her, did he?

"Well?" demanded Louis in a high-pitched clipped tone.

For answer, Queen Margaret merely turned on her heel and rejoined her party. King René descended from his throne. His counselors moved forward with him until a muttering semicircle of Angevins and Lancastrians clustered insectlike about the Queen.

Louis muttered something to Warwick, which translated sounded like "Get up!" Guienne waited for the Earl to make the first move.

"I can't!" snarled Warwick and Guienne rose gracefully and took one of his arms while King Louis held his other as if inviting him to rise. Painfully the Kingmaker tried to stand. It was obvious that one of his feet had gone numb and had they not held him as he set it upon the ground he would have toppled. Only those at the front were aware of the immense fury and frustration in the mighty Earl's face.

Margaret's son, who was not busy counseling his mother, watched, hard put to conceal his amusement. He was sucking in his cheeks in his struggle but the French King's scowl was sufficient to stifle him.

French counselors moved forward to add support to their royal master. For as long as it takes a man to walk a hundred paces, the rest of the hall waited and then impatiently began to speak at once. The hubbub was noisy, speculative.

"This is insupportable. My father once had all these French on their knees to him. How dare she!" The Countess rose tight-lipped and angry. Since her father had been one of those responsible for burning Jeanne d'Arc, she did have an argument. The Duchess, Jeanne of Laval, swiftly swept down the dais, set a detaining hand upon the Countess's wrist, and murmured something calming. Margery opportunely shrugged away from her husband's touch.

Anne, despite her short height, was looking as dangerous as a newfangled cannon that had had its fuse lit. Margery could see she was hard put not to quit the hall. The inaction of everyone else overcame her reserve and, picking up her skirts, Anne calmly glided out across the tiled floor. The men about her father parted in astonishment as she went up to him and tucked her arm defiantly through his.

"Oh, by the Saints, there is a daughter to be proud of!" exclaimed Huddleston. Margery stiffened, hurt at the comparison. "Oh, come, do not take offense. You know that only his lawful child could do such a thing."

"Do you think it is easy—wanting to but not being able?"

"The thought occurred to you also?"

She was bereft of words at his disbelief. Before she could muster an answer, the Queen moved away from her advisers. The hall hushed instantly.

"Royal cousin," Margaret d'Anjou declared, facing King Louis, pointedly directing her answer to him. "This is a great decision for me to make and I should be foolish if I did not take time and advice to make up my mind. You understand, I am sure." Having made low curtsies to each of the kings, she swept from the hall, her followers moving swiftly in a rustle of sarcenet and satin to form her wake.

Richard Huddleston stood looking after her, an uncharacteristic whistle on his lip. "An extraordinary woman!"

"Yes, indeed!" agreed Margery, selecting her words to cause him irritation. "Now my father may realize that it is Ned to whom he should bow the knee. It is too dangerous to bell a cat such as her."

"I should be careful what you say," hissed her husband, abruptly stepping back from her as if she had the plague. He glanced around swiftly to see if anyone had the English to comprehend her. "Not everyone shares your partisan opinions!" With an icy nod, he left her to join the group about her father.

Margery let out a slow breath. Next time she would make sure they all heard her.

⌒᷈⌒

Anne at least shared her opinion. "I wonder she did not expect Father to prostrate himself at her feet," she exclaimed some time later, flouncing into the chamber set aside for her. "How dared that woman embarrass him like that!" She unpinned her pearl cap and tossed it onto the back of the settle. "Where have you been, by the way? I sent pages to look for you."

"In the garden up within the ramparts. I am not sure whether it is merely for the use of royalty but there was no one around so I—"

"Avoiding your husband?"

"—trespassed," she finished. "Yes, something like that." Margery raised her head, abandoning the misbehaving link on Anne's platelet belt. It was necessary to turn the conversation. "How is our lord father? Is his pride still being massaged back into place by the French?"

"Yes, vigorously, but he was still glowering and morose when I came away. Mother kept saying not to mind and that made matters worse." She gloomily dumped herself on the window seat beside Margery. "I begin to realize how much King Louis wants this alliance. I do not think he will let the Queen or Father out of here until they agree, which means that we are pilloried here as well." She gave Margery a shrewd look. "What is going wrong between you and Richard—and do not tell me I am too young to understand!"

"I . . . I will be honest with you. I have told the King of France that I wish to return to England and that I will try and become Ned's mistress and report back what he says to me."

"Margery!"

"No, it will not be like that. I will go to England and I will tell Ned to be resolute. I want to make sure this alliance, if it happens, comes to nothing. And I *have* to leave Master Huddleston. It is the only way I can think of doing it."

"I think you are a fool, Margery, and it is quite unnecessary. We all know Ned will be on his guard."

"Will he? He is very reckless sometimes. Remember when our father held him prisoner?"

"Yes, that's true, but surely even he would not be so stupid. What will Father think if you run away to Ned?"

"You may tell him what I told King Louis. Oh, Anne, did you see the way that woman looked at our father? Such loathing. Suppose he does restore old King Harry. How long before she beheads him on some false charge?"

Anne closed her eyes painfully. "If I am forced into this marriage and the enterprise succeeds, I will be the future queen. You think she would destroy my father?"

"Of course she would." Margery flung herself on her knees before Anne and caught her hands. "Do you believe she will love you?"

"Oh, by Our Lady, of course not, but at least she cannot destroy me."

"Maybe not, but she can make your life barely endurable. They say she never allows the Prince to be away from her side. Do you imagine he will take your side against her? Oh, Anne, I cannot stand by and let any of this happen. If Ned will not believe there is danger, perhaps Dickon will listen."

Anne tugged her hands away at the mention of the Duke of Gloucester, her face pained. "But there will be no alliance, you heard her."

"Do you think she would make it that easy for our father? Allow her a little pettiness, Anne, before she truly starts the bargaining."

"Oh, Margery, no. I was hoping my prayers were answered. I do so pray you are wrong."

"I hope so too." She crossed to the door and checked there were no eavesdroppers. "In the next few days, do not be surprised at anything. I am considering voicing my loyalty to Ned."

Anne's eyes narrowed. "But that is dangerous. Even if King Louis and Father believe you are willing to spy for them, what will the Lancastrians think? And surely Richard will prevent you going?"

"Oh, he suggested the idea. It is clear he means to throw his lot in with Lancaster. He thinks the Queen is a goddess. He will be very glad to be rid of me, I assure you."

"I cannot believe how terrible this all is. The Nevilles used to be so happy and united but look at us now."

"Blame our father. First he crowns Ned king, then he wants to make George king, then he considers putting old Harry back. He uses us as pawns, Anne. Does he ever ask us what we want? Does he care?"

"You blame him for your marriage to Huddleston but he did it for the best reasons."

"Oh, yes, for the best. He sold me with some manors to gain a few men-at-arms. And he is selling you to found a Neville dynasty."

"Margery, listen, are you so sure that Richard does not care for you? I find no ill in him. He has been very kind."

"You are his future queen. He is an adventurer and openly admits it. I tell you, I can take no more of being baited, bedded, and scolded." Tears of rage sparkled in her eyes. Anne opened her arms and cradled her as if Margery were the younger sister.

"Promise me, Anne, that you will trust me, however I behave."

"Have I not always?"

"Yes, you alone. I do not deserve such a noble sister." She sat back on her heels grateful. "If I manage to set foot in England, I will seek out Dickon."

Anne smiled wearily. "Yes." Her tone was resigned. "Yes, but I think it will be too late."

Warwick's comments on Margaret d'Anjou as they sat in their chamber at private supper would have made a monkish chronicler blush and were certainly not to be repeated. He was too angry to put a rein on his tongue even in front of his unmarried daughter, despite the Countess's disapproval. If the Queen had not made up her mind in his favor within two day, he declared, then he was returning to Honfleur and everyone at Angers could go to Hell.

Next day, a dripping Saturday when the gargoyles dribbled incessantly into the moat, the Earl kept to his rooms but his martyred sulks were broken by the arrival of a charming, apologetic nobleman who stood grinning sheepishly on the threshold of the Nevilles' apartments.

Warwick rose frowning.

"How now, Dick? I am sorry," exclaimed John de Vere, Earl of Oxford, advancing into the room and tossing the droplets off his cloak like a great sheepdog. "I have just heard what happened yesterday and it is probably all my fault." He flung his arms around the astonished Earl and gave him a crushing hug. "But I shall make amends, I promise. Madam, your servant, and my sweet lady niece, Anne, is it not? You have grown since last I saw you."

One could argue that he was just saying what was polite, thought Margery, but his easy charm was hard to withstand. Within minutes he had a cup of rosé wine in his hand and was standing talking to her father by the hearth as if they were old campaigners. Of course if one thought about it, they were, but on opposite sides. And long ago, he had married one of her father's many sisters, which made him a sort of uncle.

By the end of the afternoon, Oxford's breezy optimism had blown around all the crevices of Angers. It had been Jasper Tudor whom he had singled out first and Warwick found that he had yet another caller.

"Listen to that wonderful Welsh accent, *look you*," murmured Anne as Jasper Tudor, Earl of Pembroke, made himself at home upon the settle.

"Little wonder that his father Owen managed to bed Henry V's widow," whispered Margery. "With those looks too, I will warrant. How strange that he has never married. Ankarette told me he is desperately in love with a wild Welsh shepherdess."

"Truly?" Anne regarded him with fresh eyes.

By suppertime, Warwick had entertained several more Lancastrian lords and afterward King Louis himself and his brother came. Warwick even laughed at one of Guienne's jokes—and they were as rare as hens' teeth—before the three of them disappeared downstairs arm in arm.

The women were sleepy and bored by the time the Earl returned.

"I think she's coming to heel," he declared.

⊱✿⊰

The news was announced at a reception before dinner the next day. The French were smirking jubilantly as the Prince and Anne Neville were formally introduced, each frigid with etiquette. The boy was polite but looked caught in that uncomfortable hiatus between the youthful wish not to draw attention to himself and the growing confidence of who he was and what he deserved. His face had started to strengthen into manliness, but his spasms of confidence sounded gauche.

Margery found it hard not to pass judgment. Her earlier observation that he never seemed to say anything without exchanging glances with his mother was confirmed. What the Prince needed was to taste a man's world for a while, away from Queen Margaret's intimidating control.

The banquet loosened the belts of formality somewhat and the air began to reek with premature celebration. How many Englishmen would have to die to satisfy these players? Men said that nigh on thirty thousand had been slain at Towton Field, the bloodiest of the battles between York and Lancaster. Just thinking about it nauseated Margery and her humor was not improved when she was led reluctantly to kneel before Queen Margaret. She had just seen her husband set his lips upon the Bitch's hand, his smile boiling with so much charm that her palm itched to slap him.

"We rejoice that you wear our badge about your neck, Marguerite Neville."

Was it the coincidence of the name "Margaret" or had Huddleston even calculated this? Margery wanted to rip the golden daisy from her throat. The Countess, to the left of the Queen, signaled a sympathetic caution. The Bitch d'Anjou smirked. "Fidelity is obviously not one of your husband's attributes in politics or the bedchamber, Lady Warwick." It was not queenly.

"Pardon, madame, I am my father's *eldest* daughter." Margery could not resist answering. With some calculation, it was possible to argue that her father and the Countess must have been wed as children, and she had never heard of her father straying since Isabella had been born.

Richard, watching in dismay, noted how the Queen's

eyes whipped across Margery's face. Unfortunately she caught the Countess smiling. "Indeed?"

"That is quite true, your highness." The Countess nodded serenely. "My lord has always been *sane* enough to know where his best interests lie. Perhaps his highness the Prince would like to walk with us in the gardens?" Richard awarded the Countess the winning point but the Queen gave Warwick's wife a contemptuous look.

"By St. Denis, we have not time for such vanities, Lady Warwick. My son and I cannot be dallying when there is a campaign to be planned. Come, Edouard, John." She took Lord Oxford's arm. He bent his head to her ear. "Ah yes," the Queen's French carried clearly. "Did not someone tell me she had carnal knowledge with the usurper as a child?"

To have corrected the foul lie would have been useless. Richard saw the fury lash across Margery's face and within seconds he had her by the shoulders and drew her to her feet. She was shaking within the harness of his restraining hands.

"Thank you, Margery," muttered the Countess tersely, albeit with a smug look, as the last of the Angevin entourage drifted off after the Queen, "but your father's honor needed no defense from you."

"Mother!" Anne set a comforting hand on Margery's arm. "That woman had no right to speak like that even if she is a queen, which she is not since Father took her crown from her."

The Countess gave her child an exasperated glance, flung her hands angrily in the air, and swept away.

Gripping her arm, Richard walked his wife swiftly to the side of the hall. "I thought I warned you to be circumspect. If your father's plans succeed, Margaret d'Anjou will be Queen of England again and you have just corrected her. What is more, you put Lady Warwick in an embarrassing situation."

"My lady does not like her any more than I do. *She* chose to be discourteous."

"That was her decision. But for the love of Heaven, Margery, see sense from now on. There is no point in offending the Queen."

"There is little point in mollifying her either. She looked

at me with loathing. Did you not see? She knew I was the *usurper's* mistress." Her tone was scathing enough to make him wince.

"Only in your mind. I doubt she can do you any real harm unless there is good reason and you behave foolishly. Your father has more sense than to topple King Edward for the sake of a woman with that sort of vindictiveness. There is more on her mind than bothering with you. If these negotiations succeed, she will be Queen of England again and you *will* please her."

She flinched but retaliated angrily. "I am sorry if I am thwarting your ambitions, Master Huddleston. Are you planning to give the Queen's worn shoes a daily rub?"

His face froze. "By Heaven, if we were private I would be tempted to throw you over my knee."

"And, here, have your collar back!" She struggled to open the catch but Richard gave her a contemptuous look and strode away.

cΩm

The golden marguerite burned her flesh. It was needful to wait until the hurt and anger abated, necessary to find a refuge in the nearest beckoning side chamber. Tears flowing, her arms crisscrossed defensively, fingers clutching at her bare shoulders, Margery waited miserably for the mistiness and the sniffles to clear, only to find her gaze drawn by a tapestry that hung above the doorway. The latent carnality in it penetrated her senses, astonishing her, momentarily driving away her sorrow. Men with the faces of satyrs hovered behind the fully clad noble ladies. When she looked hard, she could see the empty buttonholes, the nipples rising like suns from horizons of untidy bodices.

"You like it?" asked a voice in careful English. She realized with astonishment that King René stood behind her.

"Or is it too secular for you, Margery Neville? Did you observe the Apocalypse tapestry in St. Maurice's?" Louis of France materialized like a black wraith from a carved chair by the window.

She curtsied in panic at disturbing their intimacy. "*B-beau sire,* yes, I saw it, but it was almost too rich, too . . . powerful for me. I—I felt very small beside such a masterpiece." She could feel the betraying salt upon her cheeks; the swollen telltale rims left from weeping.

It was her host who answered. "It is good that you feel this. I am jealous, young woman. To see such workmanship, such beauty for the first time, ahh." He nodded. "I wish it was like that for me again. When I go there to mass, sometimes I do not look anymore. I think I know every thread of it and then I loathe myself for such complacency." He looked hard at her. Perhaps he was myopic. "You like it in Angers, madame?"

"Oui, beau sire, c'est . . ." She searched for a word that sounded French. *"C'est impressif."*

The King of France came across to them. "Did you know that for over seven hundred years the Holy Church denied that women had souls? Now they can be damned and redeemed like the rest of us. She reads, uncle. She shall have use of our library at Amboise if she has time." Jesu, this man terrified her. "And it is almost time for you to leave, I think, Margaret Neville," he concluded softly, his smile ambiguous.

"Yes, *beau sire,*" she asserted, lifting her chin with a tight smile.

King René, misunderstanding, gestured her through the doorway.

The ceremony in the cathedral was an outward manifestation of the results of the peacemaking, but it was velvet and silk stretched taut across the cracks in the pasted alliance. It was only during the service that the Neville womenfolk became aware that Warwick had agreed to swear his loyalty to Margaret d'Anjou on the bones of St. Laud. And it was common belief that anyone who perjured themselves on those bones would be dead within the twelve month. The Bitch was taking no chances with her old enemy, even to ensuring him a bed in Hell if he betrayed her. Her only concession was to permit the announcement that her son and Anne Neville were to be betrothed.

The tension between the Neville supporters and the exiled lords of Lancaster as they walked down the nave together was still sufficient to embarrass. Margery, too, uncomfortably forced into proximity with her personal treaty partner, resorted to whispered assertiveness. "If a papal blessing is received for the betrothal, as I am sure it will be, you will be a brother-in-law, more or less, to the future Queen of England," she observed witheringly as she and Richard Huddleston were obliged to walk together down the nave at a discreet distance behind Anne and the Prince. Her husband's smile was sardonic, she observed under her lashes.

He ignored the thrust. "But at last the web is fully cast and your father and the Queen can cease the obligatory twitches of distaste. What, of course, has not been mentioned among all the holy oaths is that if this campaign is successful, your father will be committed to war with Burgundy. This is not about England's good but the expansion of France."

"Yes." Her tone was bitter.

"You might be interested to know that Sir John Fortescue and my lord of Oxford have been trying to talk the Queen into this betrothal for some time." Richard noted the flicker of interest. "Apparently they broached the matter with your father a few years ago at secret talks outside Calais but then, of course, he was not ready for rebellion. Perhaps he was waiting for the Duke of Clarence to come of age. Or Lady Anne."

Margery groaned with disgust. Her disillusionment with her father was growing daily. "Ha, it is easy to interpret with hindsight."

"I would wager your father has been considering a Neville dynasty ever since he crowned your wonderful Ned. Either Isabella or Anne has to become a queen. Had Isabella been older and had your looks, your father might have contrived that she encountered the King in the midst of the forest. I believe that is now the known procedure for would-be queens these days. Unfortunately you were disqualified from the start. A pity old Ned ignored little Isabella, he will be quaking in his Spanish leather boots quite soon."

"I doubt it." They had reached the portal. She gracefully lifted her fingers from his gloved wrist as Matthew Long

approached with Comet. Displeased, she looked about her
for the chariot that had brought the ladies-in-waiting. Huddleston's eyes held dangerous green flames. She nearly
squealed as he put two adroit hands unexpectedly around
her waist and tossed her into the saddle. She landed with a
thud that bruised. "Was the trundle bed comfortable?" he
asked.

Forced to hang on to his belt, she gritted her teeth as he
settled before her and heeled Comet into place in the procession. At another time, she would have enfolded his waist
right willingly. "I have observed, Richard Huddleston, that
when you cannot browbeat me with words, you fall back on
your physical superiority which is extremely lily-livered of
you."

His next words knocked the breath from her. "You will
be able to claim your house in Chelsea as a concubine's pay
quite soon. The King of France has suggested I make
arrangements for you to leave."

He felt her stiffen behind him, seeming to weigh her
words before she offered them for purchase. "Welcome
news," she answered finally. "We may dispense with each
other at last but I should like to return to Amboise and collect my other belongings."

Richard smiled grimly. So she was still waiting for the
promise from the Duke, and King Edward had insisted it
must be written in the Duke's own hand. Time was running
out. If the Lancastrian lord with whom he had sat and
caroused last evening was correct, there was another extremely good reason for Margery to leave France with the
greatest urgency.

23

It was a subdued party that rode west along the road that was navigable only in dry weather. Even the River Loire seemed withdrawn and thoughtful, having shrunk across its gravelly bed. At Tours, like a cannon ready to be lit, the Duke of Clarence awaited official conveyance of the ill tidings. Margery was not there to see if he took consolation from the wine, for her father and King Louis has sent the Neville women on ahead to Amboise.

To be truthful, Isabella was relieved to see them again but the news that it was Anne who was more likely to wear the crown rendered her sullen and resentful. And poor Anne, hurt at her sister's selfish lack of sympathy, rolled herself, woodlouselike, into a little armored ball of incommunicativeness and was looking for a stone to hide under. Margery, anxious for the Duke's return and bereft of her husband's dangerous company, was restless to be quit of France.

The Duke returned to Amboise next day ahead of the Earl, and Margery, catching his glance, knew that he was poisonous with fury. Now was the time to force a promise

out of him for Ned's sake, but there was no privacy. What
concerned her too was that even if George gave her the
written promise, she could hardly leave without her father's
permission even if she did have the blessing of the King of
France and it was unlikely that Warwick would agree.

Her father rode in with King Louis a day later. Lancastrians were now swelling his retinue: Sir John Fortescue,
who was writing a political treatise on kingship for Prince
Edward, and Jasper the handsome Welsh earl. Of Huddleston there was no sign.

Given time, without the wagons and chariots, the journey
between Tours and Amboise could be pleasant. A traveler
might linger to fill his leather wine bottle at one of the vineyards east of the city. Then, approaching the village of
Langeais, there was a plethora of taverns to replenish the
sweat of the carters, laborers, and masons who were
building a fortress for my Lord Treasurer. And there was a
certain corner as the river road looped north toward the
cliffs where there were three willing cherrylips, although
the discerning rarely lingered. God knows how free of the
pox the sisters were.

Richard made an excuse to leave Tours later than his
father-in-law, having business of his own that concerned
pigeons. With good horses, Matthew and two of his Cumbrian men-at-arms, he judged himself safe enough and the
track was well trodden by the frequent passage of traffic
between the favorite residences of the King and Queen.

He was wrong. Past Langeais, they were ambushed.

It was easy to believe Blanche, Isabella's maid-of-honor,
which was why Margery left everyone else listening to viols
and poetry.

"Mistress Huddleston." Thomas Burdett followed her
out and possessed himself of her hand. "It is the Duke who
wishes you to await him, a matter of some urgency, I
believe."

The candlestick quivered in Margery's hand. This had to
be what she was hoping for, except she had no appetite to be

alone with Clarence or any of his most trusted henchmen. A written message pressed swiftly into her hand would have suited her better.

"Do not look so concerned, Mistress Margery, I give you my oath as a gentleman that the Duke means you no ill. He wishes merely to give you a letter for a friend."

The dagger within her sleeve was reassuring as she followed Burdett up the staircase and along the gallery to the Duke's bedchamber. Candles flickered on the iron circle that hung from the ceiling in the antechamber and two more sat like altar lights on either side of the small-table where clean vellum had been set out. Through the open door to George's bedchamber, she saw that the Duke's servants had turned back the emerald coverlet and lain fresh napkins upon it. The air was gentle with the perfume of rosewater, musk, and beeswax.

"No doubt you will take some wine, Mistress Huddleston? His grace sups with the Duc de Guienne and will come as soon as he may. You may find him melancholy for it went ill for him at Tours. They can offer him naught for the great help he brings them."

Margery took the chased cup he offered and savored the sweet excellence of the muscat. "Since he already owns much of the Lancastrian demesnes, I would rather imagine the original owners would like them back," she answered tartly. "With what do they plan to purchase his loyalty?"

Burdett grinned. "Ireland."

"A troublesome gift."

"And the duchy of York."

"Oh." She swallowed the wine painfully. The dukedom and title were Ned's.

"His grace can argue eloquently enow when it suits him. He and my lady Duchess are to be heirs to the throne if Prince Edouard dies without issue."

Margery pursed her lips. "Hmm, better than could be expected considering the circumstances."

"Too true, Mistress Huddleston. Best to make sure your dice lands the right way up." He refilled her goblet. "Forgive me not drinking with you but his grace will not thank me if I lack a clear head tomorrow. No doubt your husband will be joining us in the council chamber."

"I have not . . . that is, I believe so." The bells of the
valley rang the hour. "I pray you, do not feel you have
to entertain me, Master Burdett. Perhaps I can return
tomorrow." She screened a yawn.

Her companion, keeping his distance, continued to stir
the soup of conversation politely, although like most young
men, much of his telling was to glorify his own prowess,
and Margery was as drowsy as a bee in a poppy field by the
time the Duke entered the chamber some half an hour later.

Apologizing for his tardiness, the Duke flung off his tall
crowned hat and sat down wearily. He was surprisingly
sober for the late hour. Refusing wine, he lifted the goose
quill pen and studied Margery, brushing the brown tip
against the fair stubble of his cheek. Pale Plantagenet eyes
ignited into a cold grin. "Here are we met for treason. What
does my royal brother require from me, Meg?"

Margery's heart lifted. This was a wonder. She would
have predicted a more qualified compliance. Cautiously,
she glanced at Burdett. "Oh, ignore Tom. I have no better
friend."

Margery rose and came to stand at the Duke's elbow. "A
one-line promise, my lord, but it must bear your signature.
A tiny morsel of vellum that may be easily concealed."

"So be it. By St. George, sit down, will you! Your perfume distracts me and here is matter to destroy kingdoms
and make beggars."

Margery smiled, returning to the small settle to blink
sleepily as the nib scratchily wrote out the few words that
might ruin Lancaster's hopes. Then a jolt of panic twisted
her innards painfully at the responsibility she would be carrying. Jesu, every agent in France would slit her throat to
possess it. Well, at last she could put into action the instructions Ned had given her but she was too weary to think
straight tonight.

"Hold it tight, man." The Duke drew the point of his
dagger down on either side of the message as if he were cut-
ting a pastry strip. "If this"—the sides of his mouth tightened in bitterness as he wound the tiny scrap about his
finger—"falls into the hands of the Bitch's agents, I am a
dead man. They will poison me or find some other foul
means to end my life." With a swift movement, he strode

across and gripped the wooden arms on either side of where Margery sat and leaned over her until his face was level with hers. "Is it your plan to deliver this in person to my brother, for I swear on my dead father's soul that Tom here will draw his knife across your lovely throat should you betray me to my enemies." Flecks of spittle found her face.

Margery drew back. His lips, drawn back from his teeth, were far too vulpine. "N-not personally, but I have instructions. All . . . all I need to do is wear a certain token and your brother's people in Amboise will contact me."

The Duke's blue eyes glittered but he straightened and stepped back, testing the vellum strip between his fingers. "I think you should find some means to leave straightaway. I should prefer you to take this and the fewer who know of it, the easier I shall sleep."

"I think so too, your grace." She could not help but yawn again. "Do not concern yourself. I have plans laid, but it needs my father's consent for me to go. Huddleston will be no problem."

The Duke picked up his dagger, fondling the jeweled haft. "So sure of him, Meg? When we all know he oils the Bitch's hands with slavering."

"I am sure that is an . . . ohh . . . exaggeration. He will not protest so long as the French pay him enough."

"The *French*, for the love of Christ!" The Duke exchanged a look of panic with Burdett and, drawing breath, unsheathed the dagger and stuck the point beneath her chin. "Be plain with me, woman! What in God's name are you babbling about?"

Margery scowled. She wished this was finished so she might go to bed. "I told King Louis that I would spy for him in . . . in Ned's arms. So when I go from here, it will be with his majesty's blessing and Huddleston knows and will be compensated. Now let me go to bed."

The Duke's angry expression metamorphosed into disbelief before resolving itself into a nasty smile. "To bed, yes. And all this for the sake of peace, dear old Meg." He exchanged grins with Burdett before adding, "I think you lied to me last time when you spoke of England; you just want to be Ned's whore again."

"I have a whole basketful of reasons but they will feed

your purpose, never fear." She eased herself off the settle and stood unsteadily. "Pray give me the message and let me go hide it presently." She put a hand out to regain her balance.

Burdett took her arm to steady her. "The wine was too young perhaps."

Margery put her fingertips to her brow and gave her head a little shake, trying to clear the gathering cloudiness. Wine did not normally have such strong effect but there had been little to do but sip and listen to Burdett.

"Grab her garter, Tom." The Duke had moved behind her and with a swift unexpected movement dragged her arms behind her back. "Hush, Meg, it is all for our cause. We will hide the message in your garter."

She should have kicked Burdett or slammed her heel back onto the Duke's shin but her limbs weighed as heavy as ancient branches. Burdett's fingers fumbled up her right leg and pulled her garter down around her ankle and free of her leather slipper.

"Now, Meg, listen before you fall asleep. In the morning you shall leave for England. There, hush now, Tom will put the garter back in place but we must remove the rest of your clothes. No, do not struggle." She thought of her dagger but the room had acquired the vigor of a windmill sail and her mind was strapped to it. Burdett dragged the overgown up over her head. The moment it was free of her she drew breath to scream, but the Duke's fingers fastened hard across her mouth. "Be easy, Meg, this is no assault. We just will send you swiftly on your way to Ned, that is all."

Burdett was unlacing her sleeves from the underkirtle. "Carry her to the bed, your grace."

"My whore for the night." The Duke smacked a wet kiss upon her shoulder as he lifted her. "Pity Bella is privy to this," he sniggered.

"B-Bella?" Margery tried to free herself.

"And Huddleston has been inconveniently delayed but he should be back in time to wave you farewell. Clever, eh, Meg?"

"She admits she is a harlot. Are you sure one of us can't enjoy her, my lord?" Burdett lifted her legs up onto the bed and dragged her underskirts down over her hips. Margery, cursing them, saw his eyes dwell lewdly upon her nipples before lowering his gaze to the triangle of hair between her thighs.

"I-I will kill you first, wh-whoreson."

"Unstrap her weapon, man, we do not want her using it on me in the morning."

She heard no more. Her befuddled wits gave out and night came down like a great blue curtain snuffing out the candlelight.

She woke with the Countess's voice shrill in her ears. There was no meaning in the words, not yet.

"Mother, I will have this handled my way, you hear!" That was Isabella, unusually decisive in her mother's presence.

"Wake up, Margery! What is the matter with you?" An ungentle hand slapped at her face but her eyelids were pasted to her cheeks.

"I told you there was something wrong. Is is poison, do you think? Could she have drunk something intended for me?" The Duke's voice.

With a curse, Margery remembered and struggled up. It seemed that the bell being hit by a clapper was her head.

"Just look at you, you wanton," hissed the Countess, somewhere near her right ear. "How you managed to deceive Huddleston, I will never know. I hope she gives you the pox, George!"

"Just go, Mother!" Isabella snapped. "And make sure you leave me to deal with Father! If you say a word to anyone about this, I swear I will never speak to you again. I will not have the whole château sniggering at my expense."

The door slammed. Someone broke the silence with a giggle. Margery's bleared vision cleared to show the Duke and Duchess standing at the end of the bed, both in their dressing wraps, spluttering with laughter as if they had been caught at some prank.

Margery heaved her tangled hair back and dragged the sheet up tightly. "What in God's name have you agreed to, Bella?"

The Duchess folded her lips like a naughty child and

swept around toward her. "Is it not a wonderful plan? How else could we gain Father's permission for you to leave so soon? You can take George's message and all will be well."

Margery closed her eyes painfully. "Keep your distance, your grace," she warned through clenched teeth. "I have a sudden aversion to fools." It was obvious from her innocent glee that Bella had neither thought the matter through nor could grasp the fact that her bastard sister's fragile standing in Warwick's opinion, not to mention Huddleston's, would be in shards now.

"Oh, do not be so peevish. You wanted to be free of your marriage." Isabella sat down on the bed. "I promise"—she crossed herself—"that once we return to England, George and I will write to his Holiness and every bishop in England, if need be, to have you free again."

Free—and then?

"You shall retain your dowry, Meg, and a rich pension." The Duke ran his fingers through his hair. The color in daylight reminded her of fresh dog dung. "Smile, wench, and get yourself dressed while Bella and I talk to the old man. You need not face him."

Wench indeed! She grabbed a silver cup from a tray that lay upon the bed and hurled it at him. He gave his braying laugh and, arm about Bella's waist, escaped into the antechamber.

Alone, Margery put her head on her knees and wept angrily. Her tears continued to fall as she thrust back the sheets. Only the tiny twist of vellum about her garter band was some consolation. Swiftly she dressed and, finding the Duke's brushes, bullied her hair back into her headdress. Squinting into his mirror, she stared in growing horror at the love bite on her neck. Had the Countess seen that? Panic rose. Could either of the men have violated her? No, surely she would feel bruised, penetrated? Her breathing calmed and she wrapped the tail of her veil firmly around her neck. Thank God Huddleston was not back to see her shame, but where was he?

The Duke was waiting for her in the outside chamber. His servants had been dismissed except for Burdett whose grin made her turn crimson.

"Be charitable, cousin, did you not undress me in my bed

at Valognes? Wait!" The Duke put a hand out to delay her
but she slapped him away.

"What you have done was vile and to make poor Bella
agree to it too! Let me go!"

"Right willingly," whinnied the Duke. "All the way to
England."

Tears blinding her, Margery stumbled down the stairs
and stood groggily, bewildered to find the courtyard a standstill of carts and wagons being unloaded for the feast next
day: Queen Margaret was expected on the morrow. The
bustling servants stepped around her. Where could she go to
gather her thoughts and hide her shame?

"Margery!" Huddleston's voice unheard since she had
left Angers, reached her across the noisy crowd. Involuntarily she turned in his direction.

Richard froze. There was something wrong. His wife
looked distraught and unhappy, like a wobbling, spun coin
about to topple. As her gaze found him, panic contorted
her face.

He knew he was an eyesore. There was a bruise purpling
down one cheek, his jacket was torn, and his mustard hose
had a beggarly rip across the right knee.

She fled behind the pavilion that was being erected, and
by the time he had circumnavigated two laden asses and a
runaway firkin, his wife had disappeared.

Margery entered the royal library with as much awe as if
she had set foot in Heaven. Her heart was still thumping
painfully at the humiliation and shame to be faced, but the
mingled smell of ink and parchment was comforting. Here
kings' deeds were judged long after their costly ermines had
decayed and their stolen crowns were worn later by others
who never knew them.

A polite cough reminded her of where she stood.

"You are lost, demoiselle?" A tall man, as thin as if the
mighty fist of God had squeezed the fat out of him through
his soles, rose from behind a lectern. The sharp scrape of
wooden legs against stone insulted the sensibilities of the
other users. Frowning eyes under ribbed brows viewed Margery from all sides, askance at a woman's presence. She

smiled mistily and the clerks fearfully buried their heads in
their books again like moles ducking back into their hills.

"*Le Roi me veut—*" Her voice carried, offensively
female and echoing. The custodian of the books hushed
her with a gesture but at least listened with patience to
the rest of her attempt at ravishing his language. As her
words trickled to a stop and it was necessary to use a
pleading facial gesture and supplicating hands, the man's
mouth tightened.

If he turned her away, it would be the final blow into her
belly of self-esteem and tears would bring shame. It was
hard to demonstrate a sincere interest in the art of illumina-
tion when her husband and father would want to beat her for
a whore.

The scholar nearest them rolled his eyes heavenward. It
was the eavesdropper's hostility that smoothed her passage,
for, of a sudden, mischievous amusement glimmered in the
faded blue eyes above her. The custodian snapped his fingers to summon a brawny young cleric and beckoned
Margery to follow him into a forest of boards. Each was
identical, but her guide eventually lifted the huge ring of
keys that hung against his thigh and gravely unlocked one
of them. A massive volume lay upon the shelf within. Its
pages were edged with gold and the corners of its leather
cover were reinforced.

As Margery put her hand out innocently to open it, the
custodian grabbed her wrist forbiddingly. She shook her
head, raised an eyebrow like Huddleston did, and put on her
most authoritative Neville expression. The man drew his
hand reluctantly back and gestured her to proceed. She
opened the pages just a few deep and nodded with approval, as if she were some master illuminator, at the rich
colors. Briskly, she closed the cover and stood back deserv-
ingly. The custodian snapped his fingers to his assistant who
bore the book awkwardly back to the outer room. Her guide
crooked his finger at her and she obediently followed. Did
they ever actually converse, she wondered.

It was comforting to be distracted but the pain was still
with her. They did not seat her at a bench and chain the
volume to the shelf behind but set her at an individual stand.
She smiled mechanically at the custodian as he personally

turned the huge wooden screw of the lectern until the frame was at the right height for her. The book was set before her with pride and she was helped up onto the high stool and shown how to place her feet on the wooden support pedals. The latter were too distant, designed for men. She bestowed a watery smile on her helper as she twisted her ankles beneath the stool onto the cross brace. She did not fit here either. Where were women made welcome save to decorate or gratify?

The librarian, miraculously sympathetic now, drew his celibate wrinkles into a smile and inclined his head with the dignified graciousness of age before he quietly glided back to his desk. Silence resumed.

The kindness in tolerating her was almost her undoing. Tears bubbled to the surface, troublesome to hide, but at least she had her back to the others. Gold and azure swam before her vision and she kept her head back lest the salt drops mar the exquisite penmanship. To be able to sit in the learned quiet was an achievement but the wound to her reputation throbbed, open and smarting.

It mattered to her so much that Huddleston respected her. Now he could drag her before a church court that could force her to walk barefoot in her shift through the streets as a penitent harlot. She tried to concentrate on the illuminations but she must have sat there unheeding for a least most of the time between the hour bells.

"That must be a very interesting page judging by the time you have been staring at it. Are the rest pasted together or is that some incantation to turn me into a frog?"

She sniffed and blinked up in surprise at Richard Huddleston. He was a dark shadow as her sight misted again. She was too choked to answer him. No doubt his soft words were but gentle rain before he lashed out his true fury.

"How long have you been watching me?"

"Long enough." Richard sounded kind. "Let me close the book. They say prayers against water in this place."

She smudged the tears away with the knuckle of her forefinger and before she could protest, he swiftly eased her off the stool. She acquiesced—to have argued would have desanctified the silence and shocked the scholars. He almost had her past the threshold before she had the courage to hold back and speak to the custodian. It would have been clumsy to leave without whispering a promise to return.

"Where are you taking me? To chastise me before my father?"

"To admire the view, Margery. The wind from the north will dry your tears." How easily a smile seemed to weaken her, as if she wanted him to take charge of her. Ridiculous, she chided herself, that the firm hand hauling her up the spiral staircase should provide such simple pleasure.

Apart from the ripening bruise, there was now no sign that he had been fighting in defense of her honor, but there was a harshness about his mouth that told her someone must have set the information before him like a welcoming carpet. Wet-haired, his expression resilient as he compelled her briskly across the courtyard, Richard Huddleston now presented the formidable, icy sleekness of rocks beneath a waterfall—impossible to conquer.

"Wait here!" Shaking, she heard the occupants of the guardhouse adjoining Queen Charlotte's apartments exclaim in laughter and the clink of coins tossed across the board before her husband reappeared, his mouth curling at a bargain well made. Miserably, she knew that her only chance of mercy was to tell him the truth. But to do that would be to betray all that she believed in. The message to Ned was more important than saving her marriage if it prevented England being ripped once more by civil war.

She let him propel her around the curve of the tower away from the window. Here, only the baby swallows in a nest glued beneath the parapet of the turret were to be privy to her humiliation.

She looked down at the street dizzily below them and shivered.

"You are cold?" Surprisingly, he removed his cote and dropped it about her shoulders. The warmth lingering from his body was a false reassurance. She could smell the musk he favored alive in its soft folds and her heart ached. She waited, meek as Griselda, but Richard stood, his back to her, as if lost in thought, staring down the valley at the distant mirror-silver meander of the Loire.

Now stripped to his shirtsleeves, his appearance lent the occasion the informality of the solar and the bedchamber. In black from the sleek knee boots to the embroidered gipon, he appeared wilder and more threating to her than ever. The wind blew fullness into the sleeves and made a grab at his hat. He snatched it back and kept it in his hand, allowing the wind to ruffle his dark hair with the fondness of a mother's hand.

"When the thunderclouds gather and roll north, then the two kings will stand here and know the fleet will sail." It was a statement rather than a prophecy.

"Why?" she asked softly, surprised as ever, wishing that his arms could enfold her.

He turned his head and his enigmatic green gaze sent soundings into her soul. "Because it will take a great storm to disperse the cordon of ships that Burgundy has set to keep our fleet in harbor." His face lifted to the uninteresting hills. "It is decided that my brothers will escort you to England. You will leave in an hour's time."

She bit her lip at the judgment so indifferently delivered and leaned her head back against the wall, shutting her eyes against the painful world. "Do not allow anything on this Earth to delay you."

Margery's eyes opened in surprise. His lower lip was arching in distaste as if the words had been gall. He did not even want to look at her. It was all over; the bonfires that had been lit to warm her life had been trampled out and the night was cold.

But surprisingly, Richard did turn to face her and half sat against the crenellation, idly fingering the brim of his hat.

"When shall you be warming your beloved Ned's bed? Once a week? Or shall we be receiving reports more frequently?"

Her chin rose. "Tuesdays, so please you sir. Or do you require it to be more often so you may fill your coffers?"

Beneath his cunning fingers, the peacock feather was gradually torn to shreds. It belied his calm question. He rose, facing the west, away from her. "I was set upon yesterday. Tell me, was it intended to send me to my Maker or merely to keep me from returning yester eve? I should like to know if I should keep myself in a state of grace from now on." He looked around for an answer.

Her eyes widened. He watched her fingers flutter at the veil scarfed around her throat. "Jesu, Richard. If you think

I—" She jerked her face away as if seeking the right excuses from the very air. "Sir, nothing I can tell you now can mitigate the bruises to your face or your honor but I swear to you that one day if I may I will be a true wife to you again."

His smile was like a player's. "When somebody has died? King Edward? George of Clarence?" He sighed. "I thought you might show some discernment by now. I must have taught you something."

"Richard! Have mercy! I would not have had this happen for all the gold in Christendom." Astonishingly, she fell upon her knees, her palms raised to him. "Close your ears against what they are saying. Do you think I would deliberately shame you? At Angers we . . ."

He regarded her sternly. Oh, yes, he had wanted her a supplicant at his feet but not here, not now. "Angers! By all the Saints, Margery, Christendom it seems is not great enough to encompass the pair of us. Get up!" She looked so wretched and defeated. Was this his brave, beautiful Margery who had lain with the Duke last night for King Edward's sake? Was it so? Could she have writhed beneath that giggling, jealous drunkard and let him . . . Richard pushed the thought out of his mind. He dragged his gaze away. It was unbearable to watch the tears pearl at the corners of her eyes. He could not tell her he knew why she must leave, that the sand would be through the hourglass today. That the decision was right but not the manner of it.

"Life is perverse," she whispered, rising to her feet. "If only I could—" She broke off, as if unhappiness were seeping like icy water through her every pore. "Now that I cannot have you, why is it I want your goodwill? It is against all reason."

"Safeguard reason, Margery. It is less frightening than our other emotions. Forget all kings. Bid Tom or Will to take you to my home at Millom."

She bowed her head, her eyes closing with relief as if God, not he, had pardoned her. Before he could stop himself, he turned and grabbed her fiercely by the shoulders. She shook within his hands, soft lips parting, her trembling hands reaching out timidly to touch his face. He had not meant to kiss her or to touch her but God knows he could not help himself.

Her arms stole swiftly about his body and she was returning his kisses as if starved, clinging to him. "Oh, Richard, hold me." He stifled her words, his kisses wildly falling on her face, her shoulders, the curve of her breasts. Within an hour she would be gone. *Let any other man within you and I will kill him,* he wanted to snarl at her.

Margery tangled her fingers in his hair. The molten fire burned within her once again as his fingers made forays down her spine. His cote fell from her shoulders and her body felt open, ready, as his mouth came down again upon hers. He might be a traitor to the house of York but he could transport her into a realm where thinking no longer mattered.

She flung her head back as he kissed her shoulders. He held her back from him, his fingers unfastening the triangle within her collar to free a white orb of her breast into his hands, rubbing a thumb across her nipple while his eyes sought absolution in her face. As if he found his answer in the wildness of her eyes, he drew her down and pushed her gently back against his cote. His lips teased and tantalized her while the heel of his hand slid up between her legs and grasped her possessively.

Margery gasped in sheer pleasure. Had the Devil offered her a kingdom, had the archangel Gabriel arrived with a written scroll of gold assuring her a place in Heaven, she would not have listened. She was aching and hot with longing to have him thrust inside her. But his hands and mouth abandoned her, pulling her skirt over her thighs. She growled in protest, fearful that mercurial as he was, his mind had changed. He was suddenly breathing uncommonly loudly.

A dry laugh made her blood run cold. "The view is excellent from here," drawled a silky voice.

Margery's eyes snapped open.

Richard was struggling to stand while his devoted deerhound was furiously trying to hold him down for a thorough lick of devotion, and the King of France was leaning back against the outer wall, his arms crossed. The royal smile upon Margery as she sat up, her fingers sprawled defensively across her naked cleavage, was admiring. She scrambled onto her knees and grabbed the cote to her bosom, only to have Error bound across to her to launder her cheek and shoulders.

King Louis jerked his head at the Scots guard at his side to leave them.

"Not what we had expected, and yet . . ." He gave a Gallic shrug and left the wall. "Your dog appreciates your taste in a mistress."

Richard began to have sympathy for snared rabbits. How long had the King been playing the voyeur?

"Beau sire," he murmured calmly, discreetly tightening the points that had been strained an instant ago. Wonderful, was it not, how the thought of being tortured had doused his ardor? He winced inwardly as the royal fingers grabbed his wife's chin and forced her face upward.

"You think she will please the usurper Edward still?" The regal gaze marched over Margery's flushed face and the King twitched the garment out of her astonished fingers, savoring her thrusting breast.

By Christ's mercy, Richard prayed quickly, let her not look my way for guidance. He held his breath, sensing her hesitation between indignation and compliance. To his relief, she gave the King a ravishing smile and impishly held out her hand for him to help her to her feet.

"Why do you not answer, Richard?" she trilled, glancing over a provocative shoulder at him, her eyelashes moving as fast as birdwings taking off, her other hand tickling Error's back above his tail.

"You need reassurance?" He let his voice drip sarcasm and she smiled back. Without her mocking eyes moving off his face, she slowly began to fasten the fill of silk back across her bosom.

The King's eyes flickered suspiciously from one to the other, his oily mousy hair barely moved in the wind. Richard tried not to hold his breath. She had overplayed; the Spider would want to test her between the sheets, did she not realize that? Or . . . ? The ugly thought that his wife might have already passed examination sprang across his mind.

"My wife leaves for England within the hour with your

majesty's permission." He bowed belatedly but the King's attention would not be drawn away.

"You are cleverer than we thought," answered his most Christian Majesty. It seemed he was speaking to Richard and yet he was still studying Margery. "And being a king, Monsieur 'uddleston"—the dark eyes swerved to pinion him—"is quite different to being a commoner or even Dauphin. We can have anything we want"—Richard noted the cruel pause—"and we will have this union between the Earl of Warwick and the Queen of England. She is arriving today but you know that, *n'est-ce pas, monsieur,* and you know also what she will ask." He drew a fingernail lightly down Margery's cheek and poked his forefinger under her chin like a knife, jerking her head higher. "You know the two greatest currencies, Monsieur 'uddleston?"

"Yes, *beau sire.*"

"Name them!"

"Money and fear."

"Exactly." His smile would have tortured babies. "We wish you every success in the usurper's bed, madame. Continue your farewell, monsieur." He handed Margery back the garment and with a polite grin disappeared around the curve of the tower as quietly as he had come. They did not even hear his footsteps. Richard counted ten heartbeats and then followed the wall of the tower toward the courtyard. The King indeed had gone, the dog at his heels like a final insult. Richard came back to Margery. Her shoulders were heaving as she stared unseeing across the valley.

She whipped around on him and flung his clothing at him. "I feel contaminated, degraded, sullied, spiritually ravished, anything you please."

"You mean by me?" He thrust his arms angrily through the split sleeves.

"No, I do not mean by you!" she snapped. "Can you not feel the threads of his web sticking to you? It reaches to Ned's court, be sure of that. *Go to Millom?* His agents will track me down and tip poison in my wine." She swept along the rampart, every inch of her angry.

"No!" Richard halted her. "Come here, your bodice is awry." Sullenly she came back to him. "Listen to me." With husbandly concern for propriety, he undid the silk triangle and refastened it to conceal the tiny buttons underneath the broad "V" of her collar. Her eyes upon his face were wells of cynicism.

Why was it that each time he made love to her, it gave her the confidence to be disobedient and provoke him? By rights, the wench should be feeling the back of his hand across her cheek. His fingers gripped her shoulders, his mouth tightening at how rigidly she held herself. He tried to stanch the rising panic he sensed within her and to divert the direction of his own misgivings. "You do not have to do any of it. No, listen, woman! Once you are with King Edward, you will be safe. Tell him you need an armed guard and a food taster."

"The safest place in England is in his bed at Westminster. We both know that, do we not, *Monsieur 'uddleston*?" Surprisingly, she had King Louis's accent to perfection. It was her best attempt at French so far.

"If I had wanted a wasp for a wife, I could not have done better." Richard refused to be drawn. He thrust her from him and picking up his hat, tried to smooth out the woeful feather. An apologetic whining eased the silence. Error had reappeared. In panic, Margery rushed around into the courtyard, wondering if the King had returned but there were only two of the sentries sauntering back to the guardroom. "You had better go and prepare." Richard calmly caught up with her, relieved that the dog had returned alone.

Margery had recovered sufficiently to be suspicious. "What is your wonderful Queen going to ask?"

He deliberately watched a hawk circling against the clouds beyond her head. "Nothing if you are gone from here like an honest traveler. Come!" He put his hand beneath her elbow to steer her around the tower wall and across the courtyard to the logis but she caught at his hanging sleeve and forced him to look at her. "Oh, Jesu, Richard, stop playing with words. I am afraid of the King of France. He puts people in cages."

His green eyes showed kindness at last. "Yes, I know."

CHAPTER
24

Richard returned from the forest at sundown. The drawbridge was winched up as the echoes of Comet's hooves died beneath the archway. He was not expecting Matthew to materialize from the shadows and grab the bridle to bring him to a halt. Richard swore and seized him by his collar. "What in God's name—"

"My lord of Oxford ordered the mistress back. We met him on the road. Only your brothers, sir, were given leave to continue."

"The Devil take him! Did my wife give them letters or any parting gift?"

"No, sir." That at least was a relief; his brothers were not in danger. "And my lord of Warwick requires your presence straightaway."

He found the Nevilles, white-faced and silent, within the Earl's apartments. Margery, tired, raised her head bleakly. It was possible they had been haranguing her but he rather doubted it.

Clarence swung around to face him, simmering with ill temper. "You can break the news to Huddleston, Warwick, but I rather suspect he knows already." He circled Richard like a fox sniffing out prey. "Tell us, brother-in-law, is the old hag you admire so untrusting or is it my lords of Oxford and Pembroke who have advised her so cunningly?"

Richard ignored him, shifting his gaze to the Earl's adamantine gaze. "Why has my wife returned, my lord?" he asked coldly.

The Earl held out a letter to him. The wax seal, heavy upon it, was Queen Margaret's.

Anne spared him the bother of reading. "Because we sisters are to be hostages to the Bitch while Father and George slaughter Ned and Dickon." She glowered at her father.

"And Mother stays as well," snapped Isabella, from the window, her face ashen. "A wonderful alliance, is it not, Richard?"

"I protest, my lord!" Having scanned the letter, he startled them all with an uncharacteristic but calculated lack of control. "I deserve some say in this matter. Margery may be your daughter but she is my wife and I do not agree to this."

"Ha!" sneered Clarence, waggling his face near Richard's. *"I deserve some say!"* he mimicked. "Mayhap old Margaret d'Anjou does not trust you either, Richard Huddleston, despite the hand-licking. How do you manage? Do you slobber on her left hand while Father Warwick licks her right?"

"You treacherous cur!" Richard drew back his fist and launched it at the jeering mouth.

"That will do!" shrieked the Countess, coming between them with a swiftness that was rare for her. Richard's fist hit empty air as she set a calming hand upon his shoulder and looked back at her lord. "I wish we had never left England." Her voice was serrated with bitterness. "If you disobey these terms, my lord"—she took the letter from Richard and challenged her husband—"she will not make an alliance with you and if she does not, King Louis will cease to support us. We shall be destitute, my lord, but will it matter? Is it so important to you to risk those who love you most?"

Warwick's expression hardened further before their eyes. He paced to the window and turned. "Understand this, every one of you. I have no intention of giving up now that an army awaits me at Tours. I can retake England within a matter of weeks. By Heaven, all I require of you, mesdames, is a month of patience."

Not one of his daughters answered and the Countess averted her gaze with a deep sigh.

Richard broke the silence curtly. "My lord Earl speaks as though England will come wagging its tail the moment he whistles. The campaign may take months. King Edward has won every battle he has fought and Gloucester is now a man."

To his left, Anne gave a painful sigh. Warwick scowled at his daughter and raised his furious hands to them all. "Enough! It is decided. In any case, mesdames, you do not have to be hostages at Angers. I shall change the terms. If King Louis has guardianship over you, there will be no problem. I would trust him with my life. I will trust him with my children."

It was Clarence who answered venomously. "Would you now? And would you trust him with mine? Christ Almighty, you are a walking wonder, my noble lord. You have made me party to this unnatural alliance without even inviting me to the table and now you expect me to meekly comply with these foul terms. Where is the crown you swore to give me? You are a bloody traitor, Warwick, your promises are paper and lies dribble from your lips."

"Pah, a pox on the lot of you!" Warwick snarled and stormed out.

The only person who felt at ease with her was Richard's dog, reflected Margery sadly next morning, wrapping her arms around Error's friendly head. Even his soulful eyes, reproachful that he was chained, saddened her, and one of the kennelboys had crassly informed that large dogs rarely lived beyond a few years.

The news that she was to be a hostage had terrified her. Why should Queen Margaret bother to include her? She doubted her father would care now if she was left behind or not. Was it because the Queen's agents knew she had spoken with de Commynes and kept private company with the Duke of Clarence?

Her fears grew hourly. If the Duke's letter was found
among her possessions, they would hang her. If only she
were rid of it! In vain she flaunted the secret token, her St.
Catherine wheel brooch, proclaiming that she possessed the
message, but no one had left instructions for her.

Her other sorrow was that Huddleston was clearly displeased she had not left. He had not spoken to her since her
return yesterday and she wanted to resolve matters with him
and at least thank him for arguing with her father about the
hostage matter. To be with him was becoming a compulsion; to confide in him, a temptation.

She told herself that it was because she was becoming
desperate with the knowledge she carried and the desire to
exonerate herself that, like the barber who whispered "King
Midas has ass's ears" to the river reeds, she wanted to be
free of secrets. Much as he angered her, Margery wanted to
make her peace with him before the invasion army left.
They might never set eyes on each other again. If only she
might trust him.

The noise about her made further thinking impossible.
The boys were wheeling around barrows of bones and the
barking was unbearable. Miserable, she left the kennels to
face the lavish festivities for Queen Margaret and the Prince.

It seemed no one had minded her avoiding the reception.
Isabella was pretending to disdain her, Anne had withdrawn
into her own personal Hell, the Countess was genuinely
ignoring her, and the rest of the tiring ladies, taking their
cue from their betters, were not speaking to her. Only
Ankarette bothered to talk to her that morning, fishing in
vain for the reason for her disgrace and then giving her the
local gossip.

The news was piquant. A local merchant had been murdered and robbed, his premises ransacked. No doubt while
his fellow townsfolk were watching the Queen's party
approach. And there was a rumor that all the men were
leaving for the coast on Monday together with the mercenaries gathered at Tours.

Kneeling at mass behind the royal party, Margery
digested that last morsel with growing fear. Once the men
left with the invasion fleet, she would be at the mercy of

Queen Margaret. Warwick's legitimate womenfolk were protected by their high birth—but she was expendable.

"Meg!" The Duke of Clarence, attended by Thomas Burdett, stopped her outside the chapel.

"I do not want to be seen with you, your grace," hissed Margery through her teeth, skirts billowing into a coldly given curtsy.

Ankarette, halting behind Margery, overflowing, no doubt, with curiosity as well as loyalty, hovered.

"Take yourself off, Twynhoe!" The Duke, no longer caring about the common gaze, held out his wrist to Margery and led her aside to the garden. Her friend followed. "Oh, avaunt thee, Ankarette!" The Duke made a mocking sign against the evil eye. "Tom, remove her!"

Margery calmly lifted her hand from his fingers. A cluster of inquisitive maids of honor was watching. "And what have you told my father?"

"He dare not chide you." She glared questioningly at him, her face turned from the other women's prying eyes. "It is because Bella found him lustily entwined with that raven-haired wench of Queen Charlotte's, the one from Lorraine. If he rebukes you, Bella has threatened to tell Mother Warwick about him."

Well, that made two Nevilles with doubtful morals, thought Margery angrily. A fig for the pious lectures her father had dealt out. Do not trip, he had said. The hypocrite!

The Duke's smile was laconic. He raised a hand to her cheek like a lover but his words were a declaration of war. "I want my letter back, Meg. Matters have changed."

She glanced carefully about her. There were people everywhere, watching. "Like your mind?" Her smile was grave, her tone venomous.

"No, just . . . just it is becoming dangerous." The ducal finger found her chin and raised her face to his. "I do not trust anyone and that husband of yours might find it."

"I have passed it on already." God forgive me for the lie, she prayed.

The finger dropped. "You—a pox on you! How?"

"I wore a token to show I had a message. It is on its way. People are whispering, I have to go."

Had they been alone, his eyes told her he would have shaken her and slapped her in fury.

Richard watched his wife quit George of Clarence. The heir to the English crown looked as sour as a whole tree of crab apples. It was time.

"My lord!"

Clarence turned haughtily. "Painful horns, Huddleston?"

"The lady refused you, I think. Nor, I believe, did she thank you for trying to part us."

The Duke studied his face with a slow, deepening scowl. "No and it irks me," he answered finally with dangerous softness.

Richard's open grin was wolflike. "Then know, my gracious lord, that Margery and I *understand* each other very well indeed. Do not embroil her further in your fortunes."

Margery knew she had to meet Richard alone even if it meant being questioned further. But it was impossible. Her father kept him in constant attendance and the château was oozing people from every crevice. Flies would have been hard put to find rest and Margery was crammed into a bedchamber with eight other women, like salted herrings, head to tail.

At the mass in the fields at Amboise next day, she glimpsed Richard among the knights and esquires, standing beneath the great forest of waving pennons, unsheathing his sword and shouting with the rest in the roars of fealty that followed the hosannas. It was a public affirmation of unity just as the service in Angers cathedral had been—a rattle of weapons at Charles of Burgundy and the usurper Edward.

Margery had been permitted to attend, reinstated by the Nevilles for the sake of appearances. Although some distance from her husband, she was conscious of nothing but him. No matter how much she tried to harness her thoughts in the direction of holiness and pray for help in safeguarding the Duke's letter, the horse would not pull the cart of her mind.

How she managed to find herself walking beside Richard

Huddleston across the meadow afterward was due to speed and determination. He was compelled to offer her his hand across the tussocks out of good manners. They had to watch their footing; cows had been encouraged into the pasture the day before to circumvent scything the grass. Like most inspirations, there was an underside.

Albeit their gloves kept them from direct contact, the green enigmatic grin at her as they reached the laneway was a sop to Margery's impoverished spirits. She peeped sideways up at her husband, relishing the way his hair curled once more below his jawline, the just profile, the scalloped sleeves thrust back elegantly from shoulders that bent willingly to no man. It was so easy now to forget the arrogance with which he had used her, but to forget was not yet to forgive.

He caught her measuring look. "Your gown is becoming." She gave him a tight smile of disbelief, appreciative that he was being kind. "I mean it. Can I not say things like that to my wife?"

Her heart twisted painfully. "Not a wife you cannot trust. You must be pleased—you have shifted the responsibility for my upkeep entirely to the King of France. Being a hostage may irk me like a burr beneath the girth but at least it will solve all your problems. You will still be son-in-law to puissant Warwick but without the cap and bells."

Jesu, I am babbling, she thought, it is not what I wanted to say and he knows it, damn him. He is wearing that indulgent expression.

One of the Lancastrian captains appeared, ill-timed, at Richard's side, clapping him on the shoulder like an old acquaintance and Margery, disappointed at the interruption, dropped him a good-day greeting and embarked, like a good commander, on her fall-back strategy.

As Richard eventually returned across the drawbridge, listening to a joke someone was telling about the Burgundian, the Italian, and the Irishman, Matthew Long trapped him by the sleeve. "Is the mistress supposed to be riding off alone?"

"God Almighty!"

Margery knew he must come. Perhaps he would think she had a tryst. Curiosity would spur his heels, no question there. She walked her palfrey slowly, crossing the well-trodden paths between the poor cottages of the washer-women and the river. Two women, heaving a wicker basket of sodden linen back from the river edge to hoist upon the hedges, spat on her shadow. Beyond the cooking fires of the fishermen and the ragged line of the farthermost Amboise dwellings, the air was sweeter but the oaks and ashes closed in around her and she began to curse her folly in riding alone. She had made sure Matthew and at least one of the Cumbrian men-at-arms had seen her depart, but perhaps Richard would not come.

She turned toward the Loire. A broad expanse of grav-elly riverbed opened up before her as if someone had drawn back the sheet of water. Two boys were casting lines where the water ran deep and fast, and a bored dog lifted his head from his paws and stared. The children's presence was reas-suring. She urged the palfrey into the quieter water so he might drink. The sun burned hot upon her cheeks and she could feel perspiration moistening the underarm pads that protected her underkirtle. No matter, it was wonderful to be free of the court.

The water splashed up from his stallion's heels as Richard drew abrupt rein beside her, his brow sheened with sweat.

"Foolish woman! What in God's name are you at now?"

The defiant little chin rose predictably. "Oh, I am meeting six mercenaries between the hour bells. A con-dottiere, two retired *écorcheurs*, a pikeman from Vienna, and—"

"Margery!"

"I had to breathe, sir." Her voice grew sharp. "The trees and water hold no rancor." With a toss of veil, she urged the horse out of the water. "You wish, no doubt, to drag me back behind those stifling walls, or are you staying to lec-ture me?"

She was dainty as a lady in a tapestry, prettily sitting sidesaddle, her gorgeous train carefully draped across her lap. He wanted to take her into the forest to a glade where Louis of France was not likely to creep up on them, leering like a gargoyle. He wanted to finish the labor that had been interrupted but he had too many enemies now. It was not just the memory of Henri Badoux sprawled on the rushes of his storeroom, bleeding from dagger wounds in the chest and belly, but the memory of the courier pigeons lying around another man in Tours, their necks pitifully wrung, that kept Richard there beside her. If they remained by the river, he as least would have some warning before the enemy reached him.

Foolishly he dismounted, his boots crunching on the gravel as he approached her. "Goosehead, I was attacked on the road two days ago and a man was murdered last night. Have you lost all common sense?" She held out her arms and he set his hands to the slender waist. "This is against my better judgment. Can your slippers survive the pebbles?"

She solemnly slid out of his arms the moment he set her down, gathering up her train over her arm. "Who was murdered? Ankarette said—"

"That woman spoils a good story," he interrupted, his wry tone belying his words. "It was Adèle's father."

Margery crossed herself, looking at him full-faced now. "But we—"

"Met him. Yes. He traded in more than merchandise." The pause was infinitesimal. "So they say." Her face betrayed not the least hint that she knew Henri Badoux had been a link in the chain of communication with King Edward. "Monsieur Levallois is not convinced it was theft."

"And Adèle?"

"She has lost the babe. I visited them early this morning."

He watched her forehead crease beneath the wisp of veiling. "I—I would have come with you, sir, to comfort her," she blurted out.

"That is why I did not tell you." Because Margery and Adèle might endanger each other. He watched the goodwill disappear from her face. Did she know it had been Henri Badoux who had served as King Edward's main agent in Touraine?

"Why did you exclude me?" Margery fiercely swung away from him only to find the children had abandoned their sport and had crept up on them to beg for money.

"*Là!*" Margery emphatically gestured behind her and

they ran to petition Huddleston to let them hold the horses for écus. As she hastened away, she heard his laughter and their squeals of delight. Whirling around, she watched, aching, as, barehanded now, he spun the coins up into the air promising more if they performed their duties carefully.

His laughter was lacking as he left the children with the horses and caught up with her. Margery was waiting, over-spilling with anger.

"God damn you, Richard Huddleston! Why is it because you are a man, you deem your judgment in these matters better than mine?" She spread out her arms, the gorgeous sleeves reaching almost to the stone. "Look at me, sir. I can bear a child and feed it withal but I am not allowed to administer my own property or hold an opinion."

"If you will tell me why you were in Clarence's bed, lady, all that shall be yours."

She met his glance steadily. "All the kingdoms of the world? No, Richard, even you cannot change the laws nor your own nature." Her evasiveness did not please him. He needed to break her distrust. He wanted her to tell him of her own free will that she was in King Edward's pay.

"I hoped that you had lured me here to offer me the truth." A bird shot up protesting from the fringe of trees and thicket that lay futher along the shore and Richard slid his gaze uneasily along the bank before he continued, "Or is there some other more bloody reason?"

"Pah, I cannot tell you because I *will* not tell you. I am your whore, not Clarence's. You command my body but you care not a fig for my affections. You would have sent me away without even asking me my side of the matter just as you did when Ned—"

His shoulders stiffened at the mention of the name. "Then tell me now, Margery." His voice was a soft growl. "For when these hurly-burly times are done, as I pray to God they will be right soon, what of you and me?"

She gave him a deadly look bred of suspicion. "You will never trust me and so we shall be severed like a hung car-cass in a butcher's shop."

"Lady, I do not wish it so."

He could swear his gaze had pierced the armor Margery had been trying to buckle on against him. The lashes fluttered down in a devastating delight of defensiveness and enticement as she bit her lip and turned away to the lapping water.

"But as a wife, I am disobedient, wayward, contrary, and you would need to beat me at least once a week." Her glance was coy as she turned her head. Devil take the woman! She was not angry with him at all. She had lured him here for what? The kiss of peace? He watched her gracefully stoop and hurl the stick that the children's dog had deposited hopefully at her feet.

"Twice a week," he corrected her, with a smile that could melt icicles. Margery for her part felt she could not breathe. The opposite riverbank suddenly became of infinite interest to her. "And now I desire you to bare your thoughts, lady, not your body." His fingertips were stroking down her shoulders, his words against her temple. "So tell me what happened between you and the Duke."

Silence lay upon them like a coverlet.

"Margery?" She liked the way he said her name now. Before it had been a presumption, now it was a familiarity.

"Nothing that is yours is given away or sullied, sir." She closed her eyes and leaned back against him, reaching up to touch his hands.

"I want more than that," he murmured softly. "Cleanse your soul of its darkest secrets and I will champion your cause."

Neither sensed their peril until one of the children shouted and the dog barked.

Richard whirled around. He let go of her with an oath to draw his sword as two armed men came riding at them.

"Run!" he yelled.

Before she could grab her skirts, the hurtling hooves were about them. Steel hissed from above, striking Richard's blade as he tried to fend off the vicious swipes. "You're in my way! Run, damn you!"

Margery ducked low. She seized as much gravel and sand as she could within her gloved hands. It was a risk to straighten but she hurled the fistfuls into one of the horse's eyes. Directionless, it ignored the sharp hands on its bridle, reared and plunged at the water. The rider tried to bring it around.

With one foe, Huddleston had more chance. While he parried the attacker's thrusts, Margery drew her dagger, ran around the other side of the horse, and plunged the blade into the man's leg. It was a woman's force but it slid in with appalling ease. He gave a yelp and twisted around swiftly to heave a blow upon her. She shrieked, flinging herself down on hands and knees to miss the deadly scythe. The distraction was enough for Richard's blade to slip beneath the brigand's guard and into his heart. She heard herself screaming at the spurting blood. A plunging hoof cleared her cheekbone by a skin width.

Richard snatched up the dead man's sword and spun around to face the second, burlier man menacing them now on foot. Margery scrambled out of the way as steel clashed viciously on steel, withdrew and rasped again. The children were shouting.

Richard, vulnerable in his soft garments, read death in the stranger's face. This was no footpad but a trained soldier out to cut his throat and not his purse. He tried to turn the fight so that the other's eyes caught the glare of the water. The sun scorched his face as they circled like fighting cocks.

"Ride!" he bawled hoarsely at Margery.

The other laughed. "Yea, dog's piss, I am going to rape her across your corpse, stick my dagger in her belly and then her heart." The French dialect was barely intelligible but the intent was. The face was jeering below the sallet. The fist within the leather gauntlet launched a further vicious assault jolting Richard's entire body each time he parried.

Margery was sure she had stopped breathing. If Richard were to be killed . . . She forced herself to act. Edging to the dead man, she drew out her dagger from the body, stifling thought, quelling emotion.

Her action distracted the attacker and Richard's steel sliced into his shoulder. With an oath the man fought even harder, drawing blood through the tight sleeve of Richard's upper arm.

Margery, wondering if the same trick might serve, threw a handful of stones against the brigand and the dog ran close behind his heels at the sport.

Undistracted, Richard launched thrust upon thrust, driving the man backward into the shallow while his wife absurdly kept sending the dog into the water directly behind his assailant. Time slowed, limped, but at last Richard had the man on his knees. Every breath was agony as he finally plunged his sword in to the hilt.

"Oh, dear God." Margery tossed away the dagger and ran toward him as he staggered out of the river, scarlet wavelets lapping his heels.

Every gasp was torn from him. He leaned over, head bowed. The hanging sleeves, wet and mired, flopped like rags. Spatters of blood had stained the green brocade. His very stance forbade her to touch him. But at length he straightened, wearily picked up his hat from the sand, tapped it against his thigh with a sigh before he inspected the body he had just severed from its soul.

There was no livery, no hat badge, no ring. Nothing that would identify. The man's blond coloring hinted at a Schweitzer. The sword hilt suggested Nürnberg or Augsburg.

He heaved the second man from the water and lifted the edge of the leather jacket with the tip of his sword but there was no livery badge on the tunic beneath. He came back to where Margery was staring at the corpse, her arms crossed defensively across her breasts as if she were trying to hold herself together.

The boys had cautiously returned with their horses, eyeing Richard with awe. Their muttered patois was beyond his understanding as they inspected the carnage.

"You have seen him before?" They shrugged.

"Do *you* recognize him?" Margery asked huskily.

Richard shook his head and knelt to pull open the man's collar. The small leather drawstring bag contained a gold coin. He palmed it before she could read *Edwardus Quartus*, and jerked his head at the boys with an abrupt command. They took to their heels. "I have sent them for the other horse. Look for a brandmark. Check the saddles." It was important to keep her busy.

There were no saddlebags, no clues. The second horse stumbled blindly. Margery grabbed the smaller child away to safety. "The poor creature cannot see."

"Quickly!" snapped Richard. "Cleanse its eyes!"

The older boy took the reins more cunningly, dragging the animal to the river.

"Not a plaguey clue!" exclaimed Richard.

"I do not want to sound feeble but I think this is catching up with me," Margery gasped, leaning her forehead against her horse's shoulder.

"If you swoon, you can do it on your own," he replied brusquely. "Let us return to the château, soldier's wife. These may have friends." He heaved her onto her palfrey none too gently. White-faced, she clutched at the pommel of the saddle. He was alert to catch her as he paid the children but she held on, closing her eyes. Her resourcefulness in danger had been remarkable.

"Your bravery, Margery, will certainly make your father proud," he exclaimed as he swung into the saddle, "but by the Saints, you should have run when I told you to."

Margery's spirits revived at the scant praise. "What about their horses?"

He gave her a tight smile. "Enough!" And with a mighty slap, he drove the palfrey forward.

She never heard what he said to the children. He caught up with her giving no explanation. Perhaps it needed none. Nor did he draw rein until they were through the trees.

"The sand and dagger were helpful, Margery. Perhaps I should take you and a dog to war with me."

"Are you hurting?"

"My left shoulder may have work for you. You wish to play my nursemaid?" But he could see she did not believe him.

"Heaven forbid!" She wrinkled her nose but evidently her thoughts were graver. "Of what nation was the coin? Tell me who and why."

He shrugged. "They wanted to rob us. Your necklet could be sold, so could our clothing."

"Not with blood all— Oh, Richard . . ." She had not noticed the drying blood all over her bodice.

"You have been very brave but your horse will not appreciate the contents of your belly over its back, and you always put the horse's feeling first I notice." He sensed the tears stinging behind her eyes as she nodded. Then a new thought struck at her.

"Richard, do you think the Queen wants me dead?"

"The Queen? No, I do not! Your imagination is beyond belief. Just because you sense she dislikes you. No, I will hear no more." Could he tell her it was George of Clarence that he suspected?

"You will hear no more," she echoed his tone. "Plague take you! I shall think what I please and you may go whet your ambition on the French woman's slippers!"

They made the rest of the journey in silence with Margery hating him wholeheartedly.

Richard rode grim-faced, despising himself but at least her fury had distracted her from asking further questions.

Margery meekly let him conduct her to the Countess's apartments where he gave so brief a description of the attack that those who heard might have been forgiven for thinking they had been set upon by a pair of butterflies. The blood on her clothes, however, drew gasps and screams from the other women.

Her father was summoned to see her, his eyes grave and puzzled. "King Louis shall hear of this."

"No, my lord." She caught Warwick's hand. "This is too small a matter for him."

"It is the small matters that make him what he is."

Her clothes were taken away for what was probably a futile attempt to clean the blood off and she was escorted to the bathhouse to soak in hot water and be muffled in soft towels.

A page arrived from the King of France apologizing for the lawlessness. In recompense, she was to have a bed-chamber for the night. That indeed was a miracle.

She reached it eventually after sundown, wondering who had been evicted; someone had left a fistful of points upon the fur coverlet but the sheets at least were cleanly laundered. It was as she turned and stared at the carved frieze that ran along the wall behind the bed that her flesh crawled.

She forced herself to turn away, to listen to what Alys was saying, but the scene beside the river kept repeating itself in her head. It was like watching the York pageant, but every wagon that stopped before her replayed the same scene. She saw once more the expression that had flickered across her husband's face. Richard knew who had sent the assassins. She would swear that on Saints' bones.

She watched Alys snuggle down on the trundle bed and envied her innocence.

The door opened much later. Not stealthfully, but so suddenly that she hurtled across to the other side of the bed, her dagger drawn.

CHAPTER
25

"I see you are expecting visitors," murmured Richard Huddleston, setting a flickering candlestick down on the hearth.

"Do not tell me that they are offering free baths to everyone," she muttered acidly, thrusting the now clean dagger back into its sheath.

He looked relieved. "Is it not the feast of St. Swithin?"

"What?"

"The patron saint of bathwater." He received a scowl. "Alys, do you not think your mistress smells as though someone had an accident with an excess of roses?" But Alys grumbled and turned over. He was testing the bed. "Better than I have been putting up with—and a wife to go with it. Perhaps we should get ourselves ambushed more often. Is your gown redeemable?"

"I doubt it. They have removed it for cleaning." A faint frown shadowed his brow. He seemed to be staying. "I gather you are part of the compensation," she added wryly.

"Yes, but I will go if you had rather be alone. We should

have taken Matthew and five lapdogs. You could have catapulted them."

"Maybe." She clutched her arms about her and glanced
at the wooden panels. "Richard, do you know where the
nearest garderobe is?"

He stood up with a sigh. "Yes. Is this part of being
married?"

She resisted staring at the frieze. "This is nothing. When
Bella was with child—"

"No, I will hear no more." He retrieved the candle.
"Come, then."

Along the gallery, she stopped and put a finger to her lips.
"Margery! Explain, if you please."

"There was someone watching earlier behind the
panel. Do not glare at me like that!"

"There are probably a dozen people packed into a bed on
the other side of the wall. Perhaps you heard someone turn
over and rock the bedhead."

"I *saw*, not heard."

"*Sensed.* Why would anyone do that?"

"I cannot tell but I do not think we are private."

"This is not some excuse to avoid intimacy?"

"*Intimacy?*"

He sighed. "I see the thought displeases you. Come."

"Where?"

"The garderobe, lady."

Returning, he leaned against the carved frieze, examining it with a sideways glance before he set the candle
down beside the bed. She could never tell with Richard
Huddleston whether he was trying to allay her fears because
he actually believed her. She stood on the other side of the
bed, dainty in the shadows, listening.

He gave a faint shake of his head and pressed his ear
against the paneling. Then, with a shrug, he abandoned his
investigation. "Is it against the articles of your faith to help
me off with my boots?" He noted her recalcitrance. "Ah,
you wish to risk being kicked during my dreams? *Please,*
Margery."

His shoulder did hurt him. With charity, she came around
to him, her eyes demure as she sank down gracefully and set
her hand to his heel. He bit his lip and when she was done,

he recognized compassion glistening in her eyes. Smiling, he snared her fingers before she could rise and with his other hand snuffed the candle out.

She heard the door later and woke swiftly but it was no enemy. Richard had left her. Following swiftly, softly, she saw him lift the latch and slide like a wraith into the other bedchamber.

Richard kept his hand across her mouth. The woman had the sense of a snail. Only the rosewater had saved her. He tensed, waiting to see if the chamber was as empty as he had thought and then slowly released his cruel grip. Moonlight streamed across an empty bed and glinted on his dagger blade. She had the wit to say nothing, rubbing where he had bruised her, glaring at him with a revived hatred. Then she remembered why they were there and forgot to be furious.

Save for an outside door onto the courtyard, the chamber was but a reflection of theirs. The frieze was identical. Richard ran his fingers across it, noting the same holes in the tracery, then he knelt, exploring the lower panels like an admiring master joiner.

To her amazement, a low small door clicked open. "Go back outside. If anyone comes, sneeze!"

Satisfying himself that she had obeyed him, he crawled into the secret room. Its air hung with the stale smell of recent occupation and a thick woolen blanket muffled the floor. There were viewing holes into each chamber as part of the carving.

Margery sneezed.

He emerged into the passageway, tousled and panicky, in such haste that, clasping her hand to her mouth, she stanched a laugh. "I am sorry. It was a real sneeze."

"Go back to bed before I *really* strangle you!"

Richard slid back beside her a few moments later. He neither told her that a splinter of wood had snared a silken azure thread nor reminded her of the King of France's sleeves at supper.

"I confess I cannot become used to this wretched change of allegiance," Ankarette muttered as Margery returned her belongings to her original sleeping quarters that afternoon, having vowed not to spend another night in the paneled bed-chamber. "Your Master Huddleston seems to have no problem with changing sides."

Margery was well aware that the Earl of Oxford had just clapped her husband on the shoulder in the *grande salle* and that Richard had broken his fast with two of the Earl's henchmen.

"You think that if my lord father were to make a dog the King of England, Richard Huddleston would immediately produce a bone for it?"

Ankarette chose not to answer, drawing her aside. "What were you two about down by the river anyway?"

"Trying to translate *Piers Plowman* into French for itinerant peddlers." Margery bit her lip. "Your pardon, my dear Ankarette, I am so used to fencing with my husband that I draw my sword at every opportunity. I slept ill."

"And I suppose I really should stir you no further but . . ."

"Ankarette, I loathe it when you just hint at something curious. Besides, I doubt you could tell me anything new."

Tell me that I am being spied on in my own bed, that I am watched by day, that someone has just tried to kill me, and I am carrying a secret that is burning me.

"I wager I can." Ankarette tumbled into the verbal hole dug for her just like she always did. "I heard your husband speaking with the Queen in the gardens this morning and they were talking about you!"

Margery tensed, not sure she wanted to hear more. "And?" she prompted, realizing with a start that she was beginning to sound like Huddleston.

Ankarette looked around to see if any of the other ladies were likely to overhear them before she continued softly. "I could hear every word. They were speaking in English despite the fact your husband reckons himself so fluent in her tongue. So where was I? Ah yes, the Queen Margaret says as how King Louis has been telling her about you spending time in his library. You are strange sometimes, Margery." She paused, studying her friend afresh. "Anyway, the Queen says, 'This wife of yours must be clever, *hein?' Hein!* I like that word *'hein'*!"

"Ankarette!"

"Well, Master Huddleston was *très nonchalant*. 'No, not noticeably,' he replies, cool as you please. But he tells her grace as how you took lessons with the ladies Isabella and Anne and then were sent to be a nun."

"Well, that's true. Where is this leading?"

"The Queen says, 'Alors, I have been told your wife was discovered in embarrassing circumstances.' Margery, you nev—"

"Go on. At last you have reached the interesting part."

"There was a long silence and then he says, 'Yes, that's true, madam, but it was a silly device of the Duchess to make me set my wife aside.' But then the Queen answered something like, 'I will be blunt, monsieur. Whether you admit to your wife betraying you is your affair but I do not desire the future Princess of Wales to be attended by a wanton who has lain with the Yorkist usurper and all his brothers.' "

"Well, my reputation has certainly grown. How did Huddleston answer that?"

"He promised her he would make your sides ache if you displeased her in any way. And then he said that you and your sister had acted foolishly and of all the women in the world, she, Margaret, was the embodiment of all manly virtues in a woman's body, his rightful queen and his true mistress. I doubt he meant that carnally, of course, for she is too proud to lie with anyone less than a duke. Then she asked him if you were the Duchess's confidante and he said you were like true sisters."

Anger, hot as a smith's coals, smoldered within Margery, but if her friend expected a furious outburst then she would be disappointed. "I am not disputing what you heard, Ankarette, but how did you manage to overhear so much?"

"I was walking Tristan on the leash and he stopped to munch some grass and lift his leg, sniffing around the way he does. They were on the other side of a hedge with their backs to me." She set her hand comfortingly over Margery's clenched fist. "The gossip is that Huddleston has been hand in glove with Lancaster ever since he set foot in France, and he has been keeping some very odd company." She fixed her eye upon Margery. "What was your foolishness?"

"Ever to think that I had my husband's measure." Margery fingered the brooch that Ned had given her to wear as a sign her mission was fulfilled. How fortunate that yesterday's attack had forestalled her telling Huddleston the truth.

∽✇∼

She had to plan. She needed to set a pattern and be patient. If all the Englishmen and mercenaries were to leave Amboise and Tours within a few days, a beginning had to be made. Margery was not going to stay a hostage to the Bitch's whims. If the Duke's message was not taken, then she would carry it herself, whatever the cost.

She began to send Alys every day at the same hour to light a candle for her in the church across the valley. Anne, liking the notion, paid Alys to perform the same duty for her. So, God willing, by the time the guards had become used to Alys's daily passing, they might easily mistake the mistress for the maid.

As for Richard Huddleston, if he noticed his wife had managed to avoid him for two days, he gave no sign of it even if her gaze was drawn to him like a moth to a lantern.

The truth was that she was ill-armed to deal with him. She had come so close to confiding in him and her body craved him. Yet to be near him and know he was Queen Margaret's creature was torture. When Matthew brought her a command that she was to visit Error, it offered her no joy.

Richard Huddleston was waiting. As always now, she felt the stirring of desire at seeing him. Clad in half armor, the black leather brigandine and the polished steel encompassing his shoulders lent him a formidable mien, enhancing his masculinity. If only she had been able to harness his strength and intelligence in her enterprise. Why did fortune have to make them enemies once she had realized how much she wanted him?

Drawing closer, she recognized the tenseness in him like a tightened lute string. He was unsmiling but at least he had removed his gauntlets to fondle his dog's ears.

She pretended loudly that this was a chance meeting but he recognized the fear and the uncertainty in her eyes as she looked at him. By Christ's blessed mercy, would this wife of his ever lower her guard and trust him?

"It seems there is nowhere I can speak to you these days without peeping Toms or brigands interrupting. You are in health, mousekin?" His probing gaze warmed as he spoke, reminding her of the fleeting moments when they had been happy in each other's company. She busied herself with pleasing Error.

"What is it you want to say, sir?" Ice calm, was she? Perhaps that was the only way to keep the passion bridled.

Damn Edward! A thousand plagues on him for thrusting this woman into a pool of intrigue deep enough to drown them both. If only Margery could have proved to him on their wretched wedding night that she could keep a secret, then they might have worked together. Yes, and if only Louis's assassins had not murdered Badoux.

His irritation grew. "I leave Amboise within the hour."

The fingers in the dog's hair trembled as she untangled them. Richard was aware that she was trying to hide the fact his news had disconcerted her.

"I see. Then God go with you." The half curtsy was dutiful.

His jaw tightened at such a display of chilly virtue.

"I have made a will, lady. The manors you bring as dowry shall be yours in the event of my death, whoever wins the crown. My family will take you in if you require it of them." He watched her swallow nervously, nodding, her eyes modestly upon her clasped hands. This was not like Margery but some colorless cipher of a wife. "What else? Ah yes, is there any letter you wish me to carry for you? Any delivery you want made?"

At least she looked at him now, slowly shaking her head, her face expressionless.

He held her gaze. "I believe you have a message for the King of England." The blue glance shot sideways but not before he saw the panic in them. "I want it, Margery. The sand is running out and Adèle's father is murdered for it."

"What?" At least the news shook some spirit into her. Disbelief distorted her features. "How do *you* know this?"

Then the blue eyes widened. Had the hammer at last hit the anvil? "Are you trying to tell me that *you* are King Edward's man?"

"No, I am a cockroach crawling around this infernal kennel! Are we speaking English here? I am Gloucester's man. You wear the St. Catherine wheel; you have the letter."

She was shaking. By all the Saints, he should have handled this differently but time was not with him and she was watched. The man who followed her in was talking with the kennelboys.

"No, we are not speaking English, Master Huddleston. What is Henri Badoux to do with me?"

"He was the Yorkist agent in Amboise. My man in Tours was killed too. Our enemies are coming too close, Margery. It was King Louis who spied upon us in the bedchamber. It was Clarence who ordered us to be slaughtered. Pass the danger to me now. You have done your share and at far too high a price." He took a step toward her but she shrank back.

"You confuse me, sir. I do not understand any of this." She would have sped toward the door but he blocked her leaving. His fingers snatched off her headdress and drew her against him. The rivets upon his clothing bruised the soft flesh of her bare shoulders as his mouth sought hers.

Margery turned her face this way and that, knowing that within seconds she would be lost. His hands slid from her throat, traced her broad collar, and passed down her shoulders and over her forearms, tantalizing her through the sensual fabric of her sleeves, to fasten behind her and thrust her thighs against him.

She pushed against his chest. *"Let me go!"*

His painful grip snapped around her forearms. She shivered. This fury was uncontrolled. "I am not finished with you. I will have that letter, Margery."

"I have no letter, you incubus!" she snarled through her teeth, trying to free herself from his swift, iron grasp.

"Have we both come this far for naught?" he hissed. "It was not needful that you understood my presence."

This was the man who had vowed devotion to the Lancastrian Queen. The husband who had agreed to take King

Louis's gold. The lover who was never open with her, never set his affection upon the scales to be measured.

"No!" she exclaimed. "I do not follow you and there is nothing to give! *Nothing!*"

The shackles of his fingers loosened. "I trusted you, lady. And for what thanks? Horns on my head and intimate favors so chastely given. Go to perdition, Margery Huddleston, for I have done with you!" He flung her back against the barrel containing Error's bedding and stooped to retrieve her headdress. "How well this becomes you," he sneered, moving the gauze and satin through his fingers like a rosary. "A pretty, insubstantial nothingness. Here, wench, have it back! And you will not need this again." Plucking the brooch off her bodice with such ferocity that it ripped the fabric, he ground it beneath his spurred heel and left her.

Sobbing, Margery snatched up her veil and battered brooch and stumbled to her feet, her back bruised and aching from the fall. Error whined, licking her hand. It was only when one of the blushing kennelboys came across to offer assistance that she found sufficient dignity to leave.

Alys greeted her in the Nevilles' tiring-women's bedchamber, apologetic at the strewn linen and trinkets as Margery stared about her with mounting horror. "It was the master. He had mislaid something. Why, my lady . . ." Margery threw herself sobbing into her maidservant's arms.

"Oh, Alys, even my headdress."

There were no words long enough, short enough, worthy to curse with. Margery's fury was as sore as an unlanced boil, while the object of her wrath was safely on his way to Honfleur. A Judas indeed, kissing her only to search her person, having come fresh from ransacking her possessions. God deliver him to Hell! If he was truly loyal to York, then it was apparent he had never considered her worthy of his trust. While if he was a servant to Queen Margaret then . . . Jesu, she had come so close to telling him.

That was the problem. Whose side was Richard Huddleston on? The Queen's, her father's, Ned's, or merely his own? Was he the dog that waited until the lions had torn each other to pieces before he moved in and lapped up the blood?

Nothing made any sense. She sifted the conversations she could remember. There was no answer. He was a reflection in water that changed shape when the wind blew.

Sighing inwardly, she stood beside her father. Arms folded, legs astride, he was surveying the courtyard of armed men like a good peasant watching the turnip tops

breaking through the soil. Margery and her sisters had journeyed to Tours with him; anything to assuage their individual miseries. The second party was almost ready to
depart; carts lined up, fat with arms and roped with canvas,
ready to trundle north like a procession of giant maggots.

"You look pale, daughter. I think you are missing Huddleston at last."

"*Missing Huddleston*? Ha, like a barrel of sour apples!"

"No child yet?" The Earl put his arm about her and
patted her belly. The mere thought of a babe by Huddleston
powered the color into her cheeks and played havoc with
her inside intricacies.

Warwick flicked her cheek. "When I have England back
under my heel, Huddleston shall have manors in plenty."

She made no answer, narrowing her eyes against the
flashing cuirasses and shining helms amassing before them.

"Aye, they will all want rewards," her father muttered.
"Every man jack of them will need to have his loyalty
greased with titles or land. I tell you this, Margery, Neville
blood is as good as Plantagenet. By all the Saints, I could
make a better king than Ned or *him*." His gaze fell sourly on
Clarence who was making some kind of address to a cluster
of bored gunners. "Or the mother's boy."

"Think you King Harry will be fit to govern, my lord?"

He snorted. "Of course not."

"My lord, his majesty seeks you." A French page bowed
before them. King Louis waved from the other side of the
courtyard.

"My lord, there may be little chance to speak with you
again and . . ." Margery dropped into a curtsy. "I wish you
God's protection and I thank you for your care of me all
these years."

"It was the only thing I could do for your mother." Warwick's gloved knuckles stroked her cheek. "No, do not ask
it, child. I swore an oath of secrecy and her name shall never
pass my lips." He set his palm to her brow. "Until we meet
again, my blessing upon you, Margaret. Stay with Anne.
Lend her your strength. King Louis has sworn to see her
wed to the Prince and when the dispensation arrives, the
marriage must be made. She must accept her destiny."

Margery watched the men-at-arms bow to him as they

parted for him and she wondered if he would be slain within the year or whether she would be kneeling before the uncrowned King of England by the Feast of All Souls.

⁓

A few days later, Margery stood on the walls of Amboise and watched the clouds darkening and rolling venomously.

"Why are you up here alone? Did my temper become too much to bear?" Isabella fidgeted beside her, her cheeks flushed with the humidity of August.

"Look at the sky, Bella."

"Oh, yes, I see, well, the peasants will complain that their crops will be battered. I daresay there could be hail in those clouds."

"When there is a storm like this in Normandy then the invasion will begin. My hus—Huddleston said that if a tempest comes, it will scatter the blockade. Our fleet will sail the moment it is past."

"Oh." Isabella hugged her arms to her breast with a shudder despite the unnatural heat while the thunder rumbled through the valley and the heavy air carried with it an impending violence.

Indeed, thought Margery, time to go.

⁓

It was a week before God delivered what Margery was praying for, a day of full rain. Only then, clad in Alys's garments, could she pass the drawbridge with the hood of the cloak well down, covering her face.

Anne had sworn to provide lies for her absence and it had been so easy to walk along the main street to the church and kneel in prayer at the mass just as Alys always did. The hard part now would be to hire a horse but she had sufficient money to buy four hooves and silence. She would hide in the church until curfew—Alys had told her where—and perhaps seek the Levallois's help. Mayhap they would sell her a mount. If not, she must plead with a carter to take her to Tours and then hire as best she might.

It was the waiting that was the worst. Hunger and other needs gnawed at her but the old convent training of meditation returned to her. If nothing else, she could try to make her peace with God. Guilt that she could not obey her father's wishes and serve her youngest sister fought against her duty to prevent the war that might destroy England.

The hours dragged by. She heard the bells and the plain-song, the whisper of prayers and the shrieking of a distraught mother. True darkness seemed to tarry, but stiffly she eventually uncurled and crawled out guiltily from beneath the altar of Our Lady.

The evening air was sweet with rain after the incense and the dust but she was not prepared for this—a half dozen men in harness surrounded her, torches spitting in the drizzle.

They took her back into the château by the river postern and down into the very bowels of the cliff where the air was dank and fetid and there they kept her.

For over two weeks, if her calculations in this eternal night held any truth, no one had any speech with her. She had no candle. There were rats for company and a bucket that she had to feel her way to. Twice a day, ale, a trencher of coarse bread, and a cup of gruel were pushed through a grating in the door. At least they wanted to keep her alive.

Margery was left to call on every mental strength to keep her sanity. The morning they bought a flint to light the cressets, clean women's garments, and water to cleanse herself was the worst. She ate the good food they left even though she guessed they were tormenting her with hope. The King of France held her like a fly in his web.

A few hours later—was it day or night?—two soldiers hauled her roughly out and dragged her to a smoky chamber lit by wall torches and an iron brazier. Terror almost paralyzed her; a brawny man, his leather apron scarce encompassing his bulging belly, was thrusting branding irons into the glowing coals. A second fellow, sweat dripping down his naked chest, turned and looked her over with crude and gleeful lust. Then she began to scream.

The clout on the ear nearly deafened her, sending her senses reeling as they forced her onto a stool and wrenched her arms back. Struggling wildly availed her little. An iron chain, suspended from a pulley, swung into her and they bound her wrists to it with the leather straps.

It was higher than was comfortable, putting unnatural
pressure on her neck and upper back. She jerked wildly. The
chain answered with a mocking rattle behind her. Indignity,
humiliation, discomfort, anger, fear, and finally heat from
the embers, barely a man's pace from her, combined to torment her but there was more to suffer. Much more. The
guards left.

The practitioners of torture were waiting.

The second man lifted his apron and rubbed a grimy hand
meaningfully across his codpiece and the large man came to
stand leering beside him. She could imagine their filthy fingers already crawling over her body as they appraised her.

But it was not King Louis who came to stand gloating
down on the prisoner; it was Margaret of Anjou. The long-
nailed fingers tapping upon her folded arms were tuned to
the menace in her smile. Behind her, an amanuensis seated
himself upon a stool brought by a sergeant-at-arms, his
writing block upon his knee, the quill poised.

"Warwick's bastard and the usurper's whore. What a
jewel you are, Mistress Huddleston."

"Madam, what do you mean by this? I have done you no
harm." Margery tried to stand but the gaoler thrust her back
down with an ugly paw.

"Nor shall you. You do not do things by halves, do you,
Margery of Warwick? First the usurper, then his brawling
brother, Clarence. Did little Dick of Gloucester lift your
skirts as well or is he too much of an impotent runt to try?"

Margery shrugged, ignoring the gibe. "He has two bastard children, I am told, madam."

"But not by you. You are clever enough not be become
inconvenienced by your *affaires*. Is it witchcraft that makes
you so palatable to Yorkist upstarts, mistress? Your looks
do little for you."

"No, madam," Margery protested gravely. If the Queen's
mind settled on witchcraft, the local bishop would readily
light a fire in the marketplace to please her.

"We shall come to your adultery anon. We are here for a
simple interrogation, mistress. How long or what form it
takes lies within your fair hands." Margery swallowed in
fear; the smaller man smirked, his calculating eyes on her

fingers. Would they begin there? Wrenching her nails out one by one?

The Queen uncrossed her arms, spreading her hands. "We simply want to know what Clarence intends to do when he reaches England. Does he plan to be reunited with the usurper Edward?"

"You could have asked me at any time, madam. There was no need to go to this inconvenience."

The Queen's eyes glittered. "You broke your parole, your sacred word as a hostage. Where were you going?"

"I have a lover. I was going to him. As for my duty as your hostage, madam, I made no such promise nor did my half sisters. It was decided without us."

"As with all hostages since the dawn of time. If you wish to set eyes on either of those young women again, you had better consider your answers now most carefully."

"If truth will buy me liberty then, no, I do not believe the Duke wishes to be reconciled with his brothers. He has never spoken of it."

The Queen scowled. With a sudden movement, her hand flashed out to grab a fistful of Margery's hair and violently yanked her head back.

"You scream now with such little pain, you lying whore! But we have the means of teasing the truth out of perjurers. What shall it be? A brand upon your neck or breast? A knotted cord about your brows?"

"Madam, I have done you no ill. Dear Jesu, if you harm me, my father shall hear of it."

"Only if you live to tell the tale." The Queen let go with a wicked thrust that jerked her prisoner's head forward. Margery would have tumbled off the stool had the chain not cruelly held her.

Her captor bent down, her face coming so intimately close to Margery's that had the Queen's spittle been venom, she would have been blinded. "The Countess will not weep one tear to hear of your passing, will she? And the little upstart Duchess will be glad to have her drunken husband to herself again. As for my future daughter-in-law, who helped you leave, she thinks you safe on the road to England. I tell you this, if Anne does not obey me, a subtle poison will

soon rid us of her. I will have her life if your father does not
take England for me. I will have all of them!"

This was the most deadly of enemies, Margery began to
realize. Better the spider King than this unstable woman,
cankered with hatred.

"Your grace, I beg to know in what way I have offended you?"

The Queen straightened. "By living, you Neville by-
blow! Now answer! You carried secret letters to the Duke?"

"It was the condition upon which I was allowed to rejoin
my father. I carried letters to him as well."

"Harken, Margery Neville, I want evidence that Clarence
is a traitor to your father. My friends want back the lands
that rightfully belong to them. I need to know what he has
said to you or given you. Any message, token?"

"Madam, I know naught that would be of use to you. I
have nothing. No doubt you have had my possessions
searched."

"Yes, and those of your horned husband. Another matter,
why did Huddleston not publicly take his belt to you? Why
did he acquiesce in your adultery?"

Jesu, why did he?

"Because I was to spy for the King of France. Because I
was to leave France in disgrace and become the usurper's
mistress again. Pray ask his majesty yourself, madam." At
least it is partly true. Dear Christ, make her believe me,
prayed Margery. Help me look her straight in the eyes like a
clever peddler. I have to sell her lies.

"How plausible. But I need hard evidence, girl. My
agents have been watching you since Calais. We know that
you were sent to seduce Clarence. Cut her gown!"

Margery's eyes went wide with horror.

The burly gaoler came around to the front of her,
grabbed the neck of the simple gown, slicing it open to
her waist with the point of his knife. The other man behind
her wrenched the fabric over her shoulders exposing her
breasts and half her belly. To a woman of her upbringing,
such nakedness was a torment in itself. She swallowed
painfully. Were they going to brand her or squeeze her flesh
with burning pincers?

"Belle," hissed the gaoler. Margery shook her hair forward wishing it was long enough to hide her shame, but the other wretch tidied it back with callused fingers that lingered on her neck.

"You can touch her," encouraged the Queen in his own tongue. "Go on, she's a harlot." Then she changed to English. "Perhaps our guest will find the rough a refreshing change from Clarence's perfumed tumbling."

The man hesitated, then he moved a fumbling, tentative hand down her throat. Margery shuddered at the dirty nails and huge fingers. The fetid breath grew faster upon her cheek.

"You are enjoying it, are you not, Neville cherrylips? Touch her some more, fellows. You! Run your fingers along her lips." The gaoler in front of her put his huge fingers to her mouth. Margery felt bile rise to her throat. She folded her lips tightly and tried to think of anything else.

The Queen laughed and said in English, "You want more? If you do not tell me what I need to hear, I am going to give you to these wretches as a plaything until you beg for mercy."

"By God, madam, you disgrace womanhood!"

The Queen slammed her hand across Margery's cheek, her ring leaving a streak of beading blood.

"You fool, I have waited too long for this day to let you or your drunken lover get in my path. I shall win this war and I shall use any means to do so. I want evidence to prove to your father that Clarence will betray him."

"Do you want the truth, madam, or merely what you want to hear? As God is my witness, Clarence *hates* his brother."

"That is not good enough! Suckle these fellows, King's whore," snarled the Queen. "You will never have such sweet lovers. Enjoy her, you curs, feast! The King of England has tasted where you may suck."

The second gaoler stirred behind Margery. His hands scraped down her shoulders and groped her breasts. The large gaoler was salivating as his stare fed on her. She closed her eyes and tried not to feel, not to think. She wanted to retch. Her eyes flew open as a mouth fastened around the nipple of her right breast, its tongue frenzied. Margery shrieked and squirmed, shuddering back against the moving chain only to find herself held by the second man.

"Desist! Stand back again. You see, Warwick's daughter, there will be no lash marks. Your word against mine if I let you live. But maybe you would prefer a whipping? Or a taste of the Duke of Exeter's daughter? I am told that is a cunning invention by one of your usurper's minions to drag information out of traitors. Is that not true, fellow? So, shall we rack her?" She turned to the older of the men.

Margery saw his skin had dulled to a dark red. The dark centers of his eyes had dilated and his leather codpiece was bulging as he turned hungry eyes to the Queen. "*Majesté*, give her to me. She will sing sweetly afterward."

"They want you badly. Tell me where you have hidden Clarence's reply!"

"I—I have nothing, *ma reine*. I merely warmed his grace's bed and gave him comfort."

The Queen laughed. "Kiss her mouth," she snarled at the large gaoler.

He bent to comply and Margery screamed. She had not believed she could make such a sound before that awful mouth came down on her and the lascivious tongue flickered to infiltrate her mouth.

When he finally let her breathe, she spat. "I shall puke all over your skirts in a moment, madam. Will that be sufficient truth for you?"

"You wish the gaolers to ravish you till they are slaked?"

The wretch behind her grabbed each of her nipples, tweaking them painfully, and was moving himself against the back of her skirt. The chain swung. Margery closed her eyes. She did not know how much more she could bear. The thought of those vile bodies insinuating their pricks between her thighs made her nauseous.

"Ah, you wasted my time. What care I for the truth so long as I have a confession out of you and you sign it. Set down that the prisoner says she was sent to make promises to Clarence and that he has sworn to her that he will betray her father." She rounded on the scribe. "Write, you fool! Anyone would think you have never seen a woman's dugs before."

But as the man refreshed the nib with ink, there was the sound of distant arguing and a voice rising above them indignantly. Someone was running along the passageway with armed footsteps in pursuit.

Frantic hands beat upon the door, startling them all. *"Ma mére!"*

Margery's eyes snapped open. The Queen froze. Recovering in an instant, she muttered to the sergeant. He opened the door narrowly but Prince Edouard thrust him roughly aside, storming into the room like a young playful hound let out for exercise—a fair archangel entering Hell. Soldiers pushed in behind him and another man in riding cloak and boots followed behind, the liripipe of his hat still wound about his throat.

"Your grace," Margery pleaded.

Prince Edouard's eyes narrowed in horror as he took in not only who she was but that she was bound, her hair unkempt, and her gown in shreds around her ribs. He blanched as if his whole being squirmed with embarrassment at his mother's unexplained presence. For a moment he could not take his eyes from Margery's nakedness. Then he turned upon his parent as if he had caught her in bed with a lover.

"What in the name of Christ is going on here?"

The Queen seemed to swallow uncomfortably but she answered brazenly enough. "This baseborn harlot has information that could cost me England."

"But . . . this is Warwick's daughter, madam. She is a hostage left here in good faith . . ." His jaw stayed open. He turned an appalled face to the man behind him.

The other stepped forward, transferring his riding crop to his left hand. His gloved hand unwound the black cloth that scarfed his neck so that he might remove his hat.

Margery's frantic gaze looked straight into her husband's icy face. She gave a moan of shame.

Richard's mouth was a thin cold line. The surprise had already passed. He had had time to assess the situation. The cogs and wheels were turning. He raised an eyebrow in contemptuous rejection of Margery and the entire room before he bestowed his attention upon the Queen.

Margaret d'Anjou's face tightened defensively. "Master

Huddleston, there has been much mischief in your absence. We thought to interrogate your wife before handing her over to the Bishop to be punished for her adultery."

"Adultery, madam?" Huddleston drew off his gloves with seeming unconcern.

"With the Duke of Clarence. She lay with him to make him turn traitor and—"

"But, madam, I do recall the Duke left scarce after Master Hudd—" The Prince faltered as his mother thrust up her hand to silence him.

"*Before!* There are witnesses."

"She wants to behead Clarence!" exclaimed Margery, struggling to rise, but the gaoler held her down.

The Queen's lip curled in disgust. "This woman is poison within this household. A used whore sent by the usurper Edward to win his brother back. We have to be certain of Clarence's intent before we return to England and, as surely as the sun rises, this creature knows."

Richard's gaze held the Queen's while his long fingers swiftly unfastened the loops at the neck of his doublet.

"I think you will find, madam, that you have no more cause for concern. The allegation against Clarence will bear no fruit and . . ." He exchanged a meaningful look with the Prince. "In short, I have such news that will bring you so much joy that this unfaithful wife of mine will be of no matter to you.

"Gracious lady"—he dropped with reverence on one knee before the Queen's skirts and drew a folded letter from his breast—"my lords of Warwick and Clarence rejoice to inform you that England is yours."

CHAPTER
27

Margery squeezed her eyelids shut, flung back her head, and let out her breath slowly. When she opened her eyes again, it was to inwardly loathe the exultation that was slowly manifesting itself in the Queen's embittered face.

"Can this be true?" The nine years of waiting, the long exile unbelievably over? Little wonder the Queen could not halt the incredulity mixed with fervent longing in her voice.

The Prince laughed. "*Maman,* it is true. Read the letter. Two of the English heralds are in the *grande salle* waiting for you."

Margaret searched her only child's face, then with a shriek of triumph she flung her arms around him.

"Edouard, Edouard, at last." Drawing back from his embrace, she crossed herself, "Oh, God, I thank you! I thank you!" Tears sparkled behind her eyes. She turned to the kneeling messenger to drift her fingertips caressingly down Richard Huddleston's shadowy cheek.

"You shall be rewarded. But what of the usurper?"

Huddleston's heartless glance flickered sideways at Margery, chilling her to her soul. "Not heard of. He has disappeared in the north and it is believed he may be prisoner or dead. My lord Montague's messenger had not arrived when I left London but my lord of Warwick wished you to know our tidings with all speed and commanded me to leave forthwith. There is also a letter from my lord of Pembroke in his own hand confirming this."

"Wondrous, wondrous news!" The Queen crossed her arms across her chest, embracing herself with delight. "I cannot believe it. Does my cousin of France know?"

"His majesty has ordered three days of thanksgiving. We left him in Tours."

"Excellent, excellent. So my son, we must not keep the heralds waiting. Master Huddleston, to your feet. You must tell me everything as we go. No messenger ever brought me such welcome news."

Richard rose stiffly. "Madam," he replied wearily, rising. "I have been traveling these four days. Give me leave tonight. As for my wife, I will pursue this matter in my own way."

"Oh, no," countered the Queen blithely. "You must celebrate with us. A stoop of wine and good food will put new heart into you. My own servants shall prepare a bath. Yes, indeed. As for your wife, she is not good enough for you and shall remain my prisoner. Now England is mine again, you may set her aside and I shall find you an heiress. Adulterous wives should be handed over to the church for chastisement. Think well on it, sirrah."

Huddleston bowed over her proffered hand. "I shall wait on your grace as soon as I may. Have I your permission to speak with her?"

The Queen swept to the door and turned. "If you must." Her gaze fixed upon the guard. "Bestow her in a cell with a window and see that she is fed within the hour. She is not to be harmed for now."

The gaoler closest to Margery had understood nothing and slid a hand around her throat.

"Out!" snarled Huddleston, dealing the wretch such a staggering blow on the side of the face that he nearly fell upon the brazier. "Out before I turn you into a eunuch. And you, cut the bitch loose!" There was a tired jagged edge to his voice that Margery had never heard before but his fury gave her hope.

She searched his face, her lips trembling, seeking a glimmer of compassion as the soldier freed her from her bonds and hauled her roughly up.

Richard's eyes swept witheringly over her nakedness. "Well," he drawled in French. "You are even more of a fool than I took you for. It seems I shall be well rid of you." He swung on his heel and flung the door wide, nodding at the guard.

The man grabbed her shoulder and thrust her forward and the other gaoler laughed maliciously. Margery's stomach rebelled at last. She began to retch.

Her husband turned his face toward her at the sound, his eyes uncaring. He made a gesture for the soldier to stand back. When she was done, she leaned her shoulder against the wall gasping and brushed the saliva off her chin, sending him a look of poisonous hate. He waited irritably, tapping his crop against the boot leather, then he swung his cloak from his shoulders and thrust it at her. "Cover yourself!" he snarled.

His spurred boots echoed malevolently behind her as she was hauled up the tower stairs and thrust into a narrow chamber lit by a small upper grating.

Richard Huddleston was going to do nothing to free her.

Richard awoke feeling saddlesore and guilty that he had not been able to battle aganst the fatigue of four days' hard riding, especially knowing that his disobedient Margery had spent another night locked up, cursing him. Someone's servants, probably my lord of Concressault's, had heaved him onto a vacant palliase in a small circular chamber sometime before midnight. They had considerately removed his spurs and dumped his saddlebag beside the bed.

The latter was moving like a woman's belly heavy with child. Richard remembered why, groaned, and rubbed the sleep out of his eyes. One of his possessions had chewed a hole out through the bag's side, made a puddle by the wall, and was gnawing the leather strap. With an oath, Richard hauled the bag up beside him and fumbled through its contents with a swift prayer to the saints who represented the inebriated. Well, no, not the inebriated—it had been fatigue that had sent him to sleep in the middle of the Queen's peroration on her bloody plan for disposing of the person of the usurper Edward if no one else had already beheaded him.

Richard drew out the second sleepier puppy and set it down. It groggily wagged its tail at him and squatted immediately. They were to be his farewell gesture to the King of France. Even if they were not deerhounds, mayhap Louis, who appreciated such humor, might be less zealous in revenge when he learned that Richard had abducted Margery.

The rest of his hastily gathered possessions were miraculously intact. A tame apothecary in Southwark had sold him not only sufficient sleeping powder to flatten the puppies for the journey but enough to give the entire garrison of Amboise respite from guard duties. With a groan, Richard stiffly forced his much-traveled body upright, heaved the saddlebag over his shoulder, scooped the puppies up, and headed for the kennels.

From there, it was easy to slip into the town and materialize at the Levallois house in time to break his fast. He found only the merchant being waited on at the board. Adèle and Katherine were with Jacques's widowed cousin in Orléans.

"Merde!" exclaimed his surprised host. "So it was you who rode in after *couvre-feu* last night."

"Complete with festive ribbons and a surfeit of whistles. They will be celebrating all day up at the château."

"Lord Warwicque has taken Angleterre *already*?" Jacques Levallois blinked at Richard in amazement.

Richard rubbed the bridge of his nose and nodded. "Aye, like you, I thought it would be a long and bloody campaign."

"And the gorgeous Edward?"

"Fled like a servant who has feasted in his master's absence. They may have 'headed him by now. You know why I am here."

Jacques sent his servants from the room with a casual hand and chewed his bread thoughtfully before he finally spoke. "*Eh bien, mon compère,* you are reconsidering your allegiance then?"

"I may have little choice." Richard laid down his spoon, his appetite dull. "There is, however, the matter of my wife being brought before an ecclesiastical court for adultery and, Jesu forbid, other matters. By the way she boasted in her cups last night, Margaret d'Anjou will baste Margery for cooking in the marketplace."

The older man stolidly chewed on, showing no surprise at the news, but Richard felt as though he were being measured for a new cote. "What I am wondering," Jacques remarked eventually, "is just how thin you are." He glanced down apologetically at the belt encompassing his houppelande. "*Moi,* I am too large a stopper for this particular flask."

His guest raised an eyebrow. "Are you saying you and your friends might help me, Jacques?"

"Because of my father-in-law's murder and for the sake of the town? Why not? You are very fortunate that I can, *mon compère.*" The earth brown eyes glittered with amusement. "*Le bon Dieu* be praised that Madame 'uddleston has not the generous dimensions of the Queen of France."

With another meal that had taste and substance inside her, Margery felt her inner self revitalizing, like a shoot pushing skyward after a long, freezing winter. Through the barred window she could smell the autumn leaves above the wood smoke and another heavier odor that she suspected came from the nearby lions. Even a few beams of sunlight lit the floor during the morning. But *he* did not come.

Some of her belongings were brought to her, obviously at his command, among them her girdle purse containing combs and hairpins. What had he told her sisters? Not the truth.

Certes, the truth was that her husband had indeed decided for the winning side. With Ned surely dead by now, Richard Huddleston would be the last man to raise his sword to crown George for the House of York. And she had jeopardized his careful plans. To please the Queen, would he drag her before the bishops and force her to walk barefoot in a thin shift carrying a taper while the crowd hurled filth at her in a fit of hypocritical virtue? And even if he was merciful enough to petition her release, what then? The Queen had promised him a wealthy heiress. He could auction George of Clarence's message for her dowry thrice over.

Pacing the cell, she counted as she had done every day of her captivity, trying to keep her body fit, while she tormented herself. She remembered every hurt and buckled on the armor of hate and self-righteousness, vowing she would survive and the Lord God could damn her enemies to Hell! After all, had she not been steadfast in her loyalty to Ned? But with darkness, the tears flowed for what might have been. The guard banged on the door and cursed her, so she turned her face into the rough fabric of the mattress and cried silently.

✺

She woke from her tormented sleep so swiftly. It was yet night but a man had entered her cell as insidiously as an assassin. She sprang off the mattress and shrank against the wall. The door was nudged open. The single light beyond her showed her the two guards slumped against the walls, one of them snoring loudly.

"I hope these fit." Her husband's fingers closed about her wrist and drew her out into the candlelight. He was already unbuckling her belt and holding out the hose. Wordlessly she obeyed. It was he who lifted the gown up over her head and guided her fingers into the leather sleeves. Another shadow materialized beside him from the coils of the stairs and in obedience to Richard's signal, the man heaved one of the guards into the cell and onto the mattress. While Margery transferred her purse to the leather belt he had brought her, Richard, his face taut and grim, rearranged the second guard with his back to the passageway. Then he swiftly fed her discarded clothing out through the guards' arrow-slit window.

She made no attempt to question him. If he could magic her outside the castle, then she would reevaluate her safety later. What she was not expecting was to be led back down to the fouler passageways and then shoved headfirst after his fellow conspirator into a small wooden cupboard at shoulder height.

"I hope you have strong elbows." muttered Richard as he guided her knees up into a crawling position on the ledge and gave her a whack forward as if she were a testy mule.

"Dear Jesu!" she protested.

"Keep moving if you value your life!" he whispered, forcing her onward as he scrambled in after her, and cursing as he maneuvered in order to bolt the small door behind them.

The space immediately behind the wooden cupboard was broad but as Margery edged forward, following the shuffle of the other man's movements, she could feel the walls closing about her. Walls? No, it was rock.

"This is the worst part, madame," her guide reassued her.

"*We* had to do it twice," Richard pointed out, narrowly avoiding colliding with his wife's boot as she hesitated.

Crawling through burrows could safely be left to rabbits, Richard reflected as they painfully edged the next hundred paces. In patches, the limestone beneath his forearms was smooth as glaze; elsewhere a jagged miscellany of rubble bruised and bit into his knees.

His wife edged forward in the chilly darkness without complaining, but he could hear the very fear in her breathing. It seemed an eternity before he could feel the faint movement of air upon his face. He had been down in the mines his father owned and seen where their men worked. Now he vowed that if he ever set eyes on his inheritance again, he would make his father pay their labors twofold.

Margery collapsed on her arms with a gasp of relief as she emerged into the cavern where Jacques and the other men awaited them. Then she was blinking in wonderment, like an owl caught in daylight, for the roof was at least twelve paces high, knobbed with points shiny as udders, and he doubted she had ever seen the like of it in her life. But there was no time for pointing out the peculiar features of limestone. Richard set his hands upon her thighs and dragged her up onto her knees.

"*Félicitations, madame!*" Jacques Levallois caught her by the elbows and lifted her to standing before turning to clasp her husband's hand. "It went smoothly?" Of the four

men who awaited them, the merchant was the only one
unmasked.

"Aye, all to plan. The English would have lost Agincourt
had they faced you, *mes braves*." Richard's grin embraced
them all as he clapped a grateful hand on the shoulder of
the lanky man who had accompanied him. "But let us
move on." He saw Margery's jaw slacken as Jacques tugged
a cloth from his belt and bound it about her eyes. She
squeaked as one of the large men tossed her up over his
shoulder. "All part of the agreement, mousekin," Richard
reassured her.

When they finally took off his blindfold, he found himself on the bank of the river beside a small craft. An oarsman sat ready. They had lain Margery in the boat already.
He hoped she was up to the journey that faced them. In the
light of the waning moon, her face was waxen.

"What can I say?" Richard gratefully embraced the large
man and shook each of the others by the hand before he
stepped into the boat. The merchant's friends heaved the
small vessel forth; it was a little dung pellet of rebellion to
hurl against the King who was strangling their town to keep
his heir free of pestilence.

Richard said a prayer to St. Christopher and resigned his
safety to the boatman, trusting he knew the dangerous
eddies and shallows. They were at the mercy of a fast-
flowing, cantankerous river.

At his feet Margery stirred, unwinding herself from the
cocoon of his cloak, swiftly sending a panicky hand to
check that the purse at her belt was still in place. Did she
still carry the Duke's message? "Am I the ballast?" she
complained.

"No, you are the third oarsman. Keep down."

She lay still, the pike of his shoe across her hip, and sent
a prayer to St. Leonard, the saint of prison breakers, then her
argumentative nature surfaced again. She raised her head,
staring at the stranger who rowed beneath the moon with the
stoic expression of a weary horse towing a cart. "But we are
heading *upriver*."

Listening for sounds on the bank, watching for torchlit
soldiers, Richard did not answer her. He shook his head and

cautioned silence. The oarsman nodded agreement and kept close to the bank; it was the painful but only way to travel upstream against the current. At least the wind was behind them, confusing the wavelets.

Eventually Richard drew her up to sit beside him.

"I thought you were leaving me to the bishops." Her voice was like a raw wound rubbed with salt.

"It was tempting. When is the custom of women upon you again?" There was an angry hiss at the intimacy of the question. "Lady, I want to know how long I can safely keep you garbed in man's attire." His voice lightened. "Of course there are ways to ensure . . ."

It took them an hour's quarter to cross the river and as much again to free themselves from a sandbank before they struggled farther up the river's northern side. To have gone south from Amboise would have been swifter but there was a weir beneath the bridge and watchmen patrolling it and, besides, the west led to Anjou.

As prearranged, Jacques Levallois had sent horses to meet them four miles upriver and the boatman thankfully left them upon the bank.

"Are you hale enough for hardy riding?" Richard asked with concern.

"Are you?" she threw back at him.

He sighed, "I tell you I would not be a royal messenger to earn my crust. You can rub my saddle sores later, God willing. If aught parts us, seek out Adèle at the street of the silversmiths in Orléans."

"Richard." Margery reached up and kissed him. "Thank you."

By sunrise they were on the road to Blois. Jacques had already dispatched a courier the day before to Adèle in Orléans to warn her of their arrival and to have fresh horses awaiting them. But it was all too easy, thought Richard. And once word reached King Louis in Tours . . . oh, yes, a pair of cages would be made ready for them.

He was right. They had to leave the highway as frequently as an old man with a weak bladder and words became as precious as provisions between them. English, like gold, was not to be flashed in any marketplace. In Orléans two days later, Adèle welcomed them, and her hostess, a hospitable silversmith's widow of great heart, gave them food and stabled their weary horses, but by suppertime the news was bad. The King's soldiers around the city were reputed to be as numerous as worms upon a corpse and the mayor had doubled the guards upon the city gate. Richard left for the alehouses by the *quai* an hour before curfew, seeking a carter who might smuggle them out, leaving Margery hidden in the widow's cellar. He returned jubilantly before the city watch began its march.

"I think our prayers are answered. I have just become reacquainted with a donkey." His wife, not surprisingly, for once was speechless.

Well, if Warwick could kiss Margaret d'Anjou's hand, it was an age for all kinds of miracles. Richard had met up with the players who had entertained them so riotously that night at Angers, sitting at their ale but a lane away. Not only were they leaving next day, ambling northeast, but they also had a wanderer's disdain for authority and frontiers and were willing to hasten their departure to help Richard.

At his request, they sent one of their number out of the city with the fresh horses that Adèle Levallois had obtained for him; at his bidding, they caparisoned the edges of their cart with the painted cloth they used for Noah's flood so that it hung low. Then they nailed canvas to the outside frame of the underbelly leaving one end open.

"In you go, my sweet." There was no time for arguing.

Four of the players lifted Margery and pocketed her between the canvas and the boards.

"Jesu save me! *Richard!*" Slung beneath the belly of the cart like kittens in a tabby near its time, she could only pray that the driver would choose his way with care.

"Courage! Is it likely to bruise you?"

"No, and there is air enough, but will it hold?"

"With God's help if you do not wriggle. If aught goes wrong, cut your way out after nightfall."

"But what about you?"

"The Devil looks after his own," he answered blithely, crossing himself for insurance, before he took the costume and transformed himself into a masked demon like the rest.

Armed with firecrackers, the mummers left the inn noisily, juggling and clowning along the street, teasing Adèle and Katherine, catching them up like floating planks upon a wave of misrule.

It was a misfortune that the officer in charge of the northern gate appeared to enjoy the petty power that his position gave him over lesser men. He swaggered toward the wagon with the anticipatory expression of a successful bully. But the chief player was ready, positioned behind him, mimicking the man's walk. The swelling crowd loved it. The officer glanced around and saw merely an idle demon. But as he drew near the cart and leaned forward to see inside, the crowd gave a shriek of laughter as the player unbuttoned his costume codpiece and a huge black and scarlet appendage sprang out. At least a yard long, it thwacked into the officer's rear. The man turned, outraged. The onlookers screamed with laughter.

Richard set off the first firecracker and then there were fireworks everywhere, hissing and exploding in among the kirtles and boots. The crowd enjoyed running amok. They surged forward around the cart, the women, chaste and unchaste, screaming as the demons chased them with monstrous feathered pricks snaking in their hands.

Richard gave the nod to the driver and the cart creaked out slowly beneath the gateway in riotous company. He kissed his hand to the Levallois women and swung himself aboard, shaking with laughter as he hauled his costume appendage back into his codpiece. It was only when they were half a mile beyond the outlying villages and no armed horsemen had followed that he buried his head in his hands and thanked God that they had not all been arrested for disturbing the peace and alleged sodomy. He halted the cart where the player was waiting with the horses. His shaken wife was white-lipped as they drew her out like a babe from the straining canvas womb.

꧁꧂

For a week they kept with the players. Richard, straw-hatted, played at carter, and the October sun, warm and mellow, lit them past orchards and harvested fields of golden stubble. Margery, her clothing masculine, her hair cropped again, barely left his side.

Fear of pursuit stalked them. They spoke little; she thought a great deal, trying to fathom his motives, hoping that it was more than his sense of duty that had caused him to winkle her out of the fortress. She had been found wanting; she knew that and realized that the foolish admission on their wedding night—that she was carrying the letters—had burned all hope of trust. Yet there was a kindness in the way his glance touched her that carried more than the heat of sunlight.

When he announced his decision to take the horses and to leave the wagons and strike westward, she knew again the cold fear and hugged the memory of the last few days to her.

"Why did we not flee to England?" she asked him, sated with rabbit meat, turning from watching the sparks of the wood fire dance into the darkness on that last evening.

"Because I could be hanged, drawn, and quartered. The accusation of treachery has not been revoked by King Edward, and your father, when he hears from France, no doubt will let it stand." Somewhere in the forest, a wolf howled and she shivered.

"How did Ned talk you into that?" Margery whispered horrified, remembering the dismembered bodies at Southampton, and received the answer in his face of an overgenerous gift. "Oh, sweet Heaven!"

It was what she desired but, dear Jesu, the cost. She wanted to protest her unworthiness, marveling that she still could not plumb the shallowest depths of the man beside her.

But there was more: Richard idly prodded a stick into the embers. "When I was about nine or ten years old and page to your uncle, Lord Montague, I traveled in his retinue to Middleham and there was this child. About six years old she must have been, plumpish but not overly, with long hair loose down her back. I watched her rescue a little pup, the runt of a litter, from three or four boys twice her age and size. They had bagged the little creature and were threatening to throw it into the well. This little girl just stepped into their midst, her small fists upon her nonexistent hips, with a heap of courage and a belief she was right, and she grabbed the wriggling bag and cut the creature free, abusing them all the while. I who had watched with amusement and not interfered, for they were older than I, then met her indignant gaze and she thrust the little dog into my arms. 'Here, you have him,' she said, 'and take good care of him. He wants but kindness.' "

Margery frowned in amazement, her lips opening to a cherry's width. "Richard? *That was you?* All those years ago. You never told me."

"At Warwick I saw her again years later and I remembered. She had grown beautiful. I wanted to go up to her and thrust the descendant of that pup into her arms and say, 'Here, I have done what you bid me, take him and my heart with it. I want but kindness.' "

Tears sparkled in her eyes as she raised them to the dark dome of sky.

"And now we have wasted a great deal of time in quarreling." He took her hand and turned it over, rubbing his fingers across her palm. "I did not want to say this because I thought that it would hurt you more to know, and if I am slain in battle . . ." He swallowed. She did not speak and he was compelled to falter onward. "I was not going to tell you that I loved you, Margery. I thought it would be easier for you not to know if aught happened but I have learned that my judgment may be green in these matters. Am I right?"

Her smile was watery like a rainbow sky, her voice husky. "Yes, green as grass, so say it, Richard Huddleston."

"I have made many mistakes, Margery, but I know that I am not wrong in loving you."

The firelight danced upon the kind lines of his face as she reached out her hand and touched his cheek.

"In love, sir, as in death, all of us are equal." She eased him to face her and knelt before him, holding his hands in hers. "Before Almighty God, in Whom I trust, I take you Richard Huddleston in love and loyalty until death and I hereby plight you my troth." She stretched upward and kissed his mouth. "Yes?"

"Yes."

ᴄᴏᴍ

Richard's sense of being followed grew as they left the players and journeyed westward now with greater speed. Next day, they sheltered unseen in a wayside copse to watch who came behind them, but only a half-dozen toasted pilgrims, returning in scallop shell tabards from Compostela, were noteworthy. The carriers, messengers, and two merchants with an escort of armed men were not unusual wayfarers.

"Something gnaws at me," muttered Richard. "I think we should go across country."

"Without a guide but your sense of direction, so be it. But surely, we shall be more remarked if seen away from the highway, and is not the forest as perilous for but two of us?"

He nodded tight-lipped. "For a few miles only, then we will return to this road again."

He had an unfailing judgment in direction, and an hour later he led her back onto the highway. But a mile farther, they rounded a forested bend and saw the merchants and armed men drawn up ahead.

With a muttered oath, Richard grabbed both reins and hauled them off the road, hoping no one had seen them. "I knew it. Come on!"

He led her through the wood to higher ground and halted, listening. With growing fear, Margery heard their pursuers shouting in the valley. The pound of hooves came up the hill toward them.

"Dear God, not now we have come so far," she gasped, swiftly untrapping the purse. "Here, Richard, separate. Go on to Burgundy without me. This is worth two kingdoms."

He thrust it into his doublet and thwacked her horse, sending it hurtling between the trees and down the other side of the hill. She had little choice but to cling on, bent over the saddle, frantic as the branches lashed and whipped her. She heard him close behind her and then she came hard upon a river. It was too deep to ford. She tried to force her mount into the water but it balked and wheeled.

Richard had unsheathed his sword and turned his horse. She drew hers too, knowing she had the skill to parry but not the strength to thrust. Half a score of men-at-arms rode at them and ahead of them was Error.

"Go, Richard!" she cried in despair but he tossed weapons from palm to palm and sent his dagger hurtling into the nearest man's throat. Then they were beset in earnest. Two of them attacked him on either side while a third rode in on Margery. Then suddenly other horsemen hurtled from the forest, the pilgrims.

It was over swifter than it takes a beggar to drink a yard of ale. The pilgrims spared not one of the King's men, drawing their daggers across the survivors' throats and would have slain the dog, had Richard not roared in fury. Every man froze. The air was still except for the panting of the horses and the buzz of flies drawn already by the smell of blood.

Margery and Richard were surrounded.

"I thank you, *messieurs*." Richard wiped the sweat from his brow with his sleeve but he neither sheathed his sword nor relaxed his vigilance. Margery, trembling, knew then they must be *écorcheurs* bent on ransom.

"The Demoiselle Neville?" the leader asked, saluting Margery.

Richard growled in surprise. "Madame Huddleston!" he snapped but the man took no notice. They could see now by the brightness of his grin that his tan was walnut juice.

"Monseigneur de Commynes sends you greetings, demoiselle. We are here to see you safe to Burgundy."

In the light of the next dawn, Richard rose early from their camp and carried his wife's purse away from the human snores and the huff of the horses hoping to be fed.

Supervised by Error, he tipped the contents out upon the moss—two combs of bone, a silver case with needle and thread and two hairpins, a tiny pottery jar of ointment, and a leaf-shaped brooch. He picked up the larger of the two bone combs, cursing that he had never thought of it before.

The crude carving, a plethora of what might pass for leaves, was rough beneath his fingers. He turned it over and applied the nail of his smallest finger in the groove on the end. The circle moved. A hollow groove, barely thicker than a quill shaft ran within the spine of the comb. It would require a needle to auger out the hidden secret.

Without turning, he knew she stood behind him. "Oh, nobly done," she applauded, crouching to thrust her belongings back into her purse. "How many weeks has it taken you? You must have searched my clothes a score of times."

"A clever device." He weighed the comb in his hand.

"Margaret d'Anjou would give me an earldom for this scrap of treachery."

For the briefest of instants, she still doubted him. He was clever enough to turn any situation to his advantage. "You overrate yourself, Richard Huddleston," she chided lightly and swiftly prayed.

He did not answer that but reached out and caught her to him, bestowing a kiss on the tip of her nose as he pressed the comb back into her hand. "Hush, I have news that will drive all else from your head."

Margery surrendered to his arms. "Astonish me."

"They say your Ned bought a passage across the Channel with a fur-lined coat. He and Gloucester are safe in Burgundy."

"And I say she should not! She is with child." Richard Huddleston faced the crownless English King across the board in Bruges.

"You forget yourself!" snarled Edward, his color rising.

"No, your highness, I *remember*. My wife has suffered too much already in your service."

Edward sprang to his feet, towering over the rest of them. "Let the lady be sent for. I will know *her* mind."

"Ha! You know she will say yes." Richard rose also.

Gloucester set a swift hand upon his sleeve. "Let me be a stifler between you."

Which, of course, Margery reflected later, was how she came to find herself in early December foolishly riding into Westminster palace in the entourage of the embassy from Burgundy, once more carrying letters of reconciliation.

Her father, who wanted to be and could not be king because his veins held not one drop of Plantagenet blood, stood on the dais in the Great Hall beside the empty throne. The red silk cushions of the royal seat were dented as if King Henry had lately sat there, or her father, alone, had tried it out for size.

He was surrounded by noblemen, none of whom she recognized save for my lord of Oxford who eyed her with lofty astonishment. The Duke of Clarence was mercifully absent.

The Burgundians, dignified and puffed up with virtuous outrage, protested against Warwick's alliance with the King of France. Already, they complained, French soldiers had made sallies into Burgundy and there were further amassments on the border; their trading agreements had been circumvented in favor of French imports; King Louis was preparing an invasion force; and Charles Duke of Burgundy was mightily displeased.

Warwick listened as if he had heard it all before. His eyes were tired but there was a complaceny—of owning the most power—that smirked upon his mouth. "Let your master cease to give refuge to the usurper Edward and then mayhap we will have something to discuss. I see you have brought my bastard with you."

There were mutterings as Margery sank down before her father's scarlet leather shoes, at kissing level with the gold-edged hem of the gilt-threaded red houppelande. No doubt he would have worn cloth of gold if he had dared.

Warwick studied her face and noted the sealed letters in her gloved hand. "I will speak with Mistress Huddleston alone." He led her past them into the empty chamber of counsel. The lofty, star-strewn ceiling and the empty benches alongside the long oak table gave the room a haunted feeling. He seated himself in the king's great chair at the end of the table and she smiled to herself. His sense of spectacle had always impressed her.

For a moment, the whimsical notion of seating herself at the opposite end appealed but she sat down sensibly on the end of the bench at his right elbow.

"So you are here with more false promises from Ned. You broke your oath as hostage."

"I took no oath, my lord, my husband forcibly removed me, you might say, after the Queen had tormented me." That at least had trapped her father's attention. "She was seeking evidence against my lord of Clarence. Did you know she desires to bring an Act of Attainder against him so she may return his lands to the faithful?"

There was no absolution. "But that was after you tried to leave without her permission."

"True," she sighed. "It is not over, my lord. Ned will invade with Burgundy's support. He bids you and my lord of Clarence make your peace and welcome him home before Margaret of Anjou lands and it is too late for either of you."

"Let him come! I hold England now," snarled her father, bringing his fist down upon the board. "And where is that treacherous spy, your husband? Safe in Burgundy while you risk my anger? I hope he has not strayed within this realm, for by my father's soul I shall hang him and set his head upon the bridge." He saw the pain in her face and relented. "And I gave you to him against your better judgment. Are you carrying a child?" His perception amazed her; the babe was too young to be swelling her belly yet. "Is it Huddleston's?"

"No, it is mine." They both turned abruptly. The Duke of Clarence was leaning against a small doorway, his smile as broad as that of Caiaphas on Maundy Thursday. "You know she was my mistress even at Valognes, my lord." The statement accompanied him as he moved forward to make a trio beneath the painted stars.

"He is lying!" hissed Margery, taking refuge behind her father's chair. She had been braced to meet George but not like this. "You must not believe him, Father."

"Because the truth is not so beautiful as you, Meg." George reached out a caress to her cheek but she jerked her head away and he laughed. "Come, my lord, you know that Bella shunned me because she was fearful of childbirth and Meg here was harnessed to a husband that she loathed."

Looking uncomfortable, Warwick rose and strode to the broad hearth, his thumbs twitching angrily over each other behind his tense back.

"No," whispered Margery, holding on to the carved chair back for support. "Believe nothing, my lord. The child is Richard's. Why do you tell such monstrous lies, my lord duke?"

"Because Richard is an icicle. Did he not infiltrate himself into your household, my lord, by declaring a so-called desire for Meg? And we know now he is a traitor."

"My lords, there are more important matters than my virtue," she exclaimed hotly. "I have been sent by Ned to plead with you both. He promises in future to abide by your counsels. There is yet time to make amends." Her words fell upon stony ground. "My lord father," she continued, "King

Louis seeks only to make England soft while he conquers Burgundy. That is his design. He uses you."

Warwick smiled. He knew it. They used each other.

"What excellent diplomacy!" sneered the Duke. "In other words, Father Warwick, she is telling you what a gullible fool you are and we all know you are not." He smiled craftily. "Ned has nothing to bargain with. Let him come with the Burgundian mercenaries and we shall meet him on the field." Dark hate glittered in the Duke's eyes.

"England has seen enough battlefields, my lord Duke. How many innocent folk must die in such ignoble feuds?"

"Lady, your present state makes you grow peevish. Speaking of innocence . . . I think you should read this, my lord."

Margery recognized with fear the letter George was pulling from his doublet. The bloody traitor! He had come prepared. His spies must have told him of her landing. It was Ned's letter to him, the one that had been sewn within her collar. With a narrowing of his eyes at her, the Duke strode across and thrust it before his father-in-law's face. "Read it!"

The Earl snatched it ungraciously and turned. Her blood cooled to ice as she watched her father's face harden. He stuck his lower lip out. "Whence came this?"

"Meg brought it to me in Valognes." George's gaze flickered malevolently and then he leaned across and grabbed her wrist, jerking her toward him and jabbing her fingers onto the jeweled pectoral cross he wore. "There is something else, you should know, my lord. This daughter of yours is Ned's creature through and through. She begged me between kisses to forswear you. Ned sent her to Valognes to seduce me." He held Margery's fingers to the cross. "Upon the tree of our Sweet Savior, tell your father it is so. Go on, deny before Christ that you met me in secret."

"You are hurting me!" screamed Margery, her wrist writhing within his grasp.

"Dare you swear?" Warwick was at her elbow.

George's blue eyes were brilliant with malice as he held her.

The Earl's hands came down upon her shoulders. "Let her go." He reached out from behind her and laid a hand across her fingers, pressing them against the gems while the Duke maliciously waited, torturing her with his gaze, his wine-soaked breath upon her face.

"Upon the Cross, tell me, Margery. Did you ask George to betray me?"

"It was not like that. I—I wanted to bring reconciliation. I thought that if I could make my lord of Clarence change his mind, you would be forced to make peace with Ned."

George drew back from her triumphantly. "Not quite the truth, Meg, but close enough. You need not be afraid of honesty. I had as lief your father know about why you have come back as keep him in the dark. I will take care of what is mine own. You may have a house and women to attend the childbirth."

She shuddered at the way he was looking at her and struck back. "You intend me evil," she muttered. "Why do you not put your fingers on your cross and swear you are not lying, your grace. I will wager God must shudder every time you open your mouth. Tell my father how loyal *you* are, cousin . . . sweet heart. Go on, swear *that* on your soul's salvation."

"Peace, the pair of you!" Warwick paced away and turned. "Margery, not only have you broken my trust in every way, you betrayed Isabella, you refused to obey me and remain as hostage, you abandoned Anne, and now you come to me, your mouth dripping with lies from the usurper. By all rights I should have you whipped and condemn you to walk barefoot to Paul's for the whore you are."

His assumption of her guilt severed the final chains of respect that held her. "No, my lord, I ever tried to make a peace . . ."

"The trouble is"—George's arm coiled about her waist like a serpent—"I wholly believe in Meg's innocence. This is what happens when a silly wench is caught up in affairs of state. You want a perfect world, Meg, and instead we have all used you. And I, for one, will make amends. I pray you, my lord, give me custody of my sister-in-law." He rubbed his hand across her belly. "I want this child to live."

Margery froze. Richard had spoken aright. It was George who had sent the men to kill them by the Loire.

She tried to think swiftly. If she told her father of George's promise to Ned and her father believed her, the

Duke would be imprisoned and all the men he might bring
to Ned's support might be lost. If the Duke was granted custody of her, without doubt he would kill her to prevent her
telling anyone in England of his intended treachery. If her
father imprisoned her, George might seek some way to
poison her.

She tried to free herself from George's painful grip. "No!
No! I fear him. He will kill me!"

"Cousin Warwick."

The innocent voice had sufficient strength to reach them.
The Duke let her go with a curse and moved back, his chest
heaving, his hands fists. Margery, clutching her arms across
her heart, spun around to face the doorway.

The man who stood there was tall and simply clad in a
long gown of woolen cloth. The hair, streaked liberally with
silver, framed a face barely lined and eyes curiously bland
and ingenuous. Although she had never seen him before,
Margery knew that only one man could interrupt her father.
One glance at Warwick's expression frozen in fury convinced her this was her only chance.

She managed a retching sound and with her hand to her
mouth moved forward, gasping. "Your pardon, highness, I
am ill."

Once past King Henry of Lancaster, she ran. "Latrines!"
she exclaimed, thrusting the halberds of the guards aside.
The Burgundians, mercifully, had waited for her.

Unable to leave the sanctuary of St. Martin-le-Grand at
Aldersgate, Margery was to fret, a prisoner without chains,
through Yuletide into spring. As the trees and hedges began
to unfurl their buds, news came that Ned and Dickon had
landed with a small force in the north. It would be a brave
but doomed invasion, with her blood uncle, Montague,
Warwick's younger brother, waiting to swat them like
unwelcome flies. And was Richard Huddleston with them?

Rumors abounded: Margaret d'Anjou was on the Channel;
Northumberland, his troops drawn up in the north, was
waiting to see which political haystacks were alight; Oxford,
rallying the other Lancastrian earls, was moving toward
Newark. What was true was that my lord of Clarence was

hastily gone from London, armed with commissions of array, and Warwick with a huge contingent had set out for Coventry from whence he could strike at Ned and Dickon as they strove to make for London.

It was Montague's hesitation to slay the small army led by Ned that gave the Yorkists their chance. It was said they were marching swiftly south, gathering men, with Montague trailing them, torn between loyalty to his brother and his friendship with Ned.

At the end of March, the news was that Ned had offered to allow her father his life if he surrendered. If he refused then it was to be a battle to the death. Her father, snail-shelled and sullen behind the walls of Coventry, gave no answer. Was he waiting for news of Queen Margaret's landing?

A week into April, there was no word of bloodshed but tidings came that George of Clarence had drawn his force up opposite Ned's outside the castle at Warwick, keeping him guessing, and then had walked out before the battle lines and made his peace.

She heard the frantic bells in the city. Yet another of her Neville uncles, the Archbishop of York, was summoning the citizens to arm themselves. The servants at St. Martin-le-Grand told her he had fetched out the tattered banners of Agincourt to flourish behind King Henry. But the faded glory held no magic, they whispered; the son of the greatest king in English history drooped in his saddle.

London held its breath. The Bastard of Fauconberg, an ally of her father, was threatening to sail up the Thames and bombard London if the citizens declared for York.

But no one did. No city contingent ventured north. The Londoners shut the gates and waited to see who won. Rumors fluttered against the postern doors but the citizens refused to open them even a crack. But three days later on Maundy Thursday, there was an army demanding entry. It was neither exultant with victory nor bedraggled with defeat. "I want to see my son and heir," bawled Edward of York, golden and cheerful, and they let him in.

Anyone would have thought the Yorkists had already won. The entire city, and Margery with them, poured onto the streets to watch Ned escort his queen from sanctuary at

Westminster, with her new baby son and the little princesses, to his mother's house at Baynards castle by the river. He owed the citizens money, of course.

His brothers, the Dukes of Clarence and Gloucester, rode with him. There was no Richard Huddleston among the White Boars. To have reached Ned was impossible but Dickon was another matter. She sent to him requesting news of her husband and received answer. Richard Huddleston was in charge of the men who had her father's army under surveillance. Warwick, unable to wait longer for Margaret to land, was marching south on London.

All Saturday afternoon, she heard the noise of armed heels drummed through the streets and the distant trumpets sounding in the fields beyond the great walls, and then the city grew strangely quiet as if it had suddenly remembered it was the eve of Easter Day and Christ had not yet risen.

Kneeling on the prie-dieu, Margery begged to be confessed, and the Dean, knowing his guest's parentage, solemnly knelt and kept vigil with her into Easter morning. She finally stumbled exhausted to her simple room as the bells struck four. Ten miles away the two armies began to buckle on their armor.

At Barnet, Richard awoke from too brief and ill a sleep to the boom of cannon. Around him, Gloucester's camp, to the east of the battlefront, was eerily silent. The Yorkist men had wisely not used their artillery nor had they spoken above whispers as they had made camp by night as silently as they could.

His father-in-law had kept his French cannons firing intermittently all night to keep the enemy foot soldiers awake with fear. That it kept his own army from sleep, particularly the gunners, had obviously been deemed of little importance, nor had he realized that the false campfires, set up to draw his fire and attention, warmed no one. Under the booming, it had been easy for King Edward's men to insinuate themselves until by midnight they lay so close that Warwick's great force would not have space to retreat.

King Edward had to win this battle. He barely had the numbers to face the Kingmaker but he had to prevent the Earl's army from joining with Queen Margaret's invasion force that might now have landed for aught they knew.

Richard scanned the mist like a hunter but the visibility was poor, the sounds muffled. He knew that Warwick's contingent lay behind, with the forces of his allies, Montague, Exeter, and Oxford drawn up before him from west to east.

To the left of where he was standing lay the tents of the King and George of Clarence. No man dared say it but all nodded that it was wise of King Edward to keep the Duke beside him. The west flank of the Yorkist army, straddling the highway that led back through Barnet to London, was held by Lord Hastings, Edward's great friend and chamberlain.

The ground before Dickon of Gloucester's force was hazardous, worse than the hedgerows that protected the enemy's center. Gloucester's men were to skirt around to the east and come upon Warwick's force where it was drawn up in reserve before the woods and force the Earl to battle. Warwick was not to be given the chance to flee east if the day went badly. The King wanted the Earl taken.

Fighting against Warwick and Montague's men was a task that Richard dreaded. What if he recognized the soldiers he had trained at Valognes and Amboise? What if he should meet his father-in-law or Lord Montague in the heat of battle or, God forbid, his brothers? It would have been better to have been in the western flank, facing Oxford's force.

Gloucester shared his vulnerability. Would he be able to kill the man who had been like a father in his adolescent years, his beloved Anne's father? All their destinies lay in God's hands. Well, amen to that. Richard returned irritably to the tent and roused the few who still lay abed. The harsh brazen bray of the trumpets was sounding everywhere.

As an esquire, he did not carry the weight of armor that some of his companions did. Not only could he not afford it but since the White Boars were to fight on foot, he planned to be swift and agile. He wore leather boots to his knees and the *brais d'acier*, much favored by the Burgundian soldiers, to protect his thighs and upper legs. He was already sweating in the quilted brigandine that embraced him from his shoulders to where the steel mesh ended below his codpiece. His one extravagance, a breastplate, was hidden by a White Boar surcoat, and his final protection was a sallet with an extended neckguard. It lacked a visor but he preferred it so. The fog was evil enough without the blinkering of steel as well. Perhaps he had judged the matter ill but it was his first battle.

He thought of a great deal in the first few moments as they surged forward. Of Margery, carrying his child, waiting for him in London, of his brothers, of Warwick, stubborn and bitter the other side of the fog, then as his soldiers encountered marsh and mire, he concentrated on his footing and survival.

They had moved too far north and were now up against a steep slope. A trumpet burst told them to cut across to their left, swinging around to the west up the slope. Richard prayed to his namesaint and began to struggle up the hill.

As it was but ten miles from London, Lord Hastings's men and Ned's western flank, finding themselves outnumbered by Oxford's enemy force, broke and fled to the capital. The swiftest brought news of defeat, that the three Yorkist brothers were slain, their army slaughtered. The news spread like fire through dry thatch. Margery, hearing it from the casement and running downstairs to the street, fell.

They had been told to stay where they were. To retreat would have tumbled them down the hill into the marsh but they made little headway onto the plateau. The men Richard fought were strangers, he heartily thanked God, and there was no time to be sickened by the spurting blood and the screams. No reinforcements came and his mind began to plead for relief. His sword arm was tired, his intellect appalled at the Englishmen dying around him; only the mental energy for survival kept him wheeling and slashing. In the name of God, how long must this endure?

He heard the shouting to the south, the cries of treason. The enemy flank before them was on the recoil. His fellow captain, John Nesfield, flung an arm about his shoulders.

"God keep you! Have you heard the news, Huddleston? They say Montague has changed sides to join with us and Oxford has ordered his men to hunt him down. The knaves won't know their own arses before much longer." Richard smiled grimly. Perhaps God, after all, was a Yorkist.

A cheer rang in the field around him from the men in the White Boar surcoats and they began belaboring their enemy with renewed spirit. It was then he found one of his brothers, face up in the bloodied grass.

No army reached London. News did come that Lord Montague had betrayed Lancaster. A serving girl brought the tidings in a flurry of skirts that disturbed the candles in the chapel. Margery, gazing into the flickering light she had lit for the tiny soul lost to her, turned her appalled gaze to the other flames that burned beside it. London Bridge was likely to be under attack from a fleet on the Thames, the girl said, and they would be murdered in their beds if the King's army did not return soon.

Richard tumbled to his knees beside Tom, his mind screaming with fury and despair as he tried to pray. Had any of the great lords, save Gloucester, come upon him now, he would have risen with rage and hewn them down. With the back of his gauntlet, he wiped the tears aside so he might see to close Tom's eyes with reverence. He wanted to set him gently over his shoulder, take him for burial, and quit the field. It was not his quarrel nor Tom's. It never had been.

"Sir! *Sir!*" Blearily he realized that Matthew and one of his other Cumbrians were defending his back as he crouched there. There was no time to take Tom's rings back for their mother's sake. While his tortured soul knelt by his brother still, another Richard rose, machinelike, to fight beside his men.

Their assailants turned and fled as other surcoats surged up from their left, wearing the Suns of York and the Black Bulls of Clarence, rushing past them to the north. The White Boars followed.

Gloucester, panting, recognized him. "Outrun them, for

Christ's sake, before they reach Warwick!" he yelled and
stumbled onward.

There was a thud of cavalry somewhere to the west.
Richard turned northward, soul and body meshing once
more. He followed Gloucester, aware of leaping and cir-
cumventing the scarlet-and-white surcoated bodies as if
they were broken statues, dreading lest he should recognize
his brother Will's face among them. Then it was as if the
whole of the King's army was streaming up from his left.
They were running toward the woods that lay to the north. A
hoarse roar went up. It was too late. Warwick's enemies had
found their quarry.

The Black Bulls of Clarence broke up like men leaving a
cockfight. He recognized Wyke, the man who had tried to
rape Margery at Valognes, running toward him, sword dripping blood, a ripped and bloodied scarlet surcoat in his fist
and he knew; knew whose men had torn the Kingmaker
down like curs.

"The traitor's dead, now it is your turn, Queen's man!"
bawled Wyke. "I have been seeking you, you cur! You
should have died beside the Loire."

With a yell, Richard slashed his sword blade into the
other's throat. "I would it were your bloody, perjured
master," he snarled and ran onward to where Gloucester had
halted. His gaze took in the blood oozing from the young
Duke's unarmored heel before he saw what lay beyond.

"God Almighty!"

His limbs spread-eagled as if they had crucified him like
St. Peter, Margery's great father lay naked on the bent grass.
Blood was still running from his nostrils, puddling into the
congealing collar of open flesh about his throat. The Black
Bulls had slashed every piece of armor, every thread away,
leaving his breast and belly a glistening matt of bloody
wounds, so close that it was impossible to see where each
began and ended or whether they had hacked off his prick in
their foul bloodlust. His younger brother, Richard's former
lord, Montague, his presence belying the rumor of treachery,
lay face down beside him, stripped of armor, the fine hair
matted, the handsome temple gashed.

Gloucester, who had loved them both, pivoted. "Where
is Warwick's standard?" he bawled. They fetched it and

bestowed it gently across the Kingmakers's body while Gloucester knelt and closed the pained eyes that were the blue of Anne's and Margery's.

Richard stabbed his sword into the earth and leaned upon the pommel, his mind retching. Who was it lay there? A power-hungry warlord or the people's hero? Was he now marching into Hell with his ghostly soldiers, content that his quarrel had orphaned so many children, beggared so many wives? But by Christ's mercy, what a man!

"Mayhap this is better than the block," muttered Gloucester, close at Richard's elbow, as the trumpets sounded the King's progress. "I will wager my dukedom I know who would have had to sit in judgment. Holy Paul, what would I have said? 'God be with you, my darling Anne, I have just executed your father?' "

"I will tell the King I have given these Nevilles to your charge, Richard Huddleston. Get them to St. Paul's as fast as you may!" Richard looked down at the Duke in amazement. "Well, who better? And kneel when I am talking to you!"

"Kneel!" spluttered Richard, as if the young Duke's fist had just winded him, but he obeyed.

Gloucester shifted his battleaxe to his left hand and pulled Richard's sword free. At least the tip was less loathsome than the rest as it touched its master's shoulders. The ancient words of chivalry were scarce audible above the rumble of cheers that warned of the approach of the King.

The Duke embraced him as he rose. "I will never forget how much we owe you." He flung an arm about him and turned him to his men. "Sir Richard Huddleston is in command of the earls' bodies. Do as he bids!"

CHAPTER
29

Although they welcomed Margery in the chapel to grieve, the priests would not allow her to leave the sanctuary, believing she was not yet recovered from losing the babe. They were firm: the triumphant soldiers might loot or they would get drunk and behave licentiously. No doubt her husband would seek her out and if she was not here, he would be displeased. Finally, desperate for her obedience, they told her the truth: her father and uncle were being hauled through the London streets naked on a cart and she had best obey my lord of Gloucester. And Richard Huddleston never came.

He ordered the Dean's priests to wash the phlegm, mud, and excrement from the bloodless skins and to gut them discreetly. It was necessary that the naked bodies be on display for at least two days. Even though the cathedral's chill air was heavy with incense and beeswax, Richard wanted no ordure of death. He could at least give the two men whom he had respected that dignity.

No one argued with Richard Huddleston. He had the authority of Gloucester behind him. Having done the butchery, the retainers of the King and Clarence were content to carouse and leave it to the White Boar men to clean up the mess.

He hoped Margery had received his message and prayed she would have the patience to keep her distance until he could visit her.

By the time he bade his men set open the main door of the cathedral, all was in order. A ribbon of men-at-arms stood ready to open the sluicegates and let in a living canal to gawp at what Death the Leveler could perform. They were to flow around the dead Kingmaker and his brother at a distance of three paces. It was beyond spitting distance. He had tested it. No one was to be permitted closer. They were to enter from the churchyard and leave by the west door.

Huge candlesticks were placed at each corner and a row of smaller candles stood like obedient soldiers behind the earls' heads. When someone spat and commented they were traitors and deserved no such privileges, Richard replied calmly that everyone must be able to see the Kingmaker's face and know he was in truth dead. This was one man who must not rise again.

The Dean, reassured by the plan and Richard's avowal that people must be reminded it was a holy church and not a bullbaiting at Southwark, was cooperative and pleasant. When someone explained to him that the man in authority was Warwick's son-in-law, he rearranged his face in compassionate lines, gave him an instant free blessing and an appointment for absolution. Richard was not impressed.

The first in were the aldermen. The Lord Mayor of London led them although he must have seen the bodies the day before. The crowd that followed was awed and behaved impeccably but as the hours grew warmer, Richard's men began to show their irritation. None of them had breakfasted. Gloucester had promised to send troops freshened by sleep to take over but they never came. The people did though, in greater numbers, and the air was fetid with sweat as the crowd heaved like a living monster against the soldiers.

Within the square of flickering candlelight, Richard sternly watched the faces flowing past. A veiled lady in black called to him over the crossed halberds. For a moment his heart lifted, believing it was Margery. Her voice, calm as she asked his permission to kneel by Warwick and take a lock of hair, was that of an older woman. And yet the timber had a familiarity and he stared, irritated by the veil. Somehow he knew her. Was she one of the married women who had bestowed her favors upon him in the past?

"Madam, I cannot let you through. The hordes will have Warwick hairless within seconds if I let you touch his head."

"You want money, is that it?" Disgust shook her and her gloved fingers grabbed the halberds and tried to force them apart.

"No, madam. I want to keep the peace. Who are you?" He tried to keep his tone respectful. Perhaps he did not know her. Perhaps she was one of Warwick's many sisters. It could be Lady Hastings or Lady Stanley he was dealing with.

"God ha' mercy, lady, we are only trying to do our duty," exclaimed one of the men-at-arms as the crowd surged forward and the man nearly lost his balance.

"I want your name!" She was doing the demanding now. It had to be one of the Neville sisters.

He leaned forward. He was not going to shout it to the mob. "I am married to Margaret Neville, Warwick's natural daughter. Now, report me if you will, but I cannot do as you ask."

She hesitated, cast a cautious glance about her, and then said briskly and quietly, "I think you will let me through, young man. I believe I am your mother-in-law."

On Margery's insistence, one of the Dean's servants reluctantly took her pillion to Paul's yard but there the press of the crowd was so great that she slid from the saddle and was caught up in the maelstrom of people eddying around the pulpit cross in the yard and cramming through the doorway. Elbows bruised her, several hands groped, a child impersonally kicked her, lashing out screaming at everyone about him. She managed to keep upright, for to have gone under in that sea would have meant being trampled.

She had not entered Paul's before. Another time she would have marveled at the tomb of the great duke, John of Gaunt, or read the inscriptions on the monuments in the side chapels or begged leave to enter the great cloister and see the famous Dance of Death and Sherington's Library.

She recognized Richard Huddleston instantly, standing silhouetted in his armor by the candles. Her blood ran cold knowing that in the joy of seeing him again was the pain of her father dead behind him.

But this husband, whom she expected to be as laden with guilt and sadness as she, albeit he was pale with strain and lack of sleep, was taking the hand of a slim, veiled lady in both of his as she rose from kneeling on the flagstones. And he was plying the alert, glittering charm that he had bestowed on queens and duchesses. They were talking earnestly and he pressed her hand reassuringly, then finally carried it to his lips with a half bow.

Jealousy rasped her like an ill-played note. "Let me through!" Margery demanded, pressed against the halberds. "I want to speak to that officer."

"He's got company already."

"I am his wife."

"And I'm the heir to the throne. He has enough problems. Move along!" She tried shouting and waving but the noise was great and Richard, damn him, was too distracted to notice. Margery, faint more with jealousy than with the pressure of the crowd, took off her shoe and hurled it at her husband's head.

He wheeled around, snarling with anger, his hand upon his sword, and then he saw his wife.

Not letting go of the woman, he turned to her once more, speaking with some passion. Guilty as Hell, the lady took a startled look in Margery's direction and made some answer, trying to pull away. He held her there. She looked once more in Margery's direction and struggled fiercely to free herself. He was arguing with her and finally she nodded and he let her go, parting the poles so that she might disappear into the crowd.

Richard picked up the shoe and, smiling tight-lipped, came across to Margery. He was ashen with fatigue, only his eyes held any power.

"Wondering who she was?"

"Yes."

"I am delighted to hear it. Let this mistress pass."

"By Our Lady, sir. How many other women are you expecting?"

The crowd jeered and deliberately lurched against the soldiers.

Margery and Richard faced each other. The soldiers swiveled their heads, relieved by the entertainment.

"You should not have come." He meant it, scowling as he assessed cheeks deprived of sunlight, the damage done to her body, the loss.

"Face my guilt, you mean?" Her lips quivered. "Oh, I have paid for it."

So had he; she could see he bore the agony of the last week like a tomb, shell-like upon his shoulders. She had been resolute but now she was not sure she could face her father, even with Richard Huddleston, like a stranger, beside her. "Do you want to hold my hand too?" It was cruel but she was hurt, as if shot by arrows from all sides.

"Yes, it is a free commodity. I will tell you all . . . later. I . . . did my best, but it is never enough." He held out his hand, his eyes questioning her acceptance but she took it and was thankful.

"I fell . . . it was such folly." She looked away, upward to the soaring pillars, tears heavy on her lashes, dreading the loss, the loneliness that might be hers again. Compassionate fingers gently touched her face, understanding the hidden scars, absolving her.

He could feel her bones too easily, sensed her frailty. "Are you sure you are strong enough for this? I can bring you back later to be alone."

"I am a Neville."

The pressure of his fingers helped her to preserve her dignity as he led her to the foot of the cadavers.

Margery took a deep breath and looked. "Why are they not fully clothed?" She could barely speak.

The earls lay bare-chested, clad only in clean hose. Richard had dispensed with the cloths that had been wrapped around their loins in the cart. God alone knew where the expensive German armor had gone, pilfered as trophies by the dogs that

brought them down. He had ordered the wounds cleansed and
bathed until they were just sullen red slits.

"Because the men who killed them stripped every shred
away and to reclothe them is sheer hypocrisy. Margery,
know that I had no hand in killing him." She nodded; but
did she hear him? "At least I could do this for them, you
understand?"

She stood transfixed. "How long must they . . . ?"

"Two days."

She could see where they had been stabbed with swords
or daggers. Their torsos were littered with thin red mouths,
so many that they were commonplace. Christ! As if to stab
the Kingmaker ensured a seat in Heaven. The greatest was
across her father's belly, half hidden by the woolen hose.
But it was the lines of congealed blood across their throats
that made the bile rise in her mouth. Only Richard's fingers
holding hers kept her upright.

Both men's eyes were closed but a twist of agony had
frozen her father's mouth as if Death had ordained it, lest
any think he died calmly. Her uncle Montague's expression
was one of peace and he looked years younger than her
father. She could see the likeness between them, the Neville
sandy hair, the freckled skin. Bruises discolored her father's
brow and cheeks and more cuts had congealed upon his
forearms. He had had his own Passion, his own Easter. Had
God deserted him utterly? Was he now in Hell?

Margery sank to her knees, her tears falling soundlessly,
heedless of the jeers, and laid her cheek against her father's
ringless hand.

Richard, feeling the grief rising in his own eyes, turned
away, his face stony, thankful of his soldiers' backs. He
could not afford to let her stay long. The crowd was muttering, wanting mementoes.

"Come! There is something you must do." He put an
urgent arm about her but she jerked away as if he had lashed
her. "Forgive me, Margery, but this is necessary!" Ruth-
lessly, he forced her away from her father, and out through
the moving wall of humanity. Margery struggled but he
hauled her into the Lady chapel, condemning the unnatural
calm with which Margery's mother crossed herself before
she rose and faced them, not bothering to unveil her face.

"Behold your daughter!"

"What!" Margery's fingers fluttered at her throat. She could not breathe. Only the threshold of his hands supported her.

"I see you have my ring still."

Gloved hands set back the black gauze. The older woman's face was not unfamiliar. Margery knew the shape of the nose from mirrors, but the gray eyes of harder mien were those of a stranger. There was dignity, but no love asked.

"Is your curiosity sated now?" There was no giving either.

"I never dreamed you were alive. *Who are you?*"

"I cannot stay long." The words were directed at Richard as if she were doing him the favor. "Even this carries a risk that is too great a price to pay for curiosity." She looked over Margery, her lips tightening. "You have done well, Margaret, and look to do better since your husband is employed by so worthy a lord as Gloucester. I daresay you do not want my blessing. It is not worth anything." She extended a gloved hand to Richard in farewell but her eyes were still on Margery. "I doubt we shall meet again and if we do, it will be as strangers."

Richard ignored the hand and slid his arm around his wife's trembling shoulders, sensing her anger and disappointment.

"But you cannot go so soon." Margery stepped before the door, her glance beseeching Richard to add argument to hers. "You have told me nothing about yourself. I deserve that at least."

"Do you, Margaret, when fortune has blessed you already with a generous hand? What do you require to know? I have three married sons and two daughters, one wed, a husband who liveth yet and grandchildren besides. They know nothing of my sins nor shall they."

"Margery!" Margery corrected her emphatically and watched her mother—the concept still alien to her—lose control of the conversation. "Madame, they call me Margery that know me best."

The lady recovered. "I regret I cannot claim that honor. I

beg you let me pass. My husband will be missing me."
Gloved hands lightly held her shoulders and cold lips
brushed her cheek so she might set her aside. "I will pray
for you, *Margery*." The gray gaze brushed across Richard's
face before returning to her daughter's. "May God bless
both of you." She thrust back the veil and turned.

"Wait!" Richard let go of Margery. "I can give you what
you desired." He drew a fold of vellum from his breast.

Margery's eyes widened. A lock of hair lay there. She
watched, transfixed, as his fingers halved it and held out half
to her mother.

The fingers, accepting, shook. The voice that thanked
him was of a sudden heavy with pain and a hand darted up
behind the veil to stanch the tears. The lady made to go and
found control again. "*A Dieu*, Sir Richard, take better care
of her than I have."

Margery sagged against him, words useless. For a
moment his mind could not comprehend the trumpets or the
cheering.

"Absolve her, mousekin. She risked much in coming to
mourn your father. She tells me her husband is a hard,
unforgiving man."

"Oh, Richard, I am so blessed in having you." His arms
lent her the reassurance she needed. "But it hurts. She—
God damn her, she would not even give her name. Did she
tell you?"

"No. Hush, my love! Forget but above all, forgive, or the
pain will rot your soul and—"

"Sir, sir! My lord of Gloucester is come."

The Duke stood in the archway. He genuflected in deference to Our Lady, and then stepped forward, wincing still at
the pain from his wounded heel, to lay a hand on Margery's
shoulder in understanding. His face was pale as ashes.

"Nesfield has taken over, Richard, and I will see the
Dean before I go. You must take Margery to my mother at
Baynard's. She will be safe there. The Queen's grace and
the princesses are returning to sanctuary today so there is
now room."

"My mother was here, Dickon."

"Your . . ." The Duke shook his head in wonderment.

"Holy Paul! I did not know that. Here!" He glanced back to the crowds and the dead, his face pained.

But his earlier meaning had seeped through to Richard, who gently set Margery aside. "She has landed?" he whispered.

Gloucester nodded discreetly.

"Christ defend us, when?"

"At Weymouth, Easter Sunday." The Duke's glance met his in an understanding of the irony—the day of Warwick's death. "I think that God must be with us. It took them three weeks sailing from Honfleur. Go now, you must get some sleep. We march at dawn and I will need you back tonight. There is no help for it."

Richard followed him from the chapel, protesting. "The men are weary. They cannot march and fight."

"They can and they will. The King is set upon it." Gloucester gravely regarded the island of candles burning within the sea of awed faces now turned to him. "By Holy Paul, here was great honor paid, albeit subtly. Richard, you have done well. I—I could not have wished it better executed." Turning away, he blinked up at the stained glass, his young face wretched. "None of this should have happened but the Kingmaker would have it so."

Margery bowed her head with a sob.

Richard set a warning hand upon his shoulder. "My lord, the Dean approaches."

With a deep sigh the Duke turned, his sorrow visored. "Then leave me to give orders for the coffining." He looked to Margery. "Mayhap Isabella and Anne are now in England and will appreciate your company at the burial when we can free them. They will have heard the news by now, I imagine."

Margery could not answer the Duke. The tears came at last and Richard slid his arm beneath her knees and carried her out of the cathedral.

"I am hungry," he said, setting her feet on the cobblestones but keeping her within the warmth of his arms. "I cannot face delivering you to her grace the Duchess of York on an empty belly. The living must eat and I know of an honest cookshop in the Strand. What say you, *Lady* Huddleston?"

"Yes, I did listen." Her smile watery, she reached up a

trembling hand to stroke his dark hair back beneath his sallet. "And Tom and Will?"

He caught her tightly to him, hiding his face against her cap and veil, longing to feel her hair soft and comforting against his cheek. "Our poor babe will have one uncle to carry his soul to Christ."

"Oh, Richard." She eased him back, her eyes hungry on his face, as if she were trying to etch that instant into her memory for eternity, her tears falling for their dead. By morning her touch would be a memory again. "You are all I have, all I desire in this world. Sweet Jesu, Richard, what if Queen Margaret wins?"

This might be the only today left to them. He lifted his hands to her cheeks. "A few hours, mousekin, let's spend them wisely." He narrowed his eyes at the steeple of Paul's and the flock of birds wheeling around the spire. "What's done is done."

~⁜~

The year of Our Lord 1471 would be a summer to beget children and say masses for the dead, reflected Richard, as he rode out of the town of Tewkesbury in early May with fresh battle scars. The Yorkist army, racing from London, had successfully blocked Margaret d'Anjou's push northward to link up with her allies in Cheshire. The necessity of crossing the Severn at Tewkesbury had been fatal to her army, and there the two forces had locked horns.

Usually preoccupied with mustard making, their senses still sozzled from celebrating May Day, the people of Tewkesbury had stoically helped to bury the dead. They had already renamed the field across the river from their abbey, "Bloody Meadow."

~⁜~

The ride back to London with his men was not comfortable; Richard's bandaged shoulder throbbed badly, the same shoulder that George of Clarence's assassins had ripped open by the Loire, and he was haunted by the memory of the recent battle. But the House of York had won. The battle of Tewkesbury was over, not with glory, not with honor—it had been a bloody rout, the Lancastrian army out of control,

its leaders divided and suspicious. Prince Edouard, inexperienced, for once without his mother, had been slain fleeing
toward the abbey and those who had reached the sanctuary
had been hauled out to execution. King Edward would have
no more traitors.

Only the Earls of Oxford and Pembroke had sped to
safety. Margaret d'Anjou, hysterical and mad with her son's
loss, was to be held prisoner in the Tower. The Countess of
Warwick had withdrawn into sanctuary at Beaulieu Abbey
and Isabella and Anne were already on their way to Westminster, escorted by the Duke of Clarence's men. The Duke
of Gloucester had been dispatched to deal with a rising in
Kent but he had taken only the men hale enough to ride hard
and fast. "Go to Margery," he told Richard. "And have that
shoulder attended to."

Richard tried to clean the killings from his mind as he
journeyed, but every night he relived the horror. The smell
of the blood of a slaughtered sheep in one inn yard had sent
him stumbling to douse his face at the pump. And yet he
could not help but be grateful for God's mercy. Was not the
May sun warm upon his face, the fields of shooting grain
peaceful to his sight? In the villages he heard the laughter of
children and in the forests the cuckoos calling once again.
Would England be a better place?

At Baynard's castle, Margery ran down the steps to
throw her arms about him and weep with joy. Richard was
too weary to talk. Sleep in her arms would be a blessing.

≈⊙∽

The diadems had been freed from the coffers cobwebbing
in Westminster sanctuary. Silken skirts, gossamer veils,
sparkling caps, and shimmering cones, unworn during the
brief eclipse of the Yorkist sun, were shaken from the presses
and aired in the winds of summer. The season of York was
come again and the King, tall and glittering with cloth of
gold, sat feasting in glory once more in the Great Hall at
Westminster.

"You wish me to negotiate with her highness?" Richard
Huddleston asked his wife as he admired Edward's beautiful Queen. "It would give her Tuesday evenings free."

"Perhaps if you have a word with Lord Hastings, he

might write me into Ned's ledger for an hour on Wednesdays after noon."

Richard's arm tightened about her waist. "Try it and I will join Jasper Tudor and his nephew in Brittany. The University of Oxford is putting treason into the degree requirements next Michaelmas. Ah, the sun it shineth . . .."

The King impatiently descended the steps of the dais, frowning down at the Duke of Gloucester. "That Burgundian dance, brother, surely you remember? Where is my lady Huddleston?"

Since none of the bejeweled throng about him had ever heard of that person, the King crossed the floor and found her for himself. "Come, cousin." He grabbed her hand and drew her into the center of the hall. "Now, Dickon, take her left hand."

For Margery, it was like the old happy days at Warwick come again. Beaming with pride, she stood with the King of England and the Duke of Gloucester holding her hands, waiting for Ned to signal the viol players to begin.

"Who is that woman?" asked somebody rather too loudly.

"Hold!" The King carried Margery's fingers to his lips and straightened up to grin at the hallful of nobility. "We present to you our beloved kinswoman, Margery Neville, who has done us great service."

"Now they will think I am your mistress," muttered Margery, curtsying, extremely put out at the ambiguity of the statement. She sent an apologetic glance to Richard Huddleston.

"That can be remedied," laughed Dickon. "I never kiss Ned's mistresses. Cousin, your servant." He bowed and then charmingly kissed her cheek.

"Not good enough!" exclaimed Margery, letting go both their hands and folding her arms. "No dance!"

For an instant, Edward of England was taken aback. Dickon laughed, raised his hands, and silence fell again. He bowed and gestured to the King to speak.

"Our entirely beloved cousin is the natural daughter of the late traitor, Richard Neville. This lady has our favor and if any man slander her from this day forth, then he shall have quarrel with us and with our brother Gloucester."

He turned to Margery and inclined his head. "Now, sweet heart," he growled, smiling, "*please* let us show them this Burgundian dance."

"Jealous?" The Duke of Clarence had materialized like Satan at Richard Huddleston's elbow.

"No." Richard did not bother to turn his head. "But I suspect others may be." He heard the hiss of anger and knew the pointed words had slid home like a dagger.

"You think yourself more clever than the rest of us, Huddleston, but you will never rise in the world."

Richard smiled coldly. "Then at least I shall keep my head on my shoulders. God grant you contentment too, my lord."

She came to Richard as the dance ended, love in her heart, and was relieved to read no envy in his face.

"What was George saying?"

"Mischief making. By Christ's blessed mercy, I dare swear there are many here who will regret he is still with us."

"Hush." She halted and touched his lips gently with her fingers. "Dickon has asked us to go north with him and join his household after his marriage to Anne. Would that please you?" He grinned. "Oh, sweet Jesu, you know already!"

She tried to tug her hand away but Richard kept it, laughing and drawing her to him. "I love you."

Two arms crept about his waist and she nestled against him, careless of the stares of their betters. He closed his eyes briefly and sent a fleeting prayer of thanks toward the hammer beams.

Margery raised her head and peeped up at him fearfully. "I am so happy tonight. You will never stop loving me, will you? You are all I have, all I desire."

He raised an eyebrow. " 'Mon seul désir.' But what of your freedom, Lady Huddleston?"

"I must eat my words, is that it? Very well, my love, here I am more free within these walls than in my entire life." She danced her fingers meaningfully up his arms to rest on his broad shoulders.

His green gaze blessed her. "The candles are lit and the great doors are thrown wide. Can you hear the music?"

Her eyes sparkled with blue fire. "A love song?"

"Yes. Come."

Hand in hand they walked from the Great Hall. Ankarette caught Richard's arm and whispered as they went past.

Margery hesitated upon the threshold. "What was that Ankarette just said to you?"

Richard smiled. "Just a kind word about unicorns."

Sources on Sir Richard Huddleston and his family appear somewhat sparse and contradictory but it is known that he did gain high military rank; in July 1482, he was made a knight banneret by the Duke of Gloucester, the future King Richard III, during the campaign against the Scots. He was also appointed as a Knight of the Body to King Richard and held several offices in Wales, including Constable of Beaumaris castle.

Dame Margaret Huddleston was one of the few ladies invited in her own right to the coronation of her half sister, Anne Neville, and King Richard III in 1483. She and Richard Huddleston had three children who lived to adulthood, Richard, Johanne, and Margaret.

The widowed Countess of Warwick never had her lands restored to her. They were divided between her daughters. She eventually left sanctuary at Beaulieu Abbey and made her home with her daughter, Anne, and Richard ("Dickon") of Gloucester at Middleham in Yorkshire.

George, Duke of Clarence, continued to anger his brothers. According to the contemporary Ingulph's *Chronicle of the Abbey of Croyland*, he attempted to prevent Gloucester marrying Anne Neville by disguising her as a cookmaid and hiding her. Gloucester found her and took her to sanctuary at St. Martin-le-Grand while a marriage dispensation was sought from the Pope.

Isabella, Duchess of Clarence, died in 1476, probably from complications following childbirth, but a few months later the Duke of Clarence sent eighty men-at-arms to arrest Ankarette Twynhoe. She was taken to the town of Warwick and accused of poisoning Isabella. She protested her innocence but was hanged.

The Duke's high-handed action infuriated Edward IV. In retaliation, the Duke's retainer, Thomas Burdett, was found guilty of treason and necromancy by a commission of the Lords and hanged. The Duke accused the King of seeking his destruction. Louis XI further fanned Edward IV's anger by writing to him that George of Clarence was seeking to marry the heiress to the Duchy of Burgundy so that he might make war on England. Finally, for this and other reasons, Edward ordered his brother's arrest. In 1478 George was privately executed at the Tower of London, having been condemned to death for treason by the judgment of his peers.

Margaret d'Anjou was eventually ransomed by Louis XI in 1475 for 50,000 crowns on condition that she surrendered her right to inherit the Duchy of Anjou to him. Philippe de Commynes eventually deserted Burgundy and became one of Louis XI's advisers.

Error, Richard Huddleston's dog, traveled to Cumbria with Matthew Long after the Battle of Barnet and was reunited with his master later in 1471.

ACKNOWLEDGMENTS

Information, inspiration, help, and suggestions came from many people and if anyone feels they have not been properly thanked here, please forgive the oversight.

I am grateful to my parents for giving me the double whammy of history and writing DNA that has dictated my leisure and shaped my ambitions, and for indulging our shared love of history whenever we are together. My husband deserves sweet praise, especially for his patience in being hauled around so many castles in England and France on our annual leave. My daughter and son, not to be left out, insist on being thanked here for putting up with a mother whose thoughts were frequently in the fifteenth century.

It has also been my good fortune to belong to two writers groups of the Romance Writers of Australia; their friendship, constructive criticism, and unselfish support have been invaluable and I wish them every success in their own endeavors. Delamere Usher, Chris Stinson, Elizabeth Lhuede, and Antonia Lomny deserve special thanks. Wendy Brennan and the late Frank Brennan must not be forgotten either, both for the gift of their time and expertise and for teaching me how important laughter is.

Thanks are due also to the Sydney Branch of the Richard III Society, and Ricardians Geoffrey Wheeler in London and Marjorie Smith in Cumbria for information on Richard Huddleston.

Angela Iliff and Anne Phillips have been excellent sounding boards on matters historical and I am most grateful to them for their advice.

Amanda O'Connell deserves thanks for painstakingly querying everything from "brigandines" to "houppelandes."

Finally, my most sincere gratitude and thanks to my editors, Stephanie Kip in New York and Fiona Henderson in Sydney, who believed that Margery and Richard's story was worth telling.

ABOUT THE AUTHOR

ISOLDE MARTYN was born in Warwickshire, and grew up in London with the unquenchable desire to become a historical novelist. It took a while. In the meantime, she worked variously as a university tutor, book editor, archivist, freelance historian, reviewer, and parent. She specialized in the Yorkist era for her history honors degree and is a former branch chairperson of the Richard III Society. She is married to a geological consultant and lives in Sydney. Isolde is a member of Romance Writers of America. *The Maiden and the Unicorn* is her first novel; her second, set in the reign of King Edward II, is forthcoming from Bantam Books in summer 2000.

If you loved *The Maiden and the Unicorn*,
don't miss Isolde Martyn's next lush, passionate medieval
romance . . .

THE KNIGHT AND THE ROSE

When Lady Johanna FitzHenry decides to leave her unbear-
ably cruel husband, her mother offers the perfect solution:
tell everyone she was already married. The only problem?
Finding a likely hero to play the first husband. Fortunately,
a handsome rebel knight with a dangerous secret is suddenly available—and willing to exchange some false vows
for a false identity. Now, Johanna and her hireling husband
must keep the truth from a world determined to destroy
them—but it is the secrets they keep from each other that
pose the greatest threat . . .

Coming from Bantam Books in spring 2000